11-24

A GENTLEMAN OF UNRELIABLE HONOR

THE LORD JULIAN MYSTERIES

BOOK SIX

GRACE BURROWES

DEDICATION

To those whose honor *is* reliable

CHAPTER ONE

I detested house parties, and I was fairly certain my mother detested me. When Her Grace of Waltham summoned me to the gathering at Tweed House, I thus recruited reinforcements before following maternal orders.

"P'raps your lordship might explain somethin' to me." Atticus, my tiger, was perched beside me on the phaeton's bench rather than riding on the seat fashioned to accommodate him at the rear. His unruly dark hair waved in the breeze, and his wrists stuck out two inches below his jacket cuffs. "If them letters was written so long ago, why is the duchess still haulin' 'em about everywhere?"

How to explain sentimentality in a woman who seemed to harbor not a scintilla of that quality in her whole body? The duchess referred to me invariably as his lordship, or Lord Julian, never simply by my name or as her son. When I'd returned home after Waterloo, she'd tolerated a kiss to her cheek, then declared a pressing need to shop for gloves, despite owning dozens of pairs.

"The letters doubtless put Her Grace in mind of fond memories," I said. "They inspire thoughts of happier days." More likely, the duchess kept the letters at hand to safeguard them from prying eyes. "Take the ribbons."

Atticus was learning to both ride and drive. His mounted skills had lurched forward in recent weeks, and thus the time had arrived to introduce him to the whip's art. A single chestnut gelding pulled the phaeton, a sizable equine hired at the last coaching inn. Jupiter had proved himself a steady sort, and we'd reached a stretch of flat, dry road.

Atticus and I managed the exchange of reins while Jupiter trotted along.

"If I had somethin' that inspired thoughts of happier days," Atticus said, "I'd keep it safe, not drag it 'round where any porter or maid might pinch it. My arms are already tired."

"Because you are holding the reins too high. If you keep your hands near your chin, you will have no leverage should Jupiter decide to stretch his legs." I helped the boy adjust his grip, the process being something of a challenge in a moving vehicle.

"If old Jupe takes off, I'm bailin', and yer worship can do as he ruddy well pleases."

I was a mere courtesy lord rather than a *worship* of any sort. I'd begun life as an extra ducal spare, but upon the death of my brother Harry at the hands of the French military, I'd become my brother Arthur's heir. I chafed under that honor—I'd much rather have had Harry alive and hale—and dreaded the day when I might become the duke.

I was neither mentally nor physically equal to the demands of a peer's station, and I was for damned sure unwilling to surrender my only surviving brother to heaven's embrace.

"Sit up, Atticus. Posture matters as much at the ribbons, as it does in the saddle, and you will please address me properly when we are in company."

"Beggin' your lordship paw-don," Atticus drawled. "I wish we'd spent the day in the saddle."

If we'd made the journey on horseback, the contrary little

scoundrel would have preferred we'd taken the phaeton. I'd found Atticus at the last house party I'd attended, my first social outing following my return to civilian life. He'd shown unexpected brains and initiative, and a rare and precious capacity for loyalty.

I'd come home from the wars in poor shape, physically, mentally, and emotionally. My reputation as an officer had been in no better condition. Some blamed me for Harry's death. Others considered me a traitor, assuming I'd bartered my honor for my life when I'd been taken captive by the French. I'd spent much of the last year coming to terms with the whole stupid tragedy of my years in uniform.

Which was all very much old business. "Eyes up, Atticus. Look where you're going, and Jupiter will go where you look." Or so every riding instructor since Xenophon had claimed, to the amusement of many an equine.

"Not if old Jupe sees a bucket of oats," Atticus retorted. "He'll trot straight through fire to get to a bucket of oats if he's like my Ladon. That horse is a right dragon about his tucker."

Atticus was a dragon about his tucker, too, but given the boy's past—sent forth from the tender care of the poorhouse to be a general dogsbody on the staff of a country manor—I rejoiced in his appetite and in his curiosity.

"Hands out of your lap, lad. If Jupiter thinks you've gone to sleep, he's more likely to get up to mischief."

"No, he ain't. You nobs think everybody is like you, always looking for something you can filch without paying for it, or some rule you can break without gettin' caught. Most folk just want a fair wage, and a plate and a pint. Jupiter ain't fancy."

Precisely why I'd chosen him for the final leg of our journey. A duchess could summon her son in the middle of a genteel gathering, but that didn't mean the host and hostess, much less the other guests, would be glad to see him. A discreet entrance was called for.

I had timed my arrival for early afternoon, when those guests were likely to be at their amusements, napping, or enjoying amusements that involved napping in the venerable house-party tradition.

My hope was to arrive in my unprepossessing equipage, observe a few Society niceties, find Her Grace's letters tucked into forgotten a hat box, and then depart without fanfare.

My hope would prove to be in vain, of course.

"Atticus, you must not squirm. Even if you think you are holding the reins still, Jupiter can feel you scooting about on the bench, and he will wonder if something is amiss."

"Something is amiss. A lad's got to piss from time to time."

"We've had that discussion. You're to step around to the jakes at the posting inns and not inflict upon me a recitation of the state of your bodily processes."

Atticus was blessedly quiet for the duration of half a mile. Harvest was approaching completion in Kent, and the countryside had the mellow, tidy look of land at rest. Though the maples were mostly bare of leaves, the occasional oak still stood in golden glory, and the pastures were green with lush fall grass.

"You always talk fancy when you're out of sorts," Atticus said, guiding Jupiter around a long, sweeping curve.

Atticus's diction, by contrast, tended to deteriorate when he was upset. "And?"

"You been talking fancy since we left Caldicott Hall this morning. You should be glad you still got a mama, beggin' your toffship's pardon. Some of us got neither sire nor dam nor littermates."

He'd mixed his metaphors but, as usual, made his impertinent point.

"Heed me, young man. The last place I want to be is among a lot of idle peers and their admiring gentry friends, my day scheduled like a recruit in the clutches of the drill sergeants. With His Grace soon to leave for France, my place is at the Hall."

"If the duke's own mama isn't at the Hall, why should you bide there?"

Because Caldicott Hall was my home and my refuge, the one place where I wasn't Lord Julian Caldicott, traitor, disgrace, and—I'd

known some truly dark times, and still had serious memory problems
—aspiring halfwit.

"The duke's departure means much of the responsibility for the
Hall will fall to me," I said, though I should have told Atticus to mind
his infernal tongue. "I've been away from home for most of the past
five years. If I'm not to make a hash of the whole undertaking, I should
be at my brother's elbow, cramming my head with his instructions."

"Right, and himself don't have an army of footmen, farmers,
tenants, toadies, and assorted other layabouts ready to point you in
the right direction. Of course he does. You're worried he won't come
back is the trouble, and here your mama thinks she'll distract you
from all your frettin' with some harmless silliness, and you have to go
and fret about that too. Oh, the Quality."

"Her Grace wants those letters found, and that is why you must
keep a particularly sharp eye out belowstairs."

"I allus keep a sharp eye out."

In fact, Atticus did, and I'd benefited from his vigilance. "Let
Jupiter walk a bit," I said when my sharp-eyed tiger was once again
holding the reins near his chin, slouching, and watching a skein of
geese passing overhead rather than the road.

"He ain't sweatin'."

"Because the day is cool and overcast." My favorite kind of
weather, given my weak eyes. "He covered five miles in good order,
and the road is wide enough here that we can be safely overtaken by
vehicles traveling at speed."

Then too, we were nearly at the Tweed House gates by my reckoning, and if I tooled up the drive with my tiger at the reins while I
sat idle beside him, eyebrows would be raised. My plan was to have
Atticus negotiate the turn through the gateposts at a sedate walk and
then to commend him to his proper place on the back perch.

"You are puttin' off seeing your own mama."

"She has put off seeing me is more the case." Though now that
Her Grace needed to find her precious letters, and now that I had a

modest reputation for quietly solving polite society's more embarrassing problems, she had issued her summons.

And I had packed my bags. One did not ignore a duchess with impunity, especially if she was one's own mother.

"I like house parties," Atticus said. "Lots of food, everybody in a good mood, at least at first. We get run off our feet belowstairs, but it's all for one and not so strict."

"Atticus, gather up the reins and let Jupiter walk."

"Jupe, walk!" Atticus bellowed, reins loose in his lap. The horse, preoccupied with whatever passed for equine thoughts, or perhaps keen to get to his oats, trotted on.

"Lad, if you don't take up the reins, he'll trot until Domesday. We'll miss our—"

A gunshot sounded from the trees to our left. Gunfire would never again be just another aspect of the rural landscape to me, but while my body panicked, my mind knew that we were in the midst of shooting season, and the quarry was likely grouse rather than former British officers.

The explosion nonetheless had Jupiter picking up his pace, and Atticus did nothing to check the horse's speed.

"That were a gun," Atticus said, gaze slewing about. "Are there highwaymen in this part of Kent? We're near the sea, ain't we? Smugglers always have great big pistols."

"Take up the reins," I said sternly, but without shouting because Jupiter might react to a raised voice.

Atticus fumbled with the reins, and a second shot had Jupiter breaking into the canter as we sailed past the Tweed House gate.

I was torn between the urge to grab the ribbons from the lad, real worry, and the inclination to let Atticus muddle on and experience the consequences of his inattention. One more shot and Jupiter might bolt in truth. Any horse stabled at a coaching inn was likely in good condition, and Jupiter was still fresh enough to gallop for some distance.

To say nothing of the fact that gunfire inclined *me* to bolting. "Atticus, take up the reins."

Atticus sent me a blank look, and a third shot decided the matter. I appropriated the reins from him, or tried to. Alas for me, the lad had reached the limit of his considerable courage. When he should have surrendered control of the vehicle to me, he instead fought as only a boy who had scrapped for his existence since birth could fight.

"Atticus, please *let go*. Give me the reins." To speak calmly while the phaeton bumped along and Jupiter's canter gathered momentum was a skill born in battle. To my great relief, that commanding officer tone penetrated Atticus's thick skull.

He let go of the reins and promptly clutched my arm. "He's runnin' off, guv. Bastard's goin' to see us killed!"

"Jupiter, halt." I hauled stoutly on the reins, and Atticus hauled just as stoutly on my arm.

Jupiter went merrily on his way. The horse was not spooked, but he was certainly ignoring me. His naughtiness was abetted by a pair of plow horses at grass in the field next to the road, who lumbered along parallel to him on their side of the drystone wall.

"Jupiter, *halt*." Perhaps because the plow horses had to a thundering trot, perhaps because Jupiter himself had tired of the game, the gelding also abandoned the canter for the trot.

"Halt, blast you." Another hard tug that did not relent, and Jupiter finally did as he was told. I eased the reins forward, and to the extent the harness allowed it, the horse hung his head. "Walk on, you rogue in chestnut livery."

I put him through the walk/halt sequence several times, turned him at another widening in the road, and brought him again to a stop.

"You can let go of my arm, Atticus."

The boy complied and sat up straight, gaze on the horse's broad rump. "I think I'll get down and stretch my legs for the rest of the way."

Like hell he would, though lecturing the lad when he'd had a considerable fright would be unfair.

I resorted instead to the age-old adult strategy of honesty served with a dash of exaggeration. "I cannot indulge your inclination to dawdle. You are correct that the reunion with my mother looms as something of an ordeal and I want it behind me."

"Your mama is an ordeal?"

He'd inconveniently fastened on the honesty, of course, so I urged Jupiter onward and made a clean breast of it. "You are right that I have put off spending time with my mother. She has conveyed in no uncertain terms that she has no use for me. Harry was her favorite, and every time she sees me, I have no doubt that she's wishing he'd lived and I'd died."

"Yer own *ma* thinks that?"

His incredulity buoyed my spirits. In truth, Her Grace and I hadn't had a frank discussion since I'd asked her if ladies truly liked to be kissed. I'd been seven at the time and baffled by the whole business of romance.

I still was, in many particulars. "I'd been home less than a day," I said, "when the duchess asked if I'd be biding at my London town house. Her question implied that no other venue would be open to me, and I haven't seen much of her since."

"Shoddy. Duchesses ain't supposed to be shoddy."

Mothers weren't supposed to be shoddy either, though Her Grace had her reasons. "You will please drive to the gateposts, which we passed about half a mile back. Jupiter may walk or trot, though I advise walking through the turn at the gate. Halt him once he's on the Tweed House carriageway, and I will resume driving."

Atticus took the reins from me and adjusted them to a safe, proper length. He sat up, he looked where we were going, and we gained our destination without mishap and with a few yards of sedate trotting.

"Well done, lad. Well damned done." I tousled his hair so he'd have an excuse to grouse and took possession of the reins. "Ready to make our entrance?"

He scrambled onto the tiger's perch. "Ready, your toffship. Ready for some tucker, too, and I gotta piss something powerful. I still wish we'd ridden horseback."

The distance from the Hall would have been too far for the aging Ladon—much less for Atticus's fledgling equestrian stamina —but one did not denigrate a pony in the eyes of his enthralled boy.

"Atlas will be along by tonight, and if you'd look in on him from time to time and get a general sense of the situation in the stable, I'd appreciate it." I gave Jupiter leave to walk on, and we crossed the Tweed House park as calmly as a pair of dowagers returning from divine services.

To appearances.

"I were proper scairt," Atticus said apropos of nothing. "You wasn't scairt at all. Does soldiering march all the fear right outta ya?"

"I was worried too, Atticus, and your fear was justified. Jupiter is an unknown quantity, the shooting might have gone on, and the smallest bump in the road if taken at speed can result in a spill. Handling equines in any regard is not for the fainthearted."

"You wasn't fainthearted. You was nigh bored."

"Appearances can be deceptive, lad. I was unnerved by the gunfire, worried for you, angry at the horse, and wishing we'd stayed the hell home where we belong." Especially wishing we'd stayed at the Hall.

"But you were a soldier, so you kept your eyes front, forward march and all that. Right?"

How many questions could one boy ask? "I am a *gentleman*, and thus your safety and Jupiter's were a higher priority than was indulging in a pointless display of pique. I will expect you to present yourself tomorrow after luncheon for another driving lesson, weather permitting."

Atticus said nothing as the golden sandstone façade of Tweed House came into view. Willows dotted the approach, a touch of lightness when compared to the usual oaks or even to Caldicott Hall's venerable lime alley.

"So you learned not to give in to your nerves when you were fightin' old Boney?"

Would he never cease? "Something like that." I turned Jupiter along the circular drive before the wide front terrace. Potted geraniums splashed red, pink, and white color in tidy rows, and a groom stepped forward from a mounting block. "Look sharp, my boy. Listen more than you talk, watch closely, and we need not bide here for long."

Or so I prayed. In fact, the house party dragged on interminably, and before my mother's situation was resolved, I would do a great deal of keeping my eyes front and marching forward. I would also spend significant effort not giving in to my nerves—or to my temper.

My godmother, one Lady Ophelia Oliphant, would bring up the rear guard by nightfall and accompany Miss Hyperia West to the gathering. To say Miss West was my dearest friend left a world of heartfelt declarations unspoken. When I'd departed for the Iberian Peninsula, we'd been all but engaged. I'd told dear Perry not to wait for me, but she had anyway, and in a sense, she was waiting for me still.

Even she, who knew me so well, could not have envisaged the condition of my mind and body when I'd stumbled home from Waterloo. She'd marshaled her patience, and I'd marshaled my courage. Investigation by investigation, we were forging a union that had little to do with vows and everything to do with great esteem and abiding affection.

I did not deserve the degree of loyalty Hyperia had shown me, but I was determined to earn it, despite my present condition being unsuited to the demands and pleasures of wedded life.

I greeted my hostess with every intention of comporting myself as a congenial and unremarkable guest, in part because Hyperia would expect no less of me.

"My lord, a delight to welcome you." Lady Barrington's smile suggested the sentiment was genuine. "Dorothea is overjoyed that you could join us. I've put you on the west side of the guest wing. You have excellent views and considerable privacy."

She strolled along a corridor lined with ancestral portraits in gilded frames, interspersed with the occasional serene landscape. Tweed House featured prominently in the collection, as did depictions of its various features—a granite folly awash in climbing roses, a fishing cottage on a sunny lakeshore, yellow irises bobbing in a summer breeze.

"You did the landscapes?" I asked, peering at one that featured mares and foals at grass, with Tweed House providing a stately backdrop. The artist had done an excellent job of catching two chestnut colts at play, their coats gleaming, sunshine sparkling on dew-laden grass.

"I am a devoted amateur, but an amateur only. Portraits elude me." Lady Barrington was a substantial blonde of matronly dimensions and pretty features, though I had yet to see any painting of her gracing the manor's walls. "Gideon Marchant, aspiring member of Parliament, has the next apartment down, and I've asked his valet to look in on you from time to time. Dorothea says you don't use a valet proper."

At Caldicott Hall, I had a valet. His role was tending to my wardrobe rather than to my person. I liked him well enough, but we saw little of each other, and that was how I preferred it.

"I hope my imposition on your hospitality is brief," I said as we mounted a curving staircase. "Her Grace assured me she'd asked your permission before adding me to your guest list."

"She did, of course, but Dorothea has ways of asking that brook no refusal. That aside, the young ladies of the party would have mutinied had I pleaded a full house when a ducal heir could have been included in the gathering. Besides, we could billet a regiment without filling our guest wing."

Young ladies. Rubbishing hell. I was held in contempt by many former officers—taken captive, unable to save my brother, doubtless in the pay of the French all along, et cetera and so forth—but the matchmakers would overlook even those faults in a ducal heir.

My hostess led me down a corridor remarkable for being sunny. A pair of light wells in addition to alcoves boasting bow windows turned an upper floor into something of a solar.

"I'm sure I will enjoy the company of the other guests," I said. "Might I inquire as to where my godmother will bide?"

"One floor down, and Miss West's apartment is beside Lady Ophelia's. Not quite the same views, but cozy and commodious. Here we are."

She used a key to open a paneled oak door carved to depict the same folly I'd seen immortalized in oils on the lower floor. That the apartment had been kept locked struck me as odd, but every household had its habits and quirks.

Her ladyship ushered me into a parlor done up in hunter green, with dashes of green and white plaid, and plenty of oak wainscoting and sturdy oak furniture. The plaid was subdued, thank a merciful Deity, and relieved by green velvet upholstery and a bouquet of red roses on the windowsill.

The room was simply comfortable. Not fussy, not cluttered, neither overly elegant nor soberly masculine. Comfortable.

"These quarters will suit wonderfully," I said as Lady Barrington proceeded into the adjoining bedroom.

Some thoughtful maid had drawn back the drapes and left the French doors cracked. The view was unremarkable—park leading to woods, a bit of lakeshore to the west, the roof of the stable peeking through the trees to the east—but pleased me.

I could monitor anybody's approach to this side of the house. The alcoves across the corridor afforded a fine view of the front drive and the main approach. As a sentry's tower, my rooms would suffice handily.

"The bell-pull is in the sitting room," Lady Barrington said. "We gather on the back terrace before supper, and a tea tray will arrive shortly. I noticed, my lord, that you didn't ask where your mother's rooms are."

"Remiss of me." Her Grace would be staying in the grandest quarters Tweed House had to offer. "She is doubtless across the corridor, four doors up, just to the other side of the main staircase. Her sitting room will have the series of oriel windows and her bedroom the grand balcony."

I ought not to have shown off, but in the fashion of any reconnaissance officer, I had been making a mental map of the house and surrounds since my phaeton had turned through the gateposts. The staterooms, or what passed for their lesser equivalent, would look out directly over the drive and enjoy deluges of morning sunshine. The lord and lady of the manor were likely situated in comparable splendor, but at the back of the dwelling, overlooking the gardens.

"You have it precisely," Lady Barrington said as a footman bearing a tray stepped into the parlor, deposited his burden on the sideboard, bowed, and withdrew. "One heard that your time in uniform took a heavy toll, my lord, but your wits appear to be quite intact."

My wits were mostly reliable. Not so my memory. "I have recovered significantly in recent months, my lady, much to my relief." The most obvious evidence of my years in the military was a sensitivity to strong sunshine and eyes that tired more readily than I preferred. I wore blue-tinted spectacles on sunny days, and if I taxed my vision excessively, my reward was a pounding headache.

My hair, which months of captivity had turned white, now grew out in a pale chestnut shade. I kept the white part queued back, oddly unwilling to cut it.

I still tired too easily, and melancholia dogged me if I allowed myself too much idleness. I was unfit for the marital lists in the most intimate sense thanks to a bewildering lack of ability rather than an absence of willingness. The flesh and the spirit were not coordinating their maneuvers. Hyperia was aware of my many failings and regarded them as mere bagatelles.

I could not be as sanguine. I hoped that my medical indignities would abate with time. My dodgy memory, on the other hand, had been with me since before I'd bought my colors.

Lady Barrington made one last visual inspection of my quarters and of me. "I'll leave you to enjoy a hot cup of tea and some peace and quiet. Shall I inform your mother that you've arrived?"

Her Grace had doubtless been told the moment I'd set foot on Tweed House's front terrace, for all that she would act surprised to see me when we did eventually meet.

Surprised and not necessarily pleased, though she'd summoned me herself.

"If you might instead tell me how the duchess is faring? I was not expecting her invitation."

Lady Barrington, who knew the duchess well enough to refer to her by her Christian name, checked the water in the vase holding the roses.

"I suspect Dorothea is between diversions again. She has that distracted, not-quite-happy air. The spring whirl is over, summer at the shore was more tedious than anticipated, and now we come to the house-party portion of the program. How many decades of that can a woman truly enjoy, regardless of her station?"

That my mother still had *diversions* was a shock to my sensibilities. "Caldicott Hall could certainly use Her Grace's hand in the household management, what with my brother departing for the Continent."

Arthur was soon to embark on extended travel with his boon companion, lover, and friend, Osgood Banter. Where they traveled was probably immaterial to them both, provided the laws were less draconian than England's infamous bloody code.

"You expect Dorothea to count linens, my lord? To peruse menus and entertain the vicar's wife?"

Well, yes. I did, actually. Somebody had to do it, and what I knew of menus would hardly suffice for a weekday breakfast.

"I hope Her Grace will recall that she has a lovely home in

Sussex and family who would enjoy her company." The *lovely home* part was true.

Lady Barrington studied me for an uncomfortable moment. "You are so like your father. Arthur has the same quality—inscrutability on command. Dorothea hasn't an inscrutable bone in her body, heaven knows. I confess, she does not seem her usual, vivacious self. Her health, her finances, I know not what bothers her, but Gideon agrees with me, and he's known us both for ages. I'm glad you are here, because the duchess is troubled, and you stand as good a chance of sorting her out as anybody. I'll leave you to your tea."

She withdrew on a nodding sort of half curtsey and left me troubled too. I closed the door behind her and brought the tea tray out onto the balcony. While I poured myself a cup of strong, black tea, I sorted through first impressions, questions, and instincts.

If I had to use one word to describe my mother it would be *passionate*. Her Grace of Waltham could rage, laugh, sulk, and rejoice all in the course of an hour, and each sentiment would be given the fullest expression in its turn. The duchess was prone to drama, in other words.

And now she was quiet and brooding? Oh yes, I was troubled. Very troubled. When the duchess herself swept into my parlor five minutes later, I grew more troubled still.

CHAPTER TWO

"Do pour me a cup of tea, your lordship," Her Grace said, closing the parlor door and crossing to the sideboard. "You took your jolly time traveling over from the Hall. I was nigh shredded with worry to think you might get caught in a downpour and end up with a lung fever."

She lifted the stoppers in the three crystal decanters one by one, held each under her undainty nose, and made her selection.

"A dash of sugar in mine," she went on, "and a biscuit or two, if you please. One wants a restorative at this hour of the day." She took up a perch in the middle of the sofa without indicating that I was free to resume my seat, but I did anyway. Her Grace had not knocked, had not greeted me properly, and had not thanked me for risking that downpour.

A pleasure to see you too, dearest Mama.

"Arthur sends greetings." I poured a second cup of tea, added the requisite sweetener, and put two petits fours on the saucer. "He expects to take ship within the week." I'd jaunt over to Dover to see him off, downpours, enemy invasions, and biblical cataclysms notwithstanding.

"Your brother is a bit old for a grand tour." Her Grace accepted her tea and poured a dollop of brandy into her serving. A generous dollop.

I had never known my mother to tipple, and even as a boy, I would have noted such behavior.

"Don't make that dismayed face, your lordship. I am of age and enduring tribulations without number. A tonic is the least I deserve."

Whatever these tribulations, Her Grace was bearing up admirably. She was tall for a woman, and while far from sylphlike, she was well formed despite having passed the fiftieth year of her age. The late duke had referred to his duchess as a lively armful, more Hera than Aphrodite, though she was a surpassingly attractive woman. Her red hair was fading graciously to gold. Her smile could coax good humor from sulking dragons.

When Dorothea, Duchess of Waltham, chose to be charming, otherwise sensible people comported themselves with no dignity whatsoever. Harry had had the same quality, especially with the ladies.

"No brandy for me," I said, sipping my plain, tepid brew. "My journey was uneventful and Lady Barrington's welcome gracious."

"Hellie is like that." The duchess took a deep draught of her doctored tea. "A sweet soul, but nobody's fool. Dotes on her step-children a bit too enthusiastically. The girls are spoiled, but then, their papa *is* an earl and Hellie merely their step-mama. Watch yourself around that Jessamine creature. She fancies herself in a tiara."

That advice was remarkable for being halfway directed at my wellbeing. "I will make it a point not to be found alone with any unattached young ladies. Miss West will abet that goal, as will Lady Ophelia."

The duchess made a face. "Ophelia was always a bit too involved as a godmother, but perhaps that's not such a bad thing. She knows everybody, and I do mean everybody, and she never forgets a scandal."

By her own admission, my godmother had caused a few scandals in her day and enjoyed every one of them.

"Tell me about your letters." I finished my tea, poured myself another half cup, and prepared to listen to a recitation no son should have to hear.

Her Grace polished off her restorative in a few hearty swallows. "My letters are missing. You must find them."

Why me? Except I knew the answer. I had an aptitude for dealing quietly with Society's vexing little conundrums. A peer's heir gone missing, a prize hound apparently stolen, a child turning up on the ducal doorstep with no established provenance. I'd started down this path at another house party, when some unknown malefactor had attempted to wreck what had remained of my good name.

"Where do you usually keep these letters?"

"This set is with me at all times, your lordship. They travel with me, so you needn't go looking for them in Bath and Mayfair."

Her Grace was unused to interrogations. Patience was in order. "I meant, in what location did you have them here at Tweed House? Location can narrow the list of people who had access to them. The boot-boy, for example, would have had his ears boxed for presuming to venture anywhere near a lady's apartment. Even if you'd left your riding boots out for an overnight polishing, your maid would have taken them belowstairs or entrusted them to a footman."

"My lord, boot-boys in the general case cannot read. How would he have known which letters to steal, assuming he found them?"

"By the dates," I said gently, "which even illiterate boot-boys, chambermaids, and underfootmen can decipher."

She bit into one of her petits fours. "I abhor the whole situation. That is my private correspondence, and stealing is a felony."

A valid point, and a puzzling one. Whoever took Her Grace's epistles courted a small chance of being hanged for their effrontery. "When did you receive these missives?"

She finished her sweet and dusted her hands. "Years ago."

Patience was in order, so was firmness. "Madam, I understand that the matter is painful and sensitive, but I am your son and a gentleman. What you tell me remains private, though you should be aware that Lady Ophelia and Miss West are in my confidence, particularly when necessary to conduct an investigation. The more detailed your descriptions, the more likely I am to find the letters quickly."

I had never before lectured my mother, but she had summoned me to locate the damned missing mail, and we were wasting time.

"I thought you could look at the footmen's gloves or examine the maids' caps and identify the culprit."

"Divination and conjuring yield unreliable results. I draw conclusions from facts and observations, and thus far, you have given me none of either to go on. How many letters, what are their specific dates, what do they look like, did they bear any particular scent or seal, who sent them, have you seen similar handwriting or stationery anywhere else, and do you have copies of your replies?"

I waited, giving Her Grace time to choose between further prevarications and for once doing as she'd been told.

In her usual fashion, she attempted prevarication. "Of the three boys, you have always been the most like Claudius. Arthur lacked the late duke's quickness, and Harry never had His Grace's steadiness. You will find my letters, won't you, my lord?"

She turned a hopeful half smile on me that should have melted my heart. My own mother, a damsel in distress, was appealing to my gallant nature. Alas for her, my nature was gallant on occasion, but never saintly.

And—I hoped—seldom stupid.

Her Grace had deftly passed me two sideways compliments—I was quicker than Arthur and steadier than Harry—and those were valid observations. Arthur was far from plodding, but he wasn't prone to leaps of insight. Harry had been impulsive and dashing, and was likely dead in part as a result of those attributes.

The insult in her words lay in more subtle directions. She'd referred to her sons as "the three boys." Based on innuendo, over-heard conversations, and awkward silences, I had learned in my youth that Claudius, late Duke of Waltham, husband to Her Grace, and the man I'd grown up calling Papa, was not my father. The duchess had provided the heir and spare, and then assumed the free-doms a dutiful aristocratic wife was permitted, with predictable results.

I was one of three *boys*. She did not describe me as one among three ducal *sons*, and she had doubtless chosen her words to remind me of my questionable patrimony.

Or I was being ridiculously sensitive to innuendo, and Her Grace was being ridiculously evasive. "I cannot find your letters, madam, unless you provide me the information I've requested. Resign your-self to the need for honesty, or I will depart in the morning."

Her smile faded to puzzlement, then humor. "Oh, very well. You needn't scold. I'm told you keep pencil and paper handy, so prepare to serve as your own amanuensis. Three letters. Six years ago to the month, and yes, I would have been in mourning. Parents are human beings, my lord. We have flaws and foibles, and mourning is damned lonely. The handwriting was public-school penmanship, no seals—these were *billets-doux*, for pity's sake—and the wax was blue, though it has faded to gray. As for scents, I kept these epistles in my traveling desk, which includes lavender sachets, so the original damask fragrance was long since overpowered. What more do you want to know?"

This volley of generalities was a step in the direction of coopera-tion, but I'd need specifics before we concluded our discussion. I took out my little bound notebook and pencil and jotted down her litany and put a few more questions to her.

"Who was Your Grace's correspondent?" I'd kept that question in reserve, hoping Her Grace would volunteer the information.

She picked up her empty tea cup and studied the dregs. "His name was John Pickering, a mere mister. I'd taken a notion to learn the flute. My lady's maid at the time suggested that study of a musical instrument might leaven the boredom of mourning, and she was right. The flute seems easy at first, but to create beauty instead of mere notes at the correct pitch is a subtle art."

Insightful, and I was reminded that Her Grace was quick, too, when she wanted to be. "Do we know where Mr. Pickering is now?"

She set down the empty tea cup. "One does not cling to a gallant, my lord, and despite what society will gleefully imply, Pickering was only that. We were not, that is... I never allowed... oh, bosh and botheration."

"You indulged in a flirtation, a romance rather than a liaison." Some consolation to me, but Her Grace was right: Society would put the worst possible connotation on the missing letters.

"Pickering diverted me," the duchess said, "from a period in my life that was equal parts sadness and tedium, but a music master's existence is often peripatetic. He was always running off to see this cousin or look in on that former patron or a potential new one. After he'd departed on one of those excursions, I received the usual gracious, tender, ultimately selfish letter. I kept that one, too, and why shouldn't I? I own the letters. They were sent to me, and I want them back."

"You own the letters," I said slowly, my pencil posed above a new, blank page. "You do not own the right to publish them."

She glowered at me down what had been known at the Hall as the Fennington nose. "Those *billets-doux* cannot be published. I will be a laughingstock if they are published. Ruined or, worse than ruined, a joke. Nobody can publish them *ever*."

A music master dallying with his widowed employer six years ago was of no great moment. A bit sad, a bit tawdry, but not ruinous to a duchess.

"Was he married?"

"Of course not. I have standards, as you should well know."

I studied the fading beauty who had brought me into the world nearly three decades ago. Beneath her indignation lay a legitimate fear of ridicule. Her Grace would look foolish not only in Society's eyes, but in her own. I knew how bitterly self-castigation burned. What would cause this toweringly self-confident arbiter of social mores to feel ashamed of herself?

She tucked a lock of golden hair over her ear. Golden hair that had once been flaming red.

"This Pickering fellow was younger than you," I said. "Much younger."

She grimaced. "My lord is sometimes too insightful. I could have been Pickering's mother, though I doubt he grasped just how great the difference in our ages was. The memories embarrass me now, but at the time... I was angry, if you can understand that. Nobody has much use for a widowed duchess. I told myself that if I'd been a bereaved duke, the age difference would have been nigh expected. Then too, I was convinced that Pickering was smitten. I hadn't made that mistake in previous affairs, and I will never make it again."

Pickering could well have been smitten and simply realized that his love was doomed. Now, though, years later, the fellow might be short of cash and happy to blackmail a former lover or sell scandalous memoirs that traded on her social standing.

"I grasp why retrieving the letters has become a priority," I said, pouring Her Grace another tot of brandy. "I will need a few more details before I make a thorough search of your quarters."

She downed the brandy at one go. "We always pay for our pleasures, don't we?"

"Sometimes we are rewarded for our diligence too. I must talk with your current lady's maid, and Lady Barrington should know that she could well be harboring a thief."

The duchess rose and returned the decanter to the sideboard. "I want to leave. To fly off in one of my legendarily mercurial changes of venue, but that won't serve, will it?"

I got to my feet out of manners. "Not just yet, though retreat can be a useful tactic on the way to victory."

She gave me a perusal perfected by even young parents, one that seemed to see not only the person of their offspring, but their progeny's interior realities as well.

"You have his kindness too," she said. "Claudius was the kindest of husbands in most regards. Not all regards—husbands are human too—but he did make the effort to befriend me, eventually. I still miss him, and he's probably pleased to find it so."

She departed on that odd note, and I returned to my perch on the balcony. Questions swirled in my mind: Where was Pickering? How was he faring at present, if he was still extant? Had he hired somebody to retrieve the letters because the sentiments compromised *him*? Was he contemplating marriage and so very worried about his colorful past that he'd steal rather than risk the letters falling into the wrong hands?

Had Her Grace made the sort of enemies who'd blackmail her out of spite—enemies close enough to know of dear *Dorothea's* letters and determined enough to have them stolen?

Had a member of the duchess's staff come upon the letters and sold them to the penny press?

The possibilities were as alarming as they were endless, and all because a lonely widow had been a bit self-indulgent. The afternoon shadows lengthened as I sorted through next steps, and all the while, I was aware that whether I ever found the letters, I carried a question in my heart that I had never had the courage to put to my mother.

Who was my father? Who had tempted a young duchess to stray, and had that man played any role in my life? Was he extant, or had I already lost him—him too—to death?

"The design is ingenious," I said as Hyperia closed the door to the duchess's sitting room. "Papa gave the traveling desk to her for Christmas one year, and Harry and I delighted in unlocking its secrets."

"You read your mother's correspondence?" Perry sounded more curious than horrified.

"Of course not. Papa would have put us on short rations for consecutive eternities. The desk itself fascinated us."

I had already made a thorough search of Her Grace's quarters, which, while not fit for royalty, were certainly commodious. Come morning, light would pour in from the grand balcony overlooking the drive and bounce from the mirror over the sideboard, to the folding mirror at the vanity, to the cheval mirror by the door, to the dressing closet.

The quilt on the bed was burgundy velvet trimmed with a thistle-and-heather border. Pillows covered in purple satin and embroidered with the same motif were mounded at the headboard. Even the steps to the bed were carved with Caledonia's emblems.

The carpet was mulberry decorated in a predictable bouquet of cream, purple, and pink flowers with interlacing greenery, and the walls were hung in panels of cream and mulberry silk.

Not precisely a feminine room, but an exquisite complement to my mother's coloring and to her station.

"This bedchamber is designed to be quiet," Hyperia said, trailing a hand over the quilt. "All the upholstery and carpet, the silk on the walls. Your mother ought to be sleeping soundly."

By strictest protocol, Hyperia and I ought not to be alone in any room, much less one with an enormous bed and locking doors. She and I had an understanding, though. At some point, when the stars aligned and the moment was right, I would propose—again, having already done so once or twice—and she would accept.

Hyperia was well aware of my limitations—my weak eyes, my memory problems, my lack of animal spirits—and aware that despite my failings, I wanted children. The ducal succession needed children —Arthur and I were the last legitimate scions of our line—and I *wanted* them and the family life that revolved around offspring.

Hyperia was of the opposite persuasion. She was fond of children in the general case, but babies had a lamentable tendency to imperil the health and even the lives of the women who bore them. This fact had appreciably dimmed her enthusiasm for motherhood.

The topic was delicate for us both, but such was my faith in our devotion that I hoped we'd muddle through to a mutual accommodation. Given a choice between fatherhood on some distant, happy day and risking Hyperia's life, I chose Hyperia hale and whole.

End of discussion.

Given a choice between spinsterhood and marriage to me, Hyperia was choosing me with a gratifying lack of hesitation. There was hope, and great mutual esteem, and time to advance our discussion as we saw fit.

In terms of appearance, my late brother, Harry, had once described Hyperia as *not quite*. She was not quite a pocket Venus, though shortish and generously curved. She was not quite beautiful, having chestnut hair rather than the preferred blond, and green eyes rather than the requisite blue. Her features were attractive rather than gorgeous. To Harry, much taken with appearances, including his own, Hyperia had been *not quite*.

She had fooled him, along with the rest of Society, into ignoring her blazing intellect, her keen insight, and her ferocious spirit. I could not esteem her more highly if she'd been in line for the crown itself.

"What is so special about this traveling desk?" she asked, considering the object where it sat on a fussy little escritoire angled to take advantage of the natural light.

"Open it," I said.

Hyperia undid the little hook that latched the thing closed and attempted to lift the lid, without success. "Clever, and an irresistible challenge to a pair of young scamps."

She felt along the bottom and sides, eventually finding the catch secreted between a back and side panel. The lid lifted easily, revealing a tidy assortment of writing implements arranged around a red velvet writing surface. Beneath the velvet-covered lid, paper reposed in a tray sized to hold its specific dimensions. Bottles of ink, a jar of sand, lengths of wax, two pearl-handled penknives, quills, blotting paper, a small gold quizzing glass, even a slot for holding a signet ring and seal were all arranged such that not an inch was wasted and all was to hand.

"Looks serviceable and elegant," Hyperia said. "A trifle worn and sturdy, too, for all the fancy inlay."

"Italian work. I know not how old it is, but Her Grace takes it with her everywhere."

"False bottom?" Hyperia asked, tugging on dividers and tracing the velvet lining.

"Of a sort."

She needed but another minute to find the mechanism that allowed the whole interior tray to lift out in one piece, revealing a place where private letters might be stored.

"Is there more?" Hyperia asked, replacing the tray.

"At least three more hiding places, of a size to keep a piece of writing paper from view." Harry had found one. I'd located the other two.

Hyperia hunkered down to squint at the desk from eye level. She turned it slowly in a complete rotation and found the side panel that opened to reveal another narrow hiding place.

"Think of where we don't look," I said. "Of what we put aside as we explore more interesting—"

"The lid," Hyperia muttered. "Lids, rather."

Though it took her some doing, she eventually found the manner in which the lid over the box of paper could be slid apart to reveal two perfectly matching panels that fitted together to appear as one. The space revealed was sufficient for a single sheet only—a sketch or map, perhaps.

"I found that one by accident," I said. "I was holding the lid in my hand when Harry shoved me aside to get a better look at the interior of the paper tray. I dropped the lid to the carpet and happened to notice that the two panels had come ever so slightly askew. Harry was furious for days."

Hyperia set aside the paper in the tray. "Jealous of you?"

"Harry had it in his head that I was the better scholar. I wasn't. I was simply more dogged and left more to myself, so I became fond of books. What have you there?"

Hyperia pushed down on the short end of the empty tray, and the bottom flipped up.

"Gracious saints, woman. You found a new hiding place."

"This is you." She withdrew a single piece of paper going a bit yellow about the edges. A faded ink drawing graced the page, a three-quarter portrait of a gangly youth. He was bashful and sweet and all odd angles. His hair needed a trim.

Hyperia turned the page over, but no signature or date was to be found. The words *My dear Julian* were lightly penciled near a corner.

"Her Grace must have forgotten it was there," I said, ambling away from the escritoire. "The drawing has to be ten or twelve years old."

Hyperia put it back and reassembled the desk. "At least. Where is the other hiding place?"

"The whole lid. Works on the same principle as the lid to the paper tray. Swivels apart if you know where to press and twist. That's where she had the letters. Three single sheets of paper. Two swearing undying devotion, one wishing her a tender, permanent farewell."

Hyperia found the mechanism and worked it twice, then closed the traveling desk and secured the hook.

"That sketch is a good likeness of you," she said, "but you don't care for it." She joined me on a cedar chest at the foot of the enormous bed.

"I wasn't prepared for it," I said, taking her hand. "As a youth, I was so... ignorant. So unsuspecting of what life could do to a bookish lad with no vocation and a lot of privileges. Harry, as the spare, was given some warning, and Arthur was raised to step into Papa's shoes. I was neither heir nor spare, and whoever drew that sketch knew it."

A boy adrift and all unsuspecting of the currents that awaited him a few years downstream.

Hyperia bumped my shoulder with her own. "You're the heir now, my lord."

"Must you remind me?" I looped an arm around her waist. In a sense, *we* were the heirs—a duke without a duchess wasn't of much account when it came to securing the succession, was he?

She kissed my cheek, and rather than dwell on troubling sketches or ducal titles, I instead considered what the traveling desk had told us, though the topic was hardly more sanguine.

"My initial impression," I said, "is that the thief was either very much in Her Grace's confidence—had seen her working the desk's secret compartments—or the thief was an experienced felon." The sort who'd had a lot of practice opening Society's puzzle boxes and locating its safes.

Hyperia let her head fall to my shoulder. "The servants would see the duchess at her correspondence. She's not quite in Lady Ophelia's league as a letter writer, but she keeps up."

"Her Grace tends to ignore the staff and hire only the kind who know how to go about their duties quietly. Maids or footmen could have seen her reveal the desk's secrets."

"Perhaps the thief was a cabinetmaker's apprentice at one point," Hyperia murmured.

To sit with her thus settled my mental tendency to hare about, to leap from worries to questions to conjectures and back to worries. How was Atticus faring belowstairs? Had my horse made the journey from the Hall without incident? Had anybody else noticed personal effects going missing? Was that why Lady Barrington was keeping unused guest rooms locked?

What was Lady Ophelia up to? Always a worthy inquiry.

"The thief knows Her Grace well." I rested my cheek against Hyperia's hair and considered what should have been just a pretty wooden box. "To search this room earlier today took me nearly two hours, and unraveling the secrets of that box even incompletely took

Harry and me the better part of a summer. The person who stole the letters didn't have that sort of time. Their crime was the work of a few quiet moments."

Had to have been, based on the sequence of events I'd pried from my mother in my earlier interview with her. The letters had been in their assigned location after luncheon. When she'd come in from watching a bowls tournament, they'd been gone. Her room had been empty for a scant hour.

"Her Grace has many friends," Hyperia said. "I could name you a half-dozen ladies from among the guests who are of an age with the duchess and on cordial terms with her from long acquaintance. Nobody would think anything if one of them dropped by the duchess's rooms at midafternoon. She'd say she was leaving Her Grace a note and have the requisite message to support her tale."

My spirits sank. "*Ladies.* Ladies get up to mischief, and nobody suspects them. Harry relied on women for a great deal of his information in Spain. He excelled at charming neglected wives and cheering up the occasional languishing widow."

"I'll make you a list of Her Grace's familiars." Hyperia patted my knee. "You'll speak with Her Grace's lady's maid. Her name is Wisherd."

"I will speak with Wisherd tomorrow. Right now, I'd like to escort you to your room and spend a quiet hour reading to you."

I felt the change in Hyperia and knew the satisfaction of having surprised and pleased her.

"You want to read to me?"

"The day has been long for both of us, and troubling in my case. The woman who gave birth to me is all but a stranger, and yet... Her Grace knows me, Hyperia. I am mystified as to her means—we've gone for months without exchanging a word, we exchanged only epistolary pleasantries the whole time I was in uniform, but she *knows* me, and that is unsettling. A chapter or two of Mrs. Burney's wit or Mrs. Radcliffe's Gothic ridiculousness appeals, as would any handy excuse to tarry in your presence."

"Half an hour," she said, rising and shaking out her skirts. "The journey from the Hall was easy enough, but I suspect in the days ahead, we will need our rest."

A prosaic observation—I always seemed to feel short of sleep—also prescient. Before I'd concluded the duchess's investigation, I would exhaust both physical and mental reserves, and my adventures would make Mrs. Radcliffe's scribblings look dull by comparison.

CHAPTER THREE

"I am not familiar with this Wisherd person." Lady Ophelia offered that remark as we strolled formal parterres set off with squares of privet pruned to about two feet. The brick walkways had been swept, and a few other guests were enjoying the fresh autumn morning. The lack of color in the garden emphasized winter's approach, as did the lack of activity.

The hedges had been trimmed, the blooms were gone, the battle with weeds was over for a few months. The delicate plants had been marched into winter quarters in the conservatory, and the hardier specimens would face the elements as best they could.

I was in the garden by design, putting myself on display as a typical guest, paying my respects to my godmother by way of a post-prandial constitutional. The duchess, a bruising rider, had joined a hacking party intent on visiting the shops in the nearest market town.

"Would you know the duchess's lady's maid in the normal course?" I asked.

"I well might. Lady Barrington's lady's maid, Fleagle, has been with her since her first marriage. If I wanted to communicate some-thing to Lady Barrington by confidential note or word of mouth, I'd send my own lady's maid to find Fleagle to see it done. If I sought to surprise Dorothea with a holiday token, or needed to know her favorite flower, then my first recourse would be to her lady's maid."

Lady Ophelia was my mother's contemporary and, in her own way, formidable. Her ladyship appeared to be an aging original, full of naughty innuendo and harmless chatter, great fun as a dinner companion, if a bit tiring.

She was also shrewd, observant, and more discreet than most people knew. What scandals she hadn't caused she'd certainly taken the trouble to become informed about, and only she knew how many scandals she'd averted in the name of friendship, decency, or the dignity of the crown. Her ladyship was tallish and trim and much given to the sort of attire that drifted gracefully and draped elegantly.

When I'd been at my lowest, most despairing point, she had plucked me by the ear out into the fresh air and into my first civilian experience with intrigue, and that had been a mere handful of months ago.

"I should know who my mother's lady's maid is, shouldn't I?" I asked as we passed a tiered fountain that was empty save for brackish water half-covered with yellow leaves in the bottom basin.

Her ladyship steered me by the elbow down the steps that led into the park. She escorted me to a bench that offered a view of bare maples and soon-to-be bare oaks. The lawn was dotted with fat sheep, all under an azure sky that made me glad I'd worn my blue-tinted spectacles.

"Arthur might know who Dorothea has mending her gloves these days," her ladyship said, "but your mother tends to go through her personal servants like an infantryman consuming grog. They give notice, or she sacks them—always with a character and some severance. The cachet of working for a duchess soon pales in comparison to her endless haring about, her whirlwind hours, and her lively personality."

"Her Grace has a temper." She'd never raised a hand to me, but then, smacking small boys was beneath her station, and I'd given her no excuse to smack me. Ever.

"She has moods, Julian. Exhaustingly dramatic moods. Claudius was patient with her, said she was coping with a life she'd never wanted. Engaged at seventeen to a man she barely knew and wasn't sure she liked. She is not as histrionic as she used to be, but generous wages go only so far toward inspiring loyalty."

"Who is that?" I asked as a gentleman and a lady came down the steps. He was older, good-looking in a distinguished way, and she was pretty and... not older. The lady was attired in lilac, which often meant half mourning, or the sort of perpetual fading-in-place that some women preferred even years after a bereavement. Her shawl was a true violet, and the color suited her fair complexion.

"Carola Whittington and Gideon Marchant. Gideon is a permanent fixture at these gatherings, and he can be charming. Carola is the requisite pretty widow with a good portion and friendly nature. Lost her husband about five years ago. He was much older, a lieutenant general if I recall correctly. One of those fellows who could afford to buy an impressive commission earlier in life, and was then promoted by attrition and the sheer passage of time."

"Her husband would have missed most of the Iberian campaign, then. Perhaps that was a mercy. She hasn't been tempted to remarry?"

"Why would she when as a widow who has completed mourning, she's having a fine time—which we do not begrudge her? How long will it take you to find the letters?"

Lady Ophelia assumed I would find them, which was both encouraging and annoying. "Those letters could be a pile of ashes by now."

"Hard to blackmail a duchess with a pile of ashes, my boy."

The cordial couple traveled on, their conversation coming to us in snatches on the morning breeze. Mrs. Whittington had a pretty laugh, and Marchant had a tendency to pat her wrist as he spoke. For reasons that likely involved my own frustrations, I found their flirtation annoying.

"They haven't noticed us," I said. "If I were a French sniper..."

Lady Ophelia rose and moved off toward the steps. "If you're in one of those moods, then saddle your horse and go for a gallop. The start of an investigation always sours your disposition, which is short of good humor on most days. Then you go all observant, suspicious, and twitchy. I'll have Wisherd sent to the medicinal garden. You can pick some mint for a tisane to improve your spirits."

She ignored my proffered arm and set a good pace for the steps.

"Godmama, have I given offense?"

She watched the chatting couple strolling toward an octagonal gazebo along the river.

"What of Leander, Julian? The boy's mother has decamped for her home shires, and we have only her word that she'll return. Arthur is in alt, counting the hours until he takes ship for France. You've dragged me and Miss West off to this annual inanity. We're to have Highland Games at the end of next week, you know. Tossing tree trunks about, grown men hauling on ropes over mud pits. Meanwhile, Leander is left all alone at the Hall..."

Leander, age five or six, was a recent arrival at the Caldicott family seat, my brother Harry's by-blow and the subject of a previous investigation. The lad was very much at sixes and sevens, as was his mother, Millicent. Harry, in typical fashion, had procured a special license but neglected to put it to use, alas for all concerned, especially the boy's mama.

"I could not bring Leander with us," I said. "Arthur might have pulled off such a feat, but my standing doesn't admit of by-blows among my retinue."

She stopped and glowered at me. "Your standing admits of whatever feats you choose to attempt, Julian. You could adopt the marquess's title by courtesy, but you remain a plain lord instead. Leander is your responsibility, and he's a small boy all but alone in this world. Dorothea doubtless stuffed her *billets-doux* into her spare riding boots and forgot where she put them."

No, she hadn't. Whatever shortcomings my mother had, forgetfulness was my specialty, not hers.

"I will be as expeditious in my investigation as I can be," I said, "but as you've pointed out, these letters are great fodder for blackmail. The gentleman who wrote them was far beneath Her Grace in station and not exactly well situated." A music master did no manual labor, but he took coin for services and thus failed Society's test of gentility.

Godmama resumed walking. "Unless Dorothea has taken up with royal princes, a sport I do not advise anybody to pursue, nearly every trysting partner in England will be far beneath her in station. She usually shows some discernment, though."

"This was a music master, and he was quite a bit younger."

Godmama shook her head. "That one. I remember him. He was oleaginous, and Dorothea couldn't seem to help herself. First mourning drags on eternally, but in some ways, second mourning is worse. You realize you will never have back the social éclat you once had, but you haven't the stomach for remarriage, and you cannot even comfort yourself by hosting entertainments. It's as if Society draws out your misery for as long as possible."

Lady Ophelia had been widowed twice, and she'd buried two young children. Her godchildren were legion, and her surviving offspring had presented her with grandchildren. She also had nieces and nephews, cousins by the score, and friends without number.

But right now, she was concerned for one small, lonely, and likely bewildered boy, and for that, I loved her.

"I can tell Her Grace the task is impossible." I didn't want to. The missing correspondence was potentially ruinous to the duchess, and so far, no guests had disappeared in the night, no staff had taken French leave. I'd gleaned that information when Atticus had brought me hot water for shaving.

As best I knew, the thief yet abided at Tweed House, unless some particularly stealthy crook had passed by dozens of staff and guests in broad daylight and departed unseen.

Lady Ophelia slipped her hand around my elbow as we approached the steps. "If you blow retreat this soon, Dorothea will hold it against me. Just know that I would rather be at the Hall. In the alternative, you could entrust Leander to me until his mother returns from visiting her home shire."

"The boy is a Caldicott." He would also be the only family I had on hand when Arthur went traveling, and Leander was *my nephew*.

Her ladyship favored me with a crooked smile. "Fat lot of good being a Caldicott seems to do anybody."

I loved Lady Ophelia in part because she saw past titles and wealth and standing, though her perspicacity could also make me uncomfortable. "I'll make you a wager, Godmama."

"You are embarking on a clumsy attempt to wheedle. How droll."

We mounted the steps, to appearance in great good charity with each other. Ophelia had timed her display of temper for when we'd had no audience, though to call concern for Leander *temper* was not entirely accurate.

"You do your best to find the letters, my lady, and I shall do mine. Whoever locates them gets to go back to the Hall first."

"You awful boy. I have better things to do than snoop about in search of Dorothea's mail. In fairness to the duchess, that musical fellow was both attractive and talented. I'll send Wisherd to meet you in the medicinal garden."

She kissed my cheek and swanned off, and I was left to wonder exactly which of Mr. Pickering's talents her ladyship had most admired. I took myself to the medicinal garden and like her ladyship, wished I was instead bound for Caldicott Hall.

The medicinal garden, given its pragmatic focus, was located along Tweed House's northern foundation, thus guaranteeing a southern exposure and close proximity to the housekeeper's demesne and the herbal. A larger version might well be found in the acreage of the walled kitchen garden, but remedies most in demand would be grown near the house.

The sheltered location meant many of the plants yet thrived, though before the first hard frosts, some would be potted for wintering over in the conservatory, herbal, or kitchen windows.

I twisted off a sprig of peppermint and brushed it under my nose, the scent making me homesick for Caldicott Hall. Our gardens were vast and varied, and Harry and I had played in them by the hour as boys.

"My lord, good day." A woman of middling height and regular features let herself through the garden gate. "Lady Ophelia said you wanted a word?"

"Miss Wisherd, good morning." I bowed, despite the difference in our station. This woman put up with my mother, and surely she was owed a bit of deference on that ground alone? "Thank you for making the time to chat. I promise to be brief."

"Her Grace is out riding, my lord, and I'm caught up on the mending. I'm free for the moment."

I took a leaf from Harry's book and started with small talk. "A pretty day for some fresh air, though we'll soon see frost, don't you think?"

She was blond and blue-eyed, and I'd put her age past thirty. She wore not a uniform and mobcap, but rather, a plain light blue dress and a dark blue shawl. The shawl was merino wool, perhaps one of the duchess's castoffs. Excellent quality, not a snag or dropped stitch to be seen. Her attire suggested I was looking at a lady's maid who enjoyed a few of a companion's privileges.

"Frost within the fortnight, surely," she replied. "You need not be delicate with me, my lord. If you mean to ask after your mother, from everything I can tell, she's in good health and good enough spirits."

Arthur would know to pose such a question. Harry would have

offered an oblique compliment about the hue of the shawl and the
lady's eyes. I decided on a more direct approach.

"Her Grace has lost some letters," I said. "She's concerned they
could fall into the wrong hands. Shall we walk?" I gestured along the
border devoted to mints—spearmint, catmint, peppermint, and so
forth. I tossed my little specimen back among its brethren, knowing
the scent would linger on my fingers.

I did not offer my arm, lest I scandalize present company.

"Is my lord asking if I stole my employer's correspondence?"

Direct speech was to be appreciated, but that was a little too
direct even for my purposes. "I am not. In my experience, those in
domestic service seldom overstep. They are the first to be accused in
the event of mischief, and well they know it. If you and Her Grace
part ways, she will write you a glowing character and pay some
severance. Until that day, you will be loyal to your wages, if not to
Her Grace, and being transported for theft does not fit with your
plans."

Miss Wisherd kept pace with my leisurely stroll. "You have it
precisely, my lord. Those of us in service restrain our myriad criminal
impulses out of fear of reprisal, not because we're basically decent
people who know what it is to endure life's unfair turns."

Ouch. "My apologies. I deserved that rebuke. I meant to assure
you that I seek information. I am not making accusations."

"I did not take the letters. To be honest, I feel sorry for your
mother, though such sentiments would mortify her. If those missives
remind her of happier times, if they bring her any comfort, she is
deserving of that pleasure. Where's the harm in a widow finding
some distraction from her griefs?"

"Griefs, plural?"

Miss Wisherd slanted a considering look at me. "Your father had
died. His brother went shortly thereafter. Lord Harry was determined to buy his colors, from what the staff tells me, and your mother
was certain that would not end well. She was right. Then you began
nattering on about buying your colors when you'd finished your stud-

ies. Your sister Margaret had just wed that Yorkshire earl, and she and your mother were quite close."

We didn't see much of Meggie—mother of two boys and a girl—though she was a loyal correspondent, and the family opinion of her earl was affectionate.

"I take your point." Griefs, plural. "Had you seen the letters before they went missing? My mother's description was somewhat general."

"She tended to read them on the seventeenth of each month, my lord. I would see them on her vanity when I brushed out her hair at the end of the day. As far as I know, she kept them in her traveling desk, even when at home."

"Did anything about these letters strike you as distinctive?" We'd reached the far side of the garden, and I'd learned little about the object of my investigation.

"I didn't read them, my lord, and I am not in the habit of receiving personal correspondence from anyone save my sister."

Perhaps a prickly duchess needed a prickly lady's maid. "I have not seen the letters either," I said, "and my mother views them regularly. Something as unusual as being written on blue stationery might escape the duchess's recollection out of long familiarity. I have put to Her Grace a line of questions much like the ones I'm asking you, and she could tell me nothing unique about this correspondence."

"The paper was bluish, now that you mention it. Faded, but the hue was discernible. How did you know that?"

"I didn't. Some officers on the Peninsula had personal stationery in various colors. Blue for this one, cream for that one, an embossed family crest for the other. We communicate more than words when we put pen to paper, particularly when it comes to correspondence. How were the letters folded?"

Miss Wisherd stopped and stared at the peppermint. "I would say they were not creased, my lord. I saw them several times and in close proximity. Somewhat faded black ink, grayish-blue paper, and... no creases. Does that mean they weren't sent through the mail?"

"Not necessarily. If I mail you a sketch of this garden, I might send my art between two sheets of pasteboard, and the sketch would thus not be wrinkled. You have nonetheless given me the sort of detail that makes finding the letters possible, if not exactly easy." She had also raised more questions that I must put to the duchess, unfortunately.

"My guess is they were mailed," Miss Wisherd murmured. "I cannot see anybody having the temerity to deliver such correspondence in person to a woman of your mother's standing. To do so would be to risk her good name—and her wrath. A man who cared anything for a lady ought never to do that."

"Excellent point." Though the mail itself could be unreliable over longer distances, suggesting the letters had been mailed from some nearby point, if they had been mailed. "Just a few more questions, Miss Wisherd. Did you ever see my mother open her traveling desk?"

"Open the lid? Of course. The catch releases at some spot on a back corner. She treasures that item, my lord. Your father gave it to her."

"The desk has a number of ingenious compartments, places where paper can be hidden from any but a very determined observer. Are you familiar with the desk to that extent?"

She gave me another look, this one more considering than impatient. "I value your mother's privacy, my lord. I suppose that's why I've lasted longer than most of my predecessors. A lady of significant standing cannot easily dress or undress herself. She could, if she was determined on the matter, modify her wardrobe to accommodate such a necessity, but in the usual course, she won't. She requires assistance at her bath, unless she's keeping her hair very short, but even then, assistance is helpful. For your mother..."

I had no idea where this awkward gambit was heading. "For my mother...?"

"She is a private, modest person. She can be convincingly convivial, but she has learned to keep most of her thoughts and opinions to herself out of duty to her station. I suspect as a girl she was vivacious, and a duchess may not be vivacious. She cannot be overly trusting of her acquaintances, and she will have very few peers. I make it a point not to intrude on your mother's privacy. If she offers me a passing confidence, I guard it carefully. If she betrays by deed or silence some personal sentiment, I ignore it. I owe her that much."

Miss Wisherd resumed walking, and I fell in step beside her. This little homily about the privacy of the duchesses was in aid of some point, some rhetorical finale, but the gravamen eluded me.

"Miss Wisherd, might you be blunt? I am keen to find the letters, and yet, I have little insight into where they might be. I asked if you'd seen my mother access the various compartments in her traveling desk, and you replied in terms relating to privacy and duty and station."

She half smiled, revealing a quiet sort of allure. "And you want a yes-or-no answer, don't you? Your mother considers you the most sensible of the Caldicott males. The present duke is dutiful and dignified, but your mother gives you highest honors for common sense."

Interesting, and irrelevant. Why was Miss Wisherd dodging my simple inquiry? "Very well, yes or no, have you seen my mother opening hidden compartments in her traveling desk, and before you answer, my next question will be, do you know of anybody else who might have seen her doing that?"

"Any chambermaid, my lord. Any footman bearing a bucket of coal. The ducal staff is trained to be silent and invisible, if they must intrude on their betters at all. Her Grace does them the courtesy of ignoring them. They do her the courtesy of being ignorable. She could well have opened every compartment in that desk before staff and been unaware they were present, though why would family retainers bruit such a thing about?"

We'd reached the gate, which I held open for Miss Wisherd. "I am not suggesting that Her Grace was purposely betrayed in this instance. A footman, three pints down on darts night, might have made a passing reference to Her Grace's fancy desk and all the little puzzles it contains. Another footman might have tried to open the desk on a dare and met with some success. The second footman brags to a hostler, the hostler makes a passing comment to the innkeeper's wife, who remarks on the curious habits of the local duchess to the village cabinetmaker, and so forth."

Had *Mr. Pickering* seen Her Grace working the desk's secrets? From what Miss Wisherd had told me, the chances were that he had. Her Grace might have permitted him to doze on her sofa while she'd worked the latches and catches. She might have had the compartments open while Pickering pretended to compose his next string quartet at the reading table.

Pickering had much to answer for, wherever he was.

"I'm sorry I could not be more help, my lord. I know your mother is exceedingly vexed that the letters have gone missing."

"You've considered who among the other staff here might have taken them?"

"Your mother and I discussed it, and I couldn't be much help there either. Staff would not have many excuses to invade Her Grace's apartment in the midafternoon. Her bouquets had already been changed on the day in question. Nothing from the laundry was ready to be sent up at the hour when she watched the young people play bowls."

Excellent details and convincing. "Were you with the duchess when she discovered the letters had been taken?"

"I was. She'd summoned me to assist her out of her afternoon dress. She planned to work on her correspondence and have a nap. She had opened the desk and was rummaging about when she realized the letters were gone. I was turning down the bed, but Her Grace never did take that nap."

A note of disapproval colored the last observation. Miss Wisherd's devotion was apparently genuine. She guarded my mother's privacy, and she monitored how much the duchess rested.

"I apologize again for intruding on your free time," I said, mindful that Miss Wisherd likely had little enough of that commodity, "but I will ask you to turn your mind from who had an opportunity to take the letters—a broad field in one sense—and think instead about who might have had a motive. Has Her Grace annoyed anybody lately? Has she flirted with the wrong husband or foiled a matchmaker's schemes for a favorite niece?"

Miss Wisherd shook her head in the manner of a disappointed governess. "Your mother isn't like that. She doesn't poach on another lady's preserves. She has no time for the matchmakers' games. She reads a great deal. She plays the pianoforte exceedingly well. She loves to ride over hill and dale but abhors the hunt. Your father permitted her three charities, and she remains conscientiously devoted to all three and to his memory."

I was bungling this whole interview. Retreating and regrouping struck me as the wisest course. "Miss Wisherd, I mean Her Grace no insult. I am trying to solve a vexing puzzle at Her Grace's request, and somebody stole those letters. To risk hanging or transportation over a trio of old *billets-doux* suggests a very strong motive."

"The duchess would never prosecute the thief, my lord, no matter who that may be. She would not involve herself in anything so scandalous as a criminal trial, particularly when the nature of the stolen goods would become grist for the satirists. Her Grace might be best served by letting the whole business blow over."

Miss Wisherd had a point. When I referred to hanging or transportation as the price the thief would pay for his crime, I envisioned a worst case for the perpetrator. Unless I caught the blighter red-handed, he—or she—would pay no price at all.

"Consider who had motive nonetheless, Miss Wisherd. I haven't much else to go on, and delicate discussions with Her Grace are exceedingly awkward for us both."

Her smile reappeared, at about three-quarter intensity. If she ever truly beamed at a fellow, she'd be quite pretty, which she likely knew and avoided accordingly.

"This conversation has been quite awkward enough for me, your lordship, but as to that, your mother fears to further alienate you.

When you abandoned the Hall for London after mustering out, she was downcast for a fortnight. I was new to her service and thought my employer subdued by nature. She wasn't subdued. She was pining."

Bollocks to that. "Her Grace has painted a somewhat inaccurate picture of that situation for you, Miss Wisherd, but let's leave the past in the past and focus on solving the present conundrum, shall we?"

She looked like she wanted to say more, to speak sternly with me, but ended up dipping a curtsey, muttering a polite parting, and consigning me to the company of the fading medicinals.

I knew not what to make of the discussion. Miss Wisherd's view of Her Grace was very different from mine, which didn't make either one of us wrong. I decided to ponder the conversation where I did my best thinking—in the saddle—and turned my steps for the stable and the company of my horse.

If ever a creature was capable of offering wise counsel, it was my trusty Atlas, though the company I found proved to be loquacious rather than sagacious.

Also something of a tribulation to my nerves.

CHAPTER FOUR

I was prone to infrequent spells of complete forgetfulness. For a time —usually hours, sometimes not even an hour—I would forget my name. I would look about at a location I'd known since infancy and have no idea what country I was in. I wouldn't know the date or who sat upon the throne or which throne had my loyalty.

Speech was not lost to me during these episodes. The only faculty impaired was memory, which was obliterated, foot, horse, and cannon. And then, after a time, the whole book of my life returned to my keeping in every detail. The lapses had no apparent pattern. They came and went, and I did my best to weather them with some dignity. I kept a card, written in my own hand, on my person at all times explaining the situation.

Encountering Mr. Gideon Marchant stirred a vague sense of the same disorientation that afflicted me when a spell of forgetting descended. He assumed a familiarity that made me question if we'd met. If so, had we become bosom bows, and I'd somehow completely lost track of the connection?

"My lord, my lord, such a pleasure to clap eyes on you." He shoved a hand at me when our paths crossed on the walkway that led to the stable. I tolerated the presumption by shaking his proffered appendage. His smile was jovial, and if he had smelled any more strongly of sandalwood, I would have sneezed.

Sir, we have not been introduced. "Mr. Marchant, good morning." Had Godmama not identified him to me, we would have been complete strangers.

"Dorothea speaks so highly of you, and now I see that she does not exaggerate. You are a handsome devil. Be mindful of the young ladies, my boy. This batch did not bag husbands during the Season, and they are a determined lot. Has its advantages for an old campaigner like myself, but one must be careful too, eh?"

I disliked his innuendo and the cloying—expensive—scent of his shaving soap. Advantages indeed. "I am here at Her Grace's invitation, Marchant, and looking forward to some congenial company as we enjoy the last of the decent weather."

"Michaelmas summers are always a bit sad, as are the daisies left to bloom in them. Shall we enjoy a hack? Let's do. You've been least in sight since mustering out, and one wants to know why. The gossips have speculated apace in your case, and yet, they cannot be outright insulting to a ducal heir. Then too, we don't see many of that ilk permitted to preserve their bachelorhood for long, do we?"

This bumptious, jocular patter assured me that I had not met Gideon Marchant previously. I would have made it a point to keep at least two counties between us had that been the case.

"I have been recovering from my years in uniform," I said. "My eyes will likely always take exception to too much strong sunshine."

"Hence those fetching blue spectacles. They give you a scholarly, eccentric air. Has your hair always been blond?"

I could easily learn to hate this man. "Time in French custody turned my hair white. I'm assured I will regain the original color eventually. Tell me of yourself, Marchant. How did you meet my mother?"

"She took pity on me years ago, allowed me to serve as one of her gallants. Society understood that I was too busy adoring my unattainable duchess to offer marriage to a young belle. Dorothea always had a devoted escort to the theater or Vauxhall as a result. You young people don't appreciate the benefits of friendships between the sexes, but our generation perfected the art."

I did not care for the familiarity with which he referred to Her Grace. I did not care for his condescending little lecture on polite society's rosy and roaringly licentious past.

Where one's mother was concerned, some delicacy should apply. "You are also well acquainted with Lady Barrington, I understand."

"I know everybody, my boy. Absolutely everybody. Hellie wouldn't think of hosting a gathering without inviting me. We've been through the wars together, we happy few, though you won't find us reminiscing when there's so much diversion to be had. Tell me of your years under Wellington. Was he as rigid and uppish as every-body says?"

One did *not* insult His Grace of Wellington, who had indeed been rigid and uppish at times. The duke was also possessed of a droll, occasionally acerbic wit and had a genius for battle strategy. He could be endlessly charming to the ladies, and he'd had a zealot's relentlessness when it came to provisioning and clothing his army, despite Parliament's indifference to same.

More significantly, Wellington had taken quiet though public steps to quash the rumors circulating about my trustworthiness as an officer. The gossip continued, but more discreetly.

"His Grace was ever appropriate," I said, "given the hardships he and his soldiers faced. I was not often at headquarters and then only long enough to give my reports and get back to work."

We approached the stable, a two-story fieldstone edifice graced with a few pots of red salvia and yellow chrysanthemums. The stable yard was full of the ordered bustle common to well-run equine enter-prises. A groom wielded a broom in the steady rhythm of the seasoned stable boy. He sang Burns's lament for the loss of sweet Senegal, from whence the lad's ancestors might well have hailed.

Another fellow groomed a dainty gray mare to a high shine, and a farrier trimmed the front hoof of a leggy chestnut.

The scene helped me marshal my patience. I, too, had work to do. A hack with Marchant could yield useful information, and I hadn't been planning on a long or vigorous ride.

"You there," Marchant called to a lanky youth watering a pair of mares at a stone trough. "Fetch my horse, if you would. Gray gelding, about sixteen hands. Should be in stall number eight."

This told me Marchant had not sent word ahead to the stable that he'd be riding, and his offer to hack out with me had been spontaneous.

"I'll fetch my own mount." I proceeded into the dim, horsey-scented barn and found Atlas enjoying a mound of hay in a stall near the end of the row. He ceased his depredations when he caught sight of me and whuffled gently.

"Greetings, horse." I offered him a gloved hand to sniff over his half door and then a quarter of an orange I'd pilfered from the breakfast buffet.

I was inordinately glad to see him. I'd purchased him in Spain from an officer who'd been pockets to let. Atlas had the quiet fire of the Iberian breeds and the heft of his draft horse mother. We got along splendidly, both of us preferring the countryside to Town.

The grooms looked askance when I commenced currying my horse, but they left me to it. I wasn't the only former officer they'd encountered, and the typical veteran was nigh fanatical about the care of his cattle.

I saddled Atlas in the stable yard rather than in his stall. Since my time as a captive of the French, I'd harbored a profound distaste for small spaces enclosed by iron bars. Marchant watched me from the golden shade of a fading oak, his expression idle and pleasant.

As little as I knew Her Grace, I still could not see her lighting upon Marchant as her escort of choice. But then, if Miss Wisherd was correct, the duchess had been a lively, friendly young woman, and she was much changed from those earlier times.

I led Atlas to the mounting block and climbed into the saddle, then waited for Marchant to mount his gray.

"Handsome fellow you have there," I said, surveying Marchant's gelding as we left the stable yard. The beast had good bone and a refined head, though his coat was going a bit coarse with the approach of colder weather.

"Ruffian looks like a gentleman," Marchant replied, "but don't let looks deceive you. He has a wild streak. I permit nobody else to ride him, lest they come to harm. He minces along, full of airs and graces, and just when your mind wanders to the beauty of the sun upon the lake, he'll bolt."

A nasty, dangerous habit. "Why keep him?"

"He'll jump anything, he's gorgeous, and we understand each other. He no longer subjects me to his worst behaviors. Tell me about this fine specimen." Marchant gestured with his crop near Atlas's head. Atlas half shied and gave him a dirty look, but otherwise took the rudeness in stride.

"Iberian on the sire's side, draft on the distaff. Steady under fire, tireless on campaign, lovely gaits. He'll take me to Dover and back to see my brother off and be ready for the same with a day's rest. I won't tax him today because he made the journey from the Hall yesterday."

"As did you yourself, with the lovely Miss West and our dear Lady Ophelia doing likewise. One is always a bit more on the *qui vive* when Ophelia's on hand, if you know what I mean."

The *qui vive*—who lives?—was a reference to the question French sentries would put to strangers approaching the castle gates, shorthand for, *Whom do you wish to live?* The focus of the query was to discover loyalties. One should generally wish the king to enjoy a long and peaceful life, but the term now referred to any state of heightened alert.

"On the *qui vive* around her ladyship? I'm not sure I grasp what you imply. She is my godmother and a family friend of standing longer than your own. She is dear to me, and I have always found her to be good company."

Damn near insulting a lady was the quickest means for one fellow to make a bad first impression on another. Insulting Wellington was quicker.

"Oh yes, quite. Good company. Shall we let them stretch their legs?" Marchant settled his hat more firmly on his head.

"Atlas and I will keep to a sedate pace for a bit longer, thank you, but you and Ruffian should do as you please." To tax a horse before he'd had a chance to work out the kinks accumulated over a night confined in a stall was foolishness.

To imply that Lady Ophelia was less than good *ton* was rank discourtesy.

To insult Wellington to a former officer approached treason.

"Well, if you don't mind," Marchant said. "Ruffian tends to be on better behavior if I let him have his head early in a ride. I am loath to deal with his bad side, lest he have to deal with mine, so I'll leave you here. I don't suppose you're a tenor?"

"Baritone, tending to bass."

"Such a pity. I'm getting together an impromptu glee club, and we have enough of the lower register. Ah, well, perhaps we'll have to make do with sopranos for the higher register. That could be interesting." He wiggled his brows and saluted with his crop, then set his heels to Ruffian's sides.

The horse cantered off, making an elegant picture against the autumn landscape.

"What the hell was he up to?" I murmured as Atlas and I watched the pair thunder down the lane. "He came that close to goading me into issuing a challenge."

As Atlas and I ambled through the sunny morning, I was increasingly convinced that Marchant had been on reconnaissance, probing my defenses, looking for weak spots, testing the walls of my composure.

Some members of polite society were like that, viewing every encounter as a skirmish and every ballroom as a battlefield. I found such games tiresome, unbecoming, and pointless, but I was a ducal heir. My future might not see my every dream coming true, but neither did I have to scrap for Society's notice.

Atlas gave a discreet tug at the reins. Time to cease dawdling.

"Very well, but we're not pelting headlong over rabbit holes."

He snorted, and I shortened my reins. The horse was ready for a thumping good trot, if not a hearty gallop, but my stamina wasn't as reliable. I nevertheless let him have his head, and after a brisk trot and a relaxed canter, Atlas, too, was ready for more sedate paces.

I was taking off my spurs in the stable yard and watching Atlas saunter away in the care of a groom when a contradiction popped into my head.

Marchant had not asked to have his horse saddled and bridled in advance, but he had been in riding clothes when we'd met on the path, right down to the spurs on his heels. Strolling with Mrs. Whittington earlier, he'd been in morning attire. Very likely, he'd seen me out with Lady Ophelia, seen that I was dressed for a hack, and changed his own wardrobe in short order.

The whole a-pleasure-to-clap-eyes-on-you performance and the systematic attempts to annoy me thereafter had been a carefully planned engagement, if not an ambush. If Marchant had tried to make me dislike him, he could not have succeeded more handily.

Why? Why court my disdain, when most of Society felt the disdain ought to flow in my direction? And did Marchant's behavior have anything to do with Her Grace's missing letters?

"Who the devil are you?" I put the question to a young man in a plain black wool suit who was peering up the chimney of my parlor flue. He wasn't in livery, he was utterly unknown to me, and he was in *my private quarters.*

The fellow withdrew his head from the hearth and dusted ungloved hands. "Morning, my lord. I'm MacFadden, Hugh Gunning MacFadden, at your service. Gentleman's gentleman to Mr.

Marchant. I'm to inquire if you have need of valeting and to provide service accordingly."

He spoke with that blend of dignity and humor common to the Scot, and his accent placed him as a native to Perthshire. His twinkling blue eyes and mischievous smile further classified him as the typical canny laddie. MacFadden's features were just a touch craggy, even at his relatively youthful age—he couldn't have been much older than me—and his dark brows were a trifle fierce. Those brows emphasized his masculinity rather than detracted from it. My sisters, who had perfected a taxonomy of male descriptors, would have said he wasn't merely handsome, he was *attractive*.

And yet, he also spoke a trifle loudly and carried his head with the slight tilt of a man who heard better out of one ear than the other. That canted angle gave him an avian alertness that hinted of the raptor.

"MacFadden, good day. Lord Julian Caldicott, and you will doubtless be pleased to know that my tiger-cum-boot-boy acts as my liaison with the laundresses. I'm sure their efforts will be adequate for my needs."

Those dark brows drew down. "My lord, you cannot mean that you'll leave your best evening attire in the hands of *those women?* They regard the iron as a weapon rather than an artist's tool, and they think nothing of skimping on starch for the sake of economies."

His dismay came across as both amused and genuine.

"I will nonetheless take my chances with the ladies. I won't be here long, and I'm sure Marchant keeps you busy. Is inspecting chimneys a normal part of your duties?"

"Aye, milord, it is. Nothing blights clean linen like coal smoke, and we're lighting fires nightly now. I make it a point to inspect the flues for any gentleman I serve, and for Mr. Marchant most especially. A chimney that doesn't draw can give a man the most awful head upon rising, and he won't even realize the flue is to blame. If you don't believe me, run your handkerchief over the inside of the windowpanes in the music room, for example. Far from pristine."

"I have endured worse privations than a bit of coal smoke, MacFadden. Be off with you. My thanks for the offer, but your services won't be necessary."

He ran a fingertip over the mantel, tut-tutted, and bowed. "As my lord wishes, but you've only to call, and I will do my utmost to give good service."

I was a courtesy lord. Marchant was a mere mister. MacFadden would not purposely offend me, for his own sake, much less for that of his employer, and thus I forgave the man his obstinate generosity.

"I will thank Marchant for the proffered loan of your services."

MacFadden nodded and made for the door. Had he been newer to service or had our interview gone differently, he might have hesitated to give me his back. As it was, he faced me again before making his exit.

"I'll keep a lookout for the wee lad, my lord. He's a sharp one. Already has Cook wrapped around his finger, and he's getting on well with the first footman. I've seen him out in the stable, too, and he's making himself useful wherever he is."

As my eyes and ears among the lower ranks, the less noticeable Atticus was, the better. And yet, a lad could use an ally outside the safety of camp.

"Atticus has been managing on his own since he was in dresses. Your kindness toward him will be appreciated, but try to go gently. The boy has his pride."

"Wasn't much older than him when I went into service. It's not a bad life, compared to some. I'll wish you good day, my lord."

He finally took himself off, and I once again had cause to appreciate my own valet. That fellow knew how to keep himself to himself, a fine quality in a gentleman's gentleman.

I changed riding attire into formal morning wear—without the aid of a lackey, let it be noted—and was making a mental list of questions to put to my mother privately. Old enemies, suspiciously new friends... Where might I look for Pickering, and had he been close to anybody on the staff at the Hall? Did any of the guests strike Her

Grace as being short of funds, and was she truly above the match-making affray, or had she advertently run afoul of—

The door to my sitting room opened, and a lady came to a halt halfway across the carpet. "Dear me. You are not Gideon. I thought this was his room."

"Mrs. Whittington." I bowed. "Lord Julian Caldicott, at your service. Marchant has the quarters across the corridor, if I recall correctly."

"I do beg your pardon, my lord. Gideon told me you'd arrived. You and I were introduced, you know, at some regimental ball during winter quarters. Three, possibly four years ago. I was out of mourning and had gone to Portugal to meet up with some of the other wives, then I was to escort a pair of young girls home to bide with relatives. The whole business was dragging on, and... I am babbling."

I had no recollection of our encounter, but winter quarters had been anathema to me. Some officers had summoned their wives to share the seasonal tedium, but I'd preferred to be out in the country-side, keeping my Spanish in good trim and learning what I could of the terrain and of our enemies.

"You have a better memory than I do," I said, "though I am pleased to renew our acquaintance. I left Marchant intent on a lengthy hack. I'm sure you could entrust a message to MacFadden, his valet, who should be across the corridor."

Mrs. Whittington was a widow and comely. If I were found alone with her, nobody would give the situation more than a passing thought. House parties were all but intended to foster such opportunities. The lady's reputation would suffer only a light streak of tarnish, not for disporting with me, but for having been caught doing it.

My reputation, however, was sufficiently battered that I did not want to add house-party Lothario to my list of alleged shortcomings.

"Can I interest you in a sortie to the library, Mrs. Whittington? I have ever been fond of books and find that a collection can say a lot about its owner."

"You were polite then too," Mrs. Whittington said. "Lord Harry was a charmer, but you had the better manners."

Lord Harry had been a philanderer, sometimes in the line of duty, which had never sat well with me. Harry had seemed to discount the notion that his objective—gaining intelligence from the enemy—might be the lady's objective as well.

"Lord Harry was sometimes too charming," I said. "If he gave offense, I apologize on his behalf." She'd been a widow when our paths had crossed on the Peninsula, and the words *fair game* followed that status in all too many exclusively male preserves.

"A widow learns the rules of engagement, my lord, especially a military widow who was married to a man more than twice her age. Lord Harry was gentleman enough to abide by the rules. I should not have said that. Don't speak ill of the dead, and so forth."

"I have regular reason to wish my brother were alive so that I could remonstrate with him to his face. Shall we to the library?" She was a perfectly pleasant woman and apparently not Marchant's lover, or not yet his lover, for she hadn't known where his quarters lay.

I nonetheless wanted her out of my sitting room, quick time, for myriad reasons.

"I will decline your escort, my lord. I've lost my locket, and it has great sentimental value. I'm determined to find it. I am almost certain I had it on when I went walking with Gideon this morning. I mean, I am nearly certain I put it on this morning—I always wear it—and I suppose the catch gave, or I caught the chain somehow, but if I knew when it had come loose, I'd have a better idea of where to search."

The missing locket was none of my affair—I hoped—and yet, I allowed myself a few questions. "Can you describe this item?"

"It's nothing extraordinary, a trinket I've had since first mourning. Gold, heart-shaped, a simple hinge mechanism, and a short chain. The inside is inscribed but the words are so small, they are barely legible in strong sunlight with a quizzing glass. A tiny lock of dark brown hair inside."

Her late husband's presumably. Mourning lockets could be of gold, though onyx was also favored.

"You put it on when you dressed this morning?"

"I don't wear it at night, but once I have my hair up, I routinely don the locket, along with my wedding ring. I'm wearing my ring, so I must have followed my usual course, mustn't I?" Her certainty was laced with doubt.

"Check your jewelry box anyway. If you were in a hurry, if you were a bit late for your stroll with Marchant, if you were hungry and your mind was on breakfast... You might have forgotten or been distracted. Look carefully at your purple shawl too. Jewelry snags in wool so easily."

She eyed the open door. "How did you know the color of my shawl?"

"I, too, enjoyed a perambulation in the fresh morning air. I was escorting Lady Ophelia Oliphant, who happens to be my godmother. We were sitting on the bench near the foot of the steps that lead into the park, and you and Mr. Marchant passed by. I noted the color because it suited you."

Then too, a splash of violet on an autumn morning made an impression. Noting odd, out-of-place details had saved my life more than once.

"You find things," she said slowly. "You found that dog and some viscount or other, and I forget what else."

"Right now, I would like to find a good book, and then I'm off to locate my mother, if the hacking party has returned from plundering the shops."

Would you please leave? One could not say that to a lady upset over the loss of a precious keepsake, but I needed to chat directly with Lady Barrington somewhere private—a thorough, discreet search of all the guest rooms was in order, the sooner the better—and I wanted to apprise Hyperia of my morning's activities. Then too, I had a niggling desire to find Atticus and make him aware that MacFadden had taken notice of him.

"I'll have a look at my jewelry box and shawl," Mrs. Whittington said. "Those are good suggestions, my lord."

She withdrew into the corridor, and I followed her, closing and locking my sitting room door first.

"If it helps," I said as we approached the main staircase, "you and Marchant did a circuit of the privet terraces in the formal garden, then you descended into the park and made straight for the gazebo by the river. I don't recall if you went into the gazebo, and I cannot say what route you took back to the house. Marchant might have been in something of a hurry because he was intent on changing into riding attire."

"He claimed a sudden need to consult with MacFadden about next week's games, MacFadden being a genuine Scot and all."

More evidence supporting the theory that Marchant had seen me dressed for riding and changed his plans accordingly. Why? To spend a quarter hour annoying me with conversation so distasteful another man might have called him out for it?

"That tells us you made your way back to the house alone," I observed. "Perhaps you simply retraced your steps?" We'd reached the landing, and the lady paused.

"I sat for a time by the river. Seeing old friends brings back memories, and sometimes the thing to do is to be sad, let the memories have their moment, then tuck them away until they need another airing. Your mother and Lady Barrington were very kind when my Freddie went to his reward, and they'd been good friends when he was alive too. Our husbands were thrown together by parliamentary committee work, and both women allowed as how shared abandonment put us on equal footing, despite the differences in our stations. Still, grief is a burden ultimately carried alone."

Widows and soldiers marched over common ground, especially military widows and soldiers. "I find activity helps as well. Be sad, then fix an objective and get moving."

"Well said. One can see why your mother speaks so highly of you. Thank you, my lord. You've been kind as well as sensible." Mrs.

Whittington patted my arm then took to the steps, presumably to rifle her bedchamber and examine her shawl.

I had a lock of Harry's hair. I kept it in my own jewelry box. He'd given it to me before setting out on some particularly delicate mission. Such sentimentality had had little place with Harry, but I was glad to have the memento, though I seldom even looked at it. I could give it to Leander someday, and that meant worlds.

My next objective was to locate Lady Barrington, my mother, Hyperia, or Atticus. I thought to stop a footman and issue queries, but instead a footman stopped me.

"Your lordship has a visitor," he said. "In the earl's study."

"A visitor?"

"Looks a bit like you, but more serious, not so lean. Didn't want no tea, said to fetch you without making a fuss. Study is—"

"I know. Across from the library. My thanks. If you see Lady Barrington, Miss West, or Her Grace, please let them know I'd like a word."

"Aye, milord. Will do." He jaunted off, and I was left to wonder why my brother Arthur, His Grace of Waltham, was making a sneak attack on Lady Barrington's house party. Bad news, no doubt, and about that, I was utterly correct.

CHAPTER FIVE

"I've always liked Lady Barrington," Arthur said when I joined him in the earl's study. "She was between husbands when I was making the rounds, and she seemed to appreciate a bachelor with no designs on her portion or her person."

His Grace of Waltham pretended to examine the signature on a formal portrait of her ladyship, holding pride of place over the mantel. This display of idle curiosity confirmed that Arthur had a difficult topic to broach.

My handsome, shrewd, vastly accomplished brother was shy, a realization that had come as a shock to me when I'd resumed biding at Caldicott Hall. Growing up, I'd thought Arthur a prig, a dukeling, a firstborn aristocratic male, and, honestly, a bit stuffy. The six-year difference in our ages had added to my misperceptions. His Grace was simply very reserved, and for reasons.

His lofty station invited constant scrutiny, and his personal devotion to the estimable Osgood Banter could see him hanged, be he peer or peasant. I'd suggested strongly that Arthur and Banter enjoy a leisurely progress on the Continent, now that Europe was at peace.

Arthur had nigh leaped on the opportunity, and their departure was days away.

Me and my brilliant suggestions...

"How are you getting on?" he asked when Lady Barrington's portrait had been duly inspected. "Has Mama found her letters?"

She was *Mama* to him, at least in a private family conversation. "They were stolen, I'm afraid, and by somebody who could watch her comings and goings closely, somebody who knew the house party schedule to the quarter hour."

Arthur wandered to the French doors and admired the view of the park. "A guest?"

"Possibly, or somebody in the pay of a guest. Tweed House staff would be unlikely to risk the good name of the family by stealing from a visiting duchess. Sufficient coin would nonetheless turn most of us into thieves under the right circumstances. What brings you here?"

Arthur and I had begun negotiating the delicate business of parting in preparation for his travels. We'd both felt Harry's loss keenly in different ways, and we were much closer than we'd been when I'd returned from Waterloo.

Closeness came at a cost when separation loomed. I was preparing to hold the dukedom's reins in Arthur's absence and to endure the Hall on my own until he returned. For his part, Arthur was doubtless wrestling with the guilt of abandoning his post to his only surviving brother, and neither of our struggles were abetted by this unscheduled interview.

"I've had a letter," Arthur said, withdrawing a folded piece of paper from a breast pocket. "I thought you should see it before any action is taken."

"We are in the season of epistolary troubles, it seems." I took the missive from him and brought it to the window. The hand was tidy, feminine, and confident. A lady's hand.

"From Millicent," I noted, mother to our nephew Leander. She'd taken herself off to her home shire, claiming a need to catch up with family and old friends, and we'd lent her the traveling coach to make the journey. According to John Coachman's report, the reunion had gone well, her family seemed to be thriving, and the immediate parish prospered as well.

"She gets to the point near the end."

After prosing on about the delights of family ties and the pleasure of seeing dear friends, Millicent did indeed get to the point: She wasn't coming back to the Hall. After much thought, she'd decided that Leander's lot in life would be easier were he committed to the care and custody of his ducal relations, and while it broke her heart to do so, she would start anew without him and maintain the maternal tie only to the extent she could do so discreetly.

Any documents necessary to put the situation on proper legal footing would be executed at His Grace's request.

"She's not wrong," Arthur said. "We'll do right by the boy. Harry was wrong for not marrying her. Leander is our responsibility now."

"You'd rather she leave Leander behind than take him from us," I said, "but that's your conscience talking, not your heart. He's a little boy, Arthur, and his mother has been his only stability. What you and I know about raising small children wouldn't fill a stirrup cup. Leander will be devastated."

"He might also be relieved." Arthur joined me at the window, and there we stood, six inches apart, our gazes fixed on the landscape. "When I learned I was to be sent off to public school, I was about six, and somebody let it slip that six-year-olds were old enough to matriculate. Papa wouldn't hear of it, of course, so I had a reprieve until I heard that some other fellow had been packed off at age eight. My next tutor was contracted for two years of instruction—another reprieve—and by the time I finally did leave the Hall at twelve, I wasn't looking forward to public school, but I was ready to get on with it."

For *four years*, the young ducal heir had dreaded that day of parting, and nobody had bothered to explain the situation to him. He hadn't brought his worry to the attention of an adult who could have offered credible reassurances either.

"I was six when you left, and I thought you were never coming home." Arthur's letters to Papa had been weekly exercises in penmanship reporting high marks, perfect deportment, and bad, scanty rations. They were read at the supper table as a form of entertainment for the adults, but I'd heard them more as reports from an unpleasant and bewildering form of banishment.

"I am coming home, Jules." Arthur spoke gently. "The Almighty alone can alter that aspect of my itinerary."

The Almighty was notorious for altering itineraries. "Leander saw his mama off with every confidence she'd come back to us too. Lady Ophelia predicted this development, and she will not be best pleased with us for letting it happen."

"I've wondered if I didn't invite it to happen," Arthur murmured. "I settled a sum on Millicent, and thus she became more marriageable."

"I told you to settle that sum on her, more or less. I can fetch her home."

"You cannot."

How innocent my brother was. "If I roll up to her family home in all my Caldicott glory and indicate that she can either return to the Hall with me and resume her duties as the duchess's companion, or hear me lay her past before the whole village, she will get into the coach."

"You can take the soldier out of his uniform..." Arthur said, pushing away from the window and settling into the chair behind the earl's desk. "You are not to waylay Millicent in such a fashion. I can postpone my departure, and we'll see what's to be done."

The offer tempted me nigh unbearably. "You will do no such thing." Arthur had worn the shackles of duty his whole life, while Harry and I had been in uniform for a mere handful of years. We had both freely chosen to buy our commissions and been suited to our roles, for the most part.

"I am Leander's uncle, Jules, and—"

"I am his uncle as well. When it comes to the uncle business, we are equally unqualified to raise the boy and both positioned to adequately provide for him. The longer you put off traveling, the harder parting from Leander will become for you and for him. You are leaving, and that is a direct order."

"You're sure?"

He would ask that. "Of course not, but bumbling about, waiting for another letter to bring us another turn of events, or for Leander to start asking awkward questions to which we haven't formed plausible answers, won't serve. Millicent has made her decision. I will secure guardianship of Leander in your absence, and we will muddle on through the winter as best we can."

What would Hyperia make of this development? Leander liked her tremendously, though Lady Ophelia was his odds-on favorite. She'd been mine, too, in early boyhood.

"I don't like leaving this on your plate," Arthur said, rising. "I am the duke, and the child is my responsibility, and you have enough to worry about."

An oblique reference to my various infirmities of body and mind, perhaps. "Her Grace's letters are likely in the hands of a blackmailer. When demands for money start appearing, I will have a trail to follow, and I can put her malefactor to rights then."

"Speaking of which, keep that letter," Arthur said. "If Millicent turns up hesitant when it's time to sign legal papers, that letter confirms her consent to give us guardianship."

Perhaps His Grace wasn't so innocent after all. "I will put this epistle where even blackmailers won't find it."

"You're sure the letters were stolen?"

"As sure as I am of anything, and so is Her Grace. She would not have summoned me otherwise."

Arthur moved the standish two inches left so it was centered above Lord Barrington's desk blotter. "What if the objective isn't blackmail, but rather, torment? When I have had occasion to suspect that somebody noted my fondness for Banter, the result was torment. A blackmailer is a parasite. They seek coin, influence, some form of barter in exchange for silence, and I have vast resources with which to barter. Exposing my weaknesses to all of society would cut the blackmailer off from the steady flow of my wealth. My worst fear has never been blackmail per se, but rather, being in the power of somebody who could hurt Banter."

"The duchess cannot be hanged for what's in those letters, Arthur. She became entangled with a handsome young bounder. The tale is more sad than salacious."

"But somebody has risked hanging by stealing them."

"The risk arises only if I can catch the thief, as has been pointed out to me, and I have no confidence whatsoever that I can pull off such a miracle. Anybody Her Grace offended has a reason to purloin her private correspondence. Any guest or employee of a guest had some opportunity to commit the thievery. I have dozens of suspects, Arthur, and no means of narrowing the field."

"So you're in winter quarters, waiting for the enemy to move?"

Winter quarters had been more a matter of waiting for the spring rains to result in enough fodder that an army of tens of thousands could graze and provision its way across Spain.

"I am preparing to search the entire guest wing, more or less, but I must secure Lady Barrington's permission first."

"And Her Grace's. Keep her informed, Jules. Mama asks little enough of me besides a weekly report of the goings-on at the Hall, but she does like to know what's afoot. Have you inquired about her plans for the winter?"

"I assumed she did as she pleased."

"Everybody assumes a duchess does as she pleases. The same mistake is made regarding dukes. You ask her as a courtesy. You tell her of your own plans on the same basis. She answers as a courtesy, and in the course of the discussion, it might be revealed that you'd enjoy spending the holidays with our mother, et cetera."

I would enjoy spending the holidays with Hyperia, of that I was certain. "Her Grace would enjoy having her letters back." For all sorts of reasons, I'd like to be the one to return them to her.

"Retrieving missing articles is your lookout," Arthur said. "Banter wants us in Dover by Monday. We sail on Tuesday, God willing."

That soon? "Then I hope your packing is well advanced. I'll meet you in Dover."

"Offer to bring Her Grace along. She won't come—Mama has already delivered her parting lectures—but offer anyway."

"If she'll refuse the invitation, why bother to extend it?"

Arthur studied me for an uncomfortable moment. "Papa was no great prize as a husband, Jules. By the time you came along, the great marital rows had mostly ceased, and I no longer had to fear I'd walk into a room and find Mama in tears again, but His Grace had much to apologize for."

Arthur, as the firstborn, had a perspective I lacked. "Did he apologize?"

"Oh, he doubtless regularly said the words, then broke her heart all over again. If there's one thing I appreciate about Banter, it's that he doesn't play games based in jealousy and manipulation."

He didn't need to. Arthur's devotion had been as unswerving as it was discreet, but that Arthur would verbally acknowledge Banter's role in his life, even to me, was touching.

Also dangerous. "I will miss you." I said the words before gentlemanly decorum, embarrassment, or pride could stifle them.

"I leave part of my heart at the Hall, Jules, just as you did when you went off to Spain."

I absolutely had, much to my surprise, and memories of the Hall and its rural splendors had sustained me through some of my blackest moments.

"I'll see you in Dover," I said, tucking Millicent's letter into my breast pocket. "How do you plan to get out of Tweed House without being seen? The unmarried young ladies are present at battalion strength, from what I saw at supper and breakfast, and the matchmakers will be in alt if they catch sight of you."

Arthur returned to the French doors. "The matchmakers are in alt at the sight of *you*, Jules. Perhaps those blue spectacles obscure what's sitting plainly in front of you."

He undid the door latch, poked his head out, and glanced around the terrace. "The pre-lunch lull. I'm off."

"Before you go, tell me this: Does Her Grace keep copybooks from years past?"

"I don't know. You should ask her. I'll have a look about the Hall, but I am not reading my mother's mail, not even if she asks me to."

"Away with you, then," I said. "Take your time. Stroll along as if you merely want a word with your groom, or need to walk off a case of the wind before taking a meal in company. Don't hurry, don't dawdle. Give yourself a real objective—looking in on Atlas before you go—and ignore anything and anybody besides that goal."

Arthur was reserved even in his facial expressions. His displeasure came through in a mere firming of the ducal lips.

"All of life is not skulking about under Wellington's orders, Jules."

With that, he was gone, and I went in search of Her Grace, by way of a casual, if thorough, inspection of the guest wing.

"Any sign of the gloves?" I asked as Lady Ophelia, Hyperia, and I settled at a table along the balustrade. Guests were gathering on the back terrace before the evening meal, and our social obligation was to mingle and exchange pleasantries.

Since my interview with Arthur earlier in the day, my capacity for pleasantries had taken French leave. How dare Millicent abandon her son? And yet, the world being what it was, her decision made practical sense for all concerned.

"We weren't likely to find a missing pair of men's gloves among a woman's effects," Lady Ophelia replied.

I held her chair and then Hyperia's before taking my own seat facing the terrace and house. "Lady Barrington described them as old and worn," I said. "If a woman sought to pick some roses, she might appropriate them."

When I'd approached Lady Barrington about searching the guest wing, I'd told her we were looking for Her Grace's missing letters. I doubted a thief would be foolish enough to leave purloined correspondence in plain sight, but clues to the thief's identity were a different matter.

Lady Barrington had asked me to keep an eye out for a pair of men's gloves that had belonged to her first husband. She'd kept them for sentimental reasons and occasionally wore them when gardening.

An odd item to misplace, distinguished only by the monogram H-G-M branded the inside cuffs. I had examined the guest list for parties whose family name began with a G, to no avail.

"You told us to look for what wasn't in keeping with the whole," Hyperia said. "Inconsistencies, jarring notes. I did not see Lady Barrington's missing gloves, but I did learn that Lord Drayson likes to sketch young ladies without their clothes. He's quite good at it."

"His father had artistic talent," Lady Ophelia said. "Not much call for that skill in the House of Lords."

"Did you recognize the young ladies?" I asked.

"He's more interested in bodies than faces, if that's what you mean. He did one of me, but the features weren't entirely accurate."

"Not a blackmailer, then," Lady Ophelia said. "My searches were similarly fruitless. Our Gideon is either using wood stains on his boots, or he's taken to coloring his hair. Perhaps his parliamentary ambitions have turned him up more vain than usual."

Our general strategy had been that I would search the men's quarters, and Hyperia and Lady Ophelia would look over the ladies' apartments. For Marchant, Lady Ophelia had pointed out that she was the least suspicious party to be found awaiting her fellow guest in his parlor. She'd known him for ages, got on with him well enough, and would have a better sense of what to expect among his effects.

"Wood stains? What did you find?" I asked.

"A tincture of black walnut," Lady Ophelia said. "Covers up the gray, for a time, and doesn't fade at the first hint of sunlight. One must be careful not to let it touch the face or hands, though. Stains those as well, and then everybody knows precisely how your youthful locks have defied the march of time."

"I vaguely recall this," I murmured. The housekeeper at my London residence had told me that I could recover some color in my shockingly pale hair by using water in which under-ripe walnut husks had been boiled. Marchant was either sparing with his applications, or his valet was very skilled, because his salt-and-pepper hue looked entirely natural to me.

"Lady Canderport tipples," Hyperia said. "Brandy flasks under her pillow, in her spare reticule, in her workbasket. I'd tipple, too, if I had her offspring."

Twins, male and female, at the dangerous age where they were well out of the schoolroom and eager to thwart any lingering vestiges of authority over them. They knew nothing of the world and thought themselves equal to any challenge.

"Charles is younger than Lottie by five minutes." Lady Ophelia waved pleasantly to our host, who stood at the top of the terrace steps, looking jovial and benign. "Since Lottie learned to speak, every other sentence out of her mouth has begun, 'If I had been born a boy.'"

"If she'd been born a boy," Hyperia observed, "then Lord Drayson would not have sketched her in the altogether. One cannot object to a man indulging his private imagination, but those sketches were lying on the sofa in his sitting room."

"Were they meant to be a distraction?" I asked. The punchbowl was in the opposite corner of the terrace, a gloved footman ladling out glasses of some pink concoction that likely included a quantity of cheap champagne. We English favored the drink more than the French did themselves, though I avoided it.

The younger guests were apparently enthralled with their fizzy potation, which boded ill for decorum at supper.

Hyperia adjusted the shawl about her shoulders, a forest green weave that went marvelously with her eyes.

"A distraction? You mean, I walk into the parlor looking for anything unusual, anything that doesn't fit, and instead of seeing the dagger on the mantel, I'm fascinated with nude sketches?"

"Precisely." An old and effective tactic among those with something to hide. A nude sketch, a nude woman... More effective at distracting the average male than money by far.

"I've seen nude sketches before, Jules." Hyperia patted my hand. "Those drawings might have caught the attention of a young man simply idling about, but Lady Ophelia tells us artistic ability runs in the family. They fit with what we know of his lordship."

Drayson was several years my junior, and he hadn't served in uniform. To me, he was an unknown quantity and thus of interest.

"What else did you find?" I asked the ladies. The final supper bell could not ring soon enough for me. I had the beginnings of a headache, likely the result of a day of travel followed by a day of intrigue and frustration.

Who would comfort Leander when his little head hurt? Who would sing him lullabies when a vexing day left him too restless to find peace?

"I found that snooping holds no appeal for me," Lady Ophelia said. "Peeking under the bed sounds naughty and wicked, and diverting in that regard, but..."

I had more or less snooped my way across Spain and had Wellington's thanks to show for it. The average civilian, though, held my sort of snooping in contempt, as did I, on occasion.

"But then you learn things," Hyperia said, gaze on the young people flirting by the punchbowl. "Things you have no business knowing, like Lady Canderport's fondness for brandy. You cannot unknow that once you close the door to her apartment or make your report. You steal privacy even when you touch nothing and say nothing."

"You might also prevent a blameless duchess from being blackmailed," I pointed out. "You might find out who helped themselves to Lady Barrington's old gloves. They mean a lot to her." All she had to remember him by, according to her. She'd said that with such wistfulness too.

"Mrs. Whittington is bereft at the loss of her locket," Lady Ophelia muttered. "Lord Barrington will soon pitch down those steps headfirst if he doesn't cease swilling that punch. Hellie ought to know better."

"Lord Barrington ought to know better," I countered. He was amiable, hearty, and shrewd in my experience, too shrewd to be tipsy this early in the proceedings.

"Jules, perhaps you can distract him from the punchbowl," Hyperia said. "We must consider our searching to have been in vain, I suppose. Interesting, but unproductive."

"We can't know that." I rose and assisted Lady Ophelia to stand as well, though Hyperia eschewed my aid. "Reconnaissance requires patience. You sally forth and familiarize yourself with the terrain. Where will an army find grazing and water? Where could an ambush most effectively be laid? In the course of your wanderings, you see that a convent has been abandoned, and yet, the stable has recently been used."

Then you wondered if the well yet offered fresh water and found that a cache of British guns had been secreted under the well covering. Guns for Bonapartists or for Spanish monarchists or for the bandits abroad in any country ravaged by warring armies? Who had secreted them there? Who was supposed to find them?

"Julian, pay your respects to Her Grace," Lady Ophelia said briskly. "Dorothea will expect a report."

My mother had joined the gathering, timing her entrance so as not to be late, but to make an impression on the full complement of guests. She wore emerald green and wore it well, with a shimmery peacock sort of silk wrap giving her added dash.

"Notice how little jewelry she wears," Lady Ophelia said. "Dorothea has always had excellent taste. One envies her that. Greet her properly, young man, or I will tell Lady Jessamine that you are partial to silly blondes. Poor Hellie, being step-mama to such a vapid creature."

"Lady Ophelia does not make idle threats," Hyperia said, taking me by the elbow. "Let's wish Her Grace good evening, shall we? You have enough to contend with, and Lady Jessamine is a tribulation in silk slippers."

"Bless you, dear Perry." We did the pretty before my mother, who was gracious conviviality itself. Even the young blades strutting before the punchbowl beauties were distracted. When Gideon Marchant brought Her Grace a glass of pink libation, I excused myself with a promise to find the duchess again before the whist tournament began later in the evening.

Would the supper gong never ring?

"You are always restless at the start of an investigation," Hyperia said, "and then you get to haring about, too many questions, not enough answers, but you solve the riddles in the end, Jules, and Lady Ophelia and I are here to lend a hand. Now, tell me what's really bothering you."

I had promised that Hyperia would have a role in any inquiries that came my way if she pleased to assist me. I'd had occasion to try the alternative—keeping her at arm's length in the name of gentlemanly discretion—and my discretion had nearly ended in disaster. She had a way of seeing connections I missed, and of seeing *me*.

"The missing letters bother me, locked guest rooms bother me, unlocked guest rooms bother me..." Lady Barrington had given out keys, but people weren't using them. "Her ladyship knows something she isn't saying, Perry. She locks doors in her own home, and yet, when others leave those same doors unlocked, she keeps mum."

"What can she say? 'I harbor thieves on my staff'? Thieves who will steal from a duchess? If Mrs. Whittington's locket was taken, then somebody is also willing to take a widow's memento and possibly our hostess's sentimental token, assuming the gloves were taken as well."

We descended into the garden and made for the outermost path around the parterres.

I rephrased Hyperia's question. "What *should* Lady Barrington say? She should obliquely warn her guests to greater caution. She should remind them that house parties can bring together all sorts, that footmen temporarily hired from the Town agencies are sometimes not all that one would wish... If Mrs. Whittington's locket and her ladyship's old gloves were taken, our thief steals items of great sentimental significance. Spite rather than greed drives such behavior. You are keeping your door locked?"

"Of course," Hyperia replied, "and I tie a long strand of hair around the latch, and so far, nobody has trespassed, but it's only been a day."

A long, frustrating day. "You ask what's bothering me in addition to the thief *du jour*. Millicent wrote to Arthur. Says she's not coming back to the Hall. She will continue to be a mother to Leander to the extent she can do so discreetly."

A gust of laughter wafted from the terrace.

"Don't hate her, Jules. Millicent kept him safe against all odds for five years. Kept him safe when his own father couldn't."

And damn Harry for that, but Harry was dead and beyond the reach of blame. "I don't hate her, but I fear Leander might, and that she'll break the boy's heart, Perry."

Hyperia squeezed closer, though to appearances we were merely having a decorous stroll in a garden growing chilly and shadowed.

"Hearts break, Jules, but we also know that hearts can mend and be stronger than ever."

"Do we know that?"

"Yes. We are certain of it. We will convince Leander of this eternal verity as well, and he will not hate his mother. He will be properly angry with her, understandably so given his hurt feelings. But he will have us, and Millicent will remain a part of his life because you insist on it, and we will muddle on in good faith and in good heart."

Wellington himself had never known the degree of resolution Hyperia West could put into a few soft words.

"I love you so very, very much." I esteemed her, I needed her, and she was, thank all the benevolent powers, mine to love. "Let's take a turn in the park, shall we?"

Hyperia looked to be considering the notion when a voice hissed out from behind the privet border.

"You can do your smoochin' and sighin' later, guv. I got a report to make."

"Atticus, show yourself and make the fastest report of your young and storied life."

CHAPTER SIX

To appearances, I held a casual, impromptu conversation with my tiger, who had violated all decorum to catch me on the fringes of the gathering. Perhaps my horse had a loose shoe. Perhaps a final trunk had arrived from Caldicott Hall.

The truth was, Atticus could barely read and write. He was thus forced to convey pertinent information in person.

"Have you had supper, Atticus?" Hyperia asked. "One must not neglect meals at these house parties, and all and sundry likely feel entitled to order you about."

"I had me tucker, thanks, Miss Hyperia. The undercook has a baby brother what looks like me, and I know better than to hang about the kitchen when it's time to send up the meal. Staff will eat once guests are served. They take turns abovestairs, so everybody gets a chance at supper. Guv, you don't look so good."

The lad doubtless spoke out of concern—for me and for his own place in the world. If I were hit by a runaway team tomorrow, Atticus's prospects would dim considerably.

"I am tired, hungry, and out of sorts. You should know that MacFadden, the Scottish fellow who valets Marchant, has taken notice of you. MacFadden means to befriend you, but friendship can be a convenient pretext for surveillance."

"You gettin' a megrim? You're goin' all toplofty on me again."

"I have a headache, and a tiger who doesn't realize that this conversation will draw the sort of attention I'd rather avoid. Please make your report."

"Watch out for Lady Jessamine, guv. I was minding me own business along the riverbank, and I overheard her telling her friends she'll have a proposal from you before the house party ends. Says you're dicked in the nob, but your nob isn't required to 'do the necessary.' Said she always did fancy herself in a tiara."

Hyperia shot a furious glance in the direction of the terrace. "That presuming, nasty little creature."

"With whom was she speaking?" I asked.

"The mousy gal what wears specs and the chubby one with the frizzy blond hair."

"The mouse is the honorable Miss Welleeda Bivens," Hyperia said. "Frizzy is Morticia Frampton, though her friends call her Trish. Both face a third Season next year. Lady Jessamine is preying on the weak for her accomplices."

Would they steal from the older ladies? Augment their pin money with demands for ransom or threats of blackmail?

"To the extent you can, Atticus, keep an eye on Lady Jessamine. Lady Ophelia has also warned me against her, and the threat must be taken seriously. MacFadden has you pegged as canny, so don't play stupid with him."

"Not stupid, but busy. I'm allus havin' to run out to the stable to make sure Atlas's mash got made up right, or to tell the grooms you and Miss Hyperia will be hacking out tomorrow."

"I like that notion," Hyperia said. "Good thought, Atticus. Please do inform the grooms. Jules, don't fuss. You're happier when you can spend time in the saddle."

We took our leave of Atticus, and still the supper bell hadn't rung.

"I might not be on hand to ride with you tomorrow," I said as we wandered toward the house. "I'm tempted to dash back to the Hall, given developments with Leander."

"Arthur is still at the Hall, Jules. You are needed here."

"Arthur and I should explain the situation to the boy together." Though Arthur had clearly left the task to me.

"Wait until you have more particulars sorted out with Millicent. How is Leander to write to her? When can she expect letters from him? Leander will want those answers."

Hyperia was right, of course, but such was my sense of a day gone badly, a headache gathering momentum, and a plain old empty belly that I resented even Hyperia's common sense.

"I need a nap," I said, "and a tray of sandwiches in a quiet corner of a deserted library."

Hyperia wrapped her hand around my arm. "I seek refuge in week-old newspapers. The gossip has overtaken anything the penny press has to say by then, but I tell myself I'm keeping abreast of politics and fashion. I am in truth hiding."

What a lovely little confidence. "I cannot read by candlelight for too long. My eyes protest the exertion."

"Then I will read to you, Jules, and you will tend the fire and mind the tray, and we will hide together."

Yes. Yes, exactly. Even the thought of hiding with Hyperia cheered me. "But not until we find Her Grace's letters." Because until we accomplished that bit of sleuthing, Hyperia and I were stuck at this blasted house party.

"Are we looking at one thief, Jules, who steals items of sentimental value from older women, or are we looking at a thief, and a widow who misplaces her jewelry, and a hostess too busy to keep track of details?"

"Or no thief at all?" I replied. "A lady's maid who moved items and forgot about them? A footman trying to tidy up? A locket caught in a shawl and then fallen into a hedgerow? Innocent explanations would make more sense for the gloves and the locket, but very few people would know of the letters, and even fewer would know where to find them."

"You have more questions for the duchess?"

More by the hour, it seemed. "I'll catch her when the other guests gather for the whist tournament. I'd rather be eating sandwiches and hiding with you."

We had the garden to ourselves, and evening was turning into night. The gloom was deep enough that footmen were lighting torches along the balustrade, and another cheering thought struck me.

"Let's steal a moment," I said, tarrying with my beloved on the far side of the tiered fountain. I took Hyperia in my arms, and she came willingly, resting her head against my chest.

"I miss this," she said. "Miss the feel of you. If only—"

The dinner bell sounded loudly over the murmur of conversation closer to the house.

"If only?"

She stepped back and gathered her shawl. "If only we didn't have to go in to dinner and make small talk for the next hour. I believe you are to escort Lady Jessamine. You have my permission to spill your soup on her bodice."

Hyperia did not take my arm, and when we reached the top of the steps, I spotted Lady Jessamine in conversation with Miss Bivens and Miss Frampton.

"Don't underestimate her, Jules. Her mama died when she was quite small, and her father has spoiled her. She's ruthless and determined."

Perhaps what I needed was not so much rest and refreshment as a hug from Hyperia and a challenge. I smiled and waved at Lady Jessamine.

"I'm ruthless and determined too. You're promised to Drayson for supper?"

"I am. We'll talk about art. Classical nudes have always fascinated me. What of you and Lady Jessamine?"

"Have they, now? Her ladyship and I will talk about how much I value learning, integrity, and compassion in women. We will also discuss, at tiresome length, the pathetic young ladies who attempt to compromise themselves with a fellow simply because his family has a title."

"You wouldn't dare."

Lady Jessamine was making a slow, smiling progress in our direction, pausing to flutter her lashes at every gentleman who stood between us.

"I absolutely will, Perry. I don't have time for schoolgirl schemes. Lady Jessamine has apparently failed to note that once she's forced a man to meet her at the altar, that man can lock her in a tower for years, get endless children on her, and all but hold her prisoner. She thinks herself worldly and formidable—we all do at her age—but the world holds ruthlessness and determination such as she cannot imagine. She will land herself in its path if she's not careful."

"I hadn't considered that her plans could go awry like that. A dose of truth might serve better than spilled soup. Will I see you later?"

"Dodge the whist tournament. We can confer after I meet with the duchess."

Confer. I would make my report regarding further conversation with the duchess. Hyperia would share developments from her side of the table at supper. We would learn nothing helpful, and my frustration would keep me from a good night's sleep.

I would rather cuddle than confer. Perhaps we might do both.

"I favor innocent explanations for the gloves and the locket," Hyperia said as Lady Jessamine wafted closer. "A duchess, an earl's second wife, and military widow don't exactly have much in common. They are different sorts of women, dwelling in different parts of the country for much of the year. I cannot see connections, can you?"

"Not at the moment, but I'm bracing myself for the longest hour of the day. Enjoy your discussion of nudes."

Hyperia parted from me three seconds before doing so would have been a rudeness to Lady Jessamine. Her ladyship's perfume—a cloying excess of hyacinth—hit me before she held out a gloved hand.

"Lord Julian, I believe you have the honor of escorting me into supper." She fluttered her fingers as if hastening a lackey to his duty.

I bowed over her hand as briefly as possible. "Let us hope the honor, privilege, and pleasure are mutual. Tell me of your London Season, my lady. Were you amused at all the foolish young things trying to secure a match at any cost? Some of the poor dears will hide in broom closets or lure unsuspecting gentlemen into follies with forged notes. Highly entertaining, but a bit sad, don't you think? One doesn't want to label any innocent young lady as laughable, but such pathetic little schemes are certainly diverting."

I was the next thing to a bully for firing that opening salvo, but her observation to her chums—that I was not right in the upper story—had hit a bit too close to home. I winged my arm at her ladyship, and she wrapped tentative fingers around my elbow.

"Hide in broom closets, my lord?"

"I speak figuratively. One feels sorry for any party in the grip of desperation. Far better to do as you did and take one's time to look over possibilities and consider options. Tell me of these Scottish games we're to enjoy later in the gathering. Are the gentlemen expected to dance over crossed swords and throw tree trunks about?"

Her grip on my arm became more secure. "Highland Games are wonderful, my lord, and Papa is determined that we shall have caber tossing, though Lady Barrington isn't fond of the notion."

Jessamine chattered on at some length regarding cabers, hammer throws, and hill races, as the supper courses came and went, I consoled myself that her young ladyship had been disabused of any marital schemes where I was concerned.

I caught Lady Ophelia watching us from across the table and smiling faintly. Another party with whom I had to confer, though my spirits were somewhat lighter for having foiled Lady Jessamine's ambitions without a figurative shot having been fired.

~

"Tell me about Lady Barrington," I said as my mother wandered with me beneath the torches. The air was chilly, also a welcome change from the stuffy drawing room where the guests had gathered after the meal.

"Helga, Countess of Barrington, born the honorable Helga Adams, oldest daughter of Viscount Dallingham, a fine old Suffolk family. First marriage to Viscount Cobbold of the same general vicinity and a happy union. Fell from his horse just a month or two before Claudius went to his reward, though Hellie had done her duty by the succession by then. The idiot guardians consigned her to the dower house and sent the oldest boy off to public school when he was seven. They let her keep the spare until he was also seven.

"Barrington came along a few years later," the duchess went on, "looking for a mother to his children more than anything else, and Hellie had had enough of widowhood by then. She's a good soul and genuinely fond of Barrington. The boys love to visit her here now that they're grown. The elder looks exactly like her."

A report worthy of a reconnaissance officer. "You consider her a friend."

"Yes, and an ally. One must distinguish between the two. The viscount and His Grace were deeply absorbed with the work of some committee having to do with provisioning the army, or rooting out charlatans profiting from wartime contracts. Freddie Whittington consulted with them often in his experienced officer capacity, as did others. Many meetings far into the night, much brandy consumed in the name of service to the king. Claudius took it all very seriously. We ladies left them to it, and then we wished we hadn't been so understanding."

"Because?"

"We were each in turn bereaved, and then we regretted allowing our husbands so many hours of port and parliamentary prosing on. We'll never have those evenings back, will we?"

Such regret was still apparently part of Her Grace's attachment to my father's memory. "Lady Barrington is missing a pair of gloves that she claims belonged to her first husband. As apparel, they have little value, but she sets sentimental store by them."

"Odd, the things we treasure. His Grace kept a lock of baby hair from each of his offspring. Yours was flaming red by the time you were a year old. I was sorry to see you grow into more muted plumage."

"Flaming red?" This was news to me. That the duchess would refer to me as the late duke's offspring was simply familial habit, I supposed. A courtesy. That His Grace would keep a lock of my hair was a puzzle, but then, Papa had his heir and spare by then, and he'd been magnanimous by nature.

Her Grace brandished a curl at me, the end of a long lock that showed no sign of fading. "Flaming red. Both of your grandmothers were horrified."

The duchess had obviously been delighted. What must she think of the pale locks I sported now? "The sole medical man I've consulted said I should regain my previous color, but the process is taking its blessed time."

An awkward comment, but also—perhaps?—the sort of admission a grown man might make to his mother.

"If you want to hasten the progression of color, use a bit of henna. Your valet should know how to apply it skillfully."

"To have him fussing about my person would be intolerable." When I'd been taken captive by the French, my bodily dignity had been the first casualty of the ordeal. That wound, like my weak eyes, might never entirely heal.

"Your father was the same way. Forbidding others to do for him what he could do for himself. I was lucky he allowed me to tie the occasional cravat. He made a very competent lady's maid, though. Wretched man."

How had we gone from Lady Barrington's pedigree to henna to... *that*? "What do you know of Mrs. Whittington?"

"Carola Whittington would be my choice if I needed a pretty, good-humored, sensible youngish widow to round out the numbers, serve as a chaperone-at-large, and generally keep the gents from making fools of themselves. Has she lost something as well?"

Her Grace pulled the shimmery peacock wrap closer, and I recalled that my mother had always been one to take a chill. She avoided the sun with the fervor of a religious zealot, and she was ever within reach of a shawl, wrap, or robe.

"We can finish this discussion inside," I said. "Mrs. Whittington has misplaced a locket of sentimental value. A lock of hair to one side, a tiny inscription on the other. She had it this morning but cannot recall if she put it on."

"Gideon is pestering her," the duchess said. "It's only flirtation, but his persistence would be enough to make any woman misplace her wits. Let's do go inside. Tweed House is drafty, and once I grow cold, nothing short of a roaring fire will warm me up."

And Papa had indulged that habit, despite the expense. The ducal apartment at Caldicott Hall had always been cozy, as had the nursery.

I accompanied Her Grace into the house, and we availed ourselves of the music room, which was deserted, though a fire had been lit.

"The great whist tournament is doubtless under way," Her Grace said. "I have played so much whist in my life... An excuse to sit and gossip while swilling punch. Did Carola search her entire dressing closet for this missing locket? Jewelry sometimes seems to fly about on its own, which I take for the maid misplacing it, the footman finding it and putting it back with the best of intentions in the wrong location, and the owner forgetting where she originally kept it."

"Mrs. Whittington hasn't found her keepsake. What do you know of her past?"

Her Grace took a seat on the piano bench, facing away from the closed keyboard. "Carola doesn't put on airs. When some colonel-lord-somebody needed his daughters escorted home from Portugal, she made the journey and brought the girls home. She did it because the young ladies wanted for a chaperone, not because traveling to Lisbon and back in winter is particularly agreeable."

"Where does Mrs. Whittington hail from?"

Only a few sconces were lit, making a ghost of the great harp in the corner and turning the stringed instruments on the wall into shadowed forms. The meager lighting showed me both the beauty my mother had claimed in her youth and the toll of advancing years.

Papa was gone, Harry was gone, and for all I knew, Arthur was soon to make a permanent remove to the Continent. Seeing my mother perched on that piano bench, resplendent in her finery but also somehow fading, made my heart unaccountably heavy.

"Why all the questions, my lord?" she asked, turning on the bench and uncovering the keys. "I've known Carola and Helga for ages, though Carola and I aren't what I'd call close. They are good, sensible women and pleasant companions. I trust them both."

She commenced a slow movement in a minor key, one of Herr Beethoven's that I'd heard before and did not care for.

"I am looking for connections between you, Lady Barrington, and Mrs. Whittington that might tell me if a thief has struck once or more than once. Your letters, the gloves, and the locket are all sentimental items, with no particular value as objects. The missing items are not new, but you ladies apparently knew one another when they came into your lives. I seek to trace any other connections, and I need your assistance to do that."

The music emphasized the dull throbbing at the base of my skull, a relentless, slow triple meter dirging along in the lower register.

"We ladies aren't quite of an age," Her Grace said, playing on. "I'm the eldest, then Hellie, then Carola. We don't look alike—antique redhead, brunette, blond. I was married to a rascally duke. Hellie's first husband was a dashing viscount, her second an aging peer. Carola's husband was a venerable lieutenant general, if I'm not mistaken. Mutton-chop whiskers, balding, paunchy, you know the sort. Fierce in uniform, but given to sentiment and naughty jokes at home. He and Carola were genuinely fond of each other, though they weren't married long."

"How did he die?"

"Drink, as I recall. Bilious liver, or whatever the physicians call it. Too many years soldiering often ends that way."

While His Grace had died of a wasting disease and Lady Barrington's first husband in an equestrian mishap. "Might you play something different?"

She brought the music to a cadence, sat for a moment with her fingers resting on the keys, then launched into the second movement. The key was major, the tune sprightly to a fault in comparison to its predecessor.

"Since I first heard this piece," Her Grace said, "it put me in mind of Arthur, Harry, and you. This is Harry, all grace and good cheer, though not without his complications. The opening movement is Arthur, solemn, sweet, plodding if one doesn't make an effort to appreciate him. What else do you want to know, my lord? The hour grows late, and these questions aren't returning my letters to me."

More to the point, Her Grace's *answers* weren't shedding any light on the problem. "Tell me about Gideon Marchant. How did you meet him?"

She played to the end of the phrase then mercifully brought the annoyingly sprightly second movement to a close as well.

"Gideon was a friend of His Grace's, or an acquaintance, more accurately. A duke has an endless list of friends, a ducal heir nearly as many."

While a duchess had very few? "You met Marchant through His Grace?"

She studied the keys. "A house party, of all things. Up north, mostly for the shooting. Gideon had already embarked on his role as bachelor-at-large. Claudius had known him at school or university. I'm not clear on the connection, but when Claudius died, Gideon was one of few who didn't... who continued to call upon me. He has many shortcomings, but I think Carola and Hellie would agree that the man is loyal."

Was he more than loyal? The notion that he and my mother had ever been close repelled me. "Who are his people?"

She brushed her hand silently over the black keys. "You know, I'm not clear on that either. One doesn't inquire into a gentleman's means, of course, but word circulates nonetheless. In Gideon's case, I suspect he has independent wealth, about which he is tastefully discreet."

I applied my mind to the facts. "He is not considered a catch, by design. If the extent of his personal worth became known, he'd be besieged, and he prefers to do the besieging."

"Or he prefers to play that role. As charming as he can be, Gideon has also struck me as having depths. I've not pried, and neither has he, and such consideration is the stuff of a long and cordial friendship."

One attribute I would not assign to Gideon Marchant was charm. "What of Lord Drayson?"

"A sweet young man. I know his mother, knew his father. Why?"

"Sweet young men sometimes get up to foolish dares and wagers."

Her Grace peered at me over her shoulder. "So do sweet young women. Your sister Meggie was nigh infamous at her select academy for the pranks she staged. Got that from her father, of course. I was a paragon."

Said so dryly, one could not help but hear the regret in the words. "Lady Canderport?"

"In mother jail. Until she gets those twins locked up for inciting riots or properly launched—even money in my book—she is too consumed with managing them to get up to any sort of mischief."

"Would the twins get up to larceny as a diversion?" Though stealing personal items of great sentimental value was a nasty, criminal sort of diversion.

"Possibly, and as a competition. Lottie feels keenly that her brother has unfair advantages in life. She will soon see that those advantages come at a price."

"Charles is the heir, the indulged scion, the darling bachelor. I doubt he regards those privileges as costly."

My mother turned back to the piano. "Sometimes, my boy, I vow you are a changeling. Have you any more questions?"

"Not at the moment." I was being dismissed—also possibly criticized—and besides that, I was tired. I hadn't learned much, but then, I hadn't expected to.

"Lady Canderport will never send her daughter off to war," the duchess said, "or wonder what benighted corner of France has the honor of housing her daughter's remains."

Ah. That price. Her Grace had a point. "I miss him too, madam." An impulse flitted through me—to touch my mother's arm, to press a hand to her shoulder. The toll exacted for Harry's masculine *advantages* had been steep indeed, and he wasn't the only one paying it. I tended to forget that. Arthur had also lost a brother, and Her Grace had lost a son.

A favorite son.

"Seek your bed," the duchess said. "You get cranky when you're tired, but you stay up past your bedtime out of sheer stubbornness."

"I'll bid you good night and continue my search in the morning."

There seemed nothing more to say. We were two people who shared blood, some memories, and some familial connections by the accident of my birth. I could not imagine the circumstance wherein I'd seek or know what to do with maternal closeness. The duchess had been capable of that with Harry, and she was clearly fond of Arthur, but for us...

Apparently not, which made me all the more determined to find her blasted letters.

I had just closed the music room door when a thundering cascade of music poured forth, a crescendo of arpeggiated ferocity that ended in a pair of slammed chords before renewing itself and then resolving into a fury of fast, driving notes.

"The third movement." I stood for a time, listening to an expert rendition of demanding, intense, unstoppable music.

I had no earthly idea what to make of my mother's performance—the third movement was the one she associated with me—but I listened until the last note had faded into the night, and still I stood in the darkness, awash in complete and utter bafflement.

CHAPTER SEVEN

"Have you taken to lurking, Julian?" Lady Ophelia's startled me out of my reverie. She had prowled up the shadowy corridor as silently as a cat on the hunt. Marchant had noted the side of her personality that inspired wariness, and I had scoffed at him for it.

"I have concluded an unsatisfactory interview with Her Grace," I said, "who was playing the piano until a few moments ago. She's quite good."

"When your father was ill, she'd play for him by the hour. The old dances and airs from our youth. You were off at school. They didn't want you boys to have to endure the business of your father's dying."

"As a result, his death took me nearly by surprise." At Yuletide, I'd noticed that Papa had been looking older, that his weight had been down, and he'd seemed tired. His subsequent letters had been as cheerful and chatty as ever, and mine had likely been as dull and dutiful as usual. I'd spent the spring holidays with a friend, and by the time I'd next returned to the Hall, His Grace had been failing rapidly.

"Death takes a lot of us by surprise," Lady Ophelia muttered. "I hope it takes me so much by surprise that I fail to notice the change of venue until I've been assigned my harp and halo. Let's chat, shall we?"

I did not want to chat. I wanted to fall asleep on the sofa in Hyperia's sitting room while she read me some Gothic tale and I mused on suspects and motives.

"Have you something to report?" I asked.

"Oh, perhaps, and so do you, young man." She took my arm, appropriated a lamp from a sconce, and led me across the corridor to a small parlor. Not a second parlor—the room was nicely appointed, the furniture newish—but suitable for entertaining only a few guests at a time.

"The winter parlor," Lady Ophelia said. "Always on the southern side of the house, sometimes in the southeast corner, and small enough to heat easily. They've gone out of fashion, but they make perfect sense to me. Arthur called on you today."

How in blazes could she know that? "He did."

"And?"

She was my godmother rather than my commanding officer. I owed her no explanations, but she'd also been the only person willing to intrude upon my languishing version of a postwar recovery. For that, I would always owe her. Had she not literally dragged me into the light of day, my fate might have become dire indeed.

Then too, dissembling before Godmama was pointless, so I gave her the truth. "Millicent has written that she intends to remain distant from the Hall and from Leander."

"That didn't take her long."

"Arthur thinks it might be for the best."

Her ladyship passed me the lamp and took a seat in a wing chair upholstered in brocade roses. "For Millicent, getting shed of the boy is undoubtedly for the best. Will you be complicit in her scheme?"

"When I threatened to retrieve her from her home shire and return her to the Hall by main force, Arthur counseled patience."

"At least you threatened. You can do more than threaten once Arthur has taken ship."

I remained on my feet. If I sat, I would have to rise, and such was my fatigue of body and spirit that the easier course was to prop a hip on a windowsill and let her ladyship rail at me.

"The only issue from my perspective," I said, "is what is best for the boy. On the one hand, he loves his mother and will feel her absence keenly."

"You have doubtless concocted some *other hand* that conveniently excuses you from acting. Don't you dare tell yourself this is for the best, Julian. That child has no one else in the whole world. He doesn't merely love his mother as if she were a favorite set of toy soldiers. She is his refuge and the lodestar of his happiness."

"She has been, of necessity. I'm sure Millicent gave the whole matter a great deal of thought, and as his guardian, she is choosing to turn the boy over to his paternal relations. Given Arthur's consequence, Society would not criticize her for that." I did, or I had.

And yet, seeing Godmama's righteous ire, I felt compelled to argue for the defense, as Arthur had argued it with me.

"*I* criticize her for it, by heaven. She could have waited until he's older, could have given him time to adjust. She bolted at the first opportunity, Julian, and your duty to the child is to retrieve his mother posthaste, before she can dodge off somewhere you won't find her."

The hour was too late for me to dredge up any charm, and neither had I much patience left, but I did make a try for sweet reason.

"Do you know what is harder on a boy than being told his mother has chosen to dwell elsewhere, though she has promised to visit and write and remain on the periphery of his life?"

"Losing his mother and his father."

"Leander never had a father worth the name." I stated a fact and offered a silent apology to Harry. "What is harder for a small boy is dwelling under the same roof as his mother and feeling certain she resents his proximity, certain she regrets his very birth. For Leander to face his mother's regret every day, at every meal, every time she avoids divine services or refuses to dine with the family would poison his life more effectively than if she simply withdraws to a more distant place in his sphere."

Millicent had not promised to write or visit, but I would do my utmost to wring those assurances from her.

"He's not a ducal son, Julian. Your mother visited the nursery on occasion, inquired politely about your studies or your pony rides, and then swanned off not to be seen again for days. Leander's mother was his all... He slept beside her for the first several years of his life. He took every meal with her. He wore only the clothes she made for him. If you allow this... this *cataclysm* in his life, you will regret it for the rest of your days."

Early memories stirred, some of my earliest. "Her Grace always began and ended her days in the nursery. Every day, without fail. She wrote to us—individual letters, mine were printed at first—when she and Papa went up to Town, and she demanded that we write back. She kidnapped Harry and me for picnics and filled her sketchbooks with our likenesses."

These recollections welled from some mental oubliette where I'd stashed them years ago, and yet, they were vivid, complete pictures in my head. Harry had always claimed more of our mother's attention, true, but she could not be accused of the sort of remote parenting all too common among the highest aristocracy.

Not at first.

"You can defend Dorothea all you please, Julian, but I blame this whole debacle on her. Had Her Grace come to the Hall when Leander arrived, she could have insisted that Millicent remain with the boy. Millicent's role might have been governess, nurserymaid, or that of some fictitious relative, but that woman would not have defied the duchess."

Millicent had more or less defied *the duke*, and likely the inclinations of her own heart. "Debating preventive measures at this point profits us nothing." And whatever else was true, Her Grace was not to blame for Millicent's defection. "Arthur has delegated resolution of Leander's situation to me, and my next step will be to secure guardianship of the boy."

I made a mental note to add sending instructions to the solicitors to the list of tasks I'd tackle in the morning.

"I am so angry." Her ladyship skewered me with a magnificent glower. "Angry with the boy's mother, angry with Arthur for choosing the worst time to take his holiday, and angry with you, Julian. You've disappointed me, and I must consider my own next steps. I will bid you good evening."

I allowed her to have the last word and bowed to her retreating figure as she stormed out the door. In the morning, when I could think again, I'd doubtless be devasted to have earned her ladyship's poor regard. Her disappointment stung, but coming on the heels of a frustrating day and an unproductive interview with the duchess, the sting lacked sharpness.

Lest I fall asleep in the little parlor, I waited a few moments, then followed her ladyship from the room. I'd promised Hyperia a conference, and a conference we would have.

The stairs were miles too long and too steep, and a voice in my head that sounded much like Harry warned me that I was overtaxing myself, a certain recipe for disaster. At war, overtaxing oneself was excusable and even necessary, but I was no longer at war.

I tapped on Hyperia's sitting room door, heard no reply, and let myself into her apartment. The parlor was unlit, though a dim glow emanated from the bedroom. I found Hyperia asleep in a reading chair, a book in her lap. A single candle burned down to the last two inches on the table beside her. The lone taper was one of four in a candelabrum, the other three standing tall and unlit.

My beloved had been saving candles. She was swaddled in a nightgown and robe, thick wool stockings on her feet.

I gently slid the book from her lap, which earned no reaction from the sleeping beauty.

The Mysteries of Udolpho. About as Gothic as Gothic could be, though the ending was happy.

I filled the warmer with coals and did a thorough job taking the chill off the sheets, then undid the belt of Hyperia's robe.

"To bed with you, miss." She stirred slightly when I lifted her into my arms, nuzzled my shoulder, and sighed.

I set her on the bed, managed to get the robe free, and tucked her beneath the covers. She rolled to her side with another deep sigh. Her hair was a thick russet braid against the snowy sheets, and she made a sweet picture nestled against the pillows.

Don't do it. The voice was again Harry's, or his ghost. He had a nerve admonishing me to a restraint he'd not practiced himself.

"Stay, Jules." That murmured command had come from Hyperia. Her eyes were open, and she regarded me sleepily from the shadows of the bed canopy. "Stay for a time. I've missed you."

"I shouldn't. I'll fall asleep."

"One does that in beds."

To be found alone with Hyperia in dishabille would force us into a marriage on terms neither of us wanted. If I sat on the bed, if I even leaned down to kiss her good night, I'd be lost.

"I would be poor company, my dear."

"You would be delightful company. I will wake you in the morning before the birds herald the dawn."

My darling was a reliably early riser, and her assurances were sufficient to topple my reluctance.

"Very well." Call me weak and foolish, but I stripped down and made use of the wash water, then climbed into the bed and wrapped my tired self around Hyperia's warmth.

"Better," she said, lacing her fingers with mine. "Much better. Sweet dreams, Jules."

I did not dream that I could recall, but I slept deeply and woke to the merest hint of gray light filtering through the curtains.

"Jules," Hyperia whispered, "somebody's in my parlor."

I was naked but for a pair of linen drawers, and I was in the utterly wrong bed at the utterly wrong hour. The situation was impossible.

And yet, I had been in similar impossible situations. Out of habit, I'd folded my clothing in the specific order best suited to dressing at speed. Too often when making my way across the wilds of Spain, I'd had only moments to prepare for the unexpected, and those reflexes served me well. I was dressed in breeches and shirt within a minute.

I passed Hyperia her robe and slipped out onto her balcony. The cold air was a bracing slap to the lungs and the balcony chilly beneath my feet. Ghostly tendrils of mist rose from the stream in the distance, and not a single bird broke the predawn stillness. Deer grazed near the woods, doubtless ready to bolt at the first sign of activity in the house.

I stole along the building's exterior until I could peer into the parlor through a crack in the curtains.

Young Lord Drayson was making a stealthy search of Hyperia's effects, going through the drawers of her escritoire one by one. Was he looking for an item of sentimental value to steal? Would he next intrude himself on the lady's very boudoir?

I nipped back into Hyperia's bedroom. "Drayson," I whispered. "Grab a poker and ask him what the devil he's about. He won't expect you to confront him. He appears to be conducting a search."

Hyperia had already left the bed and was in her robe and stockings. She hefted the wrought-iron fireplace poker and made for the door. The look in her eye did not bode well for Drayson's prospects.

"Lord Drayson, what in blazes are you doing?" She spoke quietly but with the firm asperity of a woman prepared to dispatch a fool.

"Miss... Miss West. Good morning. Is this your apartment? I am so sorry. I thought... That is to say—"

"Do me the courtesy of being honest, and do it at once."

"I am looking for something." He'd aimed for injured dignity and ended up in the vicinity of petulance.

"Oh, clearly. You will have to do better than that."

"Something that belongs to me," his lordship went on. "Something personal and private."

"So the first place you thought to search was my personal and private apartment. How logical." Hyperia had asked a single question thus far and had otherwise adopted the interrogator's trick of allowing her prisoner to babble himself into disclosures.

"I intend to search everywhere," Drayson said. "Yours was the first apartment I came to on the ladies' floor of the guest wing."

I wanted to kick myself, hard. Hyperia had left her door unlocked the previous evening *for me*, and I'd been in such a state that I had not locked the door behind me. Excessive fatigue bred costly errors. *I knew that.* I knew that only too well.

"You passed Lady Ophelia's apartment to get here," Hyperia said. "If you came down from the floor above, the duchess's quarters were closer to yours, as were any number of gentlemen's accommodations. Your objective was to search *my* quarters, and unless you tell me why this instant, then you will be making your explanations to Lord and Lady Barrington."

Excellent next step, to rattle the sword of higher authority and worse consequences.

"You won't do that." Drayson sounded more terrified than confident. "Everybody will know I was in your rooms, and it's barely light out, and you are... not properly dressed."

"Firstly, our host and hostess will be as discreet as the crypt when it comes to the possibility of scandal arising under their own roof. Secondly, unless you want the chambermaid with her coal bucket or tea tray to find you stammering falsehoods in my parlor, you'd best explain yourself and get out."

Hyperia was really quite talented with a prisoner. I had no doubt she'd use the poker if Drayson took so much as a step in her direction.

"You were seen in the vicinity of my apartment, Miss West, yesterday afternoon."

"Who claims to have seen me committing the great crime of wandering the corridors in broad daylight?"

"One of the servants. He implied you might have been looking for me, but I was sketching by the lake, which is what I do every afternoon at this infernal... It's what I do every afternoon."

"I have been here little more than a day, my lord. I would have no idea of your regular habits." Her tone said those habits remained a matter of complete indifference to her. "Did it occur to you that the servant you spoke with might have named me to throw you off his own scent?"

A beat of silence went by. "No. No, it did not."

"You sketch nudes," Hyperia said patiently. "Based on our supper conversation, I conclude that your appreciation for the unclad form is more than passive. Perhaps you have been foolish enough to sketch nudes of people who have not consented to be so depicted, and now your self-indulgence has been found out. Very likely you are searching for some item of your own handiwork that has gone inconveniently missing. Correct me if I'm wrong."

I could nearly *hear* Drayson blushing.

"I am devoted to my art, Miss West. I know that's not fashionable, but Papa won't hear of sending me abroad to study. He says I'll outgrow my hobby as he did, but he's wrong."

"Keep your voice down," Hyperia said. "I don't have your sketches, you clodpated looby, but you are sharing a household with any number of young ladies who might delight in taking your drawings as a prank. You violated their privacy with your risqué sketches. By Mayfair's rules of engagement, the young ladies are thus entitled to violate yours. If you are imbecile enough to search the quarters of Miss Bivens or Miss Frampton, you run every risk of putting period to your bachelorhood. Depend upon it."

"You mean they might have stolen my art as a lure? As bait for an ambush?"

Such incredulity ought not to be let out without a nursemaid, and he was a peer's adult heir.

"I have no idea," Hyperia replied darkly, "what thoughts pass for ratiocination in the minds of the young ladies, but I know I do not have your sketches, I do not want your sketches, and you have been an idiot to risk my wrath and Society's censure. Slip out the door and pray nobody sees you doing it."

I heard a soft click a moment later, and then Hyperia returned to the bedroom and replaced the poker on the hearth stand.

"I saw no servant when I was in the vicinity of Drayson's quarters," she said, anticipating my first question. "I would not be that careless. Was he lying about somebody seeing me, Jules? Protecting whoever did see me?"

"Or making up the whole business, because his sketches have not gone missing, but he needed a handy excuse for plundering your belongings?"

She sat on the bed and removed her heavy stockings. "I could have another look. I leafed through his sketchbooks. I'd know if one has gone missing."

I was momentarily distracted by the sight of Hyperia's bare feet. Feet were personal, rarely on display in the normal course, and hers were long, slender, and pale.

"I cannot allow you to venture into his quarters again, Perry."

She crossed her arms. "*Allow*, Jules?"

"Do you want to end up married to him?"

"Oh." She scowled at her toes. "Suppose not, but the word you sought was 'advise' rather than 'allow.'"

Hyperia rose early, and she rose with formidable energy. "Just so, I meant to say I could not advise a second search of his rooms by you. I won't undertake one either."

"Because?"

"He's not our thief." The thought shifted from a hunch to a conclusion as I spoke. "He was too clumsy in his searching, too clumsy under interrogation. Whoever has pilfered the letters—and the locket and gloves, if they were stolen—did so skillfully. No vague mentions of fictitious servants, no stumbling around at dawn when darkness would have added some safety to the job."

"You doubt a servant spotted me?"

I had been known to claim that I investigated by reasoning from facts and observations to logical conclusions, but at certain moments, I also indulged my instincts.

"I believe somebody saw you in the corridor, and that person was not a servant. That person was a party Drayson could put an awkward question to, somebody who'd feel sympathy for him over missing sketches."

She uncrossed her arms and scooted back onto the mattress to sit cross-legged amid the quilts. "I don't know, Jules. At a gathering like this, one gets to know the other guests as a matter of courtesy. The servants, by contrast, are a faceless horde, some belonging to the house, some to other guests, some brought in from the agencies for the duration. To one of Drayson's artistic pretensions, 'servant' would be an accurate description of any person in service on the premises."

"Any male person. Drayson referred to the informant as a he, and I doubt his lordship had the wits to dissemble on the spot regarding gender."

"The house party enjoys an abundance of male persons among both guests and staff."

A silence developed, and while I was acutely aware that dawn approached, I was equally aware that Hyperia made a fetching picture in her nightclothes, lost in thought, braid gone a bit frazzled. I had not arisen in a state of procreative readiness, but I was far from indifferent to her charms.

I could not recall a better night's sleep, or a more interesting start to a day.

"I like this," she said. "I like discussing the possibilities and considering the evidence with you. I don't like when we end up with more questions than answers."

"A very wise lady told me that investigations confound and

confuse at first, sometimes that seems to be all they do, but then patterns and possibilities begin to form, and the way becomes clear."

Hyperia smiled. "And you listened to her blathering."

"I listen to her sound advice. I'd best be off."

"Yes, you had. Don't forget your coat." She bounced off the bed, passed me my jacket, and kissed me on the lips. "I'll see you at breakfast."

"You might not. Atticus is overdue for a driving lesson. Then too, I want to avoid Lady Ophelia for the nonce. She's angry that Millicent is turning Leander over to the Caldicotts, and she expects me to dragoon Leander's mama back to the Hall and inspire her to remain with her son."

"Millicent trusted Harry, and her trust was misplaced. I would rather Leander have his mother in his life, but blaming you for her choices isn't fair."

Lady Ophelia had blamed the duchess, among others. As I stole another parting kiss and then made a silent progress back to my own rooms, I wondered how often I had indulged in the same response—blaming my mother—when she had, in fact, done nothing to deserve my opprobrium?

I had deflected Lady Ophelia's criticism of the duchess, but I had not defended my only extant parent when given the chance to do so. Some of my enthusiasm for the day waned on that thought. Her Grace was a lady. I was a gentleman, and her son. I should have responded more firmly to Godmama's silly accusations, though further antagonizing her ladyship would have been both ill-advised and ungentlemanly.

By the time I reached my apartment, I was deep in rumination about where next to direct my inquiries. I wanted to find Her Grace's letters and return to my nephew and Caldicott Hall, the sooner the better. If Godmama and I were on the outs, though, the loss of her good offices as Hyperia's chaperone would mean I would return to the Hall alone.

That prospect had absolutely no appeal whatsoever.

CHAPTER EIGHT

"What are you doing here?" I asked when I found Atticus curled up in the corner of the sofa in my sitting room.

"Was trying to sleep." He rubbed his eyes and pushed his hair off his forehead. "Too cold in the stable and too hot in the footmen's dormitory." He stretched and busied himself putting on and lacing up his boots.

Atticus was shrewd, resourceful, and proud, but he was also just a boy in a big and confusing world. And he had needed a safe place to sleep.

"Shall I have a word with somebody, Atticus?"

He scowled at me. "I can take care of meself."

"A slight to your dignity is a slight to mine. That's how being in my employ works. If one of the louts in livery here made advances to you, then I am insulted on your behalf and will take appropriate measures to address the situation." Insulted and enraged.

And yet, my grand proclamation over Atticus's welfare reminded me of my failure to rebuke Godmama for casting aspersion on the duchess.

"You and your talk, guv. You make my ears tired. S'pose I fetch

you some breakfast and shaving water. Mind you don't let Miss
Hyperia know you've been roaming the house half dressed with your
cravat in your pocket. The Quality is daft, but you was brought up
better than that."

Nice try. "You will henceforth sleep on the cot in my dressing
closet, Atticus. That is a direct order. You need not wait up for me,
but you aren't to leave my quarters unattended when I'm off doing
my roaming."

He rose from the sofa. "Don't get all pistols and swords on me,
guv. Miss Hyperia won't stand for that. I just... Sometimes a lad don't
know what's friendly and what's going in a bad direction is all. Best
not to guess wrong."

"I cannot tell you how many generals have wished they'd made
an orderly retreat and regrouped until reinforcements arrived. Sleep
in the dressing closet, young man. I haven't a valet. Nobody will think
anything of you waiting attendance on me."

They'd think it strange—more evidence of my eccentricity—then
resume gossiping about Miss Frampton's prospects or lack thereof
and the ridiculous notion of young men in skirts tossing tree trunks
about in the name of sport.

"I'm for the kitchen," Atticus said, heading toward the door.
"Miss Hyperia won't like that you was out wandering when good folk
are abed, guv. Lady Ophelia is already riled at you, and you don't
want 'em both mad at you at the same time. Best watch yourself."

"How is it you know that I'm in Lady Ophelia's bad books?"

"She told her lady's maid to tell the coachy to be ready to leave by
ten of the clock this morning. Maid was up half the night packing
what she just unpacked. I was in the hall when she came down to the
kitchen around midnight for a cuppa tea and some sympathy."

"Then you will need a nap at some point today. See that you get
one."

"I'm not a baby."

"You are insubordinate, and I am hungry. Be off with you."

He made me an elaborate bow then slipped out the door while I adjusted to the notion that Lady Ophelia was breaking ranks. She was well known for her independent nature and perfectly entitled to withdraw her support at any time, but did she expect Hyperia to decamp as well?

And where did her ladyship's maneuvering leave Leander, who had grown more than passingly fond of my godmother?

A half hour later, I was shaved and properly dressed and sitting on my balcony, enjoying the day's first cup of hot tea, when voices drifted up to me. A conversation between women, cozy and relaxed, was taking place on the floor below. Amid the clatter of cutlery and the tinkle of porcelain, I gathered that Miss Frampton and Lady Jessamine were breaking their fast together.

"Her Grace is not quite..." Lady Jess paused delicately. "*Stable*, and that's why his lordship is a bit wobbly in the brainbox too. Her Grace was a Fennington, and while they are wealthy and well respected—there's an earl in the bunch somewhere—they've never been quite *quite*, if you take my meaning."

I took the little minx's meaning. She'd retreated and regrouped in her own fashion after I'd scolded her politely at supper. I could not hear Miss Frampton's reply, and neither could I make myself quit the balcony.

More old habits that refused to die. If the enemy was foolish enough to discuss her battle plans where she could be overheard, *listen*.

"I agree, Lord Julian isn't precisely bad-looking," Lady Jessamine said, "but one cannot call him handsome either. The odd spectacles don't help, he's too tall, he's bony, and his conversation is less than witty. Did you hear Her Grace attacking Beethoven last night? Never have I encountered such violent playing."

I wanted to yell over the balustrade, *Not violent, your catty-ship, passionate.*

I finished my tea and waited for the next salvo.

"I don't think I will allow his lordship to court me after all," Lady Jess said. "Blood will tell, else Her Grace's unsteady nature would not be so readily apparent in her son, would it? You should make a try for him, Trish. He's probably desperate to win free of Miss West, but nobody else will have him, and men do have their pride. Lord Julian is polite enough, and his son might well be the next duke."

I had the sense I was overhearing boys playing soldier. Little fellows knew all the commands, all the military vocabulary, but from childish mouths, the words were an eerie mockery of the adult reality. Lady Jessamine was parroting slander somebody had poured into her delicate ears, or gossip she'd made it a point to overhear.

"Well, yes, I do admit that Her Grace has aged splendidly," she allowed, "despite the red hair. But she was an inconstant wife after doing her duty to the title, and she's been a merry widow. If I am aware of her flirtations, despite being the next thing to a schoolgirl, then you know Her Grace was a bit *too* merry. Did you notice that she's gone all melancholy since arriving at Tweed House? Step-mama is concerned for her, which is vexatious in the extreme. Step-mama ought to be worried about me—about all the young ladies who haven't secured matches. If one person in the whole wide world does not need worrying about, it's a duchess."

Laughter wafted upon the morning air, laughter and guilt.

I never worried about my mother, and yet, she had detractors, if not enemies, and likely always had. With a lofty station went a near obligation to serve as an object of envy. As I went in search of Lady Ophelia, I wondered who bore Her Grace such spite that even the young ladies at the gathering felt free to slander the only duchess in their midst?

And was that unkind gossip related to the missing letters, and if so, how?

~

I tapped on Lady Ophelia's sitting room door.

"*Entrez!*"

The French took me aback, but I well knew what her ladyship's imperious tone presaged. *Once more unto the breach...* I felt as if I were about to make a dawn report bearing bad news to a general infamous for his temper and morning dyspepsia. I arranged my features into bland agreeableness and bowed.

"My lady, good day."

Godmama wore a morning gown of blue silk that brought out the blue of her eyes. A silver tea service sat before her on a low table in front of the sofa.

"You are not Marie." She set down her tea cup and visually inspected me. "I believe we've said all we have to say to each other, my lord. I will be quitting the gathering in a few hours. I wish you the best of luck retrieving the missing letters."

Her tone said she wished *my lord* would fall on his arse at one of the Regent's formal receptions.

"Who hates my mother?" I asked, taking one end of the sofa and helping myself to an apple tart.

"I nearly did," her ladyship replied, picking up her tea cup. "She had so much—a duke, lovely looks, good family—and yet, she wasn't happy. Claudius tried to be a good husband after his fashion, but his fashion was mostly gallant gestures between self-indulgent frolics. I eventually came to realize that Dorothea had made the ghastly mistake of falling in love with her own husband. I would have pitied her, except that she'd loathe the very notion."

The duchess's husband might have frolicked with Ophelia herself. Ye gods and little fishes. "Who would delight in implying that both my mother and I are mentally unsound?"

"Dorothea is no more mentally unsound... Don't look at me like that. You have that problem with your memory. Dorothea's memory is, if anything, too good. Some things are truly best forgotten." Godmama sipped her tea primly while I helped myself to another tart.

Did her ladyship allude to forgetting our spat of the previous evening or to some scandal known only to her?

"I just overheard Lady Jessamine heaping contumely on Her

Grace's head. The duchess was unfaithful to her duke, she is enjoying widowhood far too much, and she's emotionally unsteady. My own mental instability is bad blood passed down on the dam side."

Her ladyship swirled her tea. "The Caldicotts have been colorful from time to time, but a more boringly sound family than the Fenningtons does not grace Albion's shores. Dorothea was in some ways the worst possible duchess for Claudius, but she did settle him down somewhat."

"Who resents her for it? Who is angry enough with her to steal her love letters and spread evil talk about her?"

"Are you accusing me, Julian?"

Interesting question for what it said about a past that didn't concern me. "Circumstances exonerate you. You were at the Hall when Her Grace's letters went missing. You've had years to purloin her correspondence, or hire somebody to do it, and yet, the letters are a recent loss. You also would not have been on hand to take Lady Barrington's gloves or Mrs. Whittington's locket, though you might well have stolen Lord Drayson's naughty sketches, mostly to scare some sense into him."

Her ladyship poured herself more tea—none offered to me, I noted—and watched the steam rising from her cup.

"The sketches don't fit," she said. "Drayson is a wet-behind-the-ears popinjay who can claim the sketches are mere artistic exercises."

I suspected they were in truth articles of rebellion in the ongoing war between papa and heir, but her ladyship had a point.

"He's not a widow," I said by way of agreement, "and he's not older, but the sketches are dear to him and arguably compromising. You never did answer my question regarding the duchess's enemies."

"Because I cannot. You are better off asking Gideon, who knows all the latest on-dits. *How* he knows defies even my vast resources, but he does know. This is probably why he's been tapped to stand for some pocket borough."

I chose a pear tart. "I don't care for him."

"Whyever not? His drawing-room deportment is burnished to a golden glow. He never gives offense. He has the perfect quip or tale for any moment. I find him, if anything, too perfect."

That was not the man I'd ridden out with, but then, I wasn't of an age with him, and I wasn't female. "Very well, I'll speak with him, but what you call his drawing-room deportment, I call a nigh-calculated ability to either flatter or offend."

"Because you are too sensitive."

My godmother had been brusque with me, honest to a fault, and inconveniently frank, but never, ever mean.

I considered her as she sipped the tea she'd forgotten to sweeten and saw by the morning light that she'd not slept well. Last night, she'd flung irrational accusations at Her Grace's figurative feet, and this morning she was hurling barbs at me as she—whom I'd come to regard as valiant—was leaving the investigative field mid-battle.

I rose and went to the French doors, not ready to storm off in high dudgeon. The mist had drifted off the river. The deer were gone. Slanting sunbeams tried to penetrate a high overcast. The morning had a stillness unique to the start of an autumn day, a muted, senti-mental quality suited to watercolors and solitude.

Her ladyship blamed the duchess for Millicent's defection, a leap of logic that approached the ridiculous. I'd been bothered by Godma-ma's rash words the previous night, and I was more bothered by them now.

Insight befell me as a lone raven took off from a lofty perch and circled the park before disappearing into the gray sky.

"When did Patrick die?" I asked, gaze on the cloudy heavens. "He'd be nearly thirty now." Just about my age. We'd been playmates, Harry for once the odd, older fellow out.

"You hopeless, incorrigible boy. Leave at once."

I turned to find her ladyship on her feet, indignation radiating from her.

"Hurl all the thunderbolts you please, Godmama. I will never forget that I followed Harry from camp under a waning quarter moon. I try to ignore the phases of the moon, but every month, without fail, the moon reminds me of my sorrows. Next month will mark another anniversary of that night, and I feel as if I'm holding my breath until then, waiting for some dark angel to pass my house. I have no doubt that twenty years hence, this time of year will bring me to the same sorry pass."

She blinked, then seemed to wilt back onto the sofa. "Some years aren't so bad, and then you feel guilty because you aren't sufficiently miserable." She glowered at the tea tray. "I wasn't there, Julian. My little boy lay dying, and I wasn't there. I was in Town, collecting gossip from the royal dukes and being *frivolous*. Nobody thought to summon me home. A head cold, a touch of influenza... Patrick was sassing his tutors one day, and a little over a week later, he was gone. The housekeeper eventually sent word that my Patrick was poorly, but..."

"The roads were awful," I said. They were still awful for much of the realm. "He'd been poorly before, probably came down with a bad sniffle every autumn, and he was such a robust boy that you had no reason to suspect the worst. I'm sorry."

Inadequate words, but the explanation sufficed. There was Leander, alone in the world, his mother turning her back on him, Arthur larking off to France, me preoccupied with Her Grace's business, and the boy's world in pieces.

"I learned my lesson," her ladyship said. "When Catherine took ill, I was there. I did not leave her side, but she'd come too early, and her lungs had always been weak. I knew to keep my expectations humble in her case. Patrick's death was the worst blow. Still is. With a spouse, you know one of you will go first, and both of my husbands were older than me. I realize children often have only a short span, but my Patrick was such an ebullient soul. When I go to my reward, the Creator and I will have words, Julian. Harsh, loud words, just as soon as I stop hugging the angel my boy has become."

I took the place beside Godmama on the sofa and passed her my plain handkerchief. "We are supposed to leave our memories on the battlefield, but I've yet to meet a soldier who does. Try as we might, they follow us around like a stink that won't leave the nostrils."

"The memories aren't all bad," her ladyship said, dabbing at her eyes with my linen. "The good memories are supposed to help."

"Do they?" I had endless good memories of Harry, mostly from boyhood, but some from our time in uniform as well.

"I'll let you know when I make up my mind. I thought I was up to another house party, Julian, but I have overtaxed my reserves. I do plan to leave this morning."

"I would rather you fly off in a rage than take leave to grapple with sadness."

"So would I, but you foiled that plan. Was Jessamine truly slandering the duchess?"

"With malice aforethought. A dangerous thing to do when she's the unmarried daughter of a mere earl."

"Dangerous and stupid. I hope her settlements are generous, for the young lady's sake."

While I hoped the opposite, that her settlements were modest, all but compelling a love match. "Will you take Hyperia with you?" She wasn't packed, but that oversight could be remedied in an hour.

"Chaperones abound here, Julian. Lady Barrington is keeping an eye on Miss Frampton and Miss Bivens, or claiming to, and your own mother is also on hand to serve."

"So why don't you ask her?" I certainly did not want to. "I am off to chat up Gideon Marchant, for my sins."

She tucked my handkerchief into a skirt pocket. "You and Dorothea are so much alike, it's uncanny. She will be delighted you asked for her assistance, but she won't let you see that lest you be embarrassed by it. You will be inordinately relieved to have her aid, but you won't let her see that, lest she be embarrassed by your effusions. Like a spinster being courted by a schoolteacher."

Not a flattering comparison, though I suspected Godmama wasn't entirely in error either. My mother and I shared with Arthur a certain dignity that Harry and the late duke had been able to set aside on occasion.

In deference to the dignity of all concerned, I chose my next words carefully. "Very well, I will approach my mother after I've tracked down Marchant. I will miss you, but I appreciate your willingness to look in on matters at the Hall."

By the merest blink, her ladyship betrayed a satisfying hint of surprise. "The Hall? I hadn't thought... Well, yes, I suppose I could bide there until you've concluded your business here. Arthur will be gone in a few days, and one wants a responsible hand on the tiller at such times."

"One absolutely does, and I have another request to put to you." Godmama was not exactly delighted with the task I assigned her, but she agreed to take it on. We both knew the point of her excursion would be to keep Leander company, and neither of us so much as mentioned the boy.

I thanked her briefly, wished her a smooth journey, and went in search of Marchant.

Marchant proved elusive, or perhaps I wasn't that keen on locating him. What should have been a simple search for letters inadvertently stashed behind the vanity mirror was becoming a tangle of thievery, slander, sorrow, and frustration.

My night with Hyperia had fortified me with sound sleep, though, and like any soldier in the midst of a forced march, genuine repose had provided balm to the body and the spirit. When an hour of asking footmen, grooms, and other guests for Marchant's whereabouts proved fruitless, I decided to take Atticus out for a driving lesson.

He managed somewhat better, driving Jupiter around the village green, completing a looping change of direction, and getting us back to Tweed House without mishap.

"You weren't barkin' at me the whole time," he said when I climbed down to serve as his header. "I can pay better attention without you yappin' at me the livelong day, guv."

I'd been preoccupied with the question of motive. Who had motive to steal those letters? Everybody and nobody.

"Jupiter shares your opinion," I said. "He does much better when you aren't fussing with the reins, squirming on the bench, or issuing one verbal command after another. Your trusty Ladon is of the same mind. A quiet rider is much easier to please than one who can't leave a horse in peace to do the job he's been asked to do."

Atticus wrapped the reins about the brake and hopped down, violating the *no sudden moves around horses* rule for the thousandth time.

"Ladon has the right of it. I hate when everybody is telling me what to do all the time, and *everybody* does. That MacFadden fellow said I should offer to polish boots for other gents, and I might earn more vails that way."

This was a question, and deftly put. "You are certainly free to use your spare time however you choose, and extra coins are always good to have on hand."

Atticus petted Jupiter's hairy shoulder. "I'm allowed to hire out?"

A household of any size had a whole economy humming in the lower reaches. Barter in beer and candles, loans, favors, and dicing debts flew madly from pantries to kitchens to dormitories, stables, and gardens.

"You are allowed to hire out, but I'd suggest taking on one additional task at a time. When you've been paid for a job well done, take on the next, and so forth. If you're approached about work you aren't keen to do, explain that I'm jealous of your time, and you must watch your step, because that is the honest truth, my lad."

"One at a time." Atticus clearly approved of that notion. "What if they don't pay me?"

"Excellent question. First, be sure to always negotiate fees in advance so you invite no misunderstandings. If your customer refuses to pay, you tell me, and you never work for them again. You complain about their parsimony loudly in the servants' hall, where an employer's behavior reflects on his staff and conversely."

"Simmony-what?"

"Parsimony. From the Latin *parsimonia,* for thrift or miserliness, and the verb *parcere,* to save, to spare."

"You mean tightfisted, and I should bellyache in public about it. I can do that. Everybody moans about this and that in the hall. Sore feet, sore heads, the damned bells always ringin', and the housekeeper ragin'. The footmen are starting to wish the whole house party to perdition, but MacFadden says that's normal."

"You are careful around MacFadden?"

"Aye. He's friendly, but not too friendly. I'm the cheerful lad, but not too cheerful."

"Then tell him you are available to polish Marchant's boots, Atticus, and keep a very, very sharp eye when you retrieve that footwear from Marchant's apartment."

Jupiter stomped a hoof and swished his tail. "You don't like Marchant? Because he's French?"

"He's not French, that I know of. His name is French, but my grandmother was French, which makes me partly French. I don't know him, Atticus, though he seems to be a fixture in Society familiar to everybody but me."

Atticus commenced scratching under Jupiter's chin. "He's not adding up?"

"Nothing is adding up, yet." I signaled to a groom who'd been idling in the shade of the barn aisle. "Atticus, you are to become familiar with harnessing and unharnessing, and this good fellow can start you off by explaining the parts and pieces to you as Jupiter is unhitched. Spend some time organizing my dressing closet after your nooning, and take a stab at laying out my supper kit. The meal is informal, thank heavens. Supper al fresco, weather permitting."

"Organizing your dressing closet?"

The groom took the reins from me. He was youngish, the same fellow who'd been singing Burns's lament about long-lost Senegal.

I looked directly at Atticus. "Carefully and thoroughly. Take your time, keep the doors locked behind you. One cannot be too careful."

"Oh." He grinned and whacked Jupiter's shoulder. "Right. C'mon, Jean, let's get this gear off old Jupe."

"Harness," Jean replied, smiling. "You refer to the gear as harness, young Atticus."

I left them to the fascinating business of hames, traces, girths, and crupper and decided that a quiet chat with mine host was in order. Lord Barrington was recently raised to his honors, his father having lived past the allotted three score and ten.

Securing the earldom's succession had apparently resulted in three girls born one after the other, followed finally by a pair of boys.

Barrington's first wife, having done her duty, was rewarded with eternal peace before the age of five-and-thirty. The earl had muddled along for a few years, then apparently grasped that launching three daughters required commissioning a field marshal suited to the task. Lady Barrington had risen to the challenge, though no new denizens of the nursery had appeared on her watch.

I'd been told the earl was enjoying the spectacle of the young people playing pall-mall, so I made my way around the side of the house. The distant notes of a flute gave me pause well short of the grassy court. I recognized the musician and thus followed the tune across the park and down to the edge of the river.

CHAPTER NINE

Her Grace perched on a bench along the water, a flute case open beside her. Her instrument was silver, and from it issued more of Robert Burns's work. The song likened love to a red, red rose, newly sprung in June. I found the tune sad, and even ironic. After several stanzas professing eternal devotion until all the seas ran dry, et cetera and so forth, the final verse became a parting wish. *I love you truly, madly, forever, and really must be going, darling.*

And fare thee weel, my only luve!
    And fare thee weel awhile!
    And I will come again, my luve,
    Though it were ten thousand mile.

I took the place beside my mother when she lowered her instrument. "You play beautifully."

"I had a good teacher." She removed from the case the device for cleaning the flute, which put me in mind of an infantryman's ramrod.

"You don't have to stop on my account. I'm surprised nobody has press-ganged you into performing for the other guests."

"Hellie knows better. My music is personal. I don't mind taking the alto part in a chorus, but the rest of it is a private joy, not a public entertainment. You got some sleep."

How could she tell? "I did. You?"

"Some."

I did not want to launch into another interrogation, though I had more questions. I cast around for neutral ground that rose above small talk.

"Lady Ophelia has taken a notion to decamp to the Hall," I said. "She claimed to be overtaxed by yet more socializing."

"She does this almost every year. Tries to ignore the anniversary of Patrick's death, tries to soldier on, but has to call off the march for a few weeks. She'll come around, after the memories have had their due."

At least Godmama knew the specific date of her son's passing. My mother hadn't even that consolation where Harry was concerned. Nor did she know his final resting place or the particulars of his cause of death.

Which was harder, knowing or not knowing?

"Tell me about your flute teacher," I said. "His name was Pickering?"

She finished cleaning her instrument and laid the sections in their velvet bed, then closed and latched the case.

"John Pickering. One of those people who could pick up any instrument and soon get a recognizable tune from it. His least favorite was the piano. He said one could bang delicately or loudly, but the whole matter still came down to percussion. He favored the subtleties possible with the bow and breath."

Her tone was wistful, suggesting she and Pickering had argued the attributes of woodwinds over strings by the hour and enjoyed every moment.

"If he was so talented and an engaging, well-favored young fellow, do you know whether he's made his way to London?" Much easier to flit about Mayfair teaching Mozart to young misses than racket all about the Home Counties looking for work.

"I am honestly not sure what became of him. He gave no indication what his plans were. His last letter was a fond and final farewell. 'The streams of our lives are flowing in different directions,' that sort of thing. I'm sure young men learn to write those epistles at university."

No, we did not. Only a particular sort of cad had a need for such a skill. Had his name even been John Pickering? "Did he tell you anything of his people, his education?"

Her Grace settled the case in her lap and gazed across the water. "He had a gentleman's upbringing and education, clearly. He was immaculately groomed at all times, his wardrobe spotless and in good repair. Faultless manners in any sort of company. He favored attar of roses for his ablutions, and his boots were never muddy.

"Excellent Latin and French," she went on. "Enough Greek to get by. His Italian seemed more than the smattering needed to navigate a libretto. His German was very competent. He was always posting letters to Vienna requesting this or that chamber score. He spoke of Vienna as his city on a hill, and I would not be surprised if he wasn't on the Continent somewhere."

"You've never tried to find him?"

"You'll never return to France?"

The duchess put the question quietly, and her query told me two things. First, Pickering had devastated her. The manner of his defection, the finality of it, had been a low, hard, unexpected blow. A betrayal. The parting itself had perhaps been inevitable, but he'd taken from her any control over the moment and means at a time when Her Grace had needed to be in charge of her own affairs, as it were.

Second, my mother grasped the depths of my own vulnerability to the past. The notion that Arthur would be racketing around France made me queasy, despite my all but ordering him to collect Banter and travel the Continent. To hear French spoken by a native similarly upset my digestion, though I myself commanded that degree of expertise with the language.

Or I had. "I take Your Grace's point, and I hope to never set foot in the place of my captivity again."

"But you did, after Waterloo."

"Briefly. Not much call for a reconnaissance officer when the battles are all won." With my fluent French and ability to blend in among various walks of life, I could easily have made myself useful to the army still occupying Paris.

I'd been on the verge of collapse after Waterloo, having overtaxed myself during the Hundred Days, and I'd compounded all the harm I'd suffered in captivity by heeding the call to rejoin Wellington's forces in Belgium.

"What do my lord's reconnaissance skills say about my missing letters?"

"That I'm overlooking important details. I've asked Lady Ophelia to nose about at the Hall for any other letters that passed between you and Pickering."

The duchess aimed a disgruntled glance my way. "Might you have inquired of me before taking that step, my lord?"

"I did not task her ladyship with a search for personal correspondence. You retained Pickering, you set out some terms of compensation, or somebody did on your behalf. He accepted those terms in writing before making the journey to the Hall. He didn't simply knock on the door of a duchess in mourning and convince her to add him to her household. How did you hear of him, anyway?"

Had Pickering's clientele been mere gentry, he might have found employment through self-introduction and impromptu market day concerts.

One did not earn the patronage of a duchess by auditioning in the local alehouse.

"I found him through word of mouth, I suppose. One is permitted visitors after the first few months of mourning, and I do keep up my correspondence. The agencies don't typically deal in music teachers or dancing masters. Why are you so preoccupied with my past?"

Her Grace was reluctant even to say Pickering's name. Truly, he'd served her a bad turn.

"I put these questions to you because I am frustrated by a lack of progress in my efforts to find your letters. Somebody has them. I'm convinced of that. Perhaps you won't receive a blackmail demand until the party has disbanded, but your thief has to be among those present at Tweed House."

"Or the thief was hired by somebody on the guest list. Hellie has been debating how much to explain to Lord Barrington. He's nobody's fool, for all that he can play the fool convincingly. I suspect he doesn't care for Gideon, for example, but his lordship knew better than to exclude Gideon from the guest list."

"Marchant would recall the slight?"

"Lord Barrington has three daughters to launch, and Lady Jessamine was only moderately well received in her first Season. She did not exactly take."

And the sins of the sister would be visited upon her siblings. How well I knew Mayfair's delight in any pretext for rendering judgment on the innocent. I debated explaining to the duchess just why the fair Jessamine might not have impressed the hostesses with her wit and candor.

Before I found words to convey particulars, Lord Barrington came sauntering along the path that ran beside the riverbank.

"What ho!" he called. "Two more refugees from the tedium of whacking balls with wooden mallets. Your Grace, my lord, good morning. If my wife or daughters inquire regarding my whereabouts, you are both sworn to secrecy."

I rose in greeting, and Her Grace got to her feet as well.

She offered our host a warmhearted smile. "My lips are sealed. I met only Lord Julian on my rambles. I'll see you both at lunch." She collected her flute and sashayed off across the park before I could offer the requisite parting bow.

"There goeth a damned fine woman," Barrington said. "Her Grace was a great comfort to my wife when Lord Cobbold went to his reward. Shall we sit a moment? Hellie doesn't mind that I'm truant from pall-mall—I play well enough to put the bachelors to the blush, and darling Jessie would skewer me for that—but this spot is so peaceful, and peace has been in short supply lately."

I resumed my seat. "I've been meaning to seek you out, Barrington. My thanks for your hospitality. Not every host would be as gracious about three unexpected guests on top of a full house."

"House ain't full. Not by half. Place could house a regiment, and in times past, it has. Hellie and your mama are friends. Not simply gracious acquaintances, friends. When Hellie was between husbands, Her Grace remained loyal. She introduced us, in fact, or reintroduced us."

Matchmaking was a duchess's privilege, almost her duty, but Lady Barrington wouldn't have been the beautiful, much younger second wife an earl would be expected to take.

"You knew Lady Barrington in her youth?"

"She's still in her youth, my lord. They all are and always will be, and that is holy writ, if you intend to prosper on this earth. My path had crossed Hellie's when she made her come out—I was out of mourning by then, and she was a pretty young thing.

"She was smitten with her young man," he went on. "He wasn't a viscount yet, but she didn't care a thing about the title. I dismissed them as just another fatuous young couple destined to grow older and wiser. I'd forgotten all about her. I wasn't looking to remarry, but five children have a way of impressing on a man the need for reinforcements."

"Particularly when three of those children are daughters."

"Precisely. Hellie has her hands full. Jess is a bit too much like her mother, and truth to tell, I have spoiled the girls."

"Too much like her mother?"

"Headstrong. I have cousins, my lord. I am by no means the last of my line, but Inez insisted that we were to have boys. I felt no urgency, but she did. If anything happened to me, her consequence depended on being the mother of the next earl. This was impressed upon me repeatedly, and she never quite recovered from the birth of our youngest."

"Do you miss her?" My question was impertinent, but if nothing else, my sojourn at Tweed House had made me aware that many, if not most, of my elders were dealing with life after multiple grievous losses. Spouses—sometimes more than one—children, again also in the plural, friends, parents, siblings...

Later life was not the time of ease and plenty I'd apparently assumed it would be. Why did that fact have to be impressed upon a seasoned soldier?

Lord Barrington produced a flask and offered it to me. I declined with a shake of my head.

"I do not miss Inez, my lord." He uncapped his pocket pistol and took a sip. "For a time I did, but the missing was selfish rather than sentimental. Poor me, I had nobody to bicker with and tease, no marital affections to enjoy when I so chose, nobody to manage my household as I preferred. I missed a wife, not necessarily my wife. I am ashamed, of course, but that doesn't change the truth. I am sad for Inez that she is not watching the children grow up. She never had a chance to preen as the mother of the next earl."

He glanced over his shoulder at Tweed House, from whence the sound of wood striking wood and an occasional shout of laughter rose.

"Inez was not, however, a restful woman," he said. "Never content, never at peace. Hellie is a gem. I adore my current wife. She could ask me to host a state visit, and I would beggar myself attempting to amuse the Regent for as long as he chose to impose himself on us."

The earl took another swig, then banged the cork back into the flask as if to punctuate his sentiments.

I put my next question carefully, not wishing to upset a happy marital applecart. "Will you nonetheless be relieved when the house party disbands?"

"Young man, how would you like to play the genial host while your firstborn makes a complete cake of herself where her younger sisters have front-row seats, your wife is run off her feet, your larders are stripped by a plundering horde, your staff grows surlier with each day, and your stores of hay and grain are decimated before winter even arrives?"

"Point taken." Nobody's fool, Her Grace had said, and she was right.

"I'm none too pleased about the duchess's purloined letters either. Hellie hasn't said anything, but one isn't entirely rusticated. Lord Julian Caldicott finds whatever or whoever has gone inconveniently missing, and he does so quietly, according to the talk in the clubs. Your mama's letters have disappeared. Hellie has misplaced a pair of Cobbie's old gloves. Mrs. Whittington is bemoaning the loss of a locket or brooch or some other gewgaw. Drayson is moping about as if his favorite snuffbox can't be found. My valet was vague on those details. You, I take it, are here to retrieve the listed items before the talk gets out of hand."

A slight emphasis on the last phrase revealed it to be a warning.

"I am, and to enjoy good company, including that of my own mother."

"Well, mind your step around our Jessie, please. I love my daughter, but she's at an age where good sense is in short supply,. I saw her *regarding you* at supper the other night with a particularly thoughtful expression. Her Grace, to say nothing of Miss West, would take it amiss if you were to be inveigled into the warming pantry by one of Jessie's silly schemes. On that excessively honest note of paternal long-suffering, I will bid you a good morning. Oh, and welcome to Tweed House."

He strolled on his way as another gust of laughter wafted from the side garden.

I remained on the bench, contemplating the exchange, which had been pleasant, enlightening, and nowhere near as spontaneous as Lord Barrington had made it seem. He was genuinely fond of and protective toward his family, and he respected my mother as well.

He even, apparently, had some respect for me, or for my investigative skills. He did not, however, want me as a son-in-law, despite the fact that I was a ducal heir and had all my teeth.

Well, no matter. I didn't want him for a papa-in-law, and I did seek to unravel the fate of the missing letters, the sooner the better. I wandered back in the direction of the house, turning over his lordship's recitations of ancient history, a widower's regrets, and a father's warnings.

Somewhere in his lamentations had been a detail that deserved further study, perhaps several details. I was still sifting and sorting when I spied Gideon Marchant among the pall-mall throng, Miss Frampton on his arm.

Once more unto the breach. I changed course and prepared to be agreeable to my fellow guests, though I hadn't even made my way to Mrs. Whittington's side before Marchant was hailing me, exactly as I'd hoped he would.

"My lord, good day. One heard you were asking after me. You know the delightful Miss Frampton?"

"I have had the honor. Miss Frampton, good morning. Are you cheering any particular team, or remaining above the affray?"

"Quite above it, my lord. I have four younger sisters and three younger brothers. Remaining above affrays, melees, and riots has become second nature of necessity."

She had a winsome smile and lovely brown eyes, though most of Society would call her plain and chubby.

"You are doubtless a model of decorum and a temple of long-suffering," I said. "But think of all the stories you have to tell on those younger siblings when they eventually struggle toward some sort of adulthood. Your armory of embarrassing memories ensures their eventual good behavior, if you'll only be patient."

She dimpled fetchingly. "This is doubtless the strategy employed by my lord's sisters, for here you are, all good manners and drollery. If you gentlemen will excuse me, I do believe Mrs. Whittington has forgotten her parasol by the punch table. I'll return it to her before it goes missing."

She dipped us half a curtsey on that odd note and made for the gazebo, where the punchbowl had been set up.

"That one will make somebody a very agreeable wife," Marchant said, "and that somebody might even be me."

"Matrimony at long last beckons to you?"

"Not particularly, but when one contemplates embarking on a political career without a wife, one does pause to reconsider. The Framptons are a good family, but not too good. Morticia is precisely the sort of female a member of Parliament ought to have at his side. Solid, not flashy. Well connected, but never the cynosure of all eyes and so forth. She'll organize the political dinners, run the household, and be grateful for those assignments. You were looking for me."

Hyperia would detest Marchant's view of marriage and of Miss Frampton. I detested the speculative eye he'd turned on Miss Frampton's retreating form.

"The matter I'd like to discuss is somewhat delicate, Marchant."

"You weren't at the whist tournament, and I do not typically lend coin to acquaintances, my lord."

That was as close to blatant rudeness as a man could travel without getting it all over his boots. "I have no need of a loan, but I do need information." I moved away from the field of play, and Marchant ambled along at my side.

Lord Drayson delivered a stout whack to his ball and sent an opponent's ball flying yards from the ideal course. A smattering of applause and humorous insults followed as he took his next shot.

"I am at your service, my lord."

"Her Grace has lost a trio of old letters of a private nature, and I have overheard conversations suggesting the duchess is not well liked by some parties at this gathering. I seek to return her letters to her and to narrow the places I should search for them. Who dislikes Her Grace so much they'd steal her personal correspondence? Lady Ophelia herself suggested I seek your counsel on this topic, though I apologize for involving you in a family difficulty."

I expected him to reply with some ribald innuendo, but he merely looked thoughtful as Drayson took a dramatic bow.

"The problem with Dorothea," he said, "is that she has become genuinely reserved, of necessity. She's hard to like because she's hard to know. What others take for hauteur is an overly trusting nature thrust into a highly visible position. She sometimes retreats into aloof dignity when in public and gets judged for it. If she were outspoken or silly or flirtatious, she'd be judged for that, too, of course. All of which is to say I doubt Her Grace has any enemies at this gathering. She's too careful for that. Let's leave the infantry to their amusements, shall we?"

His opinion wasn't exactly at odds with anything I knew of my mother, but the insight it conveyed was at odds with what I knew of him, though in keeping with Lady Ophelia's opinion of Marchant's status as a social spectator-at-large.

"You have made a study of Her Grace's situation?"

We maneuvered around those waiting in line for punch, and we kept walking until we reached the path that led to the dormant gardens.

"I observe what's before my eyes, your lordship. I am of an age with your mother, more or less, and we move in some of the same circles."

"Hence my question about who would spread slander against her."

"What specific slander?"

I trusted Marchant would not repeat the gossip, but I was still uncomfortable with the disclosure. "That she's flighty, flirtatious, given to unnecessary dramatics."

"All of which has no basis in reality, so we must conclude that whoever maligns Her Grace does so from a place of ignorance. I nominate Lady Jessamine. She all but hates her step-mother. Hellie and Dorothea are good friends, and thus Jessamine's ill will extends to Her Grace. The girl isn't very bright."

She also wasn't a *girl*, having been presented at court and thus indelibly declared ready for marriage.

"To the contrary, the insults aimed at my mother do have a basis in reality. She can be moody. Since my father's death, she has not consigned herself to a life of quiet contemplation, and I'm told she was a more vivacious creature as a new bride."

Marchant stopped and used the toe of his boot to sweep aside some yellow oak leaves fallen to the walkway. "Thus you believe that whoever has started this whispering campaign does know your mother well and has for some time. Then we see Lady Ophelia climbing into her coach, no explanation save 'other engagements.' Very curious, that. I could add that Society believes you and your mother to be all but estranged, my lord. If you harbor filial grudges, pretending to fret over insults to your mother is the best way to hide the fact that they originated with you. Quite a tangle."

"You come close to insulting me, Marchant." Not for the first time.

I hadn't encountered this degree of expertise with verbal knives since I'd been interrogated by a diabolically clever French colonel. Girard had been equally skilled with actual knives, come to that, and he'd been my enemy. What excuse had Marchant for antagonizing me so relentlessly?

"If I am skeptical of your honor, my lord, I am merely returning a favor, hmm? I have known Dorothea since before she married your father. I am a noted observer of the passing scene and have sufficient influence that I have been asked to stand for Parliament later this year. I will doubtless win, by the by, given the nature of my sponsorship. You might conclude—erroneously, of course—that I've taken to stirring up talk where your mother is concerned. You speculate that I will then offer to quiet the talk if Her Grace will assist with my exorbitant campaign expenses."

His confidence in his electoral success meant some wealthy peer had tapped Marchant to run for a vacant seat. Lord Barrington could doubtless fill me in on those details, or I might put my questions to MacFadden. What a valet didn't know about his employer's prospects was hardly worth knowing.

"I do not question your honor, Marchant. I seek information. If you can't tell the difference between an interrogatory discussion and an insult, then I will apologize for having wasted your time." My reply was by way of an exploratory thrust, because I had put up with enough of Marchant's posturing.

He was being no help whatsoever, and his contrariness when given an opportunity to aid a lady—a lady, a widow, and friend—when she was unjustly defamed, endeared him to me not at all.

"Now, now, my lord. I do apologize. I know I can be a bit..."

I waited. I had no intention of conciliating this pompous churl, and besides that, his theorizing lacked logic. If he was truly assured of victory, he had no need—no motive—for extorting funds from Her Grace.

I wondered again who his people were and added to that query a curiosity about his means. If he was wealthy, as my mother believed, he'd not need a titled sponsor to stand for election.

"I can be arrogant," Marchant said, looking none too comfortable with the admission. "Too full of myself, overbearing even. You have neglected your mother, and the temptation to twit you bedevils me."

A weak apology wrapped in a false accusation. How had this man prospered in any setting? "You do not twit, Marchant. You egregiously overstep. I'll bid you good day."

He put a hand on my sleeve, then hastily reconsidered that

presumption. "I apparently do not have the whole story where you and the duchess are concerned, and one doesn't want to pry. I apologize again for trespassing on delicate ground. As for who might be attempting to cast Dorothea's name into the mud... I have the sort of mind that can conjure up a nefarious motive for anybody on the premises."

Now we might be getting down to business. "Go on."

"Lady Canderport needs to get her daughter launched before the fair Lottie runs off to Scotland with any available fortune hunter. The settlements involved are not large, unless a fellow is pockets to let and thinks a viscount's daughter can help him rise in the world. That sort is thick on the ground."

"And it's my mother's duty to prevent such an outcome and see Lottie wed to a German prince instead?"

"To at least aid Lady Canderport's matchmaking efforts, which Dorothea has not bestirred herself to do. The same applies where Charles is concerned. He needs a wife, posthaste, being his father's heir and an articled Bond Street nitwit. His sister does all his thinking for him, and that tells you a great deal."

"Lady Canderport has a motive to malign my mother, then." And a propensity for tippling, a disquieting combination.

"The list doesn't stop there. Barrington fancied himself in love with your mother. She's a few years his senior, but they'd both lost a spouse, and one can choose for personal reasons the second time, true? Instead, she steered the earl in dear Hellie's direction, and Barrington might regret that maneuvering now that it's time to march Lady Jessamine to the altar."

There goeth a damned fine woman. I'd taken Barrington's words for honest admiration, not the muttering of a suitor scorned.

"Interesting theory, Marchant. Anybody else?"

"The other young ladies might be culpable of dramatics out of spite and frustration, or Lady Jessamine began a campaign, and they fell in with it. Miss West might regard your mother as competition for your loyalty, or perceive that the duchess did not force you to marry her before you joined up, and thus the young lady wants back some of her own. I can attribute vile motives to almost anybody, my lord. I have watched polite society at its games for decades. Bullbaiting can be more genteel than Mayfair at play."

He spoke with a touch of humor, but what came through as well was his disdain for the performers in the dramas he watched. His was not a sympathetic critique, but rather, one bordering on contempt.

"Is this why Parliament appeals?" I asked. "You can get your teeth into reform or the Irish question or something weightier than who cheats at whist?" If so, I might have to part with a smidgen of respect for Marchant, albeit grudgingly, and only a smidgen.

From time to time, many a former soldier looked about himself and asked, *Was this what I risked my life to protect? Did good men die in their bloody and miserable thousands to ensure Prinny could waste a fortune on fireworks? Did John Bull suffer decades of privation only to find the Corn Laws threaten his children's survival more acutely than Napoleon ever did?*

"I have been asked to serve in Parliament, my lord. One is supposed to respond when called, and besides, the whole business might well be diverting. I will wish you good luck identifying your mother's detractor, but I can tell you honestly,"—he leaned close enough that I caught a whiff of sandalwood from his person—"I would not waste time suspecting either Hellie or Mrs. Whittington."

Which I had not been doing. "Lady Barrington would not undertake mischief toward a titled guest at her own house party," I said. "What of Mrs. Whittington?"

"No motive whatsoever," Marchant said, his smile wistful. "Carola married the typical gouty, balding, portly senior officer and proceeded to dote on him without limit. Old Freddie was smart enough to reciprocate to the extent he could, and she honestly mourned his passing. She hasn't a grasping bone in her body and would gain nothing by betraying a woman she considers a friend.

"Test my assessment," he went on. "Try to draw Carola into a conversation maligning anybody short of the Corsican himself. You will earn yourself a deft change of topic and the mildest of reproofs. She might not have a title, but Carola Whittington is a true *lady*."

And yet, Marchant had at least pretended to be considering marriage to Miss Frampton rather than court a woman he appeared to genuinely esteem.

"In my experience," I said slowly, "people who seem too good to be true generally are too good to be true." Informants too eager to share intelligence, servants too willing to gossip, fellow officers too willing to offer their flasks, women too available for trysting... I suspected them all of having ulterior motives, and my wariness had often been vindicated.

Marchant regarded the imposing façade of Tweed House looming up over the back terrace. "I would trust Carola Whittington with my life, my lord. I can't say that about many people and certainly about none other at this gathering, meaning no insult to present company. I'll see you at lunch."

He strode off, the picture of the mature, urbane gentleman on his dignity. He'd trust Mrs. Whittington with his life, but could not contemplate entrusting her with his future.

Interesting.

I took a seat on the edge of the tiered fountain, the air slightly perfumed with the stink of the brackish water. Tomorrow morning, that water might be ice, so clear was the sky above and so sharp the late morning light.

As I pondered my discussion with Marchant, I concluded that he'd told me nothing of value about my mother's situation. By attributing foul motives to everybody, Marchant had neither narrowed the focus of my investigation, nor exonerated himself.

He put me in mind of the Spanish resistance that had from time to time aided Wellington's army. Some of those fellows had been brave patriots, more determined to rid Spain of the Corsican menace than Wellington had been himself. Others, though, had played all sides for personal gain, worn any disguise, declared loyalty to any cause, and stooped to any subterfuge, the better to further their own ends.

I came to fear I could be too much like them, willing to adopt any means to complete a mission. Marchant, by turns annoying, honest, overbearing, and then contrite, put me in mind of those bandits in patriot's clothing. Lady Ophelia was right to give him a wide berth.

I wished my mother had as well.

CHAPTER TEN

"I am convinced my mother lived through Yuletide," Hyperia said, "and into February just so our holidays in subsequent years wouldn't carry a shadow of grief."

I thought of Harry, who'd loved the revelry and foolishness of Christmas. "The shadow lingers nonetheless, doesn't it?"

"Not as darkly as it might, but you tell me that in Lady Ophelia's case, the grief is further weighted with a mother's guilt. That must be awful."

We'd chosen to hack out in the midafternoon, when many of the guests were resting, and no particular diversions had been scheduled. No groom attended us, and the sheer pleasure of having Hyperia to myself compensated for many frustrations.

"If Arthur comes to any harm on the Continent," I said, turning Atlas onto the bridle path that led to the village, "I will blame myself. I all but told him to gather up Banter and take ship, to travel now, while they both enjoy good health and Europe is mostly at peace."

"And he's off like a bolt from a crossbow, for him," Hyperia observed. "You did not convince him to go, Jules. You merely gave him permission to do as he longed to do, and that permission couldn't have come from anybody else."

"A consolation, but I also worry he and Banter will find the Continent too agreeable. Many a titled family dwells abroad and lives far more economically than they could at home." I needed my surviving brother to come back to me, though I'd yet to tell him that.

"What has Her Grace said about Arthur's prospective travels?"

We were ambling along at the walk, having mounted less than ten minutes earlier. Atlas stopped in the middle of the path at no particular cue from me.

"I haven't asked the duchess for her opinion of Arthur's plans. She's not seeing him off, and she certainly didn't fly to the Hall when he announced he'd be sailing away." Still... Lady Ophelia had buried her Patrick nearly two decades ago, and the loss yet haunted her.

Her Grace had not *even* buried Harry, she'd mourned him without the comfort of any funerary obsequies, and now her firstborn was away to lark about the country where Harry had died.

"She has to be a bit uneasy," I said, urging Atlas forward. "The line of succession is not exactly overflowing with security. She hasn't said a thing to me about her views."

"And you haven't brought up your own misgivings. Jules, was there ever a time when you and your mother simply talked?"

"Of course. When I was a small boy, I thought nothing of intruding on either parent's peace with my myriad brilliant discoveries. A four-leaf clover, a late rose... If the kittens in the stable had opened their eyes or the oak had lost a limb in the previous night's storm. My parents heard the lot of it from me." The town crier.

I felt a pang of sadness for that little boy, always looking to impress his parents, always hoping to be the bearer of interesting news. I'd kept a keen eye out for anything that might impress Mama or Papa.

Had my reconnaissance instincts been born out of nothing more than a youngest son's fear of being ignored by his parents? Heaven defend me from such a charge, and yet...

"Her Grace always listened," I said. "Papa would make time for me if his schedule allowed, but he could also let it be known that my interruptions were inconvenient."

"Your mother listened to you." Hyperia let the words waft about on the crisp autumn air. "Not every lady of her station would have, Jules."

Her Grace had listened to Harry better, but then, Harry had excelled at commandeering adult attention. Harry had had *charm*. Once I'd understood that he also had the status of the legitimate spare, I realized he had assets in the struggle for notice and consequence that I would always lack.

Though I was now the *heir*, not merely the spare, and a fat lot of good my expectations were doing me, as Lady Ophelia would say.

"Marchant and I spoke about the letters and Lady Jessamine's gossip," I said as we emerged from the double row of stately conifers that shaded the bridle path. "He excels at viewing his fellow humans with suspicion and even presented a motive for himself."

"Say on."

"He'll slander Her Grace, using his vast social connections to smear her reputation, and then for a tidy sum, he will offer to repair the damage. Said sum will help finance his political ambitions."

Hyperia snorted. "He's backed by Lord Westerboro and quite possibly running unopposed. His political ambitions are already well financed."

"What of his personal ambitions? Nobody seems to know much about his origins or his means. He rides a pretty horse whom he claims has a naughty streak, he brought one somewhat cheeky manservant with him to this gathering, and he doesn't in any way present himself as well-heeled."

"Suggesting he is exactly that. Do you suspect him of malicious behavior toward your mother?"

"Yes, but without any evidence to support my conclusions. I simply don't care for him, and yet, he is some sort of Society darling, a favorite with hostesses throughout the Home Counties."

Was I envious of his social éclat? Lowering thought. Very lowering thought.

"I don't care for Lady Canderport," Hyperia said. "I have every reason to be sympathetic to her situation, with not one but two mutually reinforcing hellions on her hands, but she has done nothing that I can see to mitigate her own miseries."

"Aren't all those hidden flasks intended as mitigation?" Many a soldier refilled his flask twice before he even noticed he was out of biscuits. "What else would you have her do?"

"Separate the twins," Hyperia said. "Each is a bad influence on the other. They conspire and compete in equal measures, and because they hold to each other so closely, neither one has any friends to speak of."

I had my mother to thank for not allowing me to become Harry's familiar. He and I had not gone off to public school together, despite my father's preference for that plan, and we'd had different tutors and separate quarters.

Had Mama done that for me? For both of her younger sons? Had she meant to put us on equal sibling footing with Arthur, who'd had his own chambers from the moment he'd been breeched?

The village green came into view, a sparkling expanse of autumn grass flanked by Tudor shops, a smithy, and a lovely little white-washed church. The steeple was a modest gesture in the nature of a cupola putting on airs, while the bell tower was a handsome square feature that would command a view of the whole surrounds.

"I could use some lemonade," Hyperia said. "The punch Lady Barrington serves is too sweet and too strong."

"Part of its charm, I suppose. What do you make of Mrs. Whittington?" Hyperia's opinions tended to be more balanced than my own. She had the knack of assessing a situation from a few steps back compared to my own nose-to-the-ground approach.

"I like her," Hyperia said as the horses clip-clopped onto the lane encircling the green. "She doesn't put on airs. She's not stuffy or sly. Her widowhood sits on her lightly. She strikes me as the sort who was born with common sense and a kind nature, and she has maintained a firm grip on both gifts."

Much like my dear Perry, though her fortitude also deserved a good deal of credit. "Marchant claims the Whittington marriage was affectionate, that the husband was the quintessential portly, bald, gouty old soldier, and she yet doted on him."

"You believed him?"

"Any reason why I shouldn't?" Though I also suspected Marchant would be a facile liar—again, without any basis in fact.

"Jules, you described Mrs. Whittington's missing jewelry as containing a lock of *brown* hair, but Marchant told you the late Lieutenant General Whittington was bald. If nothing else, the old fellow was too much his wife's senior to have much brown hair, unless he'd kept that lock tucked away since his youth."

Possible. Highly unlikely. *My, my, my.* Hyperia's insight was exactly the sort of development that could lead to further revelations, and revelations could lead to real answers—or simply to awkwardness.

"Perry, I do believe you have caught out somebody in a lie, but that somebody is not Marchant, alas for my prejudices. The somebody is Saint Carola Whittington. Shall you question her further, or shall I?"

Hyperia looked about us at the ineffable sweetness of an English village on a pretty autumn afternoon. The oak at the center of the green still had about half its leaves, their golden hue bathing the scene in mellow light and leaving a mantle of yellow over half the expanse of grass. Too fine a day not to enjoy at least an hour with my darling Perry and too fine a day to sully with intrigue and interrogation.

"You talk to her," Hyperia said. "You have the military connection with her, and she met you in Portugal. If that lock of hair belonged to a lover, she'll find it easier to confess her peccadillo to you rather than to an unmarried woman who is all but a stranger."

"I don't want to pry."

Hyperia laughed, a hearty sound that had a boy holding a plow horse outside the smithy smiling.

"You excel at prying, Jules. Even as I speak, your mind is turning over possibilities: Is Mrs. Whittington's falsehood relevant? Does she have an amatory secret that could jeopardize her standing in Society? Is this the connection between her and the duchess—they both frolicked imprudently—and where does that leave Lady Barrington and her gloves? Am I right?"

"You have hit the bull's eye, of course." Her recitation had marched nearly word for word with my thoughts. "I can't make Drayson's stolen sketches conform to any pattern, but who knows what items will turn up missing by the time we return to Tweed House?"

"Let's have a lemonade rather than find out any sooner than we must," Hyperia said, drawing her mare to a halt before the Lynnwood Arms. "Making small talk the livelong day leaves me parched. Have you asked your mama to serve as my chaperone yet?"

I delayed my answer by assisting Hyperia to dismount and handing the horses off to a groom, with instructions to loosen girths and remove bridles, but offer only water and grass.

"I will speak to the duchess before supper," I said. "Or to Lady Barrington."

Hyperia took my arm but did not let me escort her up the steps. "Julian Caldicott, *talk to your mother*. Request her aid in this one small particular. You are asking on my behalf, after all, and it's not as if she'll have to exert any effort simply to be at the same gathering we're already both attending."

"True." My commanding officer had given me a direct order, and I would obey it, eventually.

We were honored with the use of the snug, and the lemonade was quite good, as were the cheese tarts accompanying it. When we returned to Tweed House, we learned that we'd missed a practice round of caber tossing—an occasion for hilarity, apparently—and that all gentlemen who weren't blessed to own proper Highland finery would be measured for borrowed kilts before supper.

I'd brought my plaid kilt with me, though it probably fit more loosely than it should, and thus I had plenty of time to seek out Mrs. Whittington. I anticipated that discussion with reluctance, almost as much reluctance as I anticipated asking my own mother for a simple favor.

~

"No sign of your locket, I'm afraid," I said as Mrs. Whittington accepted a glass of punch from me. "If you have a moment, I'd like to put a few more questions to you."

"You are avoiding the punch, my lord?"

"I am prone to headaches. Prudence suggests I keep my distance from the punchbowl."

We strolled along the balustrade of the back terrace, though numbers were thin for the evening buffet. Too much whacking wooden balls and tossing tree trunks, or the house party had hit the lull between opening flourishes and the farewell crescendo, and guests were fatigued from too much socializing.

Then too, the evening was brisk. The slightest breeze would feel downright chilly.

Mrs. Whittington paused at the end of the terrace, her gaze on the dull, bare squares of the garden and the footmen lighting torches along the walkways. Off to the west, a red and orange sunset suggested inclement weather on the way. She wore her purple shawl, and most of the other ladies were similarly wearing wraps.

"I keep thinking I will open a drawer," she said, "and there my locket will be. It's smaller than most of its kind, small even for a miniature. Perhaps I was meant to lose it."

"And yet, you told me that memories must be allowed their due, however painful. That locket holds memories for you, doesn't it?"

She nodded. "Good memories, for the most part. But even good memories can be sad in hindsight."

I gestured to a bench that faced the garden. At another time of year, the view would be pleasant, though it struck me as melancholy now.

"And with whom do you share those memories, Mrs. Whittington?"

She set her glass on the flagstones and remained silent for a moment. "Explain yourself, my lord."

"Mourning jewelry is seldom gold, but you said the locket came into your possession early in your bereavement and that it held a curl of dark brown hair. I assumed that you described a mourning locket, but you did not. That lock of hair belonged to somebody other than your late spouse."

She smiled faintly. "Somebody whom I loved, or thought I did at the time."

Saint Carola, whatever her faults, was no liar, nor was she a coward. "Everybody I have consulted describes your marriage as genuinely affectionate on the part of both spouses."

"We were devoted, in our way. Freddie was such a good, dear man. He wasn't handsome, wasn't young, but he was kind and sweet and faithful. I knew his life had been challenging and that his health was suffering—he'd served in India for years—and we made the best of the time we had."

"You missed him," I suggested. God knew, I missed Harry, and Papa, and I was in a near frenzy to contemplate missing Arthur for months on end.

"I missed the closeness, not just of the body. We were friends. We had the sort of jokes that a couple share with a look and a sense of being united against a silly and vexing world. Freddie said we were a regiment of two, and when he was alive, I felt that."

The usual infantry square was composed of about five hundred men, four ranks deep, packed into a fighting machine of about sixty feet on a side. The result was an impenetrable wall of weaponry, provided the soldiers did not break ranks.

"Your husband broke ranks by expiring."

She nodded. "He wasn't that old, you know. Fifty-three. I begged him to ease up on the port, to try to get through breakfast without a tankard of porter, but he was too much the military man and had been so for too long. He was never drunk, but he was never without a glass of something either."

She'd married a man more doomed than she'd understood as a bride. Ill, in a sense, and more devoted to his illness even than he'd been to her.

"I'm sorry." What else could I say? She'd given her heart to a walking ghost. "Grief under such circumstances becomes complicated."

She picked up her glass, drank, and set it back down. "Your brother Lord Harry?"

Well... yes. "My brother Lord Harry. He left camp of his own volition by dark of night and was intercepted by a French patrol, to whom he offered no resistance. He loved the risk, the daring, the near misses, and tall tales. I loved him."

"He loved you too. Depend upon that, my lord." Spoken like a woman who'd had years to consider her short marriage.

"While in mourning for your husband, did you offer your heart to another?"

"Not exactly. More like a thief came along and stole it. I was so sad, and he was so understanding. He was everything Freddie had not been. Handsome, well-spoken, unpretentious, unmilitary, young, and exuberantly healthy. He was the younger son waiting for a diplomatic post, his habits refined and his manners impeccable. He didn't even drink much. I don't regret the liaison, but it took me a long time to understand why I could be tempted."

Fate had put a nigh irresistible consolation smack in Mrs. Whittington's path, the ideal distraction from her grief.

"I loathe the thought of returning to France," I said. "Southern

France especially, but I suspect I will not lay Harry's ghost to rest until I do. You must not tell anybody I've said that." Why confide that fear—it was a fear—in her? Because she'd taken bold measures to exorcise her husband's ghost, apparently, and that had required courage.

"You might be right, my lord. I was discreetly foolish, and thank heavens, my temptation turned out to be completely unlike Freddie in another regard. Freddie was constant, faithful, devoted, and reliable. This other fellow..."

"Made you feel like the center of his universe when you were with him, and then he'd turn his regard elsewhere, and it was as if you ceased to exist. I had a brother like that. He learned not to attempt his Lord Beguiling routine with me, but I watched him work his wiles on any number of unsuspecting victims." Often to the excellent advantage of king and country and always to the advantage of one Lord Harry Caldicott.

"You have Ian to the life. I was completely unprepared for that behavior, and having watched Mayfair from the fringes for years now, I can say he was more beguiling even than the typical handsome, fortune-hunting bounder. A class apart and well suited to the diplomatic ranks. I grow wary every time I encounter the scent of roses, thanks to him. He was always sending me bouquets, and damasks were his favorites. I gave away the fans he sent me and have long since parted with his monogrammed handkerchief. The locket was my personal talisman against further occasions of masculine magic."

"How did you and he part?" This Ian fellow struck me as having a certain roguishness in common with John Pickering.

"Ian said he had to go away for a time, and because his aspirations were with the diplomatic corps, that made sense. He promised to write and intimated that were his prospects more secure, he'd be promising more than that. He'd gone on short trips previously, and we weren't in each other's pockets. I was in mourning, after all.

"Three months went by without a word," she went on, "and I concluded I'd had my first lesson in how not to conduct a widowhood. Freddie left me comfortable, though far from wealthy, and I've remained determinedly unmerry ever since."

"You have a devoted admirer in Gideon Marchant."

She pulled her shawl more tightly around her. "Gideon has been most kind. It was he who suggested I travel to Portugal, and he was right. A change of scene, a winter away from London's coal smoke, did improve my spirits. So what does any of this have to do with my missing locket?"

In all likelihood, not one thing. "Who at this gathering knows of your liaison with this Ian fellow?"

"Her Grace, though she said nothing to me at the time. She did see me and Ian hacking in the park, enjoying an ice, that sort of thing. Ian was not my only escort. Gideon knew, of course. I've said enough that Hellie doubtless suspects, and that means Lord Barrington will have heard of it. I was discreet, not secretive."

Like any good spy when conducting business in plain sight. "I have little reason to hope your locket will turn up in the usual course, but I am still searching diligently for Her Grace's misplaced letters. I might yet come across your memento."

She retrieved her glass of punch and rose. "I don't need that locket, my lord, but I do occasionally need the reminder of what I learned from Ian. Fairy tales come true at a cost, and the cost can be more than we thought to pay."

I stood as well. The conversation had been interesting, but struck me mostly as ancient history. "Marchant truly does admire you, madam."

She took my arm, and we made a progress toward the house as the fiery sky began to dim to indigo behind us.

"Miss West admires you, my lord. One gathers the sentiments are mutual?"

"Emphatically and blessedly so."

"Then get on with it, sir. Life is short, and love is all we have that matters. My husband did not expect to die when he did, despite his failing health, and I did not expect to lose him so soon."

She also hadn't expected her Ian to disappear in a puff of allegedly diplomatic smoke.

She patted my arm and left me holding her empty glass as she went to greet Lord Drayson, who looked resplendent and impossibly young in his evening finery.

CHAPTER ELEVEN

I passed the night in broken sleep, Hyperia having suggested that with her chaperone of record out of pocket, we exercise a touch more prudence. I had yet to approach my mother about serving in Lady Ophelia's stead, and thus I rose in a fretful humor.

Her Grace did not come to the breakfast parlor, and neither did Hyperia. I found myself in the company of the Honorable Charles Canderport, who looked somewhat the worse for drink.

"We've reached the grueling part of the steeplechase," he said, producing a flask and doctoring his tea. "Perhaps my lord is in better fettle for coming late to the race. I vow I will never attend another one of these gatherings again, and then Mama accepts an invitation and you see before you a doomed fellow. Care for a nip?"

He should have offered the flask to me first, and he should not have confided his frustrated state to a virtual stranger. Ah, youth. This particular specimen was, like his sister, blond, blue-eyed, and possessed of curls that owed nothing to heated tongs. Those blue eyes were a bit bloodshot, though, and the bow of his cravat was a half inch off-center.

MacFadden would have been horrified, while I merely felt old.

"I'll stick to my tea," I said. "Don't you find even the company of the other gentlemen enjoyable?"

The door was open, but we were alone, sharp morning light slanting through the mullioned windows. No footman guarded the sideboard from marauding housemaids, perhaps due to the early hour, or perhaps because the housemaids were too tired to snitch a strip of bacon and the footmen too tired to prevent them.

"The house-party contingent is for the most part not truly gentlemen," Canderport said. "We're mannerly enough when Lady Barrington is looking, but the real gentlemen were doing the pretty for the whole Season. The real gents don't just slink out of the hedges come August, looking to find some low-hanging fruit at the house parties. Ye dancing devils, whatever inspired me to put eggs on my plate?"

"If your mother walks through that door, she will notice whether you served yourself some eggs, or limited yourself to dry toast and weak tea."

He peered at me owlishly across the table. "Right you are, my lord, but then, I suppose you've had a mother somewhat longer than I have. And your mama has her wits about her, but then, your sisters are all married. Mama vows that until she gets Lottie fired off, life will be a constant string of vexations. Where's the...? Ah."

He plucked the jam from the center of the table and dabbed a generous quantity on a half piece of toast. If Charles knew my sisters were married, he'd at least perused DeBrett's at some point, and he recalled what he'd seen.

"Any likelihood your sister will marry soon?" I asked.

"Lottie don't want to marry. Says she's perfectly content to enjoy life without brats clinging to her skirts, and she says it to Mama's face. Mama responds that brats are indeed a tribulation past all bearing. A fellow doesn't know quite which pugilist to back."

"You could abandon your ringside seat, Canderport. Get yourself invited to a gents-only shooting party. Offer to accompany Drayson on an artistic tour of Paris."

"I don't speak much Frog, my lord. The tutors and governesses tended to enjoy short tenures. Lottie has some of the lingo. I was lucky to make it to the fifth declension myself."

Meaning his Latin was in better repair than his French. "Drayson can likely manage well enough for the both of you, and you'd be surprised what you pick up when a language is all around you."

He took a bite of eggs, made a face, and set his fork down. "You had to do that, didn't you? Scouting for Old Wellie? You probably know Basque and Arabic and Corsu. I missed the war. Mama says, 'Don't worry, there will be another one,' but we haven't the funds to buy me much of a commission. I am babbling. Apologies, my lord, but this is my third house party in three months."

"One sympathizes." I also had to revise my view of the Honorable Charles. He was caught between two unhappy, strong-willed women and hadn't the resources to make either one content. Better and wiser men than Charles would be flummoxed in his boots.

"I am determined to dodge the next one," he said around a mouthful of toast. "Lady Poaling is a good sort, and she won't skewer me for pleading a headache, as it were." He chewed and swallowed and sent me a gloomy look. "I said the same thing about this do. I'll develop a twisted ankle, plead a putrid sore throat, develop a bad cough. I've done it before, though not recently. One cannot overuse such a ploy."

"And yet, here you are. What changed your mind?" Not a what, a who, no doubt.

He took out his flask again, but left the cap on and traced the elaborate C engraved into the silver. "I can't just leave 'em to it, can I? Lottie strains the leash at every turn, Mama pulls all the harder because she knows Lottie is growing desperate, and somebody has to distract them from their fretting, or the spatting grows into a brawl."

Would Lady Barrington never join us? As hostess, she ought to be presiding from the foot of the table, but perhaps she, too, preferred a lie-in on her Sabbath.

Or was her ladyship avoiding me for some reason?

"You purposely draw your sister's fire," I said, "or your mother's depending on who is in the more volatile mood. I can see why you find house parties tiresome." An audience lurking in every parlor, scores of servants to bear tales, and other young men expecting Charles to find the whole exercise an endless lark.

"I suspect the right wife would get your mother and sister sorted out," I went on. "A woman of good sense and good humor would see that you had some peace."

"Odd, ain't it?" he said, putting his flask away. "We're supposed to be the protectors, but the ladies can protect us too. Mama means well. She's just weary is all. Lottie would weary Saint Peter himself when she gets into one of her moods. She's too smart is the problem, but she's not clever enough to keep the smartness to herself. Mama says she needs to grow up. Lottie says polite society needs to grow up. I wish them luck on both counts."

Perhaps I'd underestimated Miss Lottie as well. "Her settlements are modest?"

Charles poured himself more tea and stirred in a dollop of honey. "Modest, not embarrassingly so. Papa got that much right. And if we could get her launched, then I could focus on putting the acreage to rights. Have you land of your own, my lord?"

The question was wistful, suggesting Charles was a country squire at heart, and this hellion-ing about with his sister was a trial to his soul.

"I do, as a matter of fact. Two tidy estates, one in Kent, one in Surrey, each grandmother contributing to my situation. I let both properties out, and they appear to prosper. Good land is a blessing unto the nineteenth generation, according to my late father."

"Water and soil, and soil and water. You can manage without much woods and take your time with fencing, but building up the soil and arranging proper irrigation and draining are the holy grail, my lord. Depend upon it. Your fortunes can fly or fall depending on how conscientiously you marl and fallow."

He showed more animation about his fields and pastures than he had about anything else in the past three days.

"Charles, might there be some other reason why Lottie is reluctant to marry?"

He stirred his tea slowly. "She is my sister, and I love her, my lord, but I take your point. She ain't happy being dragged around to the consolation rounds at the house parties, but she pretends she'd rather play battledore and pall-mall than have her own household. What other reason might there be?"

I cast about in my imagination and said the first thing that popped into my mind. "She is worried about you?" Or she worried about her mother, but I did not say that part.

"About me? Heavenly intercessors in their winged chariots, my lord. *Me?* Salt of the earth is my middle name."

"You appear argumentative, moody, overly fond of your flask, and evidence no interest in the young ladies. You come down with putrid sore throats and the odd cough at any time of year. You enter into Lottie's mad schemes and pranks when you ought to be blowing retreat."

"I have a *very healthy* interest in the young ladies, I'll have you—oh. To appearances. Right. Well."

Contrary to his own performance, Charles was not a hopeless gudgeon in thrall to his cleverer sister. A bit plodding, perhaps, but also young and overwhelmed. Allowances should be made.

"I keep hoping somebody will sweep Lottie off her feet, but not a sweeping swain to be found, my lord. One is at a bit of a loss."

"Miss Lottie cannot show to her best advantage if she's purposely picking fights with her mother or trying to inveigle you into supporting her hoyden impersonation. I suggest you enlist the aid of Miss Frampton."

"Trish? Miss Frampton, I mean. She is a good sport and quite fetching. Too fetching for the endless whist and whingeing that passes for the average house party, but she's loyal to Lady Jess and to

Miss Bivens. Says Bivvie would be the youngest old maid in Merry Olde but for forced outings in the shires."

A Restoration farce had been going on under my nose, and me all preoccupied with missing gloves and hanging felonies.

"You explain to Miss Frampton that your mama and sister worry about your prospects, and if Miss Frampton would be so good as to seem to take an interest in you and allow you to put forth a comparable appearance where she is concerned, the rest of the house party might go much more smoothly."

"And more enjoyably," he muttered, slathering jam on a second piece of toast. "For all concerned. I vow, when Mama and Lottie go at it, they could be heard in Dover. The racket alone daunts a fellow's spirits."

"Trust in Miss Frampton, and perhaps you can alter the course of events in your own favor. Then too, when bachelors notice that a young lady has gained the escort of a particularly eligible young man, they tend to take more of an interest in the young lady. You'd be doing Miss Frampton a good turn."

I flattered him with that observation, but the lad was overdue for appreciation from some quarter.

"A gentleman is always honored to be of service to a lady," he said, munching enthusiastically. "I've seen Marchant watching Trish —Miss Frampton. Don't care for the look in his eyes, as if Miss Frampton might be persuaded to surrender her hand to an aging roué with parliamentary expectations. Nothing good happens in Parliament. Ask anybody. She can do better than the likes of that cold fish."

Lady Barrington had eluded me yet again, but the meal hadn't been entirely unproductive. Miss Frampton absolutely could do better than to become Marchant's wife, and Charles could occupy himself with pastimes more enjoyable than refereeing squabbles between his womenfolk.

"Walk the young lady home from services," I said. "At a gathering like this, the gesture doesn't have quite the significance that it would in your own parish. The rules are relaxed, and who knows how much longer the decent weather will last?"

"Mama says rain by nightfall. Her rheumatism is seldom wrong. You have given me much to think about, my lord. I don't care what Drayson says, you're a bit of all right."

I had been enjoying the conversation, a diversion from weightier matters and an exoneration of Charles's bratty reputation, but his well-intended comment sobered my mood. My lot was to have the loftiest expectations of any man at the gathering and, at the same time, to be held by many in the lowest esteem.

The only way I could navigate that confusing state of affairs was to assume at all times that I was on reconnaissance in disputed territory. A wearying but familiar strategy.

"I'll leave you to your toast and eggs," I said, rising, "but a word of advice, Canderport. Go easy on the tipple. Your mother relies too heavily on her medicinal tots, and that has been remarked. Set an example of continence for her, and she might reduce her consumption."

"She is rather fond of a dose now and again. Lottie, too, though I don't think Lottie even likes the stuff. Does it to vex Mama and me, no doubt."

"A young lady tippling is playing skittles with her reputation. Take her flask and bet her you can abstain longer than she can."

"Good heavens, she'd become head of the nearest temperance league... ah. Right. I must discuss that scheme with Miss Frampton, my lord. Two heads and all that. I'll wish you good day and see you at divine services."

Never had a young man contemplated some dreary hymns and churchyard chat with more enthusiasm, while I... To sit in a holy place with a group of people whose rooms I had searched, knowing at least one of those people was up to no good, was not a cheering prospect.

I made for the door but thought to assay one more question

before leaving. "Canderport, does either your mother or your sister have any reason to bear ill will toward Her Grace of Waltham?"

He paused, the jam knife in one hand, a slice of toast in the other. "Mama purely hates the duchess. Sorry, old fellow, but among gentlemen, there should be honesty. She thinks Her Grace ought to lend a hand getting Lottie fired off. Mama ain't none too keen on Lady B either, but at least she invited us here, so Mama keeps her powder dry where Lady B is concerned. She don't care for Her Grace one bit, though. 'The author of all my ills, the instrument of my present tribulations' and so forth. Unbecoming, but not entirely fanciful either."

"Good to know. Best of luck with Miss Frampton."

Charles nodded and beamed at his toast as a drop of strawberry jam fell from the bread to the snow-white tablecloth. "Capital female, that one. Absolutely capital."

I left, making a mental note to ask MacFadden to show young Canderport how to tie a mathematical that didn't list quite so hard to port.

I was a former soldier, a gentleman, and a dutiful son. To that list, I contemplated adding the term *failure*.

I still hadn't the first inkling who had stolen my mother's letters or why, much less whether that same person might have purloined items of sentimental value from other ladies. Drayson's missing sketches baffled me utterly.

As I made my way to Her Grace's sitting room, I reminded myself that one was obligated to report even a lack of progress, however mortifying the exercise. Then too, I had yet to request Her Grace's aid in the matter of serving as Hyperia's chaperone, and that detail required attention before I presented myself in Perry's boudoir.

I tapped on the sitting room door and was bade to enter by a soft female voice. Miss Wisherd was at the sideboard, tidying up a tea tray.

"My lord, good morning."

"Miss Wisherd." I bowed slightly, because she was owed the deference. "Is Her Grace awake?"

"Awake and at her correspondence. Shall I let her know you'd like a word?"

I was to keep my visit short, apparently, which suited me well. "Please." My mother routinely took a breakfast tray in her room, and it had never occurred to me that she might be using the early hours to tend to business.

Her Grace appeared in the doorway to her bedroom. "My lord, is something amiss?"

She wore a forest green morning gown, a darker green wool dressing gown belted loosely at her waist. Her slippers were plain and had no heels, and her hair was in a thick braid over one shoulder. Dishabille rendered her appearance no less formidable.

"Your Grace." This bow was more punctilious. "No cause for alarm, but the morning will be spent attending services, and I thought to have a quick chat."

"Come. The light is better in the bedroom. Wisherd, I can dress myself. Leave the tray for the house staff. You aren't an under-footman."

"Yes, Your Grace."

Wisherd withdrew, the sitting room door clicking softly behind her.

"She's no great fan of this gathering," the duchess said. "I expect some of the footmen think flirtation is their due. I have made it excessively plain she is under no obligation to indulge their vanity."

Wisherd, like a junior officer among seasoned veterans, had to make her peace with those footmen, else the tray would still be sitting on the sideboard this time tomorrow.

"I broke my fast with young Canderport," I said. "I gather he has come to dread house parties."

"But his mother and sister insist, and he's too kindhearted to send them on without him. They might actually learn to cooperate if he did. They squabble in a competition for his notice."

As I followed my mother into the spacious high-ceilinged bedroom, I had an odd sense of déjà vu. Her Grace's strategy had merit. A lot of merit. If mother and daughter were cast on each other's resources, they might find common ground, however small. From that toehold, greater cooperation might result.

The duchess's approach was different from the one I'd suggested—seeking Miss Frampton's aid—but simpler to effect. More efficient, and it required only that Charles have another well-timed sore throat, or perhaps—novel thought—grow some backbone. When Wellington had solicited the opinions of his generals, they'd formed plans by refining one another's suggestions.

"Should the Canderport ladies perhaps be scheming to see Charles wed?" I asked. "If his wife is sufficiently influential, she might assist in getting Miss Lottie settled."

"Valid point. Miss Canderport won't consider a husband until Charles takes the marital plunge, as it were. He probably won't consider matrimony until his sister is safely husbanded. Drayson would suit her—they both fancy themselves young rebels—but Hellie and I have agreed that, given other matters in train, we'd best not meddle."

Other matters in train, meaning thievery, of course. "About those other matters, I haven't much to report."

The duchess took a seat at the escritoire by the windows and waved a hand at a reading chair by the hearth, an overstuffed, comfortable, sofa-in-miniature. Morning light did not flatter Her Grace. As handsome as she was, my mother was nonetheless aging. She was pretty as an antique mirror was pretty, its elegance balanced with fragility and the evidence of time passing.

"The only development thus far," I said, "relates to Mrs. Whittington's missing locket. I thought it was mourning jewelry, because she said it had been given to her shortly after her bereavement. The item has sentimental value, but that sentiment is not grief." Or not only grief. Shame figured into the widow's feelings, along with regret and determination not to repeat her error.

"This has to do with Carola's dashing diplomat, doesn't it?" Her Grace said, folding her arms. "I did not care for him, though we were introduced only the once. He and Carola were at Gunter's, which is not the usual outing for a widow still in mourning, but then, Carola's husband had been a soldier, not a duke. She could be more flexible with the rules."

"What do you recall of the fellow?"

"Tall, dark-haired. Sable, not quite true black, what I saw of it. He had a hat on, of course. His voice was supposed to be plummy, but I found him oleaginous. Mind you, I formed this impression in the course of five entire minutes. He touched Carola's sleeve at least five times during those same five minutes, like a fly that won't be shooed away from the pudding."

Oleaginous, the same word Lady Ophelia had used about John Pickering.

"Ridiculously high shirt points," Her Grace went on, "which were just coming into fashion, and a cravat knotted such that his nose was always in the air. Used a jeweled quizzing glass, of all things, but then, Brummel was still ascendant, and his acolytes were legion. The diplomat's laugh was for public show: 'See how lucky this widow is to have my devoted escort.' He was performing for me and for the other people enjoying Berkeley Square."

An amazingly vivid report. "Anything else?"

"His boot heels were slightly elevated. An inch or three-quarters taller than the usual gentleman's fashion. Not suitable for riding, but suitable for strolling Vauxhall or the Mayfair shops. I noticed it when he was assisting Carola into her coach. And Society considers vanity a female failing."

Ye dancing devils, to quote young Canderport. The duchess had the eye of a reconnaissance officer, at least when it came to Society's bachelors.

"He sounds like a popinjay. The locket was a gift from him."

"He was an antidote to everything Carola married. Her Freddie was a stranger to pretension, and he would no more have followed fashion than Prinny would take up street sweeping. The diplomat was a young exquisite, witty, a bit silly, and if Carola needed to indulge in some silliness, she had earned the right."

"He told her he had a short trip to make, and she never heard from him again."

Her Grace frowned, her mouth bracketed by what might become permanent grooves in a few years. "Diplomats meet with foul play."

"He had diplomatic aspirations, but Mrs. Whittington doesn't describe him as having found a post."

"Then why travel? On business, I suppose, or to flirt with some other widow better set up than Carola. One comes to appreciate that even an indifferent husband can spare one much mischief."

Hardly high praise for the institution of matrimony or for the late duke. "You met this man once, perhaps five years ago, and yet, you recall him vividly. Why?"

She looked at me as if I'd posed a particularly complicated question, though I hadn't. Ian the Exquisite had made a lasting impression on a woman who met Society bachelors by the score.

Her Grace considered the bleak day beyond the windows, a morning that should have been misty and romantic, but instead looked merely dreary.

"My own situation with Pickering was fresh in my mind. I recall the meeting because Carola looked happier than she'd ever appeared when with her husband. She'd been content with her marriage, perhaps even pleased, but not aglow with a sense of her own value. I recall being worried for her, because she was smitten, and when we are smitten, we are vulnerable to humiliation and heartache."

An observation Lady Ophelia might have made. Dispassionate on the surface, but also attesting to a life that held some regrets.

"It strikes me," I said, "that you and Mrs. Whittington have both lost items that reminded you of liaisons you might now wish you'd not embarked upon."

Perhaps the missing letters had been Her Grace's talisman against further foolishness. By her own admission, she'd not given her heart to another since her interlude with Pickering.

"My lord, among widows such liaisons are nearly a rite of passage. The merry widow is a caricature on stage and in drawing rooms for a reason."

You are not merry. Mrs. Whittington wasn't. Lady Ophelia certainly wasn't. "Both you and Mrs. Whittington might pay a tidy sum to have the purloined goods returned. Prior to my recent discussion with her, I wasn't aware that Mrs. Whittington shared that posture with you."

Her Grace tapped a nail on the desk blotter. "So you ask yourself: What of Hellie's gloves? What could the significance of an old pair of gloves be? Perhaps it's time to stop asking questions, my lord. Nobody has been threatened with blackmail or scandal, and I consider these women friends."

That was fretting rather than a direct order to cease firing. "Lady Barrington married a viscount's heir," I said slowly. "Those fellows don't generally have courtesy titles." Either the viscountcy was the only title conferred, or, as was often the case, an underlying barony bore a similar name. Viscount Feathers was often also Baron Feathers, which would have resulted in both the peer and his heir larking about as Lord Feathers.

In an unusual fit of common sense, the viscount's heir remained a mere honorable, and thus he kept his own initials.

"Lady Barrington's first husband, Your Grace. What was his name?"

"Cobbie? Viscount Cobbold?" She tapped her nail more slowly. "Given name... biblical. Not an evangelist, but an apostle rather than a prophet... Thomas. That was it. Thomas Melton Grindelwald Cobbold, which suggests his nickname was given to him in his youth. The occasional viscount has the family name in the title as well. Why?"

How on earth did she recall these details? I'd thought Lady

Ophelia unique for her vast and accurate memory, but perhaps I'd underestimated the ladies of the prior generation generally.

"How can you remember that?"

"Melton and Grindelwald are towns, though one is in Switzerland. The family is said to have lit upon place names because they could not decide on family names. I believe the previous viscount was conceived in Melton and Cobbie in Berne, or so the gossip went. His Grace observed that if the fashion caught on, we'd have any number of Greater Backsides, Bitchfields, and Shittertons among the British peerage."

She recalled His Grace's humor fondly, and I could hear him making just that point. Clearly, she still missed her husband, despite Pickering and any of his ilk who might have come after.

Rather than observe that Harry had shared His Grace's irreverent sense of humor, I kept to the matter at hand.

"The monogram on the gloves I am to find is H-G-M. Lady Barrington fed me some taradiddle about shopping for the gloves with her intended when they were courting. Unless he bought gloves meant for another, the missing items are not the late viscount's castoffs."

"Gloves are made to order," Her Grace said. "Each one sewn individually from that customer's pattern. I cannot imagine a viscount's heir purchasing used gloves."

Neither could I, and yet, I equivocated. "At university, living on a budget, or failing to live on a budget, one compromised."

"Cobbie wasn't at university when he and Hellie courted, but again, perhaps we'd best consider allowing some sleeping dogs to lie. This is all old news, and nothing of real value has been taken."

I had not achieved the objective I'd had in mind when I'd paid this call, but I'd found—finally—a thread connecting all the items stolen from the ladies. I wasn't about to blow retreat when I might finally have sighted the enemy's advance guard.

"I will have a discreet conversation with Lady Barrington," I said. "Very discreet, unless you'd rather undertake that maneuver?"

Her Grace twirled a white quill pen between her palms. "You believe Hellie strayed?"

"Or she had a flirtation prior to speaking her vows, or a dalliance after her husband's death. The latter would put her in the same league with you and Mrs. Whittington."

"Not unless her fling was with a handsome young scoundrel who disappeared without a trace." Said with a hint of bitterness. "Lady Canderport is a widow as well. Will you poke your nose into her past too?"

My distaste for that prospect must have been visible.

The duchess laughed. "You used to make that same expression when it was time to practice your dancing."

"My sisters likely made it too." They having had to dance with me and always being more accomplished than I. His Grace would play the piano, and Her Grace would call the steps, until somebody tromped on somebody else's toes. Arthur had been exempted from these occasions, while Harry and I had had to stand up with two successive sisters apiece.

"Ginny still loves any excuse to dance," the duchess said. "Meggie thought the whole exercise beneath her until she put up her hair."

I'd forgotten these lessons, one of few times the younger siblings had been united in an activity involving both parents. Hilarity had often ensued, and we'd even learned to navigate a few of the simpler ballroom dances.

"Now you look wistful," the duchess said. "Unpredictable, the things we miss, and the memories that make us miss them."

Was she alluding to Harry? The duke? The scoundrel Pickering? *Me* as a scowling boy?

"I am courting Hyperia West," I said, apropos of nothing, save perhaps a deluge of family nostalgia. "I thought you should know." I'd thought no such thing, until the moment the words had left my fool mouth.

Her Grace's amusement shifted to a sort of puzzlement. "I should certainly hope you're courting her. The two of you are said to be very much in each other's pockets. Such a sensible lady. Perhaps too sensible. Will she have you?"

Not exactly the delight a duchess ought to express when the ducal heir spoke of matrimony. "If I ask properly and at the right time, I am likely to succeed." I hoped. "We have a few matters to clarify, but she has given me reason for optimism."

"Well, for pity's sake, my lord, *court her*. Bring her roses, quote poetry to her, and drop her fond notes even if you just shared supper the night before. I'm sure chasing old ghosts and lost letters is all very intriguing, but a woman wants and deserves some romance."

Not the advice I would have predicted from Her Grace. Look where romance had landed the duchess, Mrs. Whittington, and quite possibly Lady Barrington. For all I knew, they were about to be blackmailed or made the butt of public humiliation.

"I esteem Miss West most highly, and she is aware of my regard."

Her Grace muttered something about the Caldicott male, then withdrew a folded piece of stationery from the drawer of the escritoire. "Ophelia sent this over. She left it to my discretion whether to show it to you."

"I am in her bad books still, I suppose." I took the piece of paper, which was grayish rather than yellow with age. *Faded blue, perhaps.*

"The handwriting gave me a pang," Her Grace said. "I doubt it will shed any light on the current situation."

I read over Pickering's acceptance of the post offered at Caldicott Hall. He agreed to an engagement of three months for a sum certain, with ample leave to tend to other clients, and lodging and board to be provided at the Hall. Half the sum was to be advanced by post, the other half payable at the end of three months, at which time the parties would renegotiate.

"He stayed the full three months?"

"I had paid him the second half three days before he left for good, promising only a short absence. Said he had to run up to Town."

I took the letter over to the windows. "Public school hand," I murmured. "Bit of a flourish with his capitals. He crosses his t's with an upward stroke. You are sure he wrote this?"

She came to stand beside me and peered at the words. "Yes, as sure as anybody can be. It might be a skilled forgery, but if you look at the J in the month of June and in his signature, they are as I remember him making them. A tasteful embellishment rather than an elaborate display. He used that same paper to write his subsequent notes to me."

"You're certain of that too?"

She leaned close enough to sniff the paper and grimaced. "Camphor. Ophelia said she found it in the house steward's lumber room. She must have begun her search before the coach horses were out of their harness."

Or Godmama had had a clear recollection of dates and had known which months to focus on. "May I keep this?" I held the paper up to the light, and the faint outlines of a watermark showed through.

"You may. Don't leave it lying about, please."

As if. "Have you a quizzing glass, Your Grace?"

She produced the requested item from her traveling desk, which had been sitting closed and latched on her escritoire.

The magnification helped me discern the mark. "Heeney and Sons, Ltd. Dover, England."

"Dover?"

A thriving port of, I'd say, about ten thousand souls, also the nearest convenient point of exit for a man fleeing the country.

"Apparently so. I'll have a nose around when I'm seeing Arthur off, though stationers' shops come and go."

"He never mentioned Dover," the duchess muttered. "London, Vienna, Edinburgh, Bath, and some other spa towns, but not Dover."

"His stationery might have been a gift from a relative, or he might have purchased some paper from a London shop that bought out a Dover concern closing its doors. The watermark alone tells us little."

Her Grace wrinkled the Fennington nose. "Yes, but *Dover*. I realize that I didn't know him anywhere near as well as I thought I did, but to be confronted with more evidence of my folly... One finds the experience lowering."

"Mrs. Whittington would doubtless agree with you, but she also claims to have learned greater caution from her frolic with the handsome bounder."

"This sadder-and-wiser business is vastly overrated," Her Grace said. "I cannot recommend it."

We shared a moment of odd understanding. "Agreed, madam. Agreed. Will I see you at divine services?"

"You will not. I showed the flag last week. I will do so again before we depart. My correspondence waits for no woman, and I do believe the weather is finally turning on us."

I was being dismissed, and I needed to change into boots if I was to hike to the village. I also wanted to greet my beloved. "I wish I had more to report."

Her Grace considered me for a moment. "I wish you had no need to report at all. To think that Carola and I were similarly foolish is some consolation, but not much."

That Napoleon languished on an island in the mid-Atlantic was no consolation for Harry's death either.

"I will keep searching. We have a connection between you and Mrs. Whittington. That could be the start of a path to some answers."

"Go very carefully, my lord. Carefully and as quietly as you can. I'm beginning to think I've overreacted to a series of unfortunate coincidences."

While I was increasingly certain she had not. A silence bloomed, and I nearly made my way to the door, except that I had one more item to discuss.

"In Lady Ophelia's absence, will Your Grace serve as Hyperia's chaperone? I mean... Would you be willing to serve in Lady Ophelia's stead, as Miss West's chaperone of record?"

The duchess considered me and likely saw that my request had cost me. "Hyperia West's conscience and good sense will protect her name better than I ever could, but yes, of course. I will wave away presuming fortune hunters and intimidate any man foolish enough to present himself as a rival for her affections."

That was a yes. My relief was disproportionate. "Thank you, Your Grace."

The duchess retied her dressing gown with a firm pull on the knotted belt. "Julian, please recall that if you are truly courting a lady, then you must *woo* her. Expecting her to wait patiently while you peer behind portraits and rifle wardrobes is not wooing."

I thought of a long, sweet night spent with Hyperia in my arms, and of her assessment of Drayson and his quarters.

"Point noted, Your Grace. I'll leave you to your correspondence."

I bowed and withdrew, and not until I was halfway to the village did I realize that my mother had addressed me by my given name, albeit in the context of a scold. Still, she had called me Julian, and I had asked for her assistance.

And the sky had not fallen.

Yet.

CHAPTER TWELVE

As I added my baritone to the strains of "Old Hundredth," I felt once again the bewilderment of praising the same Deity to whom the Spanish, French, German, and Italians prayed. The Russians, Austrians, Poles, and Danes as well, for that matter.

How was the Almighty to sort out the competing prayers for vengeance and victory by all the armies who earnestly claimed to esteem Him and his Great Commandment? Did the Quakers have the right of it—one broke the Commandments when killing even in the king's name? They seemed a happy and suspiciously prosperous lot, those Quakers.

But then again, many of them had grown rich supplying the military from their tidy and efficient factories, and still more had financed the war effort from their equally tidy and well-run banking institutions. What was the Divine Authority to make of such goings-on?

I had mostly learned to set such questions aside rather than allow them to vex me at length, but today the restless weather inspired an unsettled mood. A gusty wind blew fallen leaves around the green, and coach horses shifted restlessly as gentry and guests waited their turns to quit the village. The breeze had a bite that it had lacked even two hours earlier, and the sky had taken on the look of quilted pewter.

I spotted my quarry in conversation with Miss Bivens, whose cheeks were rosy for a change, thanks to the raw air.

"My lord, perhaps you'd be so good as to accompany Miss Bivens back to Tweed House on foot?" Lady Barrington said. "She is determined on some exercise, though that overcast looks positively threatening."

"How fortunate," I said. "Miss Bivens, you will be pleased to know that Miss West is intent on walking with Miss Frampton, and Mr. Canderport has volunteered to serve as their escort. I'm sure you are welcome in that party, while I can offer my arm to her ladyship." Perry had agreed to this strategy when I'd dropped by her sitting room.

She'd also expressed an interest in assessing Charles's situation for herself.

Miss Bivens dipped me a curtsey. "A fine plan, my lord. Miss West has literary tastes similar to my own. Trish dear! Trisha, Charlie! Wait for me!"

"One would think she found the prospect of my escort disagreeable," I muttered, offering an elbow to Lady Barrington. "Shall we?"

Her ladyship marched off without touching me. "We needn't mince along, my lord. The rain will start at any moment, but the coaches are full, and needs must when one is the hostess. I trust you're finding your accommodations adequate?"

"My accommodations are delightful, but I have some questions for you that you will likely find less than pleasant."

Mine hostess picked up her pace, putting some distance between us and the throng in the churchyard chattering on despite the rising wind.

"I told Dorothea her letters would turn up in due course," Lady Barrington said, "but one doesn't argue with a duchess."

Harry had. His Grace had. I wasn't sure what it would take for me to oppose my mother, and I was loath to contemplate the prospect.

"Her letters have not turned up, neither has Mrs. Whittington's locket, or Lord Drayson's sketches. Neither have the missing gloves. You said they belonged to your late husband?"

We left the green at a pace approaching a forced march and turned along the lane that led to the bridle path.

"I did say that, but honestly, my lord, why make any bother about a pair of old gloves? They weren't even fashionable. More like work gloves or the pair you'd wear hacking out when your good riding gloves needed mending."

"And they bore his initials?"

"A monogram branded on the inside, which I gather is a simple way to make plain gloves distinguishable. They were very plain."

"And you were with him when he ordered them?"

She sent me a peevish look. "I was. We nipped into the shop on the spur of the moment, placed the order, and went on our way. Ordering gloves is not a complicated undertaking."

She was right about that. Taking a gentleman's pattern involved nothing more than tracing the outline of his hand on plain paper. The shop would keep the paper for reference and make every subsequent pair of gloves from the same outline.

"Do you recall the name of the shop?"

She was all but jogging along, and I resented the effort necessary to keep up with her. After a bad night, my stamina suffered, and last night had been restless indeed.

"I do not. We were in Town, my lord, where glovemakers and milliners adorn every street corner."

The entrance to the bridle path loomed ahead, and I waited until we were beneath the trees and out of sight of the lane to put my next question to her.

"Who was he?"

"I cannot possibly grasp what your question is about, my lord."

"The monogram H-G-M did not belong to your first husband or

to your second. I believe you were out shopping with an escort, and he did arrange to purchase these gloves while you were with him. A man does not place an order for *used* gloves, though. One explanation I can come up with for the initials not matching those of the purported purchaser is that he bought used gloves."

She came to an abrupt halt in the middle of the path. "I should never have asked you to look for those gloves."

"But you did," I said gently, "lest Lord Barrington find them first and note the discrepancy with the initials himself." She'd lied to her husband to avoid any controversy about her attachment to the missing gloves.

"I'm sure some footmen came across the gloves and, seeing their condition, assumed they belonged in the gardener's shed."

"Then why ask me to look for them when I planned on conducting a room-to-room search of the guest quarters?"

I could see her weighing the costs and benefits of further lies. She apparently chose to either trust my discretion or to avoid conflict with Her Grace's preferred snoop.

"Sit with me, my lord." She crossed the path to a fallen log at about bench height, probably a popular trysting place for the village's courting couples.

I obliged, prepared to hear more regrets in this unlikely confessional.

"Cobbie had gone to his reward and left me with two boys to raise, their guardians circling like vultures and Cobbie's younger brother making polite noises about how agreeable I'd find the dower house while he oversaw renovations to the manor house. Cobbie's parliamentary cronies had made their polite condolence calls and then disappeared from sight. I knew the boys would be taken from me the instant I'd completed first mourning.

"I was so angry at my husband, my lord. You cannot imagine my rage. Daniel was seven and such a sweet child, utterly bewildered to lose his papa, and those wretched, bedamned lawyers, abetted by

Danny's uncle... Society gossips titter about merry widows, but they ought to live in fear of murderous widows."

"A loved one's death can feel like a betrayal," I said, meaning every word. "You've been abandoned in the midst of hostilities by the one person who should have had a care lest you face defeat in solo combat."

She considered me from beneath the brim of her bonnet. "Dorothea said much the same thing when Claudius died. How dare he? I knew exactly what she meant, but at least the duke wasn't foolish enough to take a fractious three-year-old colt out after the hounds."

Or to all but walk into the guns of a French patrol by the gentle light of a quarter moon.

"You were angry," I said, "alone, and facing the loss of your children. You came across a party offering some understanding and companionship, and you availed yourself of his support."

"He said he was after pheasant and partridge. East Anglia attracts the shooting crowd, and I hadn't yet been banished to the dower house. I wanted to show off the glory of my former station, though a widow isn't supposed to entertain. It was early enough in mourning that I could not be evicted without causing talk, and I could imagine Cobbie telling me to gather rosebuds and so forth. He would have."

Years later, and a note of resentment still colored the mention of her first husband. But then, the terms of that husband's will had made banishing her ladyship's young sons to public school all but inevitable.

"Hans was good with the boys," she said, her tone softening. "He explained to Danny that public school would be cold and miserable and lonely, but that pretending to have been kidnapped by pirates and befriending one's fellow captives would help. Mama would send baskets from home, frequent baskets, and write frequent letters, and pretty soon, it would all become more bearable. Pirates are to be pitied after all, because they are doomed to sail always as outcasts, while a young peer could look forward to doing his bit to run the whole empire. Danny later said Hans's words were a comfort."

"Hans was a comfort to you as well." For a time, and possibly not even an intimate comfort, though the gossips would imply torrid trysts by the score.

By now, I knew where the story would end.

"Even a widow is allowed to shop for mourning attire, and second mourning requires a different wardrobe altogether. When Danny was snatched away and Peter and I were banished to the dower house, those outings with Hans in Town were all that sustained me."

"Can you describe him to me?"

Not a particularly relevant question, but a way to keep her focused on the past, wherein some answers might lie.

"Tallish, auburn hair, the kindest eyes... a lovely singing voice, a man comfortable in his own skin. He was a friend, my lord, more a friend than anything else, and certainly never... never a friend who trespassed beyond affection and flirtation. Whether Hans was wandering about the countryside with me or escorting me about the shops, he had a quality of self-containment, of being always in command of himself, that was such a restful contrast to Cobbie."

"Cobbie was loud?"

She shifted on our log bench. "Cobbie was the spoiled son of generations of spoiled sons. He was amazingly dear, given his antecedents, but he blew hot and cold, raged, and then jollied himself out of his tempers. He was sunny by nature, also tempestuous. Not a calm presence, for all his heart was in the right place. He was determined that being unable to serve in the military, he would pull his share of the parliamentary load, and he did. He was more conscientious about his infernal committees than most of the dukes and marquesses bothered to be. He was well liked and mourned by many."

As Harry had been. "Did you know the boys were to be raised by guardians?"

"No. I knew I would be adequately provided for, but beyond that,

Cobbie never went into details. In his world, boys went into men's hands at seven years of age. In my world, the boys were all I had, and they were wrenched from me when they needed me most."

"This Hans person understood your rage."

"He did, and he counseled a patient strategy. Take advantage of every opportunity to be the benevolent, generous, understanding mama, because there would be such opportunities. Never miss a Speech Day, a cricket championship, or a boat race, and send baskets sufficiently lavish that all the lads awaited their arrival with pleasure. I consoled myself with those measures, but they have been inadequate revenge."

The wound still ached, in other words, and might for the rest of her life. "How did you and Hans part?"

"Amicably. My attachment to him was hard to keep private once Town became the easiest place to meet. Friends quietly let me know that talk was starting, and for the sake of my sons, I could not have that. I half hoped Hans would offer marriage, though I could not have remarried that soon after losing Cobbie. I gather his prospects were limited, for all he was a gentleman, and he probably realized that my interest in him had been somewhat driven by…"

"Murderous impulses?"

Her smile was wan. "Don't judge me, your lordship. The man was handsome, attentive, a practiced flirt, and blessedly affectionate with putting untenable expectations on me. Cobbie would not have judged me, and thus I try not to judge myself."

And yet, these recollections embarrassed her. "How did you come into possession of the gloves?"

"I was still allowed to be the lady of the manor at the time. Hans and I had taken the children for a picnic, and we were caught in a downpour. One of those sunny-one-moment, a-deluge-the-next turns of weather, then back to bright sunshine and dripping boughs. Hans gave me his gloves and jacket. He took the jacket back when we reached the house, of course, but I kept the gloves, and he never asked that I return them."

"Do you miss him?"

"Yes, and no. He was truly a comfort and offered wise counsel, but he was also an indulgence. Had the guardians got wind of the variety of consolation I'd found, I'd never have seen Danny or Peter again. I was being foolish, my lord. Very, very foolish, and that realization made setting Hans aside mandatory."

Not quite the same story Her Grace and Mrs. Whittington told, but a parallel version.

"You were also wise," I said. "You exercised discretion, you did not try to make the liaison into something it couldn't be, and you let it go at the first sign it could become troublesome. Have you crossed paths with this Hans fellow again?"

"I thought I saw him once a couple years later across Bond Street. I was with Lord Barrington, and Hans apparently did not see me, or chose to exercise discretion. Then too, Hans was with a young lady. He was very attentive to her, buying her roses from the flower seller on the corner, as he'd bought me roses more than once. He might not have welcomed a greeting from me. What has all this to do with Her Grace's missing letters?"

I stood and offered my hand. "You have confirmed for me that the missing items form a pattern, and a troubling one at that."

"Oh dear. I knew about Dorothea's flute teacher fling, but Carola too?"

"A dashing diplomat." An aspiring, dashing diplomat, or so he'd claimed. "Who knew of your liaison with this Hans fellow?"

"Nobody would have known for a certainty. I was careful to occasionally accept the escort of some of Cobbie's old friends. I saw Hans in Town on a mere handful of occasions, so I hope the answer to your question is that the gossips speculated, but idly so."

"Do you believe that?"

She looked up at the pewter sky, visible through the pines. "I don't know what to believe, my lord. Those gloves are the only memento I have of a troubling time and of the joy I stole in the midst of sorrow. Nobody present now knew to whom they belonged—

nobody could know—save myself. Even if some of the usual wagging tongues began linking my name with Hans's, nobody, not even my lady's maid, would have known about those gloves."

And yet, the gloves had disappeared. No footman would risk his post pilfering a pair of plain brown gloves. No maid would have a use for them. I considered guests one by one as we made an unhurried return to Tweed House. When we came within sight of the stable, her ladyship stopped and unwound her hand from my arm.

"I'll tell Lord Barrington about the gloves, my lord. He knows I lost them, and he thinks they belonged to Cobbie. He'll understand."

"But?"

"But Barrington thinks I was the typical widow, devoted to my late husband's memory, involving myself in pious good works, and content to write regularly to my sons."

"You thought Barrington was a devoted papa, his children models of decorum, and your role as step-mama a pleasurable addition to your role as wife."

A raindrop landed on the toe of my boot.

"I did. If Jessamine doesn't sink the whole family in scandal before the next year is out, I will be very, very surprised."

The other possibility remained unmentioned: Lady Barrington's past could sink the family in scandal. Not a horrid, boiling, fresh scandal, but enough whispers and innuendos to reduce Jessamine's chances of a good match, and her sisters' chances as well.

"Putting the truth to his lordship strikes me as prudent," I said. "He is a devoted papa, but what he knew about raising daughters would probably rival what I know about raising penguins. You need his permission to use your discretion with Lady Jess—who has been maligning my mother, by the way—and to know that his lordship will support your decisions."

"Maligning *the duchess*?"

"His lordship is aware of the situation and, as far as I know, has done nothing to intervene."

A raindrop spattered onto Lady Barrington's shoulder.

"Ye suffering saints," she muttered. "I am off to have a quiet chat with my husband, your lordship. If you do find those gloves, please burn them."

She hastened away, but I called her back. "A thought, my lady. You said that part of your motivation for indulging in the company of a follower was revenge, but that the instrument was inadequate to the challenge. You were separated from your children and relegated to a lesser status in a lesser dwelling."

"Well, yes, but I should have anticipated at least a remove to the dower house."

Her son had become the viscount upon Cobbie's death. No *remove* had been in order. She could have lived out her days in the home where her children had been born, but for the meddling of her in-laws.

"What you should anticipate," I said, "is that a grandmother goes where she pleases, spoils whom she pleases, and meddles where she pleases, and there is nothing *anybody* can say against the regular and vigorous exercise of her God-given privileges."

"But the present viscount doesn't... That is to say, he's not yet..."

"He will be married, and he will make his best effort to secure the succession, and you are the mama who never let him forget her love. Grandchildren are all but inevitable, and your right to be a presence in their lives is indisputable. Best be off before the rain comes down in earnest, my lady."

Her countenance underwent a shift, like the East Anglian weather. First puzzlement, then a frown, then a smile as warm and benevolent as the English summer sun.

"Grandchildren," she said, as if she'd just now grasped the meaning of the word. "By heaven, *grandchildren*."

She hurried away, my paltry self apparently forgotten, along with gloves, bereavements, and even—for the moment—a difficult conversation looming with her husband.

My own destination lay in the stable, and by the time I gained the horsey-scented gloom of same, the rain was coming down in serious, chilly earnest.

~

"Atlas were at grass all night," Atticus said as we stood outside the gelding's stall. "Grooms knew there was weather on the way and put all the riding stock to pasture at sunset."

My noble steed dozed with one hip cocked, though he would have done his serious sleeping in the safer confines of an open paddock. Some horses were confident enough of domestication to sleep flat out in a stall, but Atlas was a former cavalry mount. I'd never seen him lost to deep slumber indoors.

"When I'm off to Dover," I said, "I'd like you to keep a special eye on my rooms. Work on your letters there, polish my spare boots, nap all you please, but guard my quarters."

The stable was deserted, the staff having gone for their midday meal before the guests would sit down to a proper Sunday supper.

"Who am I guarding them from?"

"Anybody and everybody. Miss West will remain at the house party as well, and she will keep a sharp look out too. Report anything suspicious to her."

Atlas shifted, cocking the other hip.

"Don't seem right," Atticus said, scuffing his toe on the dirt floor. "You off to the coast, Lady Ophelia gone to the Hall. I seen the duchess. She's..."

I waited, curious to hear how Atticus would characterize my mother.

"She's toplofty," Atticus said. "Like a real smile would make her shoes pinch or something."

"I'm told she's shy." A not-outlandish theory.

Atticus frowned up at me. "She's yer mum. You'd know if she was shy."

I should know, but I didn't. "She will remain here while I'm making my farewell to the duke. If you discreetly can, you will keep an eye on her as well."

"Should I put a hair on the door latch to her room?"

An interesting suggestion. Wrapping a single human hair around a door latch as a means of noting if the latch was lifted was a spy's trick, one I'd taught both Atticus and Hyperia to employ.

"Only if you can do so without being seen. Same with my quarters." Leaving Atticus behind, even for twenty-four hours, made me uneasy, but the journey to Dover and back would be grueling, and the boy would slow me down.

"Any idea who stole them letters?" Atticus asked.

"None, though a motive is becoming clearer. Some widows are apparently prone to liaisons early in bereavement that can cause them regret later on. Our thief might seek to capitalize on those regrets."

I expected Lady Canderport to be the next victim, though the handsome bachelor intent on consoling her on a fresh bereavement would have been a stalwart sort of fellow.

I still could not explain Drayson's missing sketches.

"I thought widows was a sad lot," Atticus said. "Nobody has any use for 'em, they ain't allowed to go hardly anywhere, and they're supposed to dress like ghouls, at least among the Quality."

"Mourning attire is to ensure Society accords the widow the respect her grief is due. As for the other... Sadness and loneliness can result in impulsive choices."

"You mean the ladies gave in to temptation?"

Atticus could be astonishingly delicate at times. "Apparently so." And apparently, a certain class of bachelor enjoyed tempting them. Harry had escorted more than a few widows in his day, though they had been past formal mourning.

"I wish you wasn't going to the coast," Atticus said, kicking the boards of the stall wall hard enough to make Atlas open his eyes.

"The journey will be a few hours of hard riding in either direction, Atlas is up to the effort, and I have promised to see my brother off." Promised myself, though I dreaded the prospect of putting Arthur on a ship.

"His ma should see him off. You got letters to find."

"Atticus, you are not to put yourself in a compromising position searching for the letters in my absence. That is a direct order. Disobey a direct order, and you'll be drummed out of the regiment."

"But they hafta be somewhere. A thief don't steal old letters just to toss 'em in the dustbin."

Precisely, my boy. A thief stole proof of a scandalous liaison to use as leverage against the recipient of the letters. The gloves and locket were similarly proof of past indiscretions. Lady Barrington had step-daughters to launch, and Mrs. Whittington had a pristine reputation to guard. Her Grace had significant social consequence at risk.

Then too, Mrs. Whittington had at least one admirer in a position to offer her matrimony. Marchant might well view matters differently, if Mrs. Whittington fell from grace in the eyes of society.

"You should take me with you," Atticus said. "Miss West can keep an eye on Tweed House, or yer ma can."

For a lad determined on his own independence, the prospect of two days without immediate supervision from me should have appealed strongly.

"Nonsense, my boy. You can watch from vantage points the ladies have no access to. What are you hearing in the servants' hall?"

"A lot of moanin' and whinin'. Seamstresses and lady maids is havin' to alter plaid getups for the gents. Footmen will have to wear their own plaid getups for the Highland Games. You won't put me in a skirt, will ya guv?"

"I will put myself in a kilt." And oddly enough, I enjoyed my plaid finery. The fittings had been a trial and the sensation of bare knees an adjustment, but when the tailors had turned me around to behold myself in a three-way mirror, I'd seen not an English lordling, but a *man* of style and confidence.

"Daft business, men in skirts. Do Scottish ladies wear trousers?"

"Under their riding habits, very likely. So do English ladies, I'm told. What else have you heard in the hall?"

"MacFadden says to keep clear of Lord Drayson's man. He's accusin' everybody of stealing those naughty sketches. I say he took 'em hisself, and he'll miraculously find 'em, be the hero of the day, and earn hisself extra vails."

I peered down upon my tiger-cum-general-factotum-cum-occasional-conscience. "That would explain the disappearance of the sketches. Is Lord Drayson a pinchpenny?"

Atticus let himself into Atlas's stall and took down the water bucket. "Lord Drayson is skint. All the Quality is skint, to hear the talk in the Hall. Prinny is the skint-est of them all."

"Is Her Grace in want of coin?"

"Nah. Nobody says much about the duchess. Wisherd would skewer 'em with her knitting needles. I like Wisherd. You know where you stand with her."

I liked Wisherd too. Her loyalties were not in question. Neither was her common sense. "Where is your coat, my boy? The weather has turned up nasty, and sleet is a possibility."

"Saddle room. I cleaned all your gear because you're off to the coast tomorrow. Lady Ophelia reminded me before she left."

Inspiration struck. "You might consider sending her a report. All's well, no progress, that sort of thing. Miss West will see it delivered to the Hall."

"Whyn't you send a report?"

I would do exactly that, but not because I needed to practice my letters. "Lady Ophelia quit the house party because the time of year brings her sad memories. She lost a son when he was about your age. She is also concerned for Leander, whose mother might not be returning to the Hall any time soon."

Atticus exited the stall, bucket in hand, and closed the half door behind him. "Leander said his ma might have to go away for a while. She told him that. Said she wasn't off to war, and she'd miss him and all, but you'd look after him, and she wasn't going for good and always."

And you didn't think to tell me this? But then, Atticus had no memory of either parent. His sole inheritance was a locket from his mother that he wore about his scrawny neck. In his world, parents were a dodgy lot on a good day.

"When did Leander pass this along?"

"We were playing Waterloo in the conservatory the day before you brung me here. He said his ma wasn't happy at the Hall, but that he was, and he had uncles now. Said his ma had uncles, too, and she missed 'em, and she was off to visit them, and aunties and cousins, too, but Lee-Lee liked the Hall better than anywhere else."

This exchange put a sunnier complexion on any discussions I might have with Leander, but what did it say about my nephew that he'd confided the news of his mother's exit to Atticus rather than to one of those shiny new uncles?

"Lee-Lee?"

"I call him that. Sometimes I call him Andy."

"What does he call you?"

"None a yer business, and I'm not tellin'."

I felt at once proud—Atticus and Leander were becoming friends, and a boy with a friend was a boy who found some joy and security in the world—and dismayed. I was again the outsider, the extraneous spare, and while the context was nearly silly—I did not want to play Waterloo with anybody, anywhere, ever—the feeling still took me aback.

"Write to Lady Ophelia," I said. "You may use the supplies in my traveling desk, and I expect you to keep an eye on Jupiter in my absence in addition to your other responsibilities."

"I got tuppence from MacFadden for doing Mr. Marchant's boots."

"Put the coin in my traveling desk if you haven't anywhere else to keep it."

The boy looked pathetically relieved, suggesting life belowstairs wasn't all tea and gossip. "I still wish you wasn't going to Dover."

My mother's words came back to me. "I wish I had no need to go to Dover, but His Grace will enjoy his holiday, and he's overdue for some leisure."

"And you ain't overdue for some leisure?" Atticus sauntered off, bucket in hand, and I wanted to stick out my tongue at his retreating back. Of all the cheek...

Atlas looked at me as if to ask if I was through interrupting his nap.

"Rest today, horse. Tomorrow, we fly to the coast."

Atlas replied by lifting his tail and perfuming the stable with *eau des verts pâturages*. Another cheeky lad.

My next destination was my own apartment, where I would change out of my damp attire and pen a note to Lady Ophelia. I missed her keen insights and acerbic wit, but I also needed to thank her for manning the turrets at the Hall.

She had provided a sample of John Pickering's handwriting and his stationery, and done so posthaste. That watermark on the stationery might prove to mean nothing, or it might lead to the truth—and peace of mind for three women who most assuredly deserved at least that.

When I reached the end of the barn aisle, I saw Gideon Marchant, hat pulled low, retreating along the path to the house. He was getting a thorough soaking, which begged the question: Why had Marchant, who'd dodged divine services, come to the stable? One did not typically travel on the Sabbath other than to attend church, and Marchant had chosen to visit the stable at an hour when the grooms would be absent from the barn.

I hurried after him, and when we reached Tweed House, I was surprised to see Marchant head down the steps that led to the lower reaches of the house. Not the done thing, but then, he was an old friend of the hostess and likely in want of a hot cup of tea sooner rather than later.

As was I, but I made my way to my room, where I found, to my delight and concern, that Hyperia was lying in wait for me.

CHAPTER THIRTEEN

"Jules, you're soaked." Hyperia rose from the settee and took my hat from my hand. "What could you be thinking?"

I'd been soaked for days in Spain. I'd slept in wet clothes, marched in wet boots, and would have promised my soul to Old Scratch himself in exchange for a pair of dry wool socks.

"I wanted to remind Atticus that I'll be traveling to Dover tomorrow and to catch up with the boy where we wouldn't be overheard. He's pining for Lady Ophelia and making great friends with Leander, apparently."

As I locked the door to the corridor, Hyperia set my hat on the sideboard, where the fire's heat would dry it slowly.

"Boots off, my lord."

I sat and tugged my footwear free. I did not adhere to the fashion that said a gentleman's boots must be painted onto him, such that agonies of pulling and wrenching were necessary to remove them.

Hyperia set the boots beside the sideboard. "You are missing Lady Ophelia."

True, though I hadn't quite admitted as much to myself. "She has a keen mind, she knows everybody, and she intimidates Marchant."

"Whom you do not care for. Coat."

I started on the buttons. "He annoys me for the pleasure of twisting my tail. That is the antithesis of gentlemanly behavior. How was your hike with Canderport and friends?"

"Miss Frampton has a wicked sense of humor, Miss Bivens has read everything ever written, and Charlie Canderport is surprisingly well-read too. We were a jolly party, though going by the lanes, we barely made it back to Tweed House in time to avoid the rain. What of you and Lady Barrington?"

I took my damp jacket to the bedroom and found myself a dressing gown and dry socks. Before I put them on, I divested myself of my cravat and undid three shirt buttons.

"My chat with Lady Barrington," I said, returning to the sitting room, "was exceedingly unjolly. She, too, indulged in a passing liaison while in mourning, and she, too, regrets the folly." I explained what details I'd been given. "The gloves belonged to her swain, whom she referred to only as Hans, and whom she parted from rather than allow a hint of scandal to jeopardize what little access she still had to her children."

"Children make us vulnerable," Hyperia said, which struck me as an odd observation, until I thought of Lady Ophelia... and Her Grace.

"Children also bring joy," I countered, "though Lady Canderport might argue the point. I've had a thought about her."

"Charlie was oddly silent about his dear mama, but then, I suspect you are correct that he's a gentleman, at least most of the time."

"Shall we compare notes?" I gestured to the settee, and Hyperia took a seat in the middle. I came down beside her, fatigue making itself felt, though we were yet in the middle of the day.

"Lady Canderport is a widow," I said.

"With a hoyden daughter to launch, much like Lady Barrington has step-daughters to launch." Hyperia toed off her slippers and drew up her knees.

I looped an arm around her shoulders. "By Canderport's admission, his mother despises the duchess. Her Grace should be helping to launch Lottie, and by extension, Lady Barrington and Mrs. Whittington are probably burdened with the same expectation."

"So Lady Canderport resents her fellow widows," Hyperia murmured, head on my shoulder. "She circulates in Society enough to have heard old rumors and whispers, and she is apparently less than well-off. She has motive and opportunity to blackmail the other ladies, either for coin or for their matchmaking influence."

"Precisely." I wasn't as clear on how Lady Canderport, half sozzled and supposedly focused on Lottie's prospects, could have learned of the love letters, gloves, and locket, but the half-sozzled business could be a ruse, and a canny brace of servants could learn much by lurking and watching.

"Might we share a brandy?" Hyperia asked, springing up. "The day seems to call for it."

As if to underscore her words, a gust of wind slapped a tattoo of rain against the sitting room windows.

"I dislike that sound," I said as Hyperia poured us a drink. "Too much like gunfire."

She went to the French doors and sipped, her gaze on the dreary day. "Marchant must be part duck. He's out in it again."

I joined her in time to see Gideon Marchant climbing the terrace steps. "Maybe he forgot something at the stable. I hope tomorrow isn't this wet." If Atlas pulled a shoe in the mud, I'd be hard-pressed to make Dover short of hiring a post-chaise.

Hyperia moved away from the window and resumed her seat. "Your theory, that Lady Canderport is our thief, halfway makes sense, but attributing the same motive and opportunity to Jessamine or Lottie also makes sense."

I rejoined Hyperia on the settee, turning over possibilities in my mind. "Lottie is angry enough to be foolish, and Jessamine spoiled enough, but with all three females, I cannot for the life of me grasp how they would know the significance of each stolen item."

Hyperia passed me the drink and took up her half cuddle again. "The letters speak for themselves. Whoever took them might not have known Pickering was so young, or of a station so much lower than Her Grace's, but love letters are love letters."

And another source of vulnerability, apparently. "What of the gloves and locket?"

"If Lord Barrington knew of those gloves, and some servant overheard them mentioned, that same servant could have done exactly as you did—parsed initials and come to a reasonable conclusion."

A bit convoluted, but entirely possible. "The locket?"

Hyperia stared hard at the flames dancing on the hearth. "Lady Canderport could have seen the locket and come across a portrait of the late general somewhere. Mrs. Whittington wore that item frequently, though not always where it could be seen. A casual discussion in a ladies' retiring room might have been overheard, or a few oblique questions passed along over a hand of whist."

"How old is Drayson?" I asked.

"Lady Ophelia would know. He looks like he's just down from university, and he has a convincing case of youthful self-absorption, but he was circulating about Mayfair five years ago."

"So he might also have heard stories." Men talked, though we seldom admitted that our talk amounted to pure gossip. "Hans the sportsman was familiar with Town. He might have cried into his brandy where Drayson could have heard him."

"Ian the diplomat knew London as well," Hyperia murmured, taking the drink back and sipping again. "If Drayson was of an age with these fellows, they might have belonged to the same clubs or frequented the same gaming hells."

I did prefer the notion that our culprit was a man, but had no evidence to support such a theory. "How do we connect Drayson to John Pickering?" I asked. "More gossip?"

"Pickering was a skilled musician," Hyperia said slowly, "and a skilled flatterer. If he'd worked the same scheme on some widow in Hampshire, she might have caught wind that Her Grace of Waltham had hired a young man to teach her the flute, and quiet rumors would have started."

"We're into the realm of pure conjecture, my dear. Castles in Spain."

"But not wild conjecture, Jules. Not fairy castles. If Society is bent on one activity other than frolicking, it's gossip. We are discussing possibilities rather than outlandish coincidences. Then too, if Drayson is our man, stealing his own sketches was the perfect ploy to ensure he's above suspicion. Going to the lake ostensibly to sketch every day means he had ample free time to search the ladies' belongings, and he's still apparently dependent on his father for an allowance, hence he needs money."

All very true, very plausible. "Drayson doesn't feel right," I said. "He was hopelessly clumsy about searching your quarters, and yet, the solution to an inquiry often seems outlandish at first glance. A set of coincidences, not a likelihood, until facts accumulate and connect. This is progress, Perry. I am happy to say I feel a sense of progress."

Were this my first investigation, I would not have used the word *progress*. I would have labeled a proliferation of suspects and theories *utter confusion*. I was learning, though, that investigating was a cousin to a reconnaissance mission, where close observation and patience often yielded a better sense of the land and the enemy's purpose than all the strategy discussions and map studying in the world.

"You will have to wait to apprise Her Grace of the latest developments," Hyperia said, passing me back the glass. "I stopped by her apartment on the way here, and she's napping before Sunday supper."

"Just as well. She was growing equivocal when I paid a call on her this morning. Not quite suggesting the letters had simply been mislaid, but resorting to mention of sleeping dogs."

"If blackmail is the objective, Jules, the thief has had days to make threats. Her Grace might have a point."

"If I were behind this scheme, I would wait as well, until my victims were isolated and unable to combine forces, until no reinforcements were on hand. I would want my victims to be in a position to write sizable bank drafts made out to 'bearer.' Time is on the side of the thief. If my objective were to involve the law, I might be content to wait as well."

Hyperia nodded. "You cannot involve the law. Your objective is to quietly retrieve the letters, the locket, and the gloves, regardless of who stole them, and those are likely here at Tweed House—for now. Time is your foe, or one of them. We could attempt more searching."

"Perhaps when I return from Dover, we will. I am concerned Atticus will behave rashly in my absence, though, and undertake some searching on his own. Please do what you can to dissuade him."

"And you told him to dissuade me?"

"Of course." Or I would before departing.

"I wish I were going to Dover with you, Jules."

As did I, but saying good-bye to Arthur was a private obligation. An act of faith in the future that nobody could make for me or with me.

"I should be gone little more than twenty-four hours. Wish me good weather and dry roads."

She kissed my cheek. "Safe, swift journey. You have the cards for your pocket?"

"Always." They had been her idea, else I might not have been as diligent about carrying them. "Could I talk you into napping with me, Miss West?"

Hyperia sighed gustily and straightened. "No, you could not. Too many eyes and ears about, Jules. I'll see you at supper, and if you'd like me on hand when you make your next report to your mother, I'm happy to oblige."

"Promise you'll see me off tomorrow."

She rose and took the nearly empty brandy glass to the sideboard. "Of course, and now you really ought to catch forty winks."

That way lay another sleepless night. "While you do what?"

"Get to know Lord Drayson a little better." She unlocked the door and sashayed into the corridor before I could admonish her to be damned careful.

A man who would steal from a duchess in broad daylight, who would draw any woman he pleased in the nude, and who set his valet to spreading accusations among the staff, all the while presenting himself as a sulking dandy, was not a man to trifle with.

I was paired with Miss Bivens at Sunday supper, which was delightful in one sense—she truly was widely read—and frustrating in another. This particular young lady was extraneous to the investigation. In my usual fashion, I had progressed from reluctant curiosity about some old letters, to a burning conviction that the letters, the gloves, and locket had to be found before the house party disbanded.

My mother sent regrets for supper, and when I attempted another chat with her before turning in, Wisherd informed me in hushed tones that the duchess had succumbed to a megrim. Her Grace had had such headaches periodically throughout my youth, and yet, this one was timed as if to avoid me on the eve of my trip to Dover.

No last-minute admonitions for Arthur, then, no note of parting to be delivered in person. Perhaps her ailment precluded both.

I suffered the occasional sick headache myself, and thus I left my mother in peace. I had arranged for an early departure in the morning, and after another restless night—I truly did sleep better with Hyperia in my arms—I rose, broke my fast, and prepared for some hard riding under a grim sky. The roads weren't muddy, but the day was chilly, and more rain might well be forthcoming.

"I could have Jupe hitched to the phaeton in a trice," Atticus said, leading Atlas up to the mounting block. "Or you could take yer ma's traveling coach."

"The traveling coach is heavy and thus slow. If the heavens open up, I'd be faster traveling on foot than slogging along in that contraption." The traveling coach was comfortable, though. Well sprung, cozy, packed with amenities... I hadn't wanted to ask my mother for its loan, and I truly did want the journey speedily behind me.

"Do you have the letter?" Hyperia asked, her cloak whipping in the breeze.

"In my pocket. If Heeney and Sons are still in business, I'll find them. You two, in the meanwhile, don't do anything foolish."

"Right, guv." Atticus patted Atlas's shoulder. "All foolishness will be got up to by your rubbishin' lordship. Me and Miss West, we'll be mindin' our own business and not worryin' about you a'tall."

I studied the boy, who seemed to be growing out of his clothes overnight. Both yesterday in the stable and this morning, his diction had reverted to the less articulate speech of his humbler days, which was usually a sign the lad was worried.

"Atticus, have you written your report to Lady Ophelia yet?"

"Workin' on it."

"Miss West will include it with my own epistle, which is on the sideboard in my sitting room, sealed and ready for delivery. If you've never sealed a letter before, Miss West can show you how."

Atticus brightened, as I'd hoped he would. He delighted in learning new skills, and something as simple as sealing a letter qualified.

"You'll be careful?" Hyperia muttered.

"Always, I will also be back not later than supper tomorrow. I half expect Drayson or his valet will try to plant the missing sketches in some opportune location while I'm gone. My door is locked. Atticus has the key, and the latch has been appropriately adorned."

I lingered near her, hoping for a kiss on the cheek. We were visible from the breakfast parlor windows, and a parting buss would have been a badge of honor, by my lights.

The duchess emerged from the house, a forest green cloak covering her from slippers to throat. "A moment, my lord. I'm glad I caught you."

I hadn't been running away. "Your Grace, good morning." I

waited to be given a missive for Arthur or wished a safe journey. That my mother would see me off was doubtless a display for the sake of the breakfast-parlor audience.

"I wanted you to know..." She slanted a glance at Hyperia, who met her gaze with frank curiosity. "That is, might we walk a bit?"

"Anything that must be said can be said before Miss West," I replied. "She is absolutely in my confidence." As was, in his fashion, Atticus, but he was serving in the capacity of groom at the moment and thus invisible by my mother's reckoning.

"This is personal," the duchess said, very much on her dignity.

"I will give Arthur your love and warn him that if he comes to any harm whatsoever, Banter has orders to return our duke to Merry Olde without delay. I've ensured that His Grace is amply loaded down with pigeons, coin, warm clothing, and—"

"My lord, please cease patronizing me. Arthur is a grown man and notably good at preparations. I have wished him safe journey. My present concern relates to the matter that brought you to Tweed House."

The matter that... the letters. "Yes?"

She glanced at the house, then fixed her gaze on Atlas, waiting patiently at the mounting block two yards away.

"You need not trouble yourself over the letters any further. I'm sure you will be relieved to put them from your mind."

Hyperia frankly goggled at the duchess. Atticus stared at the ground.

While I battled the urge to howl. "I beg Your Grace's pardon?"

"Your hearing is excellent, my lord, and my meaning was plain enough."

My comprehension was in fine working order too. "My services will no longer be necessary?"

She looked pained, also a bit pale and tired, but she nodded. "I apologize for sending you on a goose chase. I'm sure the letters will turn up, and they are of little moment in any case."

No, they were not. Two days ago, I would have been relieved to hear this dismissal, though I might also have been uneasy. Now, I had discerned a pattern to the thefts, I had suspects in my gun sights, and I had motives to attribute to each of them.

"Those letters represent a real risk of harm to you," I said quietly. "Have you forgotten that?"

"My memory is excellent, young man."

Mine was not, but my investigative skills were at least respectable. "You expect me to simply ride off to Dover, wish Arthur farewell, and what? Return to the Hall?"

Atticus squinted at me, while Hyperia was maintaining a diplomatic silence. The one time my mother had sought my aid, and for the one purpose that might truly suit my skills, and now I was supposed to scurry off like a footman who'd spilled wine on his livery?

"I expect you to ride off to Dover, and if you do return to Tweed House, I expect you to comport yourself as the gentleman you are for the remainder of the gathering. This is, I believe, within your abilities."

A scold. A definite, even taunting, scold.

Now Hyperia was staring at the ground, while Atticus glowered at the duchess. That Her Grace would dismiss me was frankly infuriating, but that she'd do so before the boy and before Perry...

That amounted to a betrayal, and I had had quite enough of those. Fellow officers who had known me in uniform now cut me openly. Neighbors had been notably reluctant to call at the Hall when I bided there. In London, men I'd known since boyhood hadn't bothered to call upon me when I'd dragged myself home from Waterloo.

And now this, from *my mother*. "Does it not matter to you," I said, "that Lady Barrington and Mrs. Whittington have also been victimized? If you hobble my inquiry now, those women and their families are more likely to suffer."

I kept my voice down, mindful of the windows, also mindful that

I was a gentleman, and the female so casually expecting me to forget hanging felonies perpetrated against her was due my respect.

At the moment, she had little enough of my liking and none of my forgiveness.

"I will deal with Lady Barrington and Mrs. Whittington," Her Grace replied. "I will brook no argument on this, my lord. My mind is made up. You made a good, if unsuccessful effort, and the appropriate action now is to put the matter behind us as soon as possible."

Beneath my bewilderment and outrage lay questions: Why call off the investigation now? Had Drayson got around to making his threats? Was the staff now circulating rumors that made the truth of the past look innocuous by comparison?

I considered the duchess, so dignified in her velvet-lined cloak, and I considered what I knew about all the missing items. I had made progress, with the help of those I could trust, and in a very short time. I had come when my mother needed me, and she needed me still.

"Madam, your mind is made up, and so is mine. I will be back at Tweed House, God willing, by supper tomorrow, and then I will resume my investigation."

Her gaze would have frozen the Channel from Dover to Calais. "I forbid it. You cannot."

I could, though it might cost me what remained of my connection to my only living parent. "Perhaps it has escaped your notice, Your Grace, but I am a man grown and free from any obligations to the peerage. I am a competent investigator, and you have need of same. I understand that you cannot trust me to see the matter through—"

"I did not say that."

"—and I understand that you fear I will create a scandal rather than prevent one. I promise you discretion and best efforts, but honor compels me to persevere rather than surrender to your present wishes."

I bowed, that fine speech at variance with the riot of feelings battling inside me. My mother had, before witnesses, expressed her lack of faith in me—her lack of any *use* for me. The sheer magnitude of my humiliation resonated with the enormous pride of small boys and very young men, and the intensity of my ire was reminiscent of soldiers betrayed by bad leadership.

He's going to get us all killed had all too often proved prophetic when the officer in question was some aristocratic puppy with no grasp of warfare. The duchess had no grasp of criminal mischief and apparently little comprehension of my determination in the face of same.

"I'll bid you good day, Your Grace."

"Julian, don't be like this."

She again used my Christian name, and now I could not afford to be swayed by it. "I am sorry to cause you distress, Your Grace, but I am not a footman to be dismissed at your whim. *I am your son*, the only son you have to call upon in the present circumstances, and by God I will aid you to the best of my ability."

I took the reins from Atticus and swung into the saddle. The discussion had doubtless been observed by guests, staff, and half the shire, and I wanted nothing so much as to thunder down the drive in a fit of galloping indignation. Let the duchess be blackmailed within an inch of her considerable wealth, to blazes with the letters and gloves and lockets.

But a tantrum would not do. Atlas had been standing for some time, and he had a long day ahead of him. I touched a finger to my hat brim and nodded to Hyperia.

"Until tomorrow."

Atlas offered a sedate trot as we departed, and I was mindful of eyes on my back. Hyperia doubtless pitied me, Atticus was furious on my behalf, and as for my mother... as usual, I had not the first notion what she made of the exchange.

I had the whole of a long ride to Dover to puzzle out my own feelings on the matter, and even that lengthy distance wasn't likely to be enough.

CHAPTER FOURTEEN

By the time I approached Dover, I was soaked to the skin and would have been exhausted but for the unquenchable fuel provided by roiling emotions. My mother's dismissal harked back to too many other occasions when I'd been the wrong son, with too many manners or too few. I'd lacked Harry's charm, Arthur's consequence, Harry's humor, Arthur's gravitas...

And what I had brought to the bargain—a certain tenacity of spirit, an observant nature, a mind given to pondering puzzles—had been found wanting.

As Dover Castle came into view, I kept Atlas to the walk, in deference to the bad footing and because even his great reserves of stamina had been tested in the course of the day. When the scent of the sea blended with the aroma of mud and the squawking of gulls, I felt a kind of peace settling over me.

My mother had made her feelings quite clear, and it was time to accept that those feelings would not change. We could be civil—we'd proved that much—and the people who mattered most to me would understand why civility would be the limit of our dealings. I'd have to explain the situation to Arthur, but I'd do so in a manner that let him depart England untroubled by family woes.

I was a competent investigator. My mother had sought my help because she truly needed assistance. I wasn't wrong to proceed with what inquiries I could discreetly make.

I came to a tollgate on the outskirts of Dover proper and inquired within regarding stationers' establishments. The venerable tollkeeper squinted at me with rheumy blue eyes.

"Letting the family know where to forward your allowance, young sir?" He cackled at his own humor and slapped a hand on the counter before him. "Sending a young lady your fondest regrets? We get a lot of that here in Dover, now the peace is upon us. God bless the peace."

"I merely need to buy some decent paper," I said. "Preferably before the shops close for the night."

He looked me up and down. "Oh, right. Of course. Well, you paid your toll, so I'll tell you straight we have three proper stationers, though one of them was a printer in Queen Anne's day and got notions to expand into shopkeeping. They'd be along the High Street, Peverell's by name. If you continue down the hill and past the White Horse, you'll see Heeney's on the left. That leaves Crevecoeur near the market square. Family's been here since the Conqueror's day, or so they claim. They'll all take your coin, see if they don't."

I thanked him and returned to my tired horse. Dover lacked the natural harbor that made Portsmouth a mainstay for naval operations, but the town did lie directly on the sea, a dip in the terrain between two imposing heights. On the one hand, invading forces could gain land easily from such a location. On the other, defending the town from the high ground on either side had been a priority since the days of Henry II.

I took the road that wound below Dover Castle, sitting in all its grim glory on the western heights, and descended into the town itself. What Dover lacked in natural naval features, it made up for in ferry traffic, which ran at all hours—depending on the tides—and in many directions.

I handed Atlas off to a groom at the White Horse, an establishment dating back to the fourteenth century, and made for Heeney's shop across the street and about fifty yards south of the inn. The sign swinging above the door featured an inkpot and quill pen, as well as the words *Heeney and Sons, Fine Stationery and Accoutrements* in graceful script.

The sheer density of human activity took me aback. Wherever mankind gathered in any numbers, noise and stink followed. The street sweepers hereabouts were apparently behindhand, perhaps due to a day of wet weather. An underlying odor of rotting kelp suggested recent storms were working their dubious magic on the beaches, and the raucous strains of a fiddle testified to travelers fortifying themselves against the elements in the usual fashion.

I had forgotten the bustle and crowding of this port town, and if I'd been indifferent to it on previous occasions, in my current condition, I wanted no part of such turbulence whatsoever. I craved the peace and quiet of Caldicott Hall, the slow pace of country life, and the company of my few trusted familiars.

I entered Heeney's with a sense of relief. The shop smelled good —of paper, scented waxes, and fragrant sachets intended to keep documents safe from marauding mice.

"Evenin', sir," a young lady said. "Can I help you find anything in particular?"

The shop was tidy and spacious, with samples of writing paper laid out on standing desks around the room and three sitting desks lined along the front widows displaying blotters, wax jacks, pen trays, ink bottles, and standishes.

"I'm looking to purchase a gift," I said, withdrawing the single folded paper Lady Ophelia had sent over from the Hall. "My cousin is a music master, and he hasn't been able to find his favorite writing paper in London. Blue, though this example is faded, and I believe he bought it here years ago."

I passed over the page, and the young lady held it up to the light of a flickering sconce. "Aye, he would have. This is ours. The young gents like it. Not too dear, but a bit distinctive, and the color sets a man's correspondence apart without being too fancy. Most buy half a ream at a time, though a ream is the better bargain."

The shopkeeper conveyed two pieces of bad news in her recitation. First, the paper was still made by the shop and in quantity. Second, it was a popular item among young men minding their pence and quid.

"I don't suppose you recall a music master who was particularly devoted to this type of stationery? Good-looking devil, charming, tallish, dark hair?"

She laughed and passed me back the letter. "Dover's a port, sir. We do a regular traffic in charming devils of many nationalities. I wouldn't know a music master from a Latin tutor when a fellow simply wants to let his mama know he's safely returned from his travels."

"I'll take half a ream," I said, though I had no need to lug paper back to Tweed House with me. "You can send it along to the White Horse." I'd take a few sheets for evidentiary purposes and leave the rest with the inn for the use of their guests.

I paid for my purchase and turned tired steps back in the direction of the White Horse. The inn sat next to the venerable St. James' Church, where I was momentarily tempted to seek refuge, simply for the quiet to be had.

I pushed through the door of the inn instead. This late in the day, Arthur would be worrying about me. He would also attempt to conceal his anxiety from Osgood Banter. Banter, a quick study for all his pleasant manners, would fret anyway, as one did about a loved one given over to disquiet.

I asked for a room and asked to be announced to Mr. Banter's party. Arthur was traveling with as little fuss as possible, a decision I applauded both because Mr. Banter-and-friend would gain less notice than His Grace of Waltham would, and because safety for them both lay in greater privacy.

"Jules!" Arthur came down the steps a few minutes later, appearing positively beamish. "You look like a half-drowned cat. Come along, and we'll ply you with brandy and hear all the house-party gossip. Have you found Mama's letters?"

Clearly, the holiday had already begun. Arthur's smile was open and merry, and while he might have a well-hidden streak of mischief, His Grace of Waltham was not given to jollity in the usual course.

"Brother." I held out a hand, we shook, and even my form of address seemed to add to the duke's good cheer. In the normal course, I would have *Your Graced* him and set the innkeeper's wife to goggling, if she hadn't already known the august station of her guest.

"Have you had supper?" Arthur asked as I followed him up the steps from whence he'd descended. "The food is hot, delicious, and blessedly plain. Why does travel get such a bad name when the lowliest English inn can provide such ambrosial fare? The brandy is excellent, though we must decry the coastal trade loudly while we enjoy it, and the wind and tides seem to be favoring departure by noon tomorrow."

He stopped before a substantial door, the light of the corridor sconce casting shadows over his features. "I am nigh giddy to be leaving England, Jules. What does that say about me?"

He and I were apparently gifted at wringing guilt from even the happiest of occasions. "It means you are overdue for a holiday and have planned one you can honestly look forward to."

The door opened, revealing Osgood Banter in an exquisitely embroidered waistcoat, his cravat nowhere in evidence, his cuffs turned back.

"Jules, you must come away with us. Tour the great capitals, admire ancient Rome, sample all the best vintages."

"In reverse order," Arthur said, leading me through the door and closing it behind me. "Get you to the chair by the fire, Julian. Can't have you taking a chill. How are you and Mama getting along?"

He wanted a cheerful report, and I wanted to give him one. "We're managing. Your trunks have all been stowed?"

A look passed between Banter, who was lounging elegantly on the arm of the sofa, and Arthur, who settled onto the cushions opposite me.

"Mama's being difficult?" Arthur asked as Banter rose to pour drinks at the sideboard.

Arthur was leaving me to manage the Hall and the entire family proceedings for an extended period. On the eve of his departure, I could not burden him with my injured pride and filial frustrations.

"You have a certain look about you," Banter said, handing me a glass of amber potation. "Brooding in the grand Caldicott tradition and trying not to show it."

"Out with it, Jules," Arthur said, accepting his own glass. "I learned everything I know about being high in the instep from Mama, but she's actually softhearted to a fault."

Regarding her firstborn, perhaps she was. "Her Grace and I are having a small row," I said, taking a drink of exquisite spirits. The brandy's fire was exactly right—halfway between warm and fierce—and the taste both delicate and lingering.

"Good." Arthur grinned over his glass. "About time you two learned to have a difference. I will leave England relieved to know you and Mama are behaving exactly as family ought. My money's on you, Jules. You have Miss West in your corner, while Mama's immediate reinforcements are limited to Wisherd."

"What's the spat about?" Banter asked, resuming his slouch on the sofa arm.

I was reluctant to part with details, also aware that I would miss Arthur and Banter terribly. Banter and I shared a protectiveness toward Arthur that he tolerated grudgingly, and Arthur and Banter both regarded me as a younger sibling somewhat dodgy in the brainbox from time to time, but also capable of ferreting out truths when called upon to do so.

They respected my skills, in other words, and trusted them.

"We disagree about the missing letters," I said. "Her Grace had an affair with a much younger man when serving out her mourning, and she went from demanding that I find her correspondence to demanding that I forget the whole business." Demanding in front of both Hyperia and Atticus, to say nothing of a house full of curious guests.

"What will you do?" Arthur asked, once again the sober duke.

"I don't know. The situation is serious." I explained about Lady Barrington's and Mrs. Whittington's vulnerabilities and the growing list of potential malefactors. "If I can't find the letters before the house party ends, all manner of mischief might result."

"Or it might not," Banter observed. "You assume the letters will be used against Her Grace, but they don't reflect any too well on this Pickering creature either. Took advantage of a grieving widow, toyed with a lady's affections, accepted coin into the bargain. A music master's livelihood would be forfeit if that got out."

I was finally warm after hours of cold, damp misery, the brandy was good, and Arthur's blasé reaction to news of my disagreement with Her Grace fortified me. Families did spat and argue. Harry and I had had epic arguments as boys, casting each other into an outer darknesses that could last days, only to realize that fishing alone wasn't half so diverting as fishing with a brother. A few muttered words, a suggestion, and we'd be great friends again.

I considered Banter's observation, offered from the perspective of wealthy gentry rather than the aristocracy.

"I agree that the musical miscreant has much to lose if those letters became public," I said slowly. "The same isn't as true of the other two fellows—Ian and Hans—because they were more highly placed in Society, and the ladies were not duchesses. The talk seems invariably to devolve to the lady's discredit, while the gentleman is excused on the basis of rampant animal spirits."

Arthur made a face. "If we fellows can't govern our animal spirits, what right have we to be trusted governing the realm, much less every village in it?"

Banter patted his shoulder. "No brooding, you. We embark on the noon tide, and governing won't come into it."

Animal spirits would, which made me happy for them, also envious. "I have vowed to return to Tweed House and find those letters," I said. "I'm not sure I can keep that vow."

"Return to Tweed House," Arthur said. "If anybody can locate what has gone missing, Jules, it's you, and you must begin with Mama as you intend to go on."

"Bit late for beginning," I said, "given the ages of the respective parties."

"You went off to serve in uniform shortly after university," Arthur said. "Mama went off to Bath or Lyme or the shops. You are no longer a university boy who needs fashion advice or to be slipped a sovereign at the end of his holiday. Tweed House is your adult beginning with Mama. She hasn't had firsthand experience of your investigative abilities, after all."

"I'll vouch for you," Banter said, lifting his glass. "So will my entire household and the surrounding neighborhood."

The next thought to befall me was curious: *Why would they do that?* I had the sense this man spoke of some recent history with which I should be familiar, but as I regarded the glass in my hand—brandy, presumably—I realized I did not know the fellow's name.

Another man sat relaxed on the sofa opposite my reading chair. Good-sized, age about five and thirty. Strapping in a refined way and good-looking despite a slightly prominent beak.

I looked about me with a growing sense of dismay. "I do beg your pardon, gentlemen, but could one of you please tell me the purpose of our gathering, and how I came to be here?" For that matter, I wasn't in that moment sure of my own name or where exactly *here* was. I did not feel inebriated, but surely an excess of spirits explained why my wits had gone begging.

The fellow who had offered to vouch for me was another handsome specimen in his prime, though more slender than the seated man.

"You are apparently having one of your lapses of memory," the slender fellow said, setting his glass aside. "No cause for worry. Arthur, I've seen Jules like this before. He'll be right as a trivet in a few hours. Jules—you are Lord Julian Caldicott, by the way—this is your older brother, Arthur, and I'm his friend Banter. Please consult the card in your coat pocket."

Was I an opium eater, to have a brother I could not recall? I patted my pockets and came up with a card written in a tidy hand.

"How often do I have these lapses?" I asked, staring at the card in some dismay.

"Not often," Arthur—Banter had called him Arthur—replied, "and they never last long."

"You are the Duke of Waltham?" I asked. The card had referenced seeing me into the care of His Grace, my older brother.

"The same, and I'm supposed to leave for France tomorrow."

Panic was too mild a term for the sensations enveloping me at that news. I had forgotten *my own name*, and my brother was leaving me in this undisclosed location in the morning? Was that the measure of the fraternal loyalty I was due?

"Arthur..." the other fellow said in warning tones. "France isn't going anywhere."

"We've discussed this," Arthur replied, rising. "Our trunks are on that packet, and the wind could shift again without warning."

I ought to make some demurrer and tell these two that I could manage, that they needn't bother about me, but the bloody rubbishing hell of it was, I could *not* manage. Did I have money? Where was I in relation to any sort of permanent refuge? Was another brother on hand to see me there?

Had I a wife? A private residence? My clothing was well made. I was tall and in good trim, if a bit skinny. I wasn't the family reprobate, apparently, but neither was I in any condition to fend for myself.

I nonetheless tried to emulate Banter's air of unconcern. "Put me in a coach and send me on to the family seat, assuming we have one."

Arthur was tempted, I could see that in his eyes. "Not good

enough, Jules. You are the only brother I have left, and you've never asked a damned thing of me."

So I was the proud sort, despite my faulty memory. "All I'm asking of you now is a coach, and some funds, if those are necessary."

Banter shook his head. "Arthur would fret himself to flinders, stuffing you into a carriage like some dowager who overstayed her welcome. There's time to see Julian as far as Tweed House, Arthur. I'll go. Her Grace likes me, and nobody would expect you to..."

Some sort of silent conversation took place, and it dawned on me that these two men were either very close friends, or close friends *and lovers*. I would be shocked by that just as soon as I was through being shocked at my own lack of meaningful recollections.

"Let's get you something to eat," Arthur said, tugging a bell-pull. "If we leave now, I can get you back to Tweed House and still make the packet, but we mustn't dawdle. Banter, you are to sail without me if I miss the packet. I'll catch up to you in Calais."

Banter clearly longed to argue. He instead nodded and began rolling down his cuffs. "We'll need to make arrangements for Julian's horse, and you'll want a hamper packed. You are both in for a very, very long night."

"Get him into dry clothes," Arthur said. "I'll notify the stable we need their fastest team."

He departed, and Banter sighed. "You heard him. Dry kit, a quick meal, and then we're sending you home to Mama."

I had a mother. That should have been cheering news, but for some reason, I wasn't cheered at all.

His Grace of Waltham and I traveled for hours through damp, chilly darkness. I dozed, but the rocking of the coach and unrelenting worry kept me from sleeping much. The duke—how was it possible my brother was *a duke?*—saw to the changes of teams and fares and whatnot and between stops regaled with me a recitation of my life story.

I had served honorably as a reconnaissance officer under Wellington, lost a brother to the perfidious French, been held captive for a time by same, and come home from the wars weakened in body and spirit. My pockets held two pairs of blue spectacles because my eyes objected to strong light.

They were my very own eyes, and I hadn't known that about myself.

"Did my memory problem start during the war?" I asked as a fresh team trotted out of yet another cobbled coaching yard.

"You've said the first instances occurred at university. You attributed them to overimbibing, by Harry's report, though you were nearly abstemious by university standards."

I could recall nothing about this Harry person, nothing about captivity, nothing about much of anything. Still.

"You're sure my memories will return?"

"Yes." His Grace had paused for the merest heartbeat before speaking. He was not sure. He was hopeful.

"How long will you and Banter travel?"

Another hesitation. "The better part of a year. The trip was actually your idea. You and Harry had seen some of the world, albeit for the wrong reasons, and now—you claimed—it was my turn."

"And you are going on my say-so?" What sort of brother was I to give orders to a peer?

"We are."

I would not have called His Grace a warm sort of person, but he was doing the proper thing, getting me to another family member, and he was doing it at great inconvenience to himself.

"Am I a decent sort of brother?" I asked.

One corner of his mouth quirked up. "If you were any more decent, the term 'excessive honor' would apply. Your loyalties are ironclad, your courage nearly as limitless as your determination, though to the untrained eye, you can appear merely stubborn to the point of eccentricity. You are fortunate, in that Miss Hyperia West has been training her eyes on you for some time, and she is a shrewd observer."

That sounded frankly intimidating.

"You and Banter are also traveling because your attachment to each other is unfashionably close," I said. "Or do I mistake the matter?"

The humor in the duke's expression receded but did not entirely fade. "Your powers of observation are undiminished apparently, and those are formidable as well."

I pondered what I'd learned of myself over the miles and what I'd learned of Arthur. He and Banter were devoted, despite the danger their liaison posed, and His Grace was fond of me.

"You aren't worried that my poor memory will put the family's affairs in terrible disarray during your absence?" I asked.

"Your lapses are always brief, Jules. Hours at most."

Hours had gone by, and I was still wandering in a vast mental wilderness without a single landmark. I spent the next few miles reviewing what the duke had told me and realized he'd left much out.

"Do we have sisters?" I asked some time later.

"Four, all married. You and Ginny are closest in age and close in spirit as well. The sisters all like you because you aren't stodgy, as I am, or arrogant, as Harry was. You are sensible, in their estimation, and they set great store by good sense. They all have children. I can tell you quite honestly they have come to this appreciation for good sense only after becoming mothers."

I could not recall these women or their children. I battled an impulse to leap from the moving coach and pelt out into the night in search of my memories.

"Tweed House, at last," His Grace muttered as the coach slowed to turn through a pair of stone gateposts. "I instructed the coachy to proceed to the carriage house. With luck, Her Grace will not be abed yet."

"It's the middle of the rubbishing night."

"This is a fashionable house party," the duke replied patiently. "They play cards all night, have amateur musicales until the small hours, put on ridiculous theatricals. It's a wonder Mama can tolerate it."

"She's sensible too?"

"The two of you are cut from the same bolt in so many ways, it's uncanny. Your hair used to be chestnut, by the way. Mama is a redhead."

I pulled a lock of hair forward. I was blond, the ends showing nearly white by the light of the coach lamps. "What on earth happened to my hair?"

"Your encounter with the French was something of a shock to your system. You've mostly come right, and your hair is regaining some color." He spoke briskly, suggesting I might not want to recall my *encounter* with the French, even if I could.

Except that I did want to, very much. Whatever had happened, the past was a part of me, and I wanted it put back where I could recall it, and I wanted it put back *now*.

CHAPTER FIFTEEN

The coach came to a halt, and through the window I saw a bleary-eyed stable boy emerge from the darkness.

"We're for the house," the duke said, opening the door and lowering the step. "We'll get your horse back to you in the next day or two. He needed rest before making the return journey, though Atlas is the envy of all who behold him."

I climbed out, my joints feeling about ninety-seven years old. "Why did I name my horse Atlas?"

His Grace accepted a lantern from the stable boy, a dark-skinned lad whose age I'd put at about seventeen. Grown into his height, not yet grown into his full strength.

"You didn't name him. His former owner did. You bought the horse to fund that fool's passage home from Spain," His Grace said. "Let's find our mother, shall we?"

My ducal brother knew a good deal about me, and this struck me as simply part of his nature. He would know just as much about these married sisters. He saw himself as the Caldicott patriarch, and staying informed was his responsibility.

Whereas I appeared to be nosy by nature. Not very gentlemanly of me.

We traversed a darkness punctuated by the strains of a pair of violins playing a slow air in close harmony.

"The party is not yet abed," Arthur said as we approached a sizable façade, lights showing in many of the ground-floor and first-floor windows. "That's fortunate in one way."

But also unfortunate, to the extent that my situation wanted discretion. I could puzzle out that much. "You will climb right back into the coach, Your Grace, and rejoin Banter in Dover by sunrise. If our mother bides here, I will manage adequately with her assistance." Dover by dawn wasn't likely. Dover by noon was possible.

"You would not recognize your own mother if you fell over her, Jules. Banter will sail without me if need be. Traveling is legendarily full of uncertainties."

And this brother of mine was legendarily dutiful, bless him. "I refuse to be a burden to somebody who has already—"

The duke held up a hand. "We can go in that French door. That's the estate office. I will find Mama, and you will cease bleating. You could never, ever be a burden. Banter would agree with me, and so, if he were alive, would Harry."

Harry, who had served with me, whom I could not recall in the slightest.

We entered a room that would have been in pitch darkness but for the lantern Arthur carried. He used that flame to light a branch of four candles and left me in solitude for what felt like six eternities. Music floated on the air, as did the murmur of occasional voices in the corridor, but conversations were indistinct.

I could not bear to sit, I hadn't room to pace, and I was tempted to open the door just to have a peek at this Tweed House. Perhaps familiar sights would jog some memories loose?

The door opened, and His Grace returned with two ladies and an older man. He wasn't my father—that good soul had gone to his reward years ago, according to my brother—and he was in evening attire. He looked too old to be another brother, and surely the duke would have mentioned a sibling also biding at this house party.

"Jules." The younger woman spoke first. She was a lovely creature, if a bit shorter and curvier than fashion preferred. "I'm Hyperia."

"Miss West, good evening." I bowed and looked askance at the older woman. She qualified as red-haired, and she was aging well, making the transition from striking to dignified. In addition to classic features, she was tallish, and any fool could see the worry in her gaze.

I bowed again. "Your Grace, apologies for inconveniencing you and Miss West."

The older man spoke. "You don't know who I am, do you? The rumors are true, and you have no idea who I am."

I did not know who he was, but I did not care at all for the hint of gloating in his question. Before I could remonstrate with him, the duchess rounded on him, her hands fisted at her sides.

"Gideon Harve Marchant, if you continue in that vein, you are no friend of mine. *My son* risked his life, repeatedly, to keep you and the bloviating nincompoops you aspire to join in Parliament safe from the Corsican menace. A better man than you will ever, ever be has been brought temporarily low by a malady inflicted by unkind fate, and you haven't the sense to show any compassion. If you hope to hold a prayer of moving safely in Society, you will apologize to his lordship *this instant*."

Ye gods, I was the son of a dragoness. The Marchant fellow visibly shrank as the duchess concluded her tirade. Miss West took the place on my right. Arthur stood to my left.

"Apologize," Miss West said, "then get out. This is a family matter, Mr. Marchant, and you are intruding."

Marchant flicked a gaze at the duke, who remained magnificently silent. "Apologies, my lord. I meant no offense, and I wish you a speedy recovery." He slipped out of the room.

In the next instant, the duchess had me in a fierce hug. "I am so sorry. Gideon has a bit of the ghoul in him, and he tagged along, and I was too worried..." She stepped back and looked me up and down, the anxiety still evident in her gaze. "Don't fret, my lord. You are among allies, and all will seem better in the morning. You need rest and time, and we will see that you have both."

His Grace of Waltham had spoken the truth. I would not have recognized this Valkyrie as my mother, though others probably saw a resemblance in our features. I knew two things, though, without a single memory to confirm my conclusions: These women would protect me to their last breaths, and never had a son been more fiercely beloved.

The duchess stepped back, her presumption upon my person apparently embarrassing her.

"My thanks," I said, "for your defense of me in my present state, Your Grace. I apologize for burdening you, His Grace, and Miss West with my malady."

One corner of the duchess's lips quirked up, resulting in a resemblance to her firstborn. "You haven't forgotten your manners, my boy. Perhaps we can credit your upbringing for that. Arthur, will you bide here until morning?"

Her question had a subtle neutral quality. I did not want him to leave, of that I was certain, and yet, he and Banter clearly longed to take ship.

"No need to stay," I said with as much confidence as I could muster. "Time and tide wait for no man. I'm sure Mama and Miss West will have me put to rights ere long."

I hoped they would. I prayed they would.

"You just quoted Chaucer," Miss West said. "That bit about time and tide is from 'The Clerk's Tale.' The memories are there, Jules. You'll find your way back to them as you always do."

Her reassurances carried weight with me, though I knew not why. I could not recall "The Clerk's Tale," nor the author Chaucer, but Hyperia West had made a sound point. I could retrieve the quote, ergo, the source material was still knocking around my upper story somewhere.

"And you called me *Mama*," the duchess muttered.

I was again all at sea. Arthur had called her Mama, she was my mama, but she was also a duchess. "Did I give offense, Your Grace?"

"No," she said, slipping her arm through mine. "In fact, I might hold you to it. Come, Miss West, we must see his lordship tucked into bed, and then I will have a pointed discussion with Gideon. How dare he make light of another's misfortune like that?"

"I'll have a word with Marchant," the duke said. "And then I will be on my way."

I extricated myself from my mother's grasp. "Your Grace, safe journey. My thanks for all you've done to get me here." *Please don't leave me.* I suspected that sentiment had little to do with my poor memory and everything to do with the late brother, Harry, whom I could not recall. I was down to one extant brother, and he was off to the wilds of France.

A notion I detested for no logical reason.

"Jules." Arthur took my hand, then pulled me in for a hug. "By God, sir, you shall write to me regularly, and I promise to return the courtesy. I wish you were in better fettle, but I am leaving you in the best possible hands."

I wanted the embrace to end, and I wanted to cling to this serious, solid fellow who had changed his plans without notice to see his younger brother to safety.

"Have a splendid journey," I said, clapping him on the back. "Smooth sailing and fair winds."

He let me go, kissed each lady on the cheek, and withdrew. A sense of focused energy left the room with him, and I was abruptly ready to sit again. I was capable of sleeping in a chair. I did not need my memories to confirm that fact.

"Come," the duchess said, possessing herself of my arm again. "The hour is late, the day has been interminable, and you need your rest."

"Yes, Mama."

Miss West took my other arm, and they escorted me to a comfortable parlor done up in green plaid. I was greeted by a small boy, whose scowl for some reason warmed my heart.

"I'm Atticus, and you ain't dicked in the nob, guv. You're just a might forget-ty sometimes. I'll get him to bed."

This pint-sized martinet's assurances were sufficient to see the ladies turn me over to his care. Miss West kissed my cheek—her scent was lusciously floral—while the duchess patted my arm.

"We'll have a tray sent up for your breakfast, Julian. Sleep as late as you like."

She seemed to want something from me, but in my fatigued state, all I had left were those manners she'd alluded to.

"My thanks. Good night, Miss West. Good night, Mama."

My tired eyes might have been playing tricks on me, but the duchess's gaze seemed to have acquired a suspicious shine. Miss West accompanied my mother from the room, and the boy Atticus glowered up at me.

"Did you read your card, guv? I made sure you had your card in your pocket, and when your wits go widdershins, you're supposed to read your card."

I half fell onto the sofa. "I read the card. God above, I am tired."

The boy went at my boots. "You nigh ruined these, and they are your good pair. You can't fall asleep on that sofa. You're a lordship, and lordships sleep in beds." He pulled off the second boot and glowered at it. "You shoulda never gone to Dover all on your lonesome. I'll learn to bloody drive a four-in-hand so you won't never get far from home with only a card a-tween you and the madhouse."

"Language, child." I yawned.

He disappeared into the next room. "Get yer arse in here, guv, and be quick about it."

I followed orders. I suspected I was good at following orders. "What has you in such a stir, young man?" I asked as I unbuttoned my jacket and waistcoat. "I'm told my memories always return in a matter of hours." Though what could possibly explain this cranky youngster serving as my valet?

"The memories have come back every other time," the lad replied, "but then there's this time and the next time." He disappeared into what was probably the dressing closet and emerged with a blue dressing gown. "You don't sleep in a nightshirt. You sleep in the altogether."

"In my present state, I would cheerfully sleep in a horse trough." We got me out of my clothes, I washed, the cool water a benediction beyond price, then I was abed in lavender-scented sheets. As I drifted into the arms of Morpheus, I thanked heaven for my family and marveled at the good fortune that had given me such loyal, fierce people to guard me in my hour of need.

I woke to the patter of rain on glass and to the knowledge that my world had changed irrevocably.

My mother loved me. She'd been ready to go best of three falls with Gideon Marchant over a bit of passing rudeness aimed in my direction. She'd hugged me—more than once—and when I'd called her *Mama*, she'd nearly preened and threatened to *hold me to it.*

She had not exhibited mere vestigial sentiments left over from the obligatory fondness a parent felt for a small offspring. She had shown me nothing less than mother-love, full and fierce, and her devotion had been hiding in plain sight for most of my adulthood.

Why and how had my relationship with Her Grace grown so stilted and uneasy? Even with my memories present and accounted for, I could not answer that question.

"You're awake." Atticus appeared in my bedroom doorway. "I'm Atticus. I do fer ya. You're Lord Julian."

"I know who I am, my boy, and that I had a bad spell last night, but you can cease fretting like a biddy hatching her only egg. I am quite myself this morning."

He squinted at me. "Who sits upon the throne of England?"

"That's a bit complicated. Mad George is king. His son, Fat

George, rules as Regent. Next question." I got out of bed, took down my dressing gown from the peg on the bedpost, and pretended to make a production out of scuffing into a pair of worn slippers. The relief in Atticus's dark eyes was that hard to behold.

"When's my next driving lesson?" he asked, advancing into the room and yanking up the bedcovers.

"As soon as the rain stops. Atticus, I am well. I was looked after by those who care about me. Your pocket card did its job. Skirmish concluded, victory to our side without casualties and without prisoners lost to the enemy. Now get to the kitchen, please, and find us a pot of China black and some sweet buns. I'm famished."

"I'm famished too," Atticus said. "I'll fetch yer tea and tell Miss West you've come right. 'Bout damned time too."

I permitted him a touch of rudeness born of battle nerves. He'd slept not on a cozy cot in the dressing closet, but on the parlor sofa, from which vantage point he'd been better able to guard my privacy.

"Atticus," I called as he bolted for the door.

"Aye, guv?" The caution was back, though banked.

"I meant what I said about your next driving lesson, and thank you for looking after me."

"'Tweren't nuffing." He slipped out the door as quietly as a leaf falls to earth.

By the time he returned, I was dressed but for my jacket. His haul from the kitchen included tea, sweet currant buns, ham-and-cheese tarts, and fresh orange slices, a feast fit for the gods to my hungry eyes. I took my portion to the balcony and left Atticus to break his fast while he put the bedroom to rights. He'd share a tray with me, but not *with me*, such was the dignity of my young tiger.

I could teach him to drive a four-in-hand, though my skills in that regard were merely adequate. Harry had been a noted whip, of course. Harry, whom it had been a guilty relief to have forgotten for a time.

I was pondering that admission when Hyperia appeared at the French door. "It's nigh freezing out, Jules. Are you that determined

on your dose of fresh air that you'd risk your death in this
weather?"

I rose and hugged her, and to blazes with anybody who might
have been spying. "Good morning, my dearest. I wanted some time to
think and consider recent revelations. We can discuss them in the
parlor if you'd prefer."

"The parlor is more private. This balcony is visible from the path
to the stables and from the back gardens."

Given the dreary weather, we weren't likely to be seen taking tea,
but Hyperia's caution was warranted. I was reminded of Gideon
Marchant's taunt—"You don't even know who I am, do you?"—and
his reputation as an *éminence grise* in Mayfair Society.

More of a tiresome gossip than any sort of eminence. I took my
tea into the parlor.

"Have you broken your fast?" I asked.

"I did, as did Her Grace. Nobody seems to be aware of your
condition last night."

"Marchant kept his mouth shut, then?" I gestured her to the sofa,
retrieved the tray from the bedroom, and noted that Atticus had left
two tarts and a sweet bun untouched. I brought the remains to the
parlor and set the tray on the low table.

"Mr. Marchant has kept his mouth shut for now. An aspiring MP
doesn't risk the wrath of a duke, much less a duchess with your mother's connections. How are you, Jules?"

I took the place beside her, poured a second cup, fixed it with a
dollop of honey, as Perry preferred it, and passed her the tea.

"I am in something of a muddle, to be honest."

"Give it time. Your memories are always restored to you in fairly
short order." She sipped her tea, then sipped again.

I'd got the honey right, apparently. "My memories have reported
for duty, but when they went absent without leave, some long-held
notions went missing with them."

She set down her cup. "What sort of long-held notions?"

"Inaccurate ones, regarding my mother." The conversation was about to reflect poorly on me, but this was my dear Perry, who'd dismissed Marchant from her presence like a queen disgusted with an unruly page.

"You and Her Grace are cordial," Hyperia said, taking one of the tarts. "You always have been."

"Not so. When I was a small boy, we were close. My four-leaf clovers, my skinned knees, my imaginary dragons, and little-boy dreams were all entrusted to her. Papa came in for his share of confidences, too, but my mother was devoted to her children, and to me among them."

"You are not a little boy anymore, Jules."

"True, though when I am without my memories, I am as helpless as a child, as vulnerable. Her Grace, ably abetted by your lovely self and dear Arthur, was ready to do battle with the whole French army on my behalf. She wasn't embarrassed by my situation, wasn't inconvenienced by it, wasn't the least bit ashamed of me."

"Of course not. You cannot be held responsible for a malady that—"

I took Hyperia's hand. "That malady leaves me embarrassed and ashamed, Perry, as irrational as I know those sentiments to be. If my family shunned me, they'd have half of Mayfair's blessing for doing so. I have fashioned an opinion of Her Grace that is unfair and inaccurate, labeling her an indifferent mother, when, if I can view her objectively, she is anything but."

"That's good that you can see her in a better light." Hyperia's observation held a question: Where was I going with these peregrinations?

"Perry, just before I left for Dover, Her Grace told me to cease investigating the missing letters. I recall that very clearly and recall seething with outrage that she'd dismiss me while you, Atticus, and anybody with a window looked on."

"Don't forget Atlas."

My horse, my noble steed, whom Arthur would surely see returned to me. "Exactly so. She delivered this blow to my self-regard publicly and unequivocally, though she is a woman who values her reputation, her privacy, and the regard of her friends."

"She values you as well," Hyperia said slowly. "Ah."

"Precisely. She might weather a tempest of gossip about an old affair, might even be able to smile about her own misguided folly. She would not, however, countenance harm to me. I see that now. We thus know that the threats have started, threats that include intended harm to me, and that is progress."

Hyperia let go of my hand and stood. "Progress, of a sort, and also a serious problem, Jules. Arthur, God willing, should soon be on the Continent, and his consequence won't be available to protect you or your mother. Whoever stole her letters put the fear of ruin in her—your ruin and hers, at least, and let's assume mine as well. Her Grace told you to desist, and having puzzled out her motivations, how can you do anything other than as she asks?"

Fair question, and the answer was already at hand. "My mother protected me last night, Perry, as you and Arthur did, and Atticus as well, in his slightly alarming fashion. This looking-out-for-family business is supposed to go both ways. It's still the case that Mrs. Whittington, who is apparently without family, and Lady Barrington, who cannot rely on her family, are also at risk of harm. At the least, I must ask Her Grace to rethink her decision to capitulate to these threats."

"You want to know exactly how the threats were conveyed, because you believe that will point to their source."

"True." The more awkward inquiry was harder to put into words: What had driven a wedge between my mother and me? When had it started, and why? That wedge had been a painful burden to me and doubtless to Her Grace as well. My illegitimacy figured into the mix somewhere, but pinpointing when and how was difficult.

"I wish we'd never come here," Hyperia said, resuming her place beside me. "This has all been a strain on you, and what should be a matter of some missing letters has bloomed into a small war with an enemy we cannot see. If it turns out this whole affair is the result of

Lady Canderport's hurt feelings, I will see her banished to the Outer Hebrides before Yuletide."

"With my blessing, but we've acquired a weapon of which the enemy remains ignorant," I said. Not the sort of weapon Wellington had aimed at his foes, but rather, the sort of weapon a reconnaissance officer had relied on for his very life. "Given Her Grace's behavior, her protectiveness on my behalf, we now operate with a degree of trust that at least on my part was missing previously. I hope that makes a difference to Her Grace."

Hyperia slipped an arm around my waist. "You called her Mama last night, Jules. She was in tears before we reached her apartment. She blamed it on fatigue and the tribulations of the day, but those were tears only a parent could cry for her dear child."

For me. My mother had cried for me. My throat felt unaccountably tight at the thought. I pretended to take another sip of my tea, but the cup was as empty as my heart was full.

My mother was at her correspondence when I sailed into her boudoir. To my surprise, she was wearing spectacles, which gave her a quizzical, bookish appearance.

"My lord, good morning." She removed her eyeglasses and folded them into a velvet-lined case that might have been intended to resemble a music box. "To knock before entering a lady's room is customary."

Wisherd was nowhere to be seen, but then, the morning had advanced past the breakfast hour.

"My apologies," I said. "Good day, Your Grace. I come on a matter of some urgency, and you may be assured that my memories have accompanied me." Some of them surprisingly happy. "Let us resolve the little matter of finding your letters before we proceed on to items of a familial nature."

She rose and shooed me into the parlor. "The letters don't signify. I hope you recall my telling you as much."

"You meant for half the assemblage to see you relieving me of command, as it were, even knowing that a public exchange would humiliate me far more than any private conversation could have. Why be so cavalier with my pride, Your Grace?"

I'd felt her arms around me. I'd seen the tears gathering in her eyes mere hours ago. Without that evidence, I would never have believed this reserved, nigh haughty woman was the mother who'd so generously offered me refuge.

The duchess was back on her mettle.

And so was I.

"I was not cavalier with your lordship's pride. You were shortly to depart for Dover. Time was of the essence lest you poke about the stationers' shops unnecessarily. If I spoke plainly, I did so in the interest of getting you on your way."

I tended to give my mother a wide berth, even in the literal sense, and thus I generally beheld her at some distance. Standing nearly toe-to-toe, my superior height was evident. I did not loom over her, but neither did I yield the floor.

"You were threatened," I said quietly. "You were threatened in such a manner that you feared continuing to search for the letters would bring harm to me. You ordered me to desist because you'd rather face scandal and blackmail on your own than put me at risk of the smallest harm. You put yourself between me and danger."

She scowled at my cravat pin, which featured the Caldicott lion rampant wrought in gold. "How can you know these things?"

I had made logical deductions, but those deductions had been informed by her scathing rebuke to Marchant, her immediate acceptance of my loss of memory, and her embraces. The most dangerous creature in the wild was not the lion intent on bringing down his supper or besting a rival, it was the lioness defending her cub.

"I know you were threatened on my behalf because I pay attention," I said. "Shall we sit, or would you prefer to continue this argument on our feet?"

Her scowl acquired a hint of bewilderment. "Have a seat. The letters truly are of no moment, my lord."

Call me Julian. Except that we weren't through with our first argument, and one wanted to bring a certain order to one's campaign.

"The letters matter," I said, taking a seat on the sofa and patting the cushion beside me. "They give some malcontent control over your reputation and the reputations of Lady Barrington and Mrs. Whittington. You are a duchess, and you might weather the talk with little damage, but Mrs. Whittington does not enjoy your standing or your means. Lady Barrington has step-daughters in need of husbands. For all I know, Lady Canderport is tippling madly because she, too, has been threatened, and she also has a daughter who needs every advantage in Society to make a decent match."

Her Grace took a seat at my side. "Next, you'll imply that Napoleon will escape from St. Helena if the letters aren't found."

"Harm will befall innocents, and while I esteem your maternal devotion highly, and thank you for it sincerely, I am a man grown and capable of defending myself—most days. Please tell me how the threat was conveyed to you."

"If I tell you that, you will hare off to peek under mattresses and lurk at keyholes, and I refuse to put your life at risk because I was foolish years ago."

"*My life* was threatened?"

She muttered something rude in French, which she'd been raised to speak as well as English.

Ye gods and little fishes, such stubbornness. I left the parlor for the boudoir, opened the little box that held her spectacles, and extracted a quarter sheet of foolscap folded in fourths.

Call off your hound, or you shall have a dead dog on your hands.

I brought the note back to the sitting room and held it up to the rain-spattered window. "No watermark. Cheap foolscap such as any household has in quantity." I sniffed the paper, but no particular aroma came through, and the ink was merely black. "Where did you find it?"

"You were always headstrong, in your quiet way. Arthur was dignified, Harry loud, but you kept your manners about you. You went up to bed when told to, and then you'd sneak back down to the library and read until all hours."

A diversionary tactic. She'd be sending her cavalry around my flank if I didn't make my next volleys count. "I often could not sleep, and I like to read, a predilection inherited from my mother. Please explain how this note was conveyed to you, or I will be compelled to question Wisherd."

"I found it in one of my riding boots when Wisherd brought them up from belowstairs. She insists that I use boot trees to keep the leather supple, and there it was."

Meaning the entire household, servants, guests, family, temporary hires from Town, and even the outside staff could have put the note into that boot. Somebody had chosen well.

"When did you find it?"

"The night before last, though I'm sure my boots sat about in the servants' hall for most of a day before Wisherd remembered to retrieve them. The threat to your life is plain, my lord. Continue investigating, and your mortal existence is in peril."

I resumed the place beside my mother on the sofa, lest I start pacing. "My life was in peril every day I served in uniform." Or every day I served in disguise. For much of my military tenure, I'd been a tinker's assistant, a drover, a farrier, a shepherd discharged for drunkenness, a French deserter, an English deserter...

"But you knew then who your enemy was and why you fought." The duchess glowered at the scrap of paper in my hand. "Arthur might well choose to reside on foreign shores for all the rest of his days. Harry has gone to his reward. I cannot lose you over stupid letters written to a stupid woman."

Such bitterness, such self-recrimination, was intolerable. "In the name of all that is dignified, you shall not refer to *my mother* as stupid. Sentimental, perhaps. Lonely in mourning, certainly. Overly trusting, maybe on rare occasion. Papa had gone to his reward, Harry and I were seldom at the Hall, and you encountered an attractive, talented man who listened to your dreams and woes, who appeared delighted to spend time with you, and whom you had no reason to suspect of bad motives. I see no stupidity in a temporary romantic indulgence."

The duchess patted my knee. "Never has a show of support sounded so much like a scold, but thank you. I was lonely, and Pickering was perfect, blast him. He read me poetry and brought me roses. Even his stationery was scented with roses, and he sang to me and played the violin beneath my window. Your father wasn't the roses-and-serenades type."

If she referred to the duke, he also wasn't my father. Maybe someday Her Grace and I would get around to having that donnybrook as well.

"Pickering offered you romance when you thought your last chance for romance had passed."

She peered at me with a brooding expression. "I suppose... yes. I was easily charmed. Now I am aware that a life is easily taken, my lord, and no scandal, no gossip, no toll Society could exact on my good name is worth risking your wellbeing."

I considered again the scrap of paper in my hand. "My life isn't in danger." This was an opinion, not a fact, but a strongly held opinion.

"For pity's sake, my lord, that is a threat. If you continue investigating, you will be killed."

"This is a threat," I replied slowly, "also a puzzle. Assume you are the sort of embittered soul who watches from the fringes as Society whirls along. It comes to your notice that three widows have found discreet consolation in unlikely places. You have proof of their liaisons, and each woman has access to some wealth or social influence. You crave to have that wealth and influence used for your own ends. What is your next move?"

The duchess rubbed her temples. "You want me to play chess, and I want to follow Arthur to France."

Please not France. "Do you threaten somebody who has only a very slight chance of locating that proof, or do you threaten the people with the money and influence?"

"Both? I don't know, and frankly, I do not care. Let them have the rubbishing letters. I never cared much for Mayfair in spring anyhow, and the few whom I consider genuine friends don't either."

My mother was exasperated, while I was bewildered. I had leaped to the conclusion that blackmail was in the offing—why else steal proof of three different romances involving three different Society widows? But the thief wasn't acting like a blackmailer—or wasn't acting like a blackmailer yet.

"How do you, Lady Barrington, and Mrs. Whittington know one another?"

Her Grace sat up. "Hellie and I... I knew her when she was married to her first husband, but we grew friendlier when the viscount and His Grace served together on some parliamentary committee or other. Carola's husband served on the same committee in an advisory capacity. Corruption in the military, abuse of command, those sorts of issues. Tedious, thankless, necessary work. His Grace said that whether some pilfering second lieutenant was ever brought to justice wasn't the point. The threat of investigation would make a prudent criminal think twice and go back to picking pockets rather than bilking the Navy of gunpowder."

Whatever committee Papa had served on, they'd had their hands full.

The British military had been the largest customer for nearly everything produced on Albion's shores, from mules to munitions, from wool to wheat, from cooking pots to candles. While war raged, fortunes had flowed from public coffers into private hands at a tremendous rate.

Ensuring that John Bull received value for his coin had been a hit-or-miss proposition, as any infantryman marching in a threadbare uniform had known.

"If you can think of any other connection between you and the other two ladies, please let me know," I said. "You are all widows. You are all well-received in Society. Your husbands apparently knew one another in more than passing, and there must be other common ground as well."

I rose, a sense of urgency descending upon me. "I'm off to confer with Lady Canderport."

The duchess got to her feet as well. "My lord, I have asked, I have ordered, and now I am begging you—let this go. You will make a widow of Miss West before you make her a bride, and that would be a tragedy."

A low and telling shot, but I was primed to return fire. "Do you recall how determined you were last night to see me safely through an episode of lost memory? You were ready to plant Marchant two facers, to blacken both of his eyes, and make a good start on blackening his reputation because he poked fun at me when I was defenseless."

"Gideon apologized to me again this morning, and he will not presume in such a manner *ever* again."

The man had likely groveled, and well he should have. "You still want to kick him where it counts."

"Provided I can first put on a pair of jackboots. The sheer rudeness, the barefaced, crass, lumpen, loutish, contemptible, coarse, oafish—"

"I feel the same indignation, Your Grace, twenty times over, when I think that somebody presumes to threaten the peace of a woman I esteem very highly indeed. Somebody is threatening *my mama*, and I am compelled by honor, instinct, and filial devotion to protect her. I will be careful. Hyperia and Atticus will keep a watch on me, you will, too, and even Wisherd will support our cause. Between us, we can foil this enemy."

She studied me for a long moment, her gaze unreadable. "Such stubbornness. You get that from your father. Very well, but be careful, sir. The flames of hell will be as nothing compared to my wrath if you come to harm, and much of that wrath will be directed at you."

"Understood. Any final orders before I find Lady Canderport?"

"Marry Miss West. She deserves the protection of your name, and the two of you aren't as discreet as you think yourselves."

"Our courtship remains a work in progress, Your Grace. I'll see you at luncheon." I resisted the temptation to salute and marched smartly from the room.

CHAPTER SIXTEEN

I found Lady Canderport easily enough. She answered my knock, opening the door to her own sitting room.

"If my lord is looking for Charles, he's off reading poetry to some young ladies. Lottie is supposed to be among them, but I do not flatter myself that your lordship is in search of my daughter."

A bit blunt, which I appreciated. "As it happens, I'd like to speak with you, my lady, if you can spare me a few moments."

She stepped back and gestured me into the room. "I did not steal Mrs. Whittington's brooch or locket or whatever. I cannot vouch as confidently for my offspring." Her words were laced with resignation and fatigue, also a touch of despair. "Do have a seat, my lord."

I closed the door and took a wing chair. The accommodations were certainly clean and comfortable, but somebody had taken a notion to decorate in pink and white plaid with red accents. The carpet was pink bordered with red and burgundy, and the carnations on the sideboard offered more pink and white.

The parlor was fairly bright thanks to French doors and two windows, but the abundance of pink gave the room an unsettling quality, as if her ladyship and I occupied the inside of a young girl's jewelry box or workbasket.

"Lottie claims we were put in these quarters as a test of our nerves," Lady Canderport said. "My theory is that a daughter of the house in some previous generation was excessively fond of pink, and this scheme was an attempt to cure her of her fancies. Pink requires moderation. Pink plaid is positively diabolical."

"Different, certainly. Would you prefer a stroll in the gallery?"

"With the weather turning up chilly, half the guests will be wandering about the gallery, the conservatory, or the music room. Here will do. I rang for a tray a good quarter hour ago, and—"

A tap on the door heralded the arrival of a footman bearing the requested service. Her ladyship took the end of the sofa closest to my chair and prepared to pour out.

"Hellie has done her usual excellent job as hostess," Lady Canderport said. "The tea will be hot, the biscuits fresh. How do you like yours?"

"Plain for me."

She navigated the tea tray easily, no slight tremor to her hands. Her eyes were not bloodshot, and no face powder covered tiny veins on her nose or cheeks. She did not doctor her tea with tipple, and as to that, when she leaned close enough to me that I might have caught a whiff of spirits on her breath, I did not.

No spirits, and no parsley, mint, or lemon to disguise sour aromas.

She stirred honey into her tea and regarded me frankly. "You are here in pursuit of a private word with another guest. One doesn't want to give offense, my lord, but you were not on my schedule."

"What was on your schedule?"

Her smile was wan. "Peace and quiet, a solitary cup of tea, possibly a nap. Odd, how simple our comforts become when the years begin to accumulate. I have listened to my children argue nearly nonstop for going on twenty years, and while I love them to distraction, the noise wears on one."

"Will you miss it when they leave the nest?"

"Do you miss military life?"

She asked a surprisingly difficult question. "For much of my time in the army, I did not bide in camp or at headquarters. I moved about on my own. If you refer to camaraderie in the officers' mess or the high spirits at a regimental ball, those did not figure prominently in my experience."

"But here you are again, moving about on your own. You need not be delicate with me, my lord. If you suspect that Lottie or Charles has taken Mrs. Whittington's jewelry, you are welcome to search their rooms. They are cleverer than they seem, though, particularly when they put their heads together. They would know enough to hide any stolen goods in somebody else's quarters."

"In your quarters, for example?"

She wrinkled her nose. "One certainly hopes not, but possibly. My children are clever, not brilliant."

"I doubt your children are thieves and will leave it to you to search their quarters if you think that necessary. I am more concerned that you might bear ill will toward some of the other lady guests."

Her expression turned puzzled. "I am too busy managing a pair of rapscallions to spare the effort for ill will. Do I envy Hellie her lovely house and devoted husband? Yes. Would I like to be aging as splendidly as Her Grace and have my daughter matched with an earl? Of course. Does Gideon Marchant's sniping annoy me? Most certainly. Very well, but am I ill-natured or simply human, my lord?"

I sipped my tea and mentally regrouped. Lady Canderport was not an embittered, flighty sot. She was coping with challenges and a trifle short on graciousness, but long campaigns rendered the best soldiers footsore and weary in spirit.

"Somebody stole personal letters from Her Grace and an item of equally sentimental value from Lady Barrington. The letters are not incriminating, but they are private correspondence. Whoever has these items could cause Her Grace and Lady Barrington considerable embarrassment."

She dipped a biscuit in her tea. "One assumes the same about Mrs. Whittington's missing item, then. It probably has the wrong initials beneath the inscription or came from the wrong shop on Ludgate Hill. My grandmother told me that beauty is a very mixed blessing, and I would have opportunities to appreciate the advantages of an unremarkable appearance. She was right."

Lady Canderport wasn't plain, exactly. Her attire was fashionable, if understated, her features regular. Her chin was a trifle weak, and her eyes merely brown. She wore her hair in a coronet of braids, and her figure was matronly rather than plump.

Another not-quite lady. Not quite memorable, not quite forgettable. "What does thievery have to do with a woman's appearance?" I asked.

"Your mother apparently misplaced love letters, my lord. Lady Barrington's missing item of a sentimental nature might be more romantic correspondence or a diary or journal of some sort. Mrs. Whittington's brooch or locket somehow embarrasses her as well, or we'd not be hearing from every chambermaid and underfootman that they're to keep an eye out for it. A delightful excuse for the lot of them to snoop, by the way, and yet, the trinket hasn't been found."

She took a bite from the soggy portion of her biscuit. "I was never importuned," she went on. "Not by the handsome bachelors, not by charming fortune hunters. Not as a young lady, a wife, or a widow, and thus I am free from the worry that must be plaguing your mother now."

She dunked her biscuit again and took another bite. Her attitude struck me as neither gloating nor bitter, but simply complaisant.

"You weren't tempted to leaven your mourning with a little flirtation?"

She shook a drop of tea from her dripping biscuit. "I had two small children to tend to, and my means were quite constrained until my grandmother died, Lord Canderport's papa being nothing short of a miser. To the extent that flirtation can lead to marriage, I was not, and am

not, interested. I esteemed my husband greatly and mourned him properly, but one marriage has sufficed for me. The answer to your question,
my lord, is no. No flirtations, no flings, no discreet liaisons of any sort."

"Were overtures of that nature made to you?"

A portion of her sopping biscuit fell into her tea. "Why would I
answer such a rude question about the distant past?"

Was she evading my query or reacting as any proper lady might?
"I apologize for the nature of my inquiry, but it bears on the missing
items. Each lady is widowed and found consolation in the person of a
fellow who showed up during her mourning. You are widowed,
acquainted with all three women, and like Lady Barrington, you have
a daughter to launch."

"Somebody is trying to blackmail Her Grace?" Lady Canderport
put the remains of her soggy biscuit into her mouth. "Very forward of
them, and why wait all these years to do it? That a duchess mis-
stepped years ago is interesting, but hardly compelling. Why not
threaten to expose her peccadillo before she emerges from mourning,
or just as she's resuming her place in Society?"

Put that way, I had to agree that the timing of this spree of
larceny was curious.

"I do not confirm your characterization of events," I said, "but
neither do I deny it."

"Carola was sporting about with some doting dandy a few years
back. I recall that much. She wasn't flaunting him, of course, but I
took the children for an ice, and there she was, laughing despite
wearing weeds. One envied her. He would have been good-looking if
he'd not gone in so thoroughly for the starched shirt points, lace cuffs,
and an elaborate cravat."

"Did you warn her that her deportment might be noted?"

Her ladyship chose another biscuit. "Warn her? I would have
applauded her daring, had the children not been present. She'd been
married to some old general and made a go of it, by all accounts. If a
woman cannot enjoy some freedom in widowhood, then she must

resign herself to spending her whole life as an unpaid domestic servant, must she not?"

Truly, the late Lord Canderport had not impressed his lady wife.

"I do recall that Hellie had a fling, too, now that you mention it." She dunked another biscuit and dispatched the whole thing.

"If asked, I will deny mentioning any such thing."

This smile was a bit brighter and revealed an attractiveness I would not have suspected. "You didn't need to. I heard she was also seen at Gunter's, but I forget who spotted them. She was on the arm of another tall, dark, and handsome admirer." The smile faded, and her ladyship regarded me with uncomfortable intensity. "You must sort this out, my lord. Three women, three handsome admirers, and now three incidents of theft."

"A plethora of coincidences, when what I need are logical deductions and solid evidence."

"And you were hoping I could provide you some of the latter. Sorry to disappoint. My widow's portion is quite modest. Papa-in-law is quite the pinchpenny. I would not interest a blackmailer on those grounds alone. Charles doesn't even have leave to use the courtesy title yet, that's how miserly his dear grandpapa is."

She took a considering sip of her tea. "I should be grateful that the children and relative poverty kept me safe from any philanderers, but then, I was never the romantic sort, and neither was my husband. He did nearly name our son Charlemagne—that was his late lordship's given name—but my grandmother noted that French associations might not serve the boy in our bellicose age. The derivative Charles had to suffice. My younger daughter was Charlene, though we lost her at two. Scarlet fever."

"I am sorry for your loss, my lady." I murmured the requisite platitude, and I meant the condolences sincerely. "Lady Ophelia quit the gathering in part because old losses haunt her in autumn."

"One suspected. The boy... Peter? No, Patrick. Once a child turns five, you breathe a little easier, and then they turn seven, and you hope surely the worst dangers are past. But they aren't, not for some of them. I remind myself of this every time the twins pluck my last nerve. Families argue and bicker and spat—that's normal—but we must treasure even the noise. This is gloomy talk, my lord."

"You worry about your children." She wasn't merely afflicted by her offspring, or bothered by them, she genuinely cared for their welfare.

"Charles has a good head on his shoulders, and when the right young lady catches his eye, he will cease involving himself in Lottie's wilder schemes, but my daughter is neither beautiful nor wealthy. I was content with my lot when life dealt me the same cards, but add bored and resentful to the list, and trouble is bound to follow."

I finished my tea and peered at the dregs. "The flasks belong to Lottie?"

Her ladyship grimaced at her tea cup. "You are supposed to conclude that they belong to me, because they do."

Well, of course. "Lottie tipples, and because you know that could be disastrous to her future, you do what you can to cast suspicion on yourself rather than on her."

Her ladyship sent a disgruntled glance toward the closed door. "I cannot reason with the girl, because she is justified in half of her pique and frustration. Frittering away most of the year on shallow entertainments is honestly boring, and holding out matrimony as the only worthy objective for young women of intelligence and ambition is unfair and wasteful. Lottie raises a figurative fist to all the stupid rules every time she takes a sip. I understand this, and yet, she does not know the risks she runs."

This last was said plaintively, a mother's lament. Lottie sounded in many particulars as if she and Lord Drayson were compatible spirits, equally oppressed and vexed by their elders' conventions, but I could not recommend Drayson as a suitor.

"Do you resent that Lady Barrington and Her Grace aren't taking a matchmaking hand with your Lottie?"

Her ladyship set down her tea cup. "Not now. Two years ago,

they might have been helpful, but my daughter is not aiding her own cause. Has the bit between her teeth, as the equestrians say."

"What if you declared that your efforts to find Lottie a husband were at an end?"

"I cannot give up, my lord. What I have to leave Lottie won't be enough to maintain her in the style she deserves, and Charles should not be saddled with his maiden sister for all eternity. The earldom is far from wealthy, the opposite in fact, and that assumes Charles lives long enough to inherit from his infernally vigorous grandpapa."

"I'm not suggesting you consign Lottie to the bleakest moors. Simply tell her that you are no longer engaged in the futile effort to find her a match. I have good reason to suspect that Charles and Miss Frampton enjoy each other's company, and that will leave Lottie the odd man out, so to speak."

"Ignore her. My husband used to tell me that all the time, and then he'd bring her a new storybook and give it to her whether she'd been naughty for half the day or sweet."

"May I ask if Lord Canderport aspired to serve in Parliament in any meaningful capacity?"

"Committee work, you mean? A stint in the lower house while waiting for the earl to stick his spoon in the wall? My husband dreaded the very notion of politics. That nonsense would have cramped his socializing considerably."

Not *our* socializing, *his* socializing. The distinction was not lost on me, and thus I steered the discussion back to more relevant topics.

"I'm suggesting only that you ignore Lottie's marital prospects. Let her notice that her friends are all making matches, that Charles and Miss Frampton could be next. That the house-party invitations are over for the year, and winters can be long and lonely." Or peaceful and sweet. "Give the young lady a chance to do some growing up, in other words, and time to decide for herself if marriage has any appeal."

"I have tried just about every other strategy," Lady Canderport said. "I suppose a temporary retreat deserves consideration."

"The Russians retreated all the way to Moscow and beyond," I said, rising. "Look how that turned out for Napoleon." The tsar's generals had drawn the emperor and his exhausted army straight into the face of a Russian winter, and disease and privation had achieved a victory more decisive than any the Russians had managed on the battlefields.

Her ladyship rose. "Thank you, my lord, for your suggestion. I hope you can find what's gone missing. I would not call myself warmly disposed toward your mother, nor she toward me, but I have no reason to wish her or any other guest ill."

"Does your goodwill extend to Lady Jessamine?"

"Even Lottie has found reason to criticize Lady Jess, and one feels for her step-mother."

We parted on that note, though the conversation left me frustrated. Surely, surely, I'd thought, Lady Canderport would admit to having been charmed by a handsome stranger and to having recently lost a memento of that romantic interlude.

Surely not, apparently, and I believed her. Her unsentimental attitudes, her lack of beauty, her lack of means, and even her late husband's weak allure had all conspired to make her ladyship nigh untemptable when it came to romantic liaisons.

I sorted similarities and differences all the way to the stable, a raw wind hampering my progress. All four ladies were widowed, three had titles, one did not. All four ladies were past youth, only one had remarried. All four ladies had married somewhat flawed men, three of those husbands had had parliamentary connections, one had avoided the mention of same. One was childless, three had daughters, two had daughters yet to be wed. Two had been abandoned by their lovers, one had gently sent hers packing. The fourth had disdained intimate consolations altogether.

I was getting nowhere with my search for facts and evidence, but I was forming a better picture of why my dear Hyperia might be skittish about marriage, even to a fellow who genuinely esteemed her. What sort of father sought to name every one of his children after himself, for example? What sort of husband preferred port and cigars with his parliamentary cronies night after night to the occasional quiet evening with his lady wife?

Somewhere in the middle of these ruminations, I became aware that Arthur had taken ship. The hour was noon or thereabouts, and my certainty was a matter of a hollow feeling low in the belly, almost a homesickness. I hadn't known the exact day or hour of Harry's passing, but I would have bet my grandfather's watch that Arthur's packet had just that moment filled its sails and begun the crossing to France.

"Fare thee well, brother mine, and safe journey home."

I wandered idly between the rows of loose boxes, trying to gather up the thoughts that awareness of Arthur's departure had scattered. No Atlas, no Arthur, no answers... as many differences as similarities among the victims, and too many potential malefactors.

I was standing outside the stall of Gideon Marchant's wayward gray—aptly named Ruffian— when it occurred to me that the three gallants, for want of a better term—the dashing diplomat, the doting dandy, and the flirting flutist—had all traveled under the name John or one of its many derivatives.

What else did *the three gallants* have in common, besides being tall, dark, and—to varying extents—dishonorable?

"That 'un didn't want to come in this morning," Atticus said, joining me outside Ruffian's stall. "Up on his back legs, buckin' and kickin' like perdition when Jean tried to bring him in. Nearly clocked Jean on the head rearin' at the gate."

Behavior like that passed rudeness and qualified as dangerous. "What set him off?"

"Nuffing. Jean was leading the horse to the gate, all placid and ready to come outta the wet, and then Ruffian took a fright. Jean says it were demons only the horse can see. I say the beast is too old for that nonsense."

The horse, whose coat was still dampish, munched his hay with every appearance of calm. "He's not young." In fact, the contour of the gelding's eye suggested mature years. Though handsome and doubtless fit enough for his job, Ruffian was no youngster. I opened his stall door and had a look in the horse's mouth.

"What you doin', guv? You want your fingers bit off?"

"A horse's teeth keep growing throughout his life. If he's constantly eating grass, he wears them down almost as quickly as they grow, but later in life, the teeth can be quite long. I'd put this horse's age, given the length and shape of his teeth, at past twenty."

Hardly a fashionable mount, but then, I hoped to be riding Atlas into our mutual dotage. Not a realistic aspiration, of course.

"Then he's going senile," Atticus said. "He had quite a tantrum, and Jean has wicked rope burns to show for it."

A strong, skilled rider could handle a horse who bolted, but a horse that reared, bucked, kicked... Marchant must be very attached to his Ruffian to keep that sort of mount in his stable.

I let the horse return to his pile of hay and left the stall, being very careful to latch the half door behind me.

"Keep your distance from this one," I said. "I mean that, Atticus. If he kicks out unexpectedly, he could snap your neck. Don't take him to the water trough. Don't hold him for the farrier. Don't offer to groom him because you have idle time on your hands. Jean handles horses all day every day, and Ruffian got the better of him."

"I'm too busy to have idle time on my hands." Said with bashful pride.

"Polishing boots?"

"Polishing boots. Tuppence a pair, and I'm up to sixpence in me pocket. Another sixpence and I'll have a whole shillin'."

On the one hand, I admired the boy's initiative. On the other... "Atticus, where is your coat?" I hadn't seen him in proper outer wear for some time, come to think of it.

The question earned me a fleeting scowl. "Ain't that cold, guv. Don't need a coat indoors, anyways."

The stable wasn't especially cold, but neither was it indoors. If Atticus had been busily sweeping the aisle or currying the mud off a horse, he'd be warm enough. Standing in the damp draft, he had to be chilly.

"Listen to me, my boy, because the shame belongs to those who are fleecing you. The dice were loaded, and you thought the mild weather would last forever. You were supposed to think that. Somebody suggested you bet your coat, a safe bet. You lost. Thank heavens you had the sense to leave the game before you had to surrender your boots and stockings."

"Wasn't going to bet me boots. I ain't stupid."

"No, but you are young, and the game is old. When the time comes for us to leave, you will be offered a proposition: You get your coat back in exchange for every penny in your pocket." New recruits were swindled in this same fashion almost as a rite of passage. "You did the work for the valets and boot boy, but you *earn* nothing except perhaps a sniffle. Whoever stole your coat gets *paid* for doing nothing, unless enticing you to gamble took some effort."

Which it likely had not.

Atticus scuffed a toe in the dirt, glowered at Ruffian, and then up at me. "Where can I get me summa them loaded dice?"

"Good question, but just this once I will offer a different solution. I will find you another coat, and you will return to Caldicott Hall with coin in your pocket. Whoever thought to trick you out of your coin will have a coat he can never wear and you will have your wages, but there is a price, Atticus."

He sniffed. "I'd rather have me own loaded dice."

"That way lies danger and dishonor, though I understand your frustration. Tell me who inveigled you into rolling the dice."

Another sniff. "Drayson's valet. Murray. Grouchiest old besom I ever did come across, but then he turns up all friendly after supper is served. I shoulda known he was up to something."

The entire adult staff had doubtless known, but Drayson was a lordling, and rank belowstairs derived from rank abovestairs. Nobody had warned Atticus, and nobody would peach on Drayson's man.

"And you've been cleaning Lord Drayson's boots?"

"Twice. He's allus tramping to the lake and back or off admiring nature. Murray snickers when he says that. Did Marchant's the once. Might do them again tonight if he went out today."

On the Sabbath and a miserable Sabbath at that? "Hoard your coins, my boy. Keep them in my jewelry box. They will be safer there than in your pocket."

I could see this Murray fellow thinking it acceptable to literally turn a defenseless lad's pockets out when Atticus showed no interest in redeeming his coat. Murray might well have been responsible for sending Drayson into Hyperia's sitting room, come to that.

I abruptly needed to know more about Drayson's valet, and the best person to educate me was another valet, a friendly, decent chap who had already offered to be of service to me. Upon returning to the house, I put in a request to Lady Barrington for the loan of a boy's plain, sturdy coat and took myself in search of Hyperia.

Before embarking on another sortie in the name of evidence and logical deductions, I would confer with my superior officer and gain the benefit of her wise counsel.

CHAPTER SEVENTEEN

"Lady Canderport had nothing to add," I said as Hyperia opened the cover over the piano keys. "She did not avail herself of any romantic consolations during mourning, and she hasn't since, to hear her tell it."

We had the music room to ourselves, for the nonce. I had closed the door, and if anybody asked, my motivation would have been to keep the heat of the desultory fire in the room and to keep the din of a duet rehearsal muted. At a guess, I'd say MacFadden's criticism of the flue was warranted. The room bore a faint odor of peat, and the roses in the porcelain bowl on the closed lid of the piano were drooping.

"Her ladyship admitted the details of her past to you?" Hyperia settled on the piano bench and began leafing through music stacked beside the rack.

I lit a few more sconces and poked some life into the fire. "Her ladyship was quite candid. I would not call her coldhearted—she's devoted to her children—but she's pragmatic. Her Grace, Lady Barrington, and Mrs. Whittington have reason to be concerned. Lady Canderport acknowledges the validity of their fears and, out of good sportsmanship or whatever you ladies call fair play, hopes they emerge from the situation unscathed. She doesn't consider the other ladies friends, but neither are they her enemies."

"She saves her sentimentality for her children. I caught Lady Jess trying to inveigle Miss Frampton and Lottie into smoking a cheroot. Miss Bivens was their lookout, but her nose was in a book when I strolled into the conservatory."

"Lady Jessamine needs a firmer hand on the reins."

Hyperia paused in her search for music. "You never experimented with cheroots and brandy and such?"

"I did, but my partner in mischief was usually Harry, and we were both eager and willing. I take exception to coercing innocents into folly against their better judgment." I went on to explain about Atticus's brush with Drayson's trickster valet.

"I suppose it's part of a boy's education," Hyperia said. "It's certainly part of a girl's."

What could she...? "You mean a young lady's? A new widow's?"

"Those new widows were vulnerable, Jules. Lonely, at sea, living a very reduced life before they expected to. Along comes this tall, dark, and handsome charmer, and in each case, he's exactly what the lady needs in a consolation."

"And he's traveling under some variant of the name John." I took the place beside Hyperia on the lower register end of the piano bench. "Is that coincidence—Johns are everywhere in the land of John Bull—or significant?"

"Coincidence, I'd say."

"I've focused almost exclusively on the victims, Perry. What did they have in common? Now I'm asking what the lovers had in common."

"Appearance," she said. "All tall or tallish, all dark-haired, all fair of face."

"Ian used lifts on his boots, according to Her Grace. Hans's hair was auburn, John was brown-haired, and Her Grace described Ian as having sable hair. Not quite black."

"Sun can give dark hair reddish highlights, and Lady Barrington encountered her Hans during shooting season, which starts in high summer. Sable is a version of brown."

"Very well, all three were tall, dark-haired, and handsome," I said, "but one was a skilled musician, while the other two appear to have been idle gentlemen."

"An aspiring diplomat isn't quite idle, but he is a gentleman." Hyperia set some music on the rack and laid her hands on the keyboard. "One and two and three and..."

She began to play the *primo* part of a duet, and from old habit, I came in with the *secondo*. She'd chosen the middle movement from Mozart's Sonata in D Major for Four Hands. I was rusty, and the opening *allegro* would have been well beyond me, while the concluding *molto allegro* called for speed I'd never been able to master.

The flowing and lyrical *andante*, though, was a pleasure to revisit.

"All three admirers came and went in the course of the affairs," Hyperia said, executing some intricate ornamentation with grace and ease. "John Pickering was always off visiting prospective clients or looking in on some poor relation. Ian the would-be diplomat traveled."

"Hans the dashing dandy repaired to Town, where Lady Barrington could see him only intermittently." We played on, the music exerting a calming effect on my roiling thoughts. "Each man was a perfect fit for the lady he wooed."

"Wooed, but had no intention of winning." Hyperia took a repeat the composer hadn't put in the score. "I can understand why Her Grace would not marry a music master, and Lady Barrington had her reasons for remaining unentangled, but what of Mrs. Whittington? She's comely, not destitute, and yet, her swain abandoned her."

"Almost as if the liaison had served some purpose?"

We reached the final cadence and, as had been our habit years ago, allowed a concluding moment of silence. My eye fell on the bowl of drooping roses gracing the closed lid of the piano, and I was reminded of Charles's reference to the grueling part of the steeple-chase. My enthusiasm for this thorny inquiry was certainly drooping.

Hyperia leaned into my shoulder gently. "Every liaison serves one purpose, for the male half of the duet at least."

Said with some asperity. "These fellows troubled to romance the ladies, Hyperia. Her Grace was treated to violin serenades and rose-scented love letters. Ian favored Mrs. Whittington with fragrant bouquets of damasks, and Hans..."

I fell silent as a pink petal fell from a spent bloom.

"Jules?"

"Hans had a fine singing voice," I said slowly, "and roses were his posy of preference when charming a lady. He forgot to change his favorite flower."

"What are you going on about?"

"I might well be daft, Hyperia, but I suspect all three men—John, Ian, and Hans—were the same fellow."

"That makes no sense."

Sense, maybe not, but the facts supported the conclusion none-theless. "I have been stumped for the duration of this investigation in two regards—at least two. First, what is the motive for the thievery? Blackmail serves handily, but we've received no threats of same. Threats, yes—I will be a dead dog and so forth—but no demands for money.

"Very well," I went on, thinking aloud, "perhaps the thief is biding his time, but why wait until now to purloin the stolen items? Perhaps because opportunity has arisen only now, but that begs another question: How effective would blackmail be this long after the liaisons have concluded?"

"Somewhat valuable, given that Lady Barrington is trying to find a match for a galloping hoyden of a step-daughter."

"So is Lady Canderport, and nobody has stolen anything from her."

"Because, Jules, there is nothing to steal."

I rose from the piano bench and began to pace. "Not so. Steal one of her flasks, attribute ownership to Lottie. Steal three of them, for that matter, and Lottie's chances of finding a husband plummet."

"Perhaps Lottie wants her chances to plummet."

I did an about-face before the mantel. "Then she's kept her powder dry for an uncharacteristically long time, and she has for once not involved her twin in her schemes. Charles reports that this is the third house party in as many months."

I struck off again across the music room. "The second question that has dogged me for the duration is: How could anybody, other than the ladies themselves, *know* of the love letters, the gloves, the locket? The ladies treasured these items, and gossip might have tickled an ear or two, but the suitor was also aware of each item."

"Ah. Hence you conclude we are dealing with *one* suitor who was familiar with all three women. The one who forgot to collect his gloves from Lady Barrington, who gave the locket to Mrs. Whittington, and who wrote the letters to Her Grace and well knew where she kept personal correspondence. What of Lord Drayson's sketches?"

I paused before the intricately carved great harp. "Coincidence or a diversion to muddy the waters. I vote muddy the waters."

"Because you don't like Drayson, and he's of an age to have been the suitor. Barely, but he does qualify. Would three notably astute women all fail to recognize a man with whom they'd been intimate? That's quite a stretch, Jules."

I returned to the bench, sitting at a right angle to my beloved. "We don't have all the answers yet, you're right about that, but the one suitor theory has merit. Perhaps John-Hans-Ian got to confiding in a friend, and the friend was well placed enough to put blackmail in train."

"But you don't think so."

I did not know what to think, but I knew where my instincts were leading me. "If all three women were wooed by the same man, then he was adept at disguises, as a fraud and a spy is adept. Ian used lifts to change his height, and he was also a fashionable dandy, right down to ridiculously high shirt points, a fussy coiffure, and elaborate knots for his cravat."

"What about the different hair colors?"

"Henna," I said, the answer arriving to my mind only as I mentally reached for it. "I was encouraged to use it to restore my auburn locks."

"Henna," Hyperia said, wrapping an arm around my waist and leaning against my back, "and black walnut stain."

"Brilliant, my dear. I'd forgotten about Marchant's hair tonic."

We remained in that posture, her hugging me from behind, me staring at the fire, as the repercussions of her insight reverberated in the peaty silence. Gideon Marchant possessed both tinctures, and he was of unknown patrimony. He would have heard every whisper making the rounds of polite society, and he had parliamentary aspirations that required substantial sums to achieve.

"Marchant is too old to have been the suitor, Jules, and too well known to the ladies."

"Perhaps so, but I have reason to question his financial stability, Perry, and that is an aspect of his situation I can easily investigate."

She gave me a squeeze and let me go. "Do you need a lookout?"

I rose and offered her my hand. "Bless you. If you could find Marchant and keep him occupied, that would serve even better. I need but a few minutes to confirm my hunch." I drew her into my arms and enjoyed a properly close embrace.

"What tipped you off?"

"Marchant's personal mount is not only dangerous, but literally long in the tooth. Why would any man, especially a vain man whose reputation mattered to him a great deal, keep such a beast?"

"Because he cannot afford a replacement. Not a lot to go on, Jules. Men get attached to their mounts."

As did women. "Marchant periodically fires his valet and only rehires him when another house party or social Season is in the offing. If the valet gives bad service, why not go to the agencies and find somebody competent?"

"Why does the valet accept the same post if he knows another firing awaits him?" On that worthy query, Hyperia stepped back. "Give me twenty minutes. If Marchant isn't napping in his own bed, I'll keep him occupied for at least another thirty minutes."

The gleam in her eye made me vaguely uneasy. "How?"

"I will speculate at length regarding Lord Drayson's nude sketches and where they might have got off to. In the course of my maunderings, I will let slip that his young lordship is very concerned the sketches have fallen into the wrong hands."

"And Marchant, smelling another scandal, will question you closely and hang on your every word. I really do not care for that man, Hyperia. Go cautiously."

She kissed me and patted my cravat pin. "And you, very cautiously."

"I always do." Though admittedly, sometimes going even very cautiously I'd found myself in fraught circumstances indeed.

Hyperia found Marchant in the library reading the previous day's Society pages. By the time I abandoned my listening post, she'd been leading Marchant by slow degrees to a discussion of classical art. A few minutes later, I tapped on his apartment door, announced myself, and waited on the off chance MacFadden might be within.

When that proved to not be the case, some quiet finagling with a hairpin and a pointed implement that had originally been part of a pipe-cleaning kit gained me admittance.

I wasn't looking for stolen items. I was looking for proof that Marchant had a motive for blackmailing three women who considered him a friend. I thus took myself directly to his dressing closet.

Within two minutes, I'd established that his boots had been reheeled, and while his jackets were well made and *en vogue*, his shirts were threadbare. Of spare cravats, he had only three—one still slightly damp from the laundry and hanging over the wardrobe door, one apparently awaiting starch and the iron, and one discarded after being worn. The newly laundered specimen yet had a faint pink stain that would doubtless be hidden by careful folding.

Brummel was said to have gone through six pristine starched and ironed cravats per morning dressing session because he'd been that particular about his fancy knots.

Marchant's jewelry was paste, what there was of it, though the settings were good quality and well maintained. As to that, most sensible people traveled with paste copies of any truly valuable accessories.

I needed proof Marchant was deep in dun territory rather than simply prone to excessive economies. Not until it occurred to me to look through his traveling desk did I find what I sought.

Creditors were hounding Marchant, from the bank threatening to foreclose on a property in the Midlands, to a chandler hailing from Town, to a landlord seeking to remind Marchant of arrearages on a Chiltenstone Street rental.

Marchant hadn't taken a wife, because like many a bachelor before him, he was unable to afford one. He flitted from house party to house party not simply to collect gossip, but to save on his own upkeep. The temperamental old horse, the hot-and-cold employment of a Scottish valet, the much-mended shirts... Marchant had come down in the world and doubtless hoped a stint in the Commons would improve his circumstances.

Members of Parliament were not paid for their efforts, and yet, many of them managed to turn the odd coin even so.

Well, well, well.

"Beg pardon, milord, but you oughtn't to be reading another fellow's mail." MacFadden stood in the doorway to Marchant's sitting room. With the birdlike tilt of his head, he looked more like a curious hen than an avenging angel of gentlemanly privacy, and his tone had been only mildly reproving.

"You are right, but then, somebody not only read my mother's personal correspondence, they stole it. Has Marchant paid you lately?" I closed the traveling desk as I spoke and returned the key in the lock to the precise angle where I'd found it.

"End of the month, he says." MacFadden closed the door to the sitting room and also closed the door to the bedroom. "If you hold his vowels, you have my pity."

Vowels—I, O, and U being vowels—were used for debts of honor, which the law refused to acknowledge, many of them resulting from that nominally illegal activity known as gambling.

"I avoid even polite wagers. Would you know if Marchant stole my mother's letters?"

MacFadden busied himself tidying up the hearth, which was spotless. "I might know, I might not. Himself keeps his own counsel, and my employment with him isn't what you'd call regular. The real question is, would I tell you if Marchant had turned thief, and the answer to that... I don't know, my lord. As far as I can discern, Marchant isn't a thief in the sense of taking what doesn't belong to him, but when a man doesn't pay for a top hat, when he won't give the cobbler his due, isn't that a form of thievery?"

"Yes, and that's why we have debtors' prisons."

MacFadden replaced the hearth broom and dustpan in their cast-iron stand. "I wouldn't like to see that happen to him—you catch your death at the Marshalsea, everybody says so—but I don't like lying to the tailor's boy and the coalman and the charwoman either."

"And that's why you leave Marchant from time to time?" MacFadden wasn't merely vexed on behalf of an impecunious employer, he was weary of the part he played in the whole farce. Disillusioned, even.

"He sacks me sometimes. I leave other times. Marchant pays when he can, and that used to be regularly and well, but in recent years... I don't know what will become of him, milord. He talks about Parliament, and maybe that will turn his situation around. Knows how to rob Peter and blame Paul, and that's half of what passes for government, to hear some tell it."

The late duke would have agreed. "What will become of you?" MacFadden seemed conscientious about his duties and a decent sort.

"I'll land on my feet, sir. I've had to learn the knack. Like your lad, Atticus."

"He's not my lad. He's my tiger."

A wistful expression crossed MacFadden's features. "You take up for him, he respects you, and if anything happened to the wee lad, you'd turn heaven itself inside out until you found him and brought him home safe. Doesn't matter there's no blood tie. He's your henchman."

Which had nothing to do with anything. "If Marchant asks what I was doing in his rooms, you can tell him—"

MacFadden shook his head. "He won't ask. Says nobody will trifle with him in this crowd. They are all half afeared of him, and he likes it that way."

"Are you afraid of him?"

A ghost of a smile lit MacFadden's features. "Not anymore. Best be on your way, my lord, and you needn't worry Marchant has those letters. I keep these rooms neat as a pin, and I'd know if he had them."

Fine assurances, but all MacFadden could really tell me was that Marchant hadn't stashed the letters where MacFadden was likely to stumble across them.

"I'm also looking for Mrs. Whittington's locket, Drayson's sketches, and Lady Barrington's old gloves."

"I'll keep a lookout, my lord, and have a nose around the servants' hall. Pointing a finger at the help would be just like Marchant, though I blush to admit it."

"My thanks. Don't take any risks, MacFadden, and your discretion is appreciated."

"I'll be so discreet, the pantry mice won't hear me."

I took my leave, though his words reminded me that I had seen Marchant descend into the bowels of the house on at least one occasion. I'd seen him only from the back, but his air of haste had been evident nonetheless.

By the time I rejoined Hyperia in the library, I had a working theory of the situation: Marchant had hired some actor or fortune hunter to inveigle all three women into questionable liaisons and, in each case, had left incriminating evidence of the affair in the woman's hands. He was retrieving that evidence now because his parliamentary plans were moving forward.

My theory was less than brilliant, but it fit with blackmail as Marchant's motive—one he'd attributed to himself, oddly enough—and explained both Marchant's timing and for the John-Hans-Ian similarities.

The first question became what Marchant would do with the stolen items now that he'd retrieved them. The second question was why he'd embarked on such a long, complicated game, and as to that, I had some ideas. When I returned to the library, I sent off another epistle to Lady Ophelia at Caldicott Hall and paid the groom Jean to deliver my letter posthaste and wait for a reply.

When I told him he might have to kick his heels for a day or two at the Hall, the rejoicing in his eyes was plain to see.

CHAPTER EIGHTEEN

For three days, I watched and waited, my trusted familiars joining me on sentry duty. Her Grace, Hyperia, and I kept Marchant under surveillance, but he did not return to the lower reaches of the house, unless he did so in the dead of night.

Wisherd undertook a discreet search of the servants' hall and surrounds. At my suggestion, she first secreted an unfinished embroidery project behind a stack of plates in the china bureau and then made a great show of looking everywhere else for her missing stitchery.

Always ensure an alibi is as credible as possible. She found two lurid novels and a dusty penny, but neither gloves, nor locket, nor letters.

I set MacFadden to the same sort of exercise in the footmen's dormitory, because I also wanted to locate Drayson's sketches. Bawdy drawings he found aplenty, but none executed with Drayson's skill and none depicting guests at the gathering.

Atticus suggested we adorn Marchant's door latch with a single hair to monitor his nocturnal comings and goings, and that worthy strategy suggested Marchant wasn't roaming in the small hours.

In short, my investigation was going nowhere, and I had only a few days left to find the goods and hold the thief accountable.

"Where haven't we looked?" Hyperia murmured as rain pattered gently against the dark windows of the conservatory. The glass was steamy with condensation, and the strains of a male vocal quartet drifted from the music room. Supper had been a buffet, punctuated by the announcement that our Highland Games were canceled due to unrelenting precipitation. Three days of autumnal downpours that showed no sign of relenting meant we had to content ourselves with Highland finery at the grand ball scheduled for the conclusion of the party.

When Lord Barrington had made that announcement, the company had at first been silent—nobody, it seemed, had looked forward to scrambling up hillsides or being dragged through the mud with five other fellows clinging to the same rope. Then Miss Bivens had begun clapping, followed by Charles and Miss Frampton, and general applause had risen to deafening heights.

Highland finery without the Highland Games won the evening handily.

Drayson had suggested an evening of amateur music honoring Scottish composers, and I was reminded again of Charles's steeple-chase analogy. With the Highland Games off the agenda, the grueling part was over, and the horses could anticipate the race's conclusion with renewed joy and spirit.

Though my own spirits were sinking by the hour. "I searched the ballroom," I muttered, "and the gallery and this conservatory, the drains of which need a good cleaning."

"I've revisited the rooms of the lady guests," Hyperia said, bending to sniff a precocious camellia. "Miss Bivens has more books than the rest of the ladies combined have slippers. Why a mind like that is judged unfit for Oxford, I do not know."

"You are sympathetic to Lottie's frustrations?"

"I always have been, and my dear brother Healy is the first exhibit for the prosecution. He nearly brought the family to grief with his dimwitted machinations, and yet, nobody considers putting the West fortune in my hands, do they?"

I opened a door in the outer wall and let in a cold, damp breeze. "Stars to the west. We might get a reprieve from the rain after all."

Hyperia took a deep breath of chilly air. "You had to keep an eye on the weather in Spain at all times, didn't you?"

At the moment, my eyes were on her. On the dear, familiar contours of her features, on the inherent reserve that kept her thoughts and emotions private from the world and sometimes even from me. I took her in my arms, and we stood in the door, the brisk night a contrast to the warmth of our embrace.

"Is this when I propose again?" I asked, stroking the fine bones and sturdy muscles of her back.

"I think not," Hyperia murmured. "We are vexed by missing items that refuse to be found and a thief who refuses to be caught. We'll want to make a proper celebration of our official engagement, and the moment isn't right."

In her demurral, she comforted me by innuendo. We apparently had an *unofficial* engagement well in hand. On that cheering thought, I kissed my beloved, and she kissed me back. We got half a soaking exchanging further proof of mutual affection, while visions of a night spent cuddled in my four-poster danced in my tired head.

I eased away, both frustrated by and pleased with the moment. "Are we still being prudent about our sleeping arrangements?" I asked, arms loosely around Perry's shoulders.

"I don't want to be."

More consolation. "But?"

"But Marchant could choose tonight to prowl about unchecked, and when next I treat myself to dreams in your arms, I would rather be preoccupied with thoughts other than 'where are the letters?' and 'where haven't we looked?'"

I kissed her cheek. "Your dratted logic is valid."

I pulled my thoughts back to the matter at hand. Where hadn't we looked? An excellent question with not enough answers. In my supposedly idle hours, I'd done a thorough inspection of the stable, the springhouse, the summer kitchen (still in use owing to the large number of guests), the brewery, game locker, and laundry.

"I had a peek at Lord and Lady Barrington's quarters," Hyperia said, stepping back. "Bad of me, but we hadn't looked there."

"Thorough of you." I closed the door and secured the latch. "I did a cursory pass through Mrs. Whittington's rooms. She's a tidy soul." With a penchant for shockingly lovely underlinen. Confiding such a detail even to Hyperia felt unnecessary and ungentlemanly.

Hyperia laced her arm through mine, and we moved in the direction of the camellias. "I made a try at Drayson's quarters, but the odious Murray was lurking."

"I managed to have a look while Murray was at supper. Atticus helped me with the timing. His lordship should give landscapes a try."

"Or honest employment," Hyperia said. "How I do blaspheme when vexed." She stopped me at the next set of doors for another hug. "We're running out of time, Jules."

The duchess had grown quiet, and Lady Barrington's gaiety had taken on a determined quality. Mrs. Whittington's serenity bore an undertone of anxiety, and I had yet to hear any news from Lady Ophelia.

"I'll see you up to your rooms," I said. "Perhaps inspiration will strike us while we're dreaming our separate dreams."

"Insomnia is more likely. How about if I see you to your rooms, and we can share a nightcap?"

My experience with nightcaps was that they hastened one to sleep, then resulted in a fitful night, but Hyperia's company calmed my spirit at any hour.

"A scandalous nightcap rather than a scandalous night. I will content myself with lesser measures," I said, ushering her through the door. "The gents are in good voice."

"I think Burns is often the better for being sung by men. 'Green

Grow the Rushes, O' just doesn't ring as convincingly from a soprano."

The quartet had a good ear for harmonies, and they weren't rushing through "Jock O'Hazeldean."

"This one has a happy ending." Why I should recall that, I had no idea. "The Scottish lover spirits the lady away from her wealthy English suitor and his annoying father."

"And you like that?" Hyperia started up the main staircase, which abruptly loomed before me as daunting as the Pyrenees in winter.

"I like that the lovers are happy and nobody had to be shot at dawn. Has a certain sentimental appeal. If we do catch Marchant with the goods, what then?"

Hyperia paused on the landing. "We won't catch him with the goods, Jules, and Her Grace never asked that of you. Return her letters to her, and she will count that a victory."

I would count that fighting to a very frustrating draw, but better than a defeat. The whole way across the Iberian Peninsula, Wellington and his generals had known exactly how to define victory —invade France. Take the fight to the Corsican who had inflicted violence on much of an entire continent and beyond. Liberate France from the Corsican oppressor and from his continental system of trade, of course, and return her to the oppression of a king whose reign would be more profitable for Albion.

Perhaps I blasphemed when vexed as well.

"I must decide what our victory will entail," I said. "What would Marchant consider a defeat?" Even if I managed to locate the stolen goods and return them to their respective owners, Marchant apparently had learned of the affairs in detail and still held a place in Society where he could instigate very inconvenient gossip.

We gained the top of the steps, fatigue hitting me at gale force. "I've been overdoing," I said. "I know better."

"But you push yourself, because you think surely you won't have another bout of forgetting so soon, and your mother is depending on you, and time grows short. Should we forgo our nightcap, Jules?"

I should have said yes, but I was too selfish. "Join me for a moment. I've come to regard my green plaid apartment as my sanctuary. I can't say the décor has grown on me, but neither does it jar."

From across the corridor, we heard a man's raised voice. Marchant berating his valet, perhaps. MacFadden apparently returned fire, though the words were indistinct.

"Does nobody at this house party get along with anybody else?" Hyperia muttered. "That sounds as acrimonious as Lady Canderport and her dear Lottie."

"The ladies are family. Family members have a license to bicker. Harry, along with every one of my sisters, assured me it was so." I used my key on the latch of my sitting room door, noting that the single hair was unbroken. Atticus was still on his appointed rounds, then, which was cause for some concern, given the lateness of the hour.

"Brandy for you?" I asked, handing Hyperia into a wing chair, "or something else?"

"Is it still the good brandy, or are the more pedestrian vintages on offer this late in the gathering?"

"Good, not spectacular." I passed her the stopper from the decanter, and she took a sniff.

"Good will do. I've been looking forward to seeing you in your kilt."

"I might have to rely on MacFadden's good offices to tend to the details. He's an interesting sort. More philosophical than the average valet."

I poured a single serving and passed it over, then busied myself with the fire, which had been allowed to go out. For the staff, the steeplechase wasn't over.

I used the poker to establish that the flue was, in fact, open and went through the exercise of piling tinder and kindling on the andirons. By rights, I should have summoned a footman to make a proper job of it, but I'd built countless fires in the Spanish wilderness. Why bother those already overburdened?

"We haven't searched the kitchen," Hyperia said, sipping her brandy. "Easy enough to plead a growling belly."

"How could Marchant hide anything in the kitchen?"

"You said he went belowstairs, and that suggests he was in the kitchen."

"Marchant's trespass into the lower reaches was probably noted and observed by three footmen, two maids, the undercook, the scullery maid, and a disapproving valet. With a crowd of witnesses such as that, he'd not have tried to hide anything."

I used a taper to bring the flame from a wall sconce to the hearth and watched my tinder—paper, some pinecones, and sticks—catch. I was having to build this fire because I'd eschewed MacFadden's aid upon my arrival, and he would have reported my rejection to the ranks.

Lord Julian liked his privacy and wouldn't require or tolerate much fussing. Not a guest likely to part with generous vails, and thus I could be neglected to a point with impunity. Atticus made my bed and managed my coal and laundry.

Of all the staff, only MacFadden himself had ventured... I was abruptly reminded of walking into my private quarters and finding MacFadden fussing with my flue.

Ye blushing gods and goddesses.

"Hyperia, where is the last place you'd look for something that my mother expressly directed me to find?" As I spoke, I shoved a heap of ash over my inchoate fire.

"Jules, what are you doing?"

"Looking in the one place we haven't searched." I rose and gestured to the room at large. "The last place anybody would look." I peeled out of my evening jacket and gathered up the loose sleeve of my shirt. "The first place I should have thought to inspect."

I stuck my arm into the chimney, felt around the ledge, as

MacFadden must have, and brought out a metal box latched with a simple hook.

Hyperia passed me a handkerchief. "Well done, Jules."

"Well done, MacFadden." Rather than risk getting soot on the box's contents, I used the washstand in the bedroom to clean my hands.

"You open it," Hyperia said. "You found it."

The gloves and letters lay on the bottom, the locket atop them, the little collection at once prosaic and profound. My sense of victory was keen, also incomplete.

"The ladies will be relieved." I was relieved. I'd complied with orders and found Her Grace's letters. Mission accomplished, which wasn't the same thing at all as victory won.

Hyperia gently closed the lid of the box. "You are fretting because the ladies, though relieved, all departed from strict propriety, and somebody has learned of their adventures. Worse, that somebody collected evidence of those liaisons."

Mentally hurtling from facts to conclusions along straight lines of logic and reason was work for a fresh mind. I was tired enough that hurtling eluded me, mentally and physically.

I could state the obvious, though—obvious in hindsight, of course. "MacFadden put this evidence where nobody was likely to find it."

"On Marchant's orders?"

Across the corridor, through two closed doors, they were arguing still, which was bad form, to say the least. MacFadden getting ready to quit again, or Marchant preparing to sack him.

"Marchant could have hidden the goods himself and then not even his valet would know their whereabouts. I suspect MacFadden was operating on his own initiative."

As I stared at the little locket winking in the candlelight, my sluggish imagination lurched sideways into an incontrovertible fact: The ladies had each known of their individual mementos. *Only the suitor would have known of all three and been able to easily identify them in the course of a swift spree of thievery.* The suitor, who was tallish, dark-haired, charming, canny, and facile with disguises.

"Do you find MacFadden attractive?" I asked, closing the lid of the metal box.

"What sort of question...? I suppose he would be, but he has that stooping, head-cocking air, which puts me in mind of chickens and crows. His features are well fashioned. I grant you that."

"And he's Scottish rather than English, and a valet, rather than accomplished at the gentlemanly arts... but I do believe he's our man, Perry."

HGM, *Hugh Gunning MacFadden,* and not a monogram for Hans M. Gadabout, or some such patronymic. Simple initials in the usual order.

"As a valet," Hyperia said, "MacFadden isn't likely to cross paths with the lady guests, is he?"

She wasn't rejecting my theory outright, and the more I mentally probed the notion of MacFadden as John-Hans-Ian, the more support I found for it.

"He's tallish when he isn't bringing an obsequious stoop to the party, dark-haired, has access to walnut stain. A valet would know all about fashion, as Hans the doting dandy did."

Hyperia considered her brandy. "A valet would not be a talented musician, much less have diplomatic aspirations."

"Robert Burns was a talented musician, and he came from a long line of farmers." I rebuilt my little fire, and this time let it catch. "My father was a duke, at least in name, and yet I made a credible intelligence officer as did my brother. When necessary, I was also a believable drover, deserter, monk, or sot."

"Fair point. Then MacFadden's accent and Scottish name are as false as his humble demeanor?"

I tossed a square of peat on the flames and settled on the arm of Hyperia's wing chair. "I don't know. Perhaps MacFadden had a gentleman's education and fell on hard times. Perhaps he's an actor of superb skill. Perhaps Marchant has some hold over him."

Hyperia sipped her drink. "That fits. I don't know as anybody associates with Marchant enthusiastically, but the hostesses keep him in plain sight rather than allow him to skulk about behind their backs."

I looped an arm around her shoulders, and we sat for a good half hour, evaluating possibilities and coming to no definite conclusions, for all that we'd found both our thief and the purloined mementos. When Hyperia's head was a sleepy weight on my shoulder, I escorted her to her room and kissed her good night.

By the time Atticus reported for lights out, the bickering from Marchant's side of the corridor had subsided to an irritable rumble. I was reminded of those times Harry and I had sniped at each other for days and sulked for more days.

That recollection gave me another potential answer and yet still more questions. I stashed the stolen items in the squeaky drawer at the bottom of my wardrobe and passed a fitful night in anticipation of battle in the morning.

I rose with a map in my head of the terrain that had to be covered, but no clear route to my destination. All I knew was that I must begin by consulting Mrs. Whittington.

The strain of the past two weeks was telling upon her, putting a tension about her eyes and mouth. I took the place next to her at breakfast and suggested she accompany me on a stroll to the stable. The rain had let up, though the skies remained gray and threatening.

"The stable, my lord?"

"I like to confer with my horse early in the day. Gives me an excuse to stretch my legs and catch up on the stable gossip. I sent a groom over to Caldicott Hall earlier in the week, and I'm hopeful that he's returned."

She topped up my tea cup. "I suppose a bit of fresh air won't go amiss. I must change out of my slippers, and I'll meet you at the door to the back on the hour."

Lady Jessamine and Miss Frampton joined us, and talk turned to how much plaid was too much (if the plaid was pink, the only possible answer was *any* was too much, in my opinion). When the subject shifted to the necessity of finding a piper for the grand ball, I made my exit and conferred with my reinforcements.

I waited until Mrs. Whittington and I were a good distance from the house before I stopped beneath a towering stand of rhododendrons and passed her the locket.

"I found this stashed in the chimney of my sitting room."

She opened the locket and peered at the inscription. "This is mine. This is the piece I thought I'd misplaced. What of the other items?"

"Found in the same location, all stored in a box that would keep them safe from soot and flames. The stolen goods were secreted in my quarters by one MacFadden, valet to Gideon Marchant."

Fine brows drew down, and a feminine fist closed around the locket. "Gideon stole my locket? I was walking with him the morning I noted it was missing. A pickpocket could manage such a thing, I suppose, but Gideon Marchant?"

"To snatch the locket off your person would generally result in the chain or clasp breaking. Both are intact. Marchant could easily have slipped into your quarters and helped himself to the contents of your jewelry box, just as you slipped into his quarters when first you and I met."

She sent a fulminating glance in the direction of the house. "Gideon has an unpleasant side, but he leaves me alone. I am no threat to anybody. I am exactly what Society believes me to be—a contented widow of modest means."

Gideon did not leave the lady alone in his thoughts. In his thoughts, and possibly in what passed for his heart, he esteemed her sincerely, and that had been his first real mistake.

"I apologize for the question I'm about to ask, and I would avoid it entirely were the answer not key to setting matters to rights. When you were enjoying the occasional company of Ian the aspiring diplomat, did you have occasion to... That is, how close did you and he become?"

She snapped the locket closed. "Very. We were lovers in the physical sense of the word. Why?"

"Would you be able to identify Ian if you saw him again?"

"Of course. I identified him a little over two years ago from across a busy thoroughfare."

"Have you seen MacFadden?"

"Who? Oh, Gideon's valet? No. I have no occasion to consort with the entourage male guests might bring to a gathering such as..." She turned from me and frankly glowered at Tweed House's graceful façade. "You are saying that Ian has been underfoot at this gathering, and I've not recognized him?"

"If MacFadden is your Ian, then he has much to answer for. He would have taken great pains to avoid you, the duchess, and Lady Barrington."

Mrs. Whittington bowed her head, adopting a posture often seen in those who grieved deeply. "I refuse to believe what you're implying. Ian could be frivolous—I needed frivolity desperately—and his schedule was erratic, but he wouldn't—he absolutely would not—be so cavalier as to pursue other women, other widows, while we were close."

"If I can believe my mother and Lady Barrington, he did not play you false to that degree. You are the only lady with whom he indulged in the intimacy you've described. With the others, he encouraged affection and trust, and certainly friendship. He lavished time and attention on them, but he took few liberties beyond those permitted a typical gallant."

She rounded on me. "Few is not none."

"You consider yourself a woman scorned, but I suspect that Ian's esteem was genuine." I even had some grudging sympathy for the

conflicting loyalties that drove MacFadden to his deceptions. Some.
A little.

Harry had literally slept with the enemy and with the enemy's
wife. He'd claimed never to have seduced an innocent, but I'd still
found his behavior repugnant and stupid. To save the whole British
army, I might have attempted the same, but Harry's amours had never
been in aid of so worthy an objective, at least as far as I could tell.

I'd lived in fear that some brilliant lady spy was beating Harry at
his own game, and for all I knew, a woman had inveigled him into
leaving camp on the night he and I had met with disaster at the hands
of a French patrol.

"If Ian's esteem was genuine," Mrs. Whittington said, "then why
disappear from my life like the proverbial thief in the night?"

"Because Ian *was* a thief in the night, and he didn't want you to
learn that about him. He genuinely cared for you and probably never
meant for matters with you to become as involved as they did." I was
speculating, offering Mrs. Whittington the dubious fruits of insomnia
and imagination.

"Where is he now?" she asked. "Ian, or MacFadden, or whoever
he is? They might not be the same man, you know. Gideon seldom
keeps any employee for long. He's always complaining about wages
and characters and the agencies."

As if on cue, Atticus's piping tones heralded his approach. I drew
Mrs. Whittington deep into the foliage and put a finger to my lips.

"The guv'nor claims Murray will offer to sell me back my coat for
every penny in my pockets," Atticus said. "I got sixpence, MacFadden. Jolly, jolly sixpence. I'm as rich as I've ever been."

"Will you ransom your coat, Master Atticus?"

"Just Atticus." He stopped near where Mrs. Whittington and I
lurked and pulled tuppence from his pocket. "I dunno. Guv says let
him keep the coat, I'll keep me money, and that'll teach old Murray to
fleece the likes o' me. I fancy that coat, though. Miss Hyperia said it
fit me somethin' handsome."

"Tell you what," MacFadden said. "You leave the coat to me, lad. Murray will find when he goes to pack his lordship's duds on Sunday that the coat has mysteriously found its way back to you. Murray can explain to Lord Julian why you ought not to have possession of your own clothing with winter on the way. His lordship doesn't suffer foolishness."

I would have been flattered by even a thief's praise, except that MacFadden was also a convincing and experienced deceiver.

"Guv will sort him out proper, I promise you that. Murray took Drayson's dirty pictures."

"Young Atticus, how could you possibly know such a thing?"

"I don't know it, but I seen him skulking about. Mind your step, MacFadden, or he'll put them pictures under your cot."

"You have a vivid and criminal imagination, laddie. Off to the stable with you, and keep a keen eye on what shows up under your own cot." He tousled Atticus's hair—Atticus hated such presumptions—and jaunted off in the direction of the house.

Another piece of the puzzle fell into place as I watched MacFadden's retreating form. His posture was impressively upright until he gained the edge of the park, at which point a subtle angle crept into the way he held his shoulders and head.

"You comin' out, guv?"

I put a hand on Mrs. Whittington's arm when she would have revealed herself. "You heard MacFadden, my boy. Off to the stable. Find out if Jean has returned, and report developments posthaste one way or another."

"Aye, guv." Atticus pelted off with the energy of a lad who had no concept of the weighty matters in train all around him.

"Mrs. Whittington?" I drew her from among the dripping eaves. "Can you identify that man as your Ian?"

Her features were pale and composed, but her voice shook slightly. "That was Ian, but he is not mine and apparently never was. You will excuse me, your lordship. I have a trunk to pack and—"

"Please don't go. Keep to your room with a megrim, visit the village shops, look in on the vicar's wife, or attempt a quiet hack between showers, but please do not call attention to yourself by departing. Not yet."

"You have no idea," she said, "what the sight of that man provokes in me, my lord. He isn't safe if I bide at Tweed House."

Hell hath no fury, and Carola Whittington had reached the end of a very long and, for the most part, lonely tether.

"Let me give you the benefit of my further conjectures," I said, "and then you can decide the best course. I have yet to broach any of this with Her Grace or Lady Barrington, though I am assured that their involvement with Ian was in the nature of protracted flirtation only."

I was betting that Carola Whittington would yield to the pull of fair play and propriety, the lodestars of her existence thus far, but for one flaming aberration.

"Very well. I will bide here for now, but I make no excuses for Ian's fate should his path cross mine in a deserted corridor."

"Fair enough. Let's find someplace warm and dry, and I will acquaint you with the larger picture as I envision it, though, mind you, I might have the whole business absolutely wrong."

I offered that gesture in the direction of modesty for the sake of her pride. In truth, the longer I pondered and observed and gathered evidence, the more certain I was that a very great scandal was in the offing, and I would find myself at the center of it, exactly where I did not want to be.

CHAPTER NINETEEN

The elusive Jean had not returned from Caldicott Hall by the time I finished conferring with Mrs. Whittington, but then, the roads had been miserable, and his mission had had no assurance of success.

I'd tasked Lady Ophelia with an investigation within an investigation, and her efforts might never yield the evidence I sought. Like any good reconnaissance officer in unfamiliar terrain, I would forge ahead on the strength of logic, determination, and what information I had in hand.

I returned the gloves and the letters to their respective owners. The box reposed in its previous location, awaiting MacFadden's efforts to retrieve it. I had confirmed with both my blushing mother and an equally self-conscious Lady Barrington that their involvement with John-Hans-Ian had been flirtatious rather than carnal, and I'd explained to them that their former gallant was Gideon Marchant's valet.

"His valet?" Lady Barrington said. "I don't think I've seen the man. Gideon sang his praises, agreed to lend him to you if needed, and that... Gideon did that on purpose, didn't he? Does MacFadden tell Gideon what to do, or the other way around?"

A fair question, one I hadn't a definite answer for. Lady Barrington had bustled off to confer with her husband. I had counseled against destroying the gloves quite yet, as much as she wished to see them tossed into the flames.

The duchess, whom I'd found once again at her correspondence, similarly threatened to burn the letters.

"These letters are evidence of gross folly, my lord. Foolishness of a magnitude I hope never to repeat."

She wore an afternoon dress, though we had yet to enjoy the noon meal. Her spectacles were perched upon the Fennington nose, making her look scholarly and severe.

"You claim you kept them as a reminder of how close to disaster you sailed," I said, taking the chair opposite her escritoire. "You also kept them because you were fond of John Pickering." I was apparently comfortable taking a seat without Her Grace's permission, and I hoped that was a sign of progress in our dealings.

The duchess removed her eyeglasses and folded the earpieces. "He was a good flute teacher. Very talented."

"He was a friend when you needed one."

"What is this defense of the accused in aid of, my lord? He deceived me, Hellie, and Carola. If he didn't exactly play us false at the time, he's stolen from us and very likely colluded with one of the worst gossips in Mayfair to put us under his thumb."

"That might be the case. All I'm asking is that you don't destroy the letters just yet. Come Monday, you can start a bonfire with them, but until we've confronted the thief, please guard the evidence of his perfidy well."

"I haven't even seen this valet you claim Gideon is towing about."

"I'm sure MacFadden has been least in sight by design."

She tucked her spectacles into the little box where she kept them. "What are you planning, my lord?"

"To deceive the deceiver, if I must, and for that, I will need your trust."

"You already have it." She closed the box with a decisive snap.

"Hasn't this whole exercise demanded that I repose my entire confidence in you? You need not ask your own mother to trust you, for pity's sake, and you will insult us both if you repeat the request."

Who had noted that reassurances could take the form of a scold? "My apologies, Your Grace. The last thing I want is to quarrel with you, and I do appreciate that you've been bearing up under a great strain."

She balled up a page of foolscap and pitched it at my chest. "Cut line, sir. Families bicker. You found my letters. If you want me to hold on to them for a bit, I'll ask Wisherd to secure them among her effects."

"Good thought." I explained the rest of the situation as I saw it and how, exactly, I hoped to turn the tables on MacFadden and Marchant. Her Grace wrinkled her nose once or twice and frowned frequently, but I had her trust and, by the end of the discussion, her consent as well.

And yet, that wasn't quite enough either.

"I've been meaning to broach a topic with you," I said, rising to collect the crumpled foolscap and toss it into the dustbin. "Feel free to ponder your response or decline my request."

"If you must travel on the Continent, please wait until Arthur is home. One son racketing around France is one too many, in my maternal opinion."

"I hope never to set foot in France again," I said. "This has to do with more immediate concerns."

She tapped a nail on her blotter. "Out with it, sir. I can certainly offer relief if you are short of coin—"

I help up a hand. "I am short one mother." Not what I'd planned to say. "For the Yuletide holidays, I mean. They will be upon us before we know it, and in Arthur's absence, I know there are traditions to uphold and so forth, and..."

My mother stared at the fading letters folded by her wax jack. She saw her past, no doubt, her regrets, and a time when fate had seemed to provide an unlooked-for comfort, only to turn comfort into woe.

"What is it you seek from me, Julian?"

I hadn't the words, or perhaps the courage, to answer simply. "There's a boy at the Hall, a small boy, and his world has become daunting. He's without allies, or so he thinks, but for an uncle or two who always seem to be charging off on mysterious adult business. He doesn't understand why his situation has become so isolated and odd, he hasn't made many new friends yet, and he'll lose heart if I can't... if *we* can't be family to him. He doesn't deserve the cards fate has handed him, and I am asking you to be family with him... with him and with me."

The duchess rose and faced the window. A weak sun was trying to chase off the clouds, with indifferent success. "Leander?"

I managed a nod. "Leander and... I. Please join us for the holidays, Your Grace. He's illegitimate, I know, and I am not good *ton*, and I am well aware that you have many other options over the Yuletide season, but I'd appreciate it if you could spend it at the Hall."

She turned, her arms crossed, her gaze speculative. "With the boy Leander?"

"And with me." To reiterate the request had cost me, but trust went both ways, if it was the genuine article.

"Yes," the duchess said, blinking at the carpet. "I will be pleased to join you fellows at the Hall for the holidays. We will make Arthur regret his desertion and spoil the lad to the very best of our ability. He will have a legendary tummy ache, and be Lord of Misrule, and sneak hens into the house, and enjoy a proper Christmas."

"You'd tell Leander about Lady Biddy?" I'd smuggled my favorite laying hen into the house to protect her from the stewpot. She'd lived to a grand old age, though at my mother's insistence, her ladyship's earthly span had been served in the henhouse rather than in my dressing closet.

Her Grace's smile would have illuminated the seventh heaven.

"For starts. You will invite Miss West so she gets all the best stories as well, and I think perhaps Ginny should provide the necessary dash of mayhem. Her Declan is of an age with Leander, and the two of them will be polishing the banisters within a quarter hour of meeting."

Sliding down the long, smooth railing on the grand staircase in the time-honored Caldicott tradition.

"I will look forward to ineffectually scolding them both. My thanks, Your Grace."

Her smile dimmed. "Might you cease with the honorifics? I am your mother, after all. I understand proper address in company and will afford you the same if you've become such a stickler, but really, Julian, we are family."

I had yet to eliminate the threat of looming scandal, but I had found Her Grace's letters, and I had found the start of a path back to the pleasure we'd taken in each other's company earlier in life.

"We are family," I said. "And I will look very much forward to your company later in the year, Mama."

"See that you do."

She extracted her spectacles from their box, and I went upon my way, my step lighter and my heart lighter too.

The grand ball came and went, complete with skirling pipes to add to the din and vast quantities of Lady Barrington's infernal punch. The latter generosity ensured a very thin turnout for divine services on Sunday morning. Convention forbade most entertainments on the Sabbath—cards, theatricals, charades, glees, and choruses of a secular nature—and blustery weather deterred those inclined to hack out or stroll the grounds in aid of recovering their health.

Even the Sunday feast—industry belowstairs benefiting little from biblical proscriptions—was sparsely attended.

And yet, Tweed House was full of activity. Maids and footmen scurried up and down their respective stairways. Porters wrangled trunks to the porte cochere. Valets, grooms, boot-boys, and gardeners paraded steadily between house, stables, gardens, and laundry.

The kitchen staff was kept busy preparing hampers to the extent those could be filled a day before anticipated travel, and in the carriage house, harness was cleaned, organized, and rehung in order of expected departures.

I remained in my sitting room throughout the day, claiming fatigue and a sore head. The fatigue was sincere, as was my determination to catch MacFadden in the act of retrieving his contraband from my chimney.

I had given up hope that young Jean would return from Caldicott Hall. Perhaps he'd never aspired to reach his destination, in which case the lad might well have committed horse thievery. I hadn't read him as inclined to felony offenses, but then, I'd taken MacFadden for a friendly, philosophical sort of valet rather than a consummate deceiver.

"Best get some sleep, guv," Atticus said, setting a tray on the low table before the sofa. "Going to be a long night, and me arms will fall off if I have to drive us the whole way back to the Hall tomorrow."

"You wish. I see your coat has been returned to you."

Atticus executed a graceful pirouette. "MacFadden pinched it from Murray's trunk. Said Murray also has a pair of lady's Sunday gloves among his effects and another set of loaded dice."

The tray included a tower of sandwiches—ham and cheddar, may Cook and all her kin perpetually prosper—a dish of fried pickles, two small pints of ale, and a half-dozen cinnamon biscuits.

"What have you learned from going temporarily coatless, Atticus?" I passed him one of the pints and took a seat on the sofa. Arthur preferred simple fare, and in this, he and I agreed.

"I won't be dicing with no more scoundrels." Atticus took a sip of his ale and went to the French doors. Night fell earlier and earlier, and all beyond the windows was darkness and damp. "But how do you tell who's a scoundrel?"

"You can't be sure in most instances, and the logical precaution is to avoid the dice altogether."

"Murray was a scoundrel, cheatin' like that," Atticus said, "but whyn't anybody tell me what he was about?"

Thus did the budding philosopher begin to parse degrees of evil. "Would you have listened?"

"Maybe, or I mighta hung about, watching long enough to see how Murray always won in the end. He let you get in a few good throws first, but he always won. We came late to the party. The other lads and footmen knew what Murray was about."

"Eat something. Don't just stand over there pondering the foibles of human nature."

"What's foibles?"

"Failings, shortcomings, like finding humor in a boy losing his only coat to a crooked valet who doesn't need a coat."

"Winter's coming," Atticus said, swiping a sandwich and returning to his brooding by the French doors. "Nothing funny about a lad without a coat when the snows start."

"I would not let you face the elements unprotected, Atticus, and the poor treatment you endured probably had to do with the low regard the staff feels toward me."

He glowered over his shoulder. "Your ma's a duchess. You fought Boney and nigh lost your wits doing it. Your horse follows you around like a dog. Nobody got any call to look down on you."

A touching endorsement. "But I came to find missing letters, and the staff likely thought I'd accuse one of them of the theft. Then the locket and gloves went missing, and I began snooping about the entire premises. Murray doubtless resented my very presence, and you were tarred with the brush of his ill will toward me."

"Tarred him right back, dint we?" Atticus saluted with his mug and nearly sloshed ale on the carpet.

"MacFadden retrieved your coat. I hope you thanked him."

"Offered him all my pennies, and he wouldn't take 'em. Said I was to look out for the next hapless laddie I came across. I don't know any hapless laddies 'cept me."

I was a hapless lad, in some corner of my soul. The duchess and I —Mama and I—had come to a new and better understanding, and for that I was grateful, but we still had difficult terrain to cover. Perhaps at Yuletide we could make more progress.

"Find your cot when you've finished eating," I said. "I'll take the first watch."

My parlor door was unlocked, though the chimney flue had been crisscrossed with strings of bells. MacFadden could not retrieve his little box without creating a din worthy of a Morris dancer in full regalia.

Atticus and I finished our cold supper, the boy sought his bed, and still I waited. MacFadden must even now feel the passing of every hour, as I'd felt time growing short while I searched in vain. Marchant ought to be half mad with worry and frustration, and that notion cheered me considerably.

Heaven knew, the ladies had suffered undue worry thanks to Marchant and his minion.

I nonetheless also had frustrations. I still wasn't convinced that the various mementos had been stolen to support a blackmail scheme. First, no demands for money had been received, and second, I could not see MacFadden allowing Mrs. Whittington in particular to be victimized like that. From a pragmatic perspective, she hadn't much in the way of means or social influence, she had no daughters to launch, she wasn't a fashionable hostess, she wasn't on the verge of making a splendid match herself and, in fact, did not seek to remarry...

The thought struck my imagination like a candle flaring in pitch darkness. Mrs. Whittington was emphatically not in search of another spouse. True enough, but perhaps the boot belonged on the other foot.

Well, well, well and *eureka*.

With yet another set of possibilities to ponder, I found myself a semicomfortable position recumbent in a dark corner of the parlor and blew out the last candle. Let MacFadden come, and he and I would have a long and very interesting discussion.

CHAPTER TWENTY

I went through the pretense of climbing into the duchess's traveling coach when it lumbered up to the porte cochere. I remained within its confines as trunks were strapped to the boot and roof, and I was still in my appointed location when the coach lumbered off to retrieve Her Grace from the front steps.

When the coach arrived before Tweed House to collect Her Grace, who was resplendent in a carriage dress and fashionably veiled bonnet, I was lurking among the camellias in the conservatory, having exited the moving vehicle after it had pulled around the corner of the house. I crept back to my quarters in a house gone eerily quiet and used a prearranged tap on the door to alert Mrs. Whittington to my return.

She and her familiars waited in my bedroom, while I repaired to the balcony from whence I kept watch over the parlor.

MacFadden cut the timing fine, waiting until the last trunk had been sent down from Marchant's rooms. He opened my parlor door, bold as you please, closed it behind him, and went straight to the chimney.

The bells tinkled quietly, and I let myself in through the French doors. "MacFadden, what have you there?"

He frankly stared at me. "My lord. Good day. Thought you'd left."

"You were supposed to think I'd left. Have a seat, if you please."

"Best not, sir. Mr. Marchant gets into the worst sort of taking if his departure is delayed. I've got my box—put it here for safekeeping when this room was vacant—and I'll just be on my way." MacFadden's tone was as brisk and cheery as ever, but he was also eyeing the French door to my left.

"It's a good twenty feet down to the terrace. You'd break something, probably something important. The ladies would not want your death on their consciences. Look in the box, MacFadden."

He obliged, his demeanor subtly changing as he viewed the empty interior. "Did Marchant get here first?"

"I got here first. Mrs. Whittington got here second. Ladies, if you'd join us?"

Lady Barrington, Mrs. Whittington, and Her Grace emerged from the bedroom with Hyperia bringing up the rear.

MacFadden sent another longing glance to the French door and stared resolutely at nothing.

"Sorry, *Mr. Pickering*," Her Grace said, putting ironic emphasis on the name. "You saw Wisherd climbing into my coach. Veiled hats are ever so convenient, and one takes a tiny bit of satisfaction out of deceiving the deceiver, to quote my son."

"We want answers," Lady Barrington said, "and we shall have them."

The parlor door swung open. "What the hell is taking you..." Gideon Marchant stopped short, then made to withdraw.

"Don't you dare scurry off now," Her Grace said. "We have questions for you too, sir."

"That is a pity," Marchant said, "because I really cannot tarry. If you must detain MacFadden, feel free. I've sacked him for the last time, and you can't believe a word he says. He'd betray his own mother for tuppence, and—"

"I rather think," I said, "that it was you, Marchant, who betrayed his mother. You've betrayed your son as well, by any reasonable measure."

Carola Whittington marched across the room and glowered at MacFadden, then at Marchant. "By God, there is a resemblance. I shall be sick."

"The ages are right," Lady Barrington murmured. "They could be father and son if Gideon was quick off the mark."

"They bicker like family," Her Grace noted. "Was that how you knew, my lord?"

"The bickering was a clue, true, but I also mistook MacFadden for Marchant when I watched him return to the house last week. From the back, they have exactly the same walk. The person I mistook for Marchant went directly belowstairs rather than up to his apartment. I thought that unusual, but I was nonetheless thoroughly convinced I'd been watching Marchant."

Even when the real Marchant had come into the house a few moments later, I'd not realized my error.

"Why steal old mementos?" Her Grace asked, and she aimed her question at Marchant. "Why do this to us and to your own son?"

"You have no right to question me," Marchant retorted. "I have done nothing wrong, and I do not answer for the behaviors of my valet—my former valet. Now if you will all excuse me, I have promised Lord Westerboro—"

"My mother asked you a question, Marchant. You refuse to answer her, but I can offer some considered speculation. Run along to curry favor with your parliamentary sponsor if you must, but know that I will call upon him too."

"You would not dare. You are the next thing to a traitor, according to half of Mayfair. Got your brother killed by the French, to hear Horse Guards tell it, came home a wreck, and I've seen with my own eyes that you're as dotty as a drunken—"

My mother slapped him to silence. I could feel the ladies and perhaps even MacFadden restraining applause as the crack of her palm against Marchant's cheek reverberated in the otherwise quiet room.

"Whack him again," Carola Whittington said. "Lest I do worse yet."

"He'll find a way to whack you back," MacFadden muttered. "Every time I thought I was done with him, he'd come up with a new scheme, a new promise, all is forgiven and let's-begin-again-my-boy. I fell for it every time."

The ladies regarded MacFadden with a mixture of puzzlement and disdain.

"Did his victims include the national exchequer?" I asked, because finally, finally, I'd found enough connections to see past the convenience of a blackmail motive. Marchant had been a naughty fellow indeed, if my suspicions were correct. Treasonously naughty.

"I tried not to think about what he got up to," MacFadden said. "I knew all the same. He made sure I knew so it's my sin too. He claimed Parliament was looking for scapegoats, when all he'd done was try to provision our soldiers for a fair profit."

"Wool?" I asked. The infantry had been desperately short of uniforms and good British wool the preferred fabric.

"Aye," MacFadden said. "He'd buy cheap up in the Highlands— coarse stuff, barely fit for carpet—then top a shipment with some decent Cheviot fleeces and send the lot of it from Edinburgh. The inspectors would approve the whole, and dear papa would pocket a princely sum while the factories asked no questions."

"Lying," Marchant said breezily. "Exactly as I predicted. Complete falsehoods intended to distract you from his thieving and swindling."

"He wasn't swindling," I said evenly. "He was snooping, and at your behest, Marchant. You sent him to the grieving widows of those committeemen rooting out fraud on the military. You wanted to know if your name was coming up in those late night meetings, if your scheme was about to be toppled by criminal charges and a warrant for your arrest."

The disdain the ladies had expressed toward MacFadden paled compared to the disgust they aimed at Marchant.

"In short," I said, "while MacFadden had a thorough look through old journals, copy books, and meeting minutes, he'd offer the widow distractions of a compelling sort, and then he'd move on to the next assignment. Perhaps he also tried to court a daughter here and there, provided her papa sat on the same committee."

"No daughters," MacFadden said. "Daughters move about in public. Widows keep to themselves. I drew the line at allowing all of polite society to see what a bounder I'd become."

"He's lying," Marchant said. "He's no relation of mine, and I wash my hands of him."

MacFadden waved a hand. "Right, and the next time you want a footman to lurk at some ambassador's soiree, collecting gossip in four languages, or a groom to sneak about a gentleman's stable, you will be back, with more promises and excuses. I wish we weren't related, but alas for me, we are. I owe you, you claim, because you had your bastard son educated when you could easily afford the expense. You expect a return on every investment. Well, it appears your investment will be lucky to get transported, Papa dearest, and I am honestly not as daunted by the prospect as I should be."

"Transportation?" Carola Whittington gave the word a horrified air. "For stealing a locket that you'd given me in the first place?"

"A pair of gloves isn't worth your life," Lady Barrington observed. "I am displeased in the extreme to have been lied to and used, but those are not crimes in the eyes of the law."

They turned to the duchess, and as the entire assemblage waited for Her Grace's opinion on the matter of MacFadden's fate, I realized I had been asking myself the wrong question. The relevant query was not what constituted victory from my perspective, but rather, what constituted justice in the view of the ladies, if justice was even possible.

"John Pickering," the duchess said slowly, "longed to travel to Vienna, but I think in this, we must defer to Carola's wishes."

MacFadden waited with the stoic resignation of a prisoner in the dock.

"Explain to me," Mrs. Whittington said, "exactly why my locket was stolen."

MacFadden shook his head. Marchant eyed the door.

"Correct me if I'm wrong." I took up the narrative rather than waste more time on pointless histrionics between father and son. "MacFadden apparently stole the items rather than leave Marchant a clear field for the same larceny. The gloves, the letters, and the locket were the only proof of liaisons each of you ladies might regret. If Marchant had them, he'd have influence over you and thus access to your jewelry boxes, so to speak."

"Damn you for a meddling, cork-brained fool," Marchant snarled. "You are determined to embroil me in nonsense I had no part of."

"The real problem arose," I went on, "when MacFadden realized that Marchant is genuinely enamored of Mrs. Whittington. My guess is, Marchant would not have threatened scandal outright, but he would have started rumors and mentioned to his dear friend Carola how easily a lady's reputation could be brought low. Mrs. Whittington, knowing that somebody had her incriminating locket, would have viewed Marchant's offer of marriage as an honorable kindness. MacFadden, who does appear to have a conscience of a sort, found marriage for Mrs. Whittington to Marchant on those terms intolerable."

"This is all very entertaining," Marchant said, "but your lordship can vouch for the fact that I held no matrimonial aspirations toward Mrs. Whittington—meaning no offense, madam."

MacFadden rounded on his father, and Marchant shrank back against the door. "Do you know what I inherited from you? Not the languages, not the music, not the maths—that was all from my mother. From you, sir, I inherited the ability to *act*, to put on performances worthy of Drury Lane, but I never developed the knack you have of believing your own lies."

MacFadden shifted to face the ladies. "My father assured me he had no marital aspirations toward Mrs. Whittington, and he's also said that I was all but on my way to Vienna. He's said every job was the last one. That it would be a cold day in hell before he aspired to sit in Parliament. He's said he never sent the army cheaper wool than they bought. He says and says and says—half of it's lies, and half of it will become lies, and he himself cannot tell the difference. I could not risk that he'd get his hands on that locket, or on the gloves or the letters."

"Why give them to us in the first place?" Lady Barrington asked.

"I shouldn't have. I'm sorry. If I hadn't, then you would have had no cause for all this bother and worry, but my esteem for each of you was genuine, and I wanted you to have something real from me. He," —MacFadden jerked his chin toward his father—"was wroth with me for the mementos, and that was a consolation to me. I should never have done what I did, should never have fallen for his promises, should never have deceived anybody. A token of true regard makesthe deceptions less vile, in my mind. I am sorry."

That last was offered with a fleeting glance at Mrs. Whittington, who appeared lost in very serious thoughts.

"All quite touching," Marchant said, "and ridiculous. If you're bringing this fellow up before the magistrate for his larcenous actions, I will cheerfully testify that he gave bad service and could not be trusted with coin. Hearing no more unfounded accusations, matrimonial or otherwise, then I will just—"

"Shut your mouth." Carola Whittington spoke with the finality of an experienced governess reduced to her last remaining nerve. "You stole from every infantryman to sweat and stumble his way across Spain. Soldiers died of the heat, and some of them doubtless died wearing the cheap, heavy wool you bilked the army into accepting. You have much to answer for. My husband was a soldier, and I am not convinced by your display of disdain, Gideon Marchant."

"Nor am I," Her Grace observed.

"The jury is unanimous," Lady Barrington added. "But what are we to do with him?"

"I have a suggestion." What I actually had up my sleeve was in the nature of a bluff, a threat along the lines of an empty pistol. I'd hoped for proof from the Hall, and I still might find proof at the Hall, but for the present, I was prepared to dredge up my own thespian talents.

Somebody tapped on the door. Marchant stepped away and might have bolted through the subsequent opening had not MacFadden moved to check him.

A dusty and worn Jean stood in the corridor, along with a butler trying to look utterly disinterested and failing mightily.

"Beg pardon," Jean said. "I have documents that I am to surrender to Lord Julian, in person, and only Lord Julian. Lady Ophelia was most insistent."

"As only she can be," the duchess muttered. "Julian, have a look, and somebody find this young man some food and a quiet place to sleep."

I took a packet from him wrapped in oilcloth and secured with a red ribbon. "Well done, sir. You heard the duchess. Tucker and a nap."

He bowed, and I closed the door on the scowling butler. I opened the packet and scanned the contents and sent a silent prayer of thanks in Godmama's direction.

"From the late Duke of Waltham's personal records," I said. "Meeting notes, signed minutes, agendas. Our very own Gideon Marchant's name figures prominently, but not—one blushes to admit —in a flattering light."

The last of Marchant's insouciant air evaporated, leaving a furtive, frightened creature in our midst. "You can't prove anything."

"We don't have to," I said gently. "Just as all the reputations you ruined merely for sport, all the friendships you soured because it amused you to make trouble between innocent parties, were spoiled without proof. Three honest women need only whisper a few hints, and not a club in London will open its doors to you, Marchant. Please do finagle your way into Parliament. I'm sure Mrs. Whittington has a cause she'd like you to tirelessly champion."

Mrs. Whittington caught her cue with admirable alacrity. "Our veterans and retired seamen," she snapped. "There is no Britannia without them, and yet, we discard them like lame coach horses when they can no longer serve."

"Climbing boys," Lady Barrington said. "They are barely out of infancy, and we turn a blind eye to their suffering."

"Get the women and children out of the mines," Her Grace added, surprising me. "You men are so convinced your greater physical strength entitles you to run the whole world. Well, run it, one load of coal at a time, please, and leave the women and children to live their feeble lives above ground."

Marchant's mouth worked, but he said nothing.

"You're giving him a choice?" MacFadden asked.

"Not really," I replied when the ladies disdained to do so. "If Marchant can get himself into Parliament, and if he espouses the causes enumerated by the ladies, and if he's also above reproach in every other regard, he will enjoy a reprieve. At any point, if he fails to perform to expectations, traitor and dimwit that I am, I will take the evidence that I have straight to Wellington, assuming my proposal meets with the approval of the ladies."

"His lordship means the duke," Her Grace added. "Of Wellington."

"Wellington?" Marchant barely managed three coherent syllables.

"Wellington, for starts," I replied. "The penny press might come into it, and I'm sure the ladies could suggest a few other interested parties."

"You won't get transportation," MacFadden said. "I'd get myself into Parliament posthaste, Marchant."

"But I..."

Lady Barrington made a shooing motion. "You have a pressing engagement with Lord Westerbumpkin. Leave my house, and don't expect to be invited back."

Marchant scurried out. I predicted he'd become a first-class scurrier in coming months. He'd learn to toady as well and perhaps do some actual good with his talent for manipulation and artifice. Stranger things had happened.

"I am for Caldicott Hall," the duchess said. "John, or whatever your name is, I bear you ill will only for the way you parted from me. Lord Julian saw through your attempt at a death threat, so we will classify that as bungling." She stuck out her hand, he bowed over it, and then Her Grace made a quiet, dignified exit.

"I will see my guest off," Lady Barrington said. "As for you, *Hans...* We can learn from the past. I hope you do." She followed the duchess into the corridor, leaving Hyperia and me with MacFadden and Mrs. Whittington.

MacFadden seemed to know better than to renew his apologies. He simply regarded Mrs. Whittington with the air of a man who had been cast out of Eden and knew he must dwell in the land of Nod forevermore.

"I'll help you finish packing," Hyperia said, taking Mrs. Whittington's arm.

The widow didn't immediately accept the invitation, but rather, regarded MacFadden impassively. "I loved you. I honestly, truly loved you, and I was in love with you." On that devastating blow, she quietly passed into the corridor, Hyperia on her heels.

MacFadden stared at the door, then seemed to realize his performance wasn't quite over. He tried for a weary smile in my direction.

"We're for the magistrate, my lord? I'd like for the boy, Atticus, to have what vails I've earned." MacFadden took some coins from his coat pocket and put them on the mantel. "I don't expect the rest of the staff will want my effects, but perhaps the local vicar will have a use for them."

"Nice try, MacFadden, but your sentence won't be that light. Collect your vails save for tuppence and sit down."

He ignored the money on the mantel—give the man credit—and took a seat.

~

"You sent MacFadden to Vienna?" Hyperia asked as the phaeton rattled down the Tweed House carriageway. "*Vienna*, Julian?"

"Mrs. Whittington wasn't willing to see him transported, and MacFadden insisted a life sentence in the Antipodes was the least he deserved. I suggested a compromise. A remove from Britain, across land and sea, far from all that is familiar."

"Across the Channel. Far from his wretched excuse for a father's importuning. Not too far if Mrs. Whittington should take a notion to travel in the next year or so."

"Now who's matchmaking?" Though, for the sake of both parties, I hoped Mrs. Whittington did take a notion to travel and that MacFadden was wise enough to accept forgiveness if she offered it.

I steered Jupiter through the gateposts, glad to have the last two weeks behind me, gladder to have Hyperia at my side. Atticus had been bribed to make the journey to the Hall with the duchess's coach and four.

John Coachman would doubtless demand a raise before day's end, and I would pay it without a qualm.

"Why make MacFadden's dream come true?" Hyperia asked. "He deceived three women, abused their trust, even if he couldn't find the documents he was supposed to steal for Marchant."

"I suspect he did find the documents. He simply could not bring himself to destroy them, which would have guaranteed Marchant safety. Neither could he bring them to light, which would have seen Marchant hanged."

"And revealed MacFadden for the rogue and thief he is. You believe he purposely failed in his efforts to protect his even more roguish father. Why does that entitle MacFadden to tour the great capitals?"

We tooled along, the day chilly without shading into bitter cold. I appreciated this opportunity to discuss the Tweed House investigation with dear Perry, who would be honest even when the truth didn't flatter me.

If we aired the whole business thoroughly enough, I could turn my sights to the holidays and to the arrangements necessary to host guests and family at the Hall.

"MacFadden was betrayed by his father," I said as Jupiter fell into the businesslike trot that would get us to the first posting inn in little more than an hour. "He should have hated Marchant, but that's not how family works. When siblings or parents turn from us, we seek to win them back. We can't help it."

Hyperia bumped her shoulder against mine. "I am wroth with Healy, but he's my brother. If you invite him to your Christmas revels, I will be civil to him and likely even give him a token."

"And I will welcome him graciously." An aspiration, not a promise. "We cannot choose our family, but we desperately want them to choose us. The duchess and I... She needed me, and I came."

"You and Her Grace seem to have resolved some misunderstandings."

"Some, not all. I decided that my mother held me in low esteem and then found every piece of evidence necessary to support my conclusion and ignored evidence that did not. I have that much sorted."

Another shoulder bump. "Human nature. Will you ever let me have a turn at the ribbons?"

We executed the transfer of the reins with practiced success. Hyperia was a skilled whip, and to be honest, the whole Tweed House excursion had tired me in body and spirit.

"Trot on, Jupiter," Hyperia called, which earned her a flick of a horsey ear and a slightly smarter pace. "Your mother says Ginny will join us at Christmas."

"I expect all sorts will come out of the family hedges to look me over. I was least in sight last year." We fell to discussing the cousins, in-laws, and informal relations who might grace the Hall at Yuletide. Some of them were twice as old as Father Christmas and not half so jolly.

The miles passed pleasantly, and a gradual sense of a job well done settled over me.

With the aid of my friends and family, I'd found the letters, found the truth, and found the start of better footing with my mother. Not a bad effort, not bad at all.

Hyperia and I made two changes of horse and traded the reins frequently by the time we were back on Caldicott land.

"I did something last night, Perry, and I wanted to let you know." I'd left this confession as late as I could.

"Last night, you were keeping watch over MacFadden's empty box."

What a metaphor. "Atticus took a shift, and when I was free, I went to your rooms."

She glanced over at me and guided our horse—Taranos, a Caldicott steed—through the Hall's gateposts, then handed me the reins. "You came to my room and didn't waken me?"

"I was tempted, of course. Sorely tempted and considered curling up with you, but I would have had to ask your permission first, and that would have meant waking you, so I completed my errand and decamped for another forty winks in my own bed."

"Jules, get to the point."

"When you unpack your effects, you will find a brief missive in my hand. A personal missive. I tucked a lock of my hair with it. Your trunk was unlocked, else I would have put it in your reticule."

I was glad for the reins in my hands. They gave me an excuse to stare hard at the horse's ears and pretend I had to steer him along a lane he'd been traveling since foalhood.

"A missive?"

"And a lock of my hair, even though my hair isn't the right color these days and might never again be as it once was. The note is in the style of a tame *billet-doux,* or tending in that direction." I was babbling, also blushing.

"I love your hair, no matter what color it is. You've written me a love letter?"

"Something of that sort. Harry gave me a lock of his hair. I have letters written in my father's hand. Leander gave me a four-leaf clover I will treasure until it turns to dust. I wanted you to have something of mine to keep." I'd thought long and hard before committing a few heartfelt sentiments to paper, and I had stared at my reflection in the mirror for a quarter hour before snipping off a length of straw-colored hair.

I guided Taranos around the circular drive and brought him to a halt at the foot of the terrace steps.

"My mother said I owed you a courtship. I gather His Grace didn't give her much of one. If ever you and I parted, I want you to have some proper courting to look back on. A lot of proper courting. Investigations matter, but they aren't everything or even the most important thing."

I trailed off into silence, expecting laughter, teasing, or even a dismissive pat to my knee.

Hyperia kissed my cheek. "I love you so, Julian Caldicott. Prepare to be courted in return. Christmas is coming, and you have been an exceedingly good fellow."

We sat for a moment, enveloped in a mutual glow of loving regard, and then I assisted my beloved from the bench and escorted her into the Hall. Christmas did come, bringing that mutual courtship Hyperia and I had promised each other, and mischief and mysteries in abundance came along as well.

But that, as they say, is a tale for another time!

Made in the USA
Las Vegas, NV
04 October 2024

96284812R00157